brud

Kenneth J. Harvey

beware, Jordan,
the world is hollow and filled with fools.

brud

Kenneth J. Harvey

Little, Brown and Company Canada

Boston   New York   Toronto   London

Canadian Cataloguing in Publication Data

Harvey, Ken J. (Ken Joseph), 1962-
Brud :

ISBN 0-316-34977-1 (bound) ISBN 0-316-34980-1 (pbk.)

I. Title.

PS8565.A6785B78 1992   C813'.54   C92-094567-8
PR9199.3.H37B78 1992

Cover Design: Debbie Adams Associates
Editing: The Editorial Centre
Interior Design and Typesetting: Pixel Graphics
Printed and bound in Canada by Gagné Printing Ltd.

Little, Brown & Company (Canada) Limited
148 Yorkville Avenue, Toronto, Ontario, Canada

part one

belief

chapter one

fall and goodbye

Brud knew the world was spinning. Sometimes he could sense it, gently easing him through the still air. Standing in an open field like a heavy ship lost at sea, swaying with the wind and to the forces of nature, he could sense it; the world, circling.

Brud's body had taught him about the spinning of the world. His body and his mother and father had been his only teachers through thirty-one years.

The orbit of the earth and other less complicated facts were set for certain in his mind. However, most common knowledge escaped him.

Alone in the field, not far from where his father quietly fed the horses, Brud would kneel, bend his rotund body forward, and press his wide oval face to the flowers. His eyes — set close to the bridge of his small nose — were narrow and slanted playfully when he smiled. There was great joy for him in the satiny texture of the petals. He would touch them against his face, rub them affectionately with his lips as if kissing. The sensation tingled and he would laugh quickly and move to swipe the thrill away with his stubby fingers.

The flowers charmed him for hours. They were like tiny miracles, like God faces. Brud knew about God. As sure as the world was spinning, so too was there a heaven and hell.

"Heaven is peaceful, calm, and clear," his father had told him. "Hell is the worst imaginable opposite. Hell is fire, smoke, and noise."

Brud stared up from the flowers and lovingly watched his father. His fingers brushed back and forth along the petals, savouring the feel of them. Endowed with a powerful sense of smell, he gloried in the fragrance that rose to him. The scent was sweeter than it could be to any other man. He drew in a deep breath. His nostrils twitched and widened like those an animal; a simple creature whose intelligence was measured by the scope of his senses.

His mind was sharp and uncluttered. Unlike normal men, Brud was incapable of thinking complicated thoughts. His slow-moving eyes witnessed surfaces, perceiving colours and shapes. He saw only the purity of his surroundings. All images were well defined. The great natural beauty of the land was certain to set his fleshy lips quivering, until he was forced to smile, his top lip rising higher, exposing his crooked teeth.

Brud never thought of leaving the land. He was content. In all of his years, he had wandered from the farm only once. As a young boy, he had dallied along the dirt road, thumping his fingers against the slats of the wooden fence and watching his hands, knowing how his thumbs

were gone, how he was born without them, and understanding he was special because of this, different from his
mother and his father, but like them, too. The white, well-
maintained fence ran along the edge of his father's sprawl-
ing farmland.

Brud wandered, counting his footsteps — not with the
numbers he had been taught, but with his own private
sequence of measurement — until he arrived at a place
past the fence where the road turned black and smooth.

He stepped cautiously upon the surface. It was like
nothing he had stepped upon before. He felt strangely
level and solid. The false sensation was full of trickery. He
looked ahead. The black strip of unearthliness curved off
into the distance before disappearing behind a small,
grassy hill.

With a disturbing start, Brud realized he must be standing upon the beginning of something evil. The extreme
blackness of the wide pathway assured him of this. He
stiffly jutted back and spun on weakening knees. Running
clumsily, he stumbled several times while forcing himself
ahead with limbs flailing.

His breath tangled in his throat, raging hot and frightened as he raced back to the farm. Sweat plastered his
shirt against his chest. His eyes were wide as if he were
being pursued by a darkness that leaked from the pathway, by a sinister apparition that swam amidst the blackness. Although he could not see it, he could sense it,
screeching up behind him to enter his flesh with its bony,
metal-sharp fingertips.

Brud stood still and silent, listening to the sounds of crickets in the field. It was late afternoon and the air was sweet
and cooling. Brud felt the air in his shirt. He smelled his

sleeve and smiled. Tilting back his head, he watched two crows swirling and looping past, their carefree caws beckoning Brud to join them in flight. Brud stretched up on his toes and raised his fingers as if to touch the winged creatures. He followed their effortless trails until they disappeared into the trees at the edge of the field. Leaving the crows there, he looked down at the flowers.

"Can't fly," he admitted, casually shaking his head. The flowers seemed to nod in the breeze. They dipped limply and shivered. Brud laughed, covering his mouth with his hand, blinking and smiling with squinted eyes. "Yes," he said to them. "Yes is all. Can't fly." He shook his head several times until he heard his father's distant voice calling to him. Brud's face became serious. He turned to look. From far away, the corral appeared as a miniature. His father's body was small. It seemed infinitely useless as it fell to the ground, tumbling awkwardly like a horse with its legs buckling.

Brud's fleshy lips parted in shocked recognition, but it took several seconds for the word to come.

"Dad?"

His feet shifted, bracing the earth. Had the earth tossed his father down? Brud stayed quite still, but sensed no movement. A wave of solitude and apprehension filled him.

Finally, as if his father — in absolute stillness — had called to him again, Brud quickly trudged across the field, moving closer to the farmhouse and barn. With each step, his body insisted he must hurry. His breath changed. He was aware of its loud quick rhythm in his ears as he made his way down the gradual incline. He was uncertain and slowed his footsteps no more than twenty paces from the fallen image of his father. Two hesitant steps, he stopped, his hands holding each other.

"Dad," he said, staring at the crippled form lying beneath the corral's bottom railing. Brud knew something had happened. His father was not moving. A long time ago, he had seen the same thing happen to his mother. She had fallen to the ground and Brud had not seen her again. He sensed that she still lingered on the farm, but she was not visible. She was in the air. Sometimes, he could smell her there and he would remember her face, as if she had come to him and filled the pictures he saw inside his head. She was here or, perhaps, on another farm similar to this one, only set elsewhere on an equally pleasing landscape.

Brud's eyes searched the grassy area around the barn, expecting to see his mother reappear, her figure floating close to delicately lie beside Brud's father. The word "Dad" moved around inside of him but washed thinner before settling between his lips. Although he could still see his father, Brud knew the form would soon disappear, vanish like the word he could no longer speak.

Brud stood for hours. He rubbed his palms together, joined his fingers, then released them, watching, expecting his dad to fade before his eyes. He kicked at the dirt and felt laughter rise in his chest, remembering what his father had said about the end, how it was a happy time, not a sad time. A happy time.

Covering his mouth with his entire hand, Brud giggled, his face saddening at the unruly humour that played with him. He did not understand the emotion. Standing there, he sometimes laughed, sometimes cried, and as night grew upon them, his dad began to dissolve into the darkness. Everything became hard and shadowed, disappearing beneath the gravest clouds.

"Gone." Brud spoke into the immaculate blackness. Kneeling by the veranda of the house, he sensed the refreshing night ground beneath him. He listened to the sounds of horses moving behind the corral and imagined them galloping, free and silent across the fields where his father would let them run.

Closing his eyes, he called goodnight to his father, then curled himself into the shape of innocence and nestled close to sleep.

"Son?" A hand shook Brud's shoulder.

Brud woke instantly and sat up, pulling his legs in close to his chest.

"Yes," he said. He blinked and squinted, waiting for his eyes to focus on the figure before him. The outline was washed white, then vague and uneven, slowly filling in. Within seconds, he saw Mr. Neighbour, bent on one knee, watching him.

"You okay?"

Brud nodded hesitantly. He nodded again, this time more sure of himself, and began to yawn, but stopped himself and smiled instead.

"We've got your father on board." The man pointed at the pickup truck parked beside the corral. His son was sitting inside, staring off across the field of dull yellow grass. Each wisp seemed straight and faultless in its reach for the sheer blue sky.

"Your father's gone," said Mr. Neighbour. He briskly surveyed Brud's plain features, then firmly settled on his eyes. "I'm sorry, Brud."

"Yes," Brud said, regarding the place where his father had fallen, seeing he was no longer there. His eyes crept toward the farmhouse. The door was closed, the window vacant.

"He's in the back of the truck. We better get him to town." Mr. Neighbour straightened up, wagging his legs to set the circulation flowing. Almost as an afterthought, he added, "You'd better come too." Brud wiped his face with a generous sweep of his hand. Small pieces of hay fell loose, while several others remained stuck in his thin, uneven brown hair. Over the years, the sun had streaked his hair blond so now the wisps of hay could be mistaken for thick unruly strands.

"Must've been a heart attack," said Mr. Neighbour, tapping his own chest. "His heart was weak. He knew it. Could only take so much. The way things are going around here. The land giving up on him."

Brud's forehead wrinkled and he licked his lips, "Mr. Neighbour, Dad fall and goodbye." He ran his hand back and forth over his hair. Laughing, he shook his head and made a quivering sound with his big lips. A few more wisps drifted to the ground. He looked down at them, wondering what they had been doing hanging onto him.

"It's okay," the man said, smiling just a touch at being called Mr. Neighbour. "I'll take you to the lawyer. Your father had it planned." His body tightened as he gripped Brud's elbow and helped him to his feet.

"We'll go in the truck."

"Truck." Brud pointed at the truck.

"That's right, truck," said Mr. Neighbour, picking a strand of hay from Brud's green-and-black checkered shirt. He twirled the strand in his fingers, then slipped it between Brud's lips.

"Your father's in the back. We'll all go together. Okay?"

Brud stared at the empty space on the ground and nodded senselessly. From between his dry lips, the strand of hay slipped loose and fell toward the ground, landing on the toe of his brown cowboy boot.

"You'll be alright," Mr. Neighbour declared, squeezing Brud's arm. He hooked his thumbs in his pockets and said, "Anyway, it's about time you saw the city. Have to move off here now. We're moving." Mr. Neighbour pointed across the field. "Sold our place to the same construction guy that wants your place. Crops are useless now. No sense farming. If you ask me, that's what's the matter with the world. No land under anyone's feet. Nothing natural they can claim as theirs. The land's gone all wrong. There's no way of working it any more."

"It's all coming this way," said Mr. Neighbour, watching through the windshield for bumps in the pot-holed back road. "The city's coming this way. No use holding out against it. It's impossible. Land is something out of story books now. Farming." Turning his head, he saw that Brud was tensely pushed against the passenger door, and he remembered. "Listen, Brud, I'm sorry about your father. I really am." His son inched along the seat, moving away from Brud, closer to his father's side. The boy didn't like the big idiot, didn't know if what he had was contagious.

"Dan'll be going into high school in September." Mr. Neighbour smiled and tossed a thumb toward his son. He glanced at Brud, then back at the road, realizing how Brud didn't even know the meaning of the words "high school."

Brud heard nothing of Mr. Neighbour's conversation. He only heard the tone of his voice, like a drone. He was watching the road. He'd never been in a truck or car before. It felt like he was riding the smoothest horse or drifting like a bird ruffled by a steady gale.

"He's laughing, Dad, look." The man leaned to take a look. Brud's lower jaw was quivering as he bounced on the seat, rocking with the uneven ride of the road.

"I think he likes it," Dan said. "Look at him." He tilted his head toward Brud and smiled, staring down at the hands with no thumbs. "What a..." He stopped himself from saying "weirdo," fearing disapproval from his father.

"I don't think he was ever in a truck before." The neighbour coughed to clear his throat, then shouted as if Brud were deaf, "Never been in a truck before, hey?"

Brud continued bouncing, hands on his legs, elbows swaying freely.

The man shook his head as he dug into his shirt pocket with two fingers, searching for his package of cigarettes.

"Can I have one?" asked Dan.

The man offered the pack to his son. He did so with a touch of pride. His boy was growing up. He'd be a man in no time at all.

Dan pulled loose a cigarette, and they both lit up.

"Cigarette, Brud?"

Detecting the smoke, Brud suddenly stopped rocking. He looked suspiciously at the two faces, his languid eyes fixing on the cigarettes dangling from their lips. Dubiously, he watched the smoke drift and linger around the ceiling.

"You smoke?" Dan asked, plucking the cigarette from

his lips, extravagantly blowing smoke at the windshield. "Nothing like a good smoke, huh?"

"Smoke?" Brud said, his eyes commencing to glaze with water. Smoke was suddenly, effortlessly, streaming from the two mouths beside him. Their insides must be on fire. He knew that fear was close to him, sniffing, searching.

"Nasty habit anyhow." Mr. Neighbour looked back at the road. The pavement was just ahead. "Smooth sailing coming up."

"Smoke," Brud said, remembering what his father had explained to him about fire, smoke, and noise. He glanced at the road, his eyes charged with terror. The pavement, the charred stretch leading...

Dan nudged his father, "Look at him," jerking his head toward Brud. He glanced at the weirdo's hands. They were all wrong. They were amazing.

"Civilization," said Mr. Neighbour, smoke billowing from his lips. He clamped the cigarette between his teeth and smiled. "It's all that's left." Quivering childlike emotion welled up from Brud's chest, rushing into his throat. It shuddered in his jawbone and set his teeth rattling against each other, clicking slowly, then ferociously as if he had fallen into the lake in wintertime.

Mr. Neighbour's smile faded, but Dan found the idiot's distress more and more amusing.

Through all the frenzied emotion contorting Brud's simple features, one word untangled itself to bound free. The word came as an almost inhuman grunt; a sound so filled with fear it seemed impossible to have erupted from such a plain face.

The sound was one raging word, growling from him without mercy, "HELL!"

The wheels struck the pavement's dividing bump.

Brud scrambled for the door handle and threw himself out into the land that blurred by. He cried out, rolling in an uncontainable whirl of turmoil, tumbling into a vicious tangle of bushes that seemed to hold him. The sharp branches scraped the backs of his hands, and his knee struck something hard, a boulder lodged in the ground. Ignoring the pangs of pain that defiantly stayed with him, he rose hurriedly, stumbled and tripped, collapsed, pushed himself up, and limped hurriedly through the bushes until he saw the gravel road, the potholes, and the familiar fence along the boundaries of his farmland.

The pickup truck had bucked to a stop. The neighbour regarded Brud's fleeing form in the rearview mirror. He stubbed out his cigarette and thought of going after him, but then he thought of more urgent matters.

"Have to leave him," he sighed. "Get this body to the place where it belongs."

"He's crazy!" Dan watched through the back window with his elbows up on the seat. "What's he scared of?"

"Leaving, I guess." The man pulled the gearshift down and thanked God — despite the years of hardships with his farm — for his one great blessing, the deliverance of a healthy son.

The truck rolled to a start, gliding smoothly. Dan watched Brud scramble around a bend and disappear, then he looked down at the body lying face-up in the back of the pickup. Startled, he quietly turned around in his seat to stare at his father, not knowing what to say.

His father blinked. His father watched the road.

Dan joined his fingers in his lap. He glanced at his father's big hands on the wheel and wondered about being empty like the man in the back.

chapter two

everything you could possibly imagine

Brud set a place for himself at the kitchen table. Everything was meticulously laid in order. Spoon, fork, knife, plate, and glass. Each item fit into a certain space as if he were aligning the planets, the lights in the sky.

His father had explained it to him. "When you look up at night, you see the stars. They never change positions, do they, Brud?"

Brud replied, "No."

"Tell me," his father prompted.

"Just move around, but always the same. Stay the same."

"That's right. Good. You're a smart boy. They stay the same, but move around. And they look perfect, right? This is very important. Many things in life are like this. Everything must be in its place.

"When everything is in its place, then the world is at ease. It's calm. I'll be honest with you, Brud. Not very often this happens. But we try. Just little things, they add up, you know. The fork goes here, the spoon here, the knife, plate, glass here. This is one thing you can control, Brud. One little piece of perfection. So you should do it, set it in its place. It's like a little piece of perfection right here on the kitchen table. Simple, right? Am I right, or am I right?"

"Simple," Brud said, chuckling. "Right."

"So simple and nice it'll make you smile. See, you're smiling."

Brud smiled now, knowing how perfect the kitchen table looked. He lifted the remnants of a cooked chicken and a bowl of mashed turnip and carrots from the refrigerator and plunked it down in the center of the table.

"Food like the sun," he said. "Everything around it." He made a circular gesture with his finger and sat opposite the place he had set. He wanted to watch it, make sure it was laid out properly. While eating, he stared intently at the order of the articles he had set out. This place was his father's and was not to be disturbed. Without giving much attention to his food, he picked at the chicken carcass and then ate the mashed-up carrot and turnip with a wooden serving spoon.

Brud surveyed the kitchen as his heavy jaw worked. His mother and father were here somewhere. He could smell his father, sense the heat of his body from the chair where he usually sat. The sweet and earthly odour of the farm lingered in the walls.

Finishing his meal, Brud dumped the carcass and the scraps of vegetables into the garbage. The waning light beyond the window told him he was late for feeding the animals. They were making restless grunts and cluckings from their places on the farm.

Staring out the window, he watched the horses moving around the corral as if on guide wires. They should be in their stables. Brushed and fed. This is what he must do. Or he would let them loose. Let them run into the dusk, across the summer fields.

He glanced back at the table, admiring the place he had set. It was as perfect as the stars, outlining an image of his father. He left the table as it was and walked through the wood-panelled hallway to the front door.

Outside, the air was cool and sweet with the smells of dusk. The fragrance overpowered and lulled him so potently he became unsure of which animals were to be fed. He stood and closed the door behind him, wandered off, and watered and fed all of the animals with extra buckets of feed. Then he sat on the wooden front step with his elbows on his knees and his fists tucked under his chin.

He wondered about the darkness, how it thickened before him. Shutting his eyes, he thought of the flowers closing up the way he had seen some of them do. The image was comforting. By simply closing his eyes, it was as if he, too, were a part of this majesty.

He heard himself laughing, dully and seeming far away. Opening his eyes to watch the black sky, he sensed a gentle hush of breeze merging with the creaking of crickets and the quieted animal sounds. Brud dared not stir from where he was sitting, afraid that the slightest movement would disturb this perfect balance.

Sleep did not touch him. It nuzzled close like a satisfied dog, briefly sniffing his fingers, before it lay down at his side. Brud waited. Time did not bother him. There was no definition. He heard the birds stirring and the animals come to life as dawn blossomed pink and orange before his eyes. He did not feel tired at all watching the brightening light, only wider and wider awake.

The gradual unfolding of daylight revealed itself with brilliant clarity. Brud was fascinated by the sharpening of images around him, seeing through the trees off across the dirt road, the sunlight sifting and slanting down, the rushing flights of birds. His eyes moved from limb to limb and barely noticed the car pull up beside the corral. Turning his head toward the vehicle, he caught flashes of its metal body, sunlight glinting across its curves.

Two men were sitting in the front seat. One wore a uniform, the other a suit. Brad could see them talking and then laughing behind the windshield, the glass reflecting a vague reverse image of the blue sky and the white, full clouds. Brud smiled and stood. He had been expecting something, and he settled on the fact that this was it.

The two men stepped out of the car and remained still, watching Brud trudge toward them. The man in the uniform stopped smiling. The one in the suit smiled wider, extending his hand.

"Hello, Brud, I'm your father's lawyer," he said.

Brud nodded, then glanced uncertainly at the uniformed man standing with his hands on his hips.

The lawyer looked where Brud was looking. He cleared his throat.

"Steve," he said to the policeman. "Come on, now." He nodded toward the man's hands.

The policeman reluctantly moved them from his hips. He sighed and casually pulled on one of his thumbs, then folded his arms across his chest.

"Yeah, that's much better," the lawyer said, disappointed. He turned to Brud and took his arm. "Let's go inside and talk."

Brud walked toward the farmhouse, but stopped to glance back, over his shoulder, at the man in the uniform who was smiling behind dark glasses. Brud knew better. His body told him something was wrong. He had seen cars before, but never one with lights on the roof and important-looking symbols on the doors.

The policeman moved away from the car, but continued watching Brud. When Brud waved and nodded, he turned and leaned on the corral, making funny noises to the horses.

"Brud," said the lawyer. "This way." He carefully tugged on Brud's arm and tilted his head encouragingly.

Brud looked down and saw the man's shoes. They were a shiny black in the sun and reflected light like stars against a night sky. Brud had watched those same shoes during the man's previous visits. The man had come many times to speak with his father.

Brud had never heard the lawyer's name, but he remembered the man's big, bright blue car with the light powder of dust along the doors. He remembered chopping wood for the stove, then pausing to watch the man enter the house. The man would come at the exact same time. The time when Brud swung the axe. Chopping time. And the man would leave just as Brud had finished. Brud's father would be standing in the doorway, watching the car back away. His father would always nod before stepping back into the house. But the man's car was different today and the man wanted to talk to Brud, not Brud's father.

The man in the suit carried a case. It was held firmly

in his hand and was glossy and black, just like his shoes. Brud always wished that one day he would touch the case. He wondered what was inside and imagined the magic that must be trapped within — something so special the man had to carry it everywhere that he went.

The lawyer stopped on the porch, waiting for Brud to enter first. Brud stopped beside him, staring down at the case. He looked up at the lawyer and smiled through two intently peaceful and worriless eyes.

Brud led the man down the wood-panelled corridor and into the kitchen. He stood beside the table, noticing the place he had set for his father. The man sat in his father's chair.

"No," Brud insisted, frantically pointing at the next chair. "There."

"Yes?" The lawyer stood, quizzically regarding the chair, then the table setting. "I see what you mean. Can't lay my briefcase there with that plate in the way." The man moved to the chair closest to Brud and lifted his briefcase onto the table.

Sheepishly reaching forward, Brud ran his fingers over the smooth leather. He smiled at the man in the suit.

"Like night," Brud said. "But no stars. Can't touch night like this." He shook his head confidently. The lawyer looked down at the blackness of the case and let an understanding smile warmly shape his lips. He watched Brud's earth-worn, stubby fingers glide along the surface.

When he pressed the two buttons, the steel latches popped up on tight springs. The sudden sound startled Brud. His mouth hung open and he quickly pulled his fingers away, pinning them between his thigh and the chair.

The lawyer paused before opening the case. He

glanced out the window and saw the field stretching off, its grassy depths stirring him to recall childhood visits to places just like this, the memories of school trips and animal farms nimbly installing a nostalgic feeling in his stomach.

Brud watched in anticipation, waiting to see the marvels of the universe flood out from within the case. The lawyer pulled his gaze from the window. The top of the briefcase eased open and Brud was noticeably dejected to see nothing more than a collection of white papers.

"Your father has left you a great deal of money," said the lawyer. "No doubt you probably know..." He paused for a moment, overly conscious of the manner of his speech. "The city has been working its way toward your land." He made a sweeping motion with his arm in the direction of the city. Brud looked at the wall where the man had pointed. "Very close to your property. Your land is worth a great deal of money." The man took a document from his case and turned the page, drawing his finger along specific lines. Brud smiled at the man, his eyes narrowing. He nodded and moved his lower lip up over his top one, holding it there.

Turning the paper fully around, the lawyer scanned the words and decided it would be useless to read them verbatim.

"You can live very, very well for the rest of your life." The lawyer's smile was reassuring. Brud smiled. The man nodded. Brud nodded. The man licked his lips. Brud did the same.

"Live," Brud said. "Good. Like to live."

"Your father has chosen a person to live with you. A live-in helper. A woman." He waited to see how Brud would respond to this, but there was no change in the sad little-boy eyes.

"Your father wanted you to stay in the country, but there's no way you can stay here and be supported, get the things you need. Welfare. You could claim...but the system is horrible... Your father didn't want you to be a part of that. And there's no land around here that we can buy and still support you. It's too expensive. Contractors pay the big dollars for it. You know."

Brud closed his lips and held them firmly shut. Blowing out, he filled his mouth with air, feeling the space above and below his lips curving out.

"The barn and all the land will be sold, easily. Developers have been trying to buy this land for years. The price has gone up and up."

Brud glanced up at the ceiling. He thought he saw something moving there. It was only a fly.

The lawyer smiled and turned another page, as if reading from the document. "As I said, a great deal of money will be yours. One particular developer is very interested, very rich. The owner of Quagmire's Construction, Quagmire's Towing, The Quagmire Tower. The list goes on and on. He's been trying for years to purchase this land. But your father wouldn't hear of it as long as he was alive." The lawyer examined Brud's face, hoping for a sign. "You're a rich man." The man smiled. Brud smiled. "Very, very rich. You understand?"

"Very, very rich." Brud looked at the place he had set for his father, expecting to see him there. He glanced around the kitchen, knowing his father was here somewhere. He looked at the corners of the room, then up at the ceiling again. Another fly, or maybe the same one.

"Our firm has been appointed guardian..."

"Awww!" Brud cried, holding onto the edge of the table. "Guardian angel!"

"Not quite." The lawyer blushed, embarrassed by the misunderstanding. "We'll just take care of the money and release funds as you need them. Whatever you want, anything within reason, you can have. A penthouse suite — you have that already. It's yours. Something people dream of. If you want a limousine, a big car." The lawyer stretched out his hands and then made two loose fists and rocked them, holding an imaginary steering wheel. "Anything. Your father told me that you'd never been off the farm, so I understand it's going to take a little getting used to. He meant to take you there years ago, get you accustomed to everything, but he didn't want to change you, couldn't face it. It was against his beliefs, so he put it off, even though I'd keep after him when I came out here. He'd always say he was going to do it, bring you into the city, but he didn't care much for the idea. Your father..." The lawyer frowned and shook his head. "I'm sorry. I really am. I keep forgetting it was only yesterday. It may not be easy at first. I know money is not really much of a consolation, but it's a help. It'll help you."

Brud studied the papers in the lawyer's hand. He reached for them with his thick fingers.

"See?" he asked, nodding toward the papers.

It was his father's will. The lawyer placed the document in Brud's hand, cautiously observing the wide, unblemished face for signs of emotion.

Brud tightly gripped the papers with both hands. He looked down at the even rows of lines. Letters. The alphabet all mixed up. He often wondered why his father tried to teach him all the letters in a certain order, repeating them over and over. Whenever Brud saw them again they were arranged differently, like the ones on this paper. He turned the pages, trying to find the right order, until he came to a signature at the end. He recognized the imprint like a track in clay. His father had scraped it with a stick in the dry dirt. It was like a part of his father, the thing that lived forever.

"Dad," Brud said. "Fall and goodbye, like Mom." A tear formed in one eye, then in the other, before several droplets trickled loose to stream down his cheeks. The tears came without noticeable emotion, hanging from the bottom edge of his jaw before dropping, one by one, to patter against the paper, blotching the ink.

The lawyer coughed to clear his throat.

"Better take that now," he said, reaching for the document. "You'll be okay." He paused for reflection, uncertain if he really believed his own words. They came automatically. He had said them before and now he said them again without genuine concern. "You can come to the city with us now." A resigned smile settled in a corner of his lips, unethically defying him. He felt uneasy, grappling with emotion like this. "See your new apartment. It's a wonderful apartment. Like nothing you've seen. It has everything you could possibly imagine. I bet you're excited."

Brud watched the lawyer gently tug the paper away from him and lay it in the briefcase.

"We should get going," the lawyer insisted, slowly closing the top. He stared at Brud, saw how the simpleton was quietly watching the case, wondered how much he knew, before pressing the latches back into place.

That's the end of that, the lawyer reasonably assured himself. *It's over now. It hadn't been so difficult after all. Look at him. He understands.*

chapter three

entry

After a long half-hour of coaxing, Brud finally sat in the back seat of the police car. He felt different from when he had been riding in the truck. He was closer to the ground and the ride was smoother. He felt like a loon skimming across the glassy surface of a lake. The ride gradually comforted him. He felt vaguely sleepy. Shutting his eyes, he pictured himself in flight on the back of a loon. His fingers pried into the seat beneath him, attempting to hold on.

"Take him back with you?" the policeman inquired, "or drop him at his apartment?"

"My office, I guess." The lawyer glanced at the policeman and offered a brief cordial smile. "I appreciate this, Steve. I didn't know how Brud would react to it all."

"He seems okay."

"Yes, let's hope so."

The policeman straightened his sunglasses. He sucked air in through his teeth and stroked the steering wheel.

"The boy's father is being buried today," the policeman declared.

The lawyer nodded and stared through the windshield.

"Shouldn't the boy be there?"

"No." He looked down at his briefcase. It was propped against his leg and the edge of the police radio. "His father didn't want him there. He's never been to a funeral before and his father wasn't sure how he'd take it. He said it didn't matter. Once he was dead that was it. He was gone. What was left of him was in Brud's head."

The policeman stared at the road. He refused to pass comment.

"I never forgot that. That's pretty good, huh?"

"Sure." The policeman snickered.

"Actually, his father was hoping Brud would die before him. It sounds cruel, I know, but it makes good sense."

The car hit the pavement's dividing bump, rolling along the asphalt.

Brud's eyes were still closed. He felt the change in movement and remembered how he used to slide over ice in winter. He was sliding now, but his feet were not moving. Three harsh laughs pumped from his throat. He let go his grip on the seat, his hands coming out at his sides to steady himself, holding his balance against a fall.

The policeman glanced in the rearview mirror and saw the smile and the movements of his stout passenger.

"You're going to let him live on his own?"

"There's someone living with him. A woman."

"And you say he's never been in the city?"

"No. I mean yes, that's what I said. He hasn't been."

The policeman drew in air and slowly shook his head. "Oooow boy." He looked back at the road. "Good luck to you, brother Jimmy."

"He'll be fine," the lawyer casually insisted. "We'll see to that."

"I think we've got enough to see to already."

"I don't want to get into it with you today. Alright? Let's just try to be civil."

The policeman straightened his sunglasses and ran his fingers down his thick moustache. "The city's a whole different ball game. If you weren't my brother, I wouldn't touch this with a ten-foot pole. You don't know what that...what he's going to do. What he's doing now. Look at him. He doesn't know anything. Turn around, one minute, he'd snap someone's neck and still be smiling. Not a clue. That's the kind he is."

The lawyer glanced over his shoulder and saw the smile curled on Brud's purplish lips. It was a smile filled with absolute delight. Seeing Brud's closed eyes and the heavy arms swaying to the ride, he had to smile himself.

"He'll learn," he said, turning back. "He's not dangerous, by any means. There's no way you can tell me that. And besides, he's one wealthy man. He can buy his way out of anything. You know the law."

"I thought you said we weren't getting into that." The policeman pulled off his sunglasses. His eyes flashed in the rearview mirror. Brud was swaying from side to side, his arms held horizontally. "It's a shame about all that money though. What is it, millions?"

"Easily."

"And he doesn't even know the difference. Seems the money could go to a lot better use. Sick people. Food banks. I see it every day. The need for it. Real need."

"I see it too. A foundation is going to be set up for charities. That was a provision in his father's will."

The policeman thought for a moment. "I don't think

32

you understand what can happen here. You're not that naive, Jimmy. Come off it. You know the possibilities. A rich stupid guy in the city. You going to take him for walks? Keep him on a leash? Don't tell me you haven't thought of what can happen. The set-ups. The scams."

"We'll just have to keep it quiet then. Right?"

"Quiet? What are you? Stupid? There are people who read the data sheets on every legal purchase. They know the money changing hands. It's all published in the financial pages, as soon as the land is sold, every jerk and con man knows. He's a target. Think about it. Put him away somewhere. A place where they'll feed him his pudding and shove a pacifier in his mouth so he can suck his time away. Put him in a place where he'll be safe."

Brud opened his eyes. The sights were moving quickly. He sensed an unnatural spinning, forces moving against the familiar circlings of the earth. He felt disoriented and weak, sick to his stomach.

The car sped along a black stretch of pavement surrounded by houses and concrete pathways, sloping lawns, parked cars, and different sets of lights coloured green, yellow, and red. He saw a dog sitting on some steps. It was a small dog, wearing funny clothes, and it would not stop barking at the passing cars.

A murky huddle of buildings towered in the distance. They looked sleek the way they rose toward the grey haze hanging like smoke in the sky. The sunlight was strained and flatly gleamed off the glass. Things seemed pushed together, exiled to a tiny area as punishment for being so big.

Brud panicked. Desperately he reached for the door handle, but there was no handle to be found. The lawyer heard the scurrying movements and turned in his seat.

"What's the matter, Brud?"

Brud quickly pointed, stuttering and nodding with determination to the buildings in the distance.

The lawyer looked quizzically toward where Brud was pointing.

"It's okay," he calmly said. "It's the city. Looks kind of messy from here."

Brud shook his head with short, jittery movements. His toes moved around in his boots, the tiny digits aching with restlessness and fright.

The policeman looked in the rearview mirror. He smugly puckered his lips.

"I told you," he snapped, slipping one hand from the wheel and lowering it toward his hip. "You watch."

"Brud?"

The policeman's hand tightened around his holster. He could feel the hard steel shaped beneath the leather. He thought of his partner. Maybe he should radio for backup, before it was too late.

"One false move and I'm putting in a call."

"Please." The lawyer cast an irritated glance at his brother, catching sight of how he was clutching the holster. "You're going to use a gun on him. Is that it?"

The policeman raised his hand in a gesture of surrender.

"Okay. Okay," laughing away the idea. "Just looking out for my little brother."

"That's great, Steve. Save your concern for someone else."

Brud yelped.

The lawyer tried to reassure his client. "It'll be okay." Then addressing the policeman, "Maybe you should pull over."

"Find me a place." His eyes searched the asphalt. "You see a place?"

"Watch the road, okay. I'll take care of this. It's nothing."

Brud sat back, resting his hands firmly on the seat and trying to steady his trembling.

"What's his problem?" the policeman scoffed.

Brud grunted, "Hhhhhelalalallll."

"Boy oooow boy." The policeman's laugh was tinged with cynicism.

"Steve!"

"Can you believe it?"

Brud pushed himself into the springs of the seat. He thrust as hard as his arms would allow. Pushing and pushing, he hoped he would slip past all of this, tumble free, and roll back to the farm.

"Maybe if I turned down the window. Get some air," the lawyer said, slowly cranking the handle, letting the breeze rush against Brud's face. The noise of passing traffic streamed in. Brud clamped his hands over his ears and jammed his eyes shut. He saw visions of smoke and fire, colourful pictures from the Bible. He heard the noises, great noises like no other sounds he had ever heard.

The car stopped for a traffic light on the outskirts of the city. Aware of the stillness, Brud carefully opened his eyes to steal a peek. The buildings were closer, looming overhead. To his right, a concrete stack intruding high into the clouds billowed thick white smoke.

Brud's mouth dropped open, his breath turning raspy and short. The lawyer could hear Brud's breath groaning out, and then his quick intake like a shivering sob, but it was dry. Brud's eyes scrunched shut. His forehead wrinkled as his bottom lip rose, almost touching the base of his nose.

"Hhhhelalalll," he uttered, "no go." He lashed his head from side to side.

"Hell!" Laughing with disbelief, the policeman enthusiastically wiped his moustache with the back of his hand. "The boy's smarter than I thought."

"Great, just great." The lawyer turned on his brother. "You're a barrel of laughs, you know that, huh?" He stared bitterly, then focussed his attention on the back seat in an attempt to calm Brud. Brud was moaning and holding his face, his meaty lips shivering,"bu, bu, bu, bu." Between his thick fingers, glimpses of the stark white sheen of his eyes. He rocked back and forth, shaking his head, "bu, bu, bu, bu, bu..."

chapter four

heaven in hell

"I can only suppose he'll be okay," the doctor speculated, standing with his hands in the pockets of his white lab coat. His hair was red and combed to the side. He spoke quietly and straightened his glasses with his thumb and forefinger before joining his hands behind his back.

"He's just frightened, I think," the lawyer said.

The doctor nodded and glanced at the floor. He seemed completely exhausted when he looked up again. "We gave him a shot of Demerol. A low dosage. Nothing to put him out."

"Can he go now?"

"It's best if he stayed for a little while longer."

"I can't allow him to stay for more than a few hours," the lawyer indicated. "His father wouldn't have it. I assured him that Brud would never stay in a hospital."

"Why's that?" The doctor took a deep breath. Slowly

exhaling, he shifted from one foot to the other, bending one knee to take the pressure off his lower back.

"His religion. They don't believe in hospitals. Only God's will."

"I see. Well, if I understand what you've already told me, taking him from his house like that should have been done on a more transitional basis. I'm sure you understand what I'm saying about his nature."

"Yes, I understand, but I have my instructions. I have to follow them."

"And what about serious illness?"

The lawyer shook his head. "Nothing," he insisted. "No compromise. His father said, `The Lord is the only healer.' He shouldn't have been medicated, either. No impurities introduced to his body."

The doctor sighed and straightened his glasses. "He's under my care."

"I have lists of special foods. What he can and can't eat. Everything has been planned for him."

"So he thinks this place, the city, is hell. This is what I understood from him. That's rational thinking. How do you expect him to live here without the guidance of medical professionals?"

"I see his point, about hell."

The doctor chuckled. He was working a long shift and did not want to argue. "A touch tragic."

"I don't know. You tell me."

"You're his legal custodian?"

"Yes."

"You'll have to sign for his release, taking responsibility out of my hands. I'll do as you say. I'll sign his discharge." The doctor turned and walked to the reception desk. Stepping behind the counter, he slid out a chart, sat, and flipped it open. Without regarding the lawyer, he said, "You can see him if you want." Then he turned in his chair, his elbow resting along the back. "I'd appreciate it if you left him here for the maximum time allowed. Whatever your rules are. He needs to settle."

The lawyer stared at the doctor. He seemed to be at war with this man and he could not determine why. The doctor was only concerned for Brud's health. A confrontation seemed implausible, but he was following orders, the teachings of a faith set out by Brud's father, translated from the words of the Bible.

"Thanks for your help," the lawyer offered, feeling he should say more. After all, what the lawyer believed was far different. He had to make the distinction. He did not want the doctor to think that he sympathized with these backward ideas.

The doctor was studying a chart. He nodded, mumbling, "Um-hmm," in a dismissive tone that implied the lawyer believed in what he seemed to be defending and subsequently had no respect for the medical profession.

"I appreciate it," the lawyer added, meeting eyes with one of the nurses. The doctor nodded again, this time offering no words.

Brud was sitting upright in bed. He had refused to change into the hospital gown, playfully slapping away the nurse as she tried to undress him. She was a matronly woman and looked very much like his mother. Her actions made him feel like a silly little boy, but only until she left the room, then he felt older again, alone.

He had smiled at the nurse, believing she was his mother. This was one of the main reasons he thought he was in heaven. This calm, quiet place was even more perfect with the shot of tranquil fluid lagging through his veins.

Despite this sense of easiness, he still would not comply with the nurse's insistence that he put on the green gown. He sensed that she was treating him like a child and so he slapped her hands away, wanting to turn the situation into a game.

The nurse had halted her actions with a sudden red-cheeked huff and shook a fist at him before deciding to leave. She disappeared through the smooth door like a ghost slipping from one plane to another.

"Funny," Brud blurted out, laughing with quick raspy heaves of his chest. He looked lazily around the room and watched the whiteness of the walls merging in the corners. The whiteness of the sheets blending with the whiteness of the floor.

"Whooooooo!" Brud gripped the sides of the bed with an awkward lunge. He felt as though his body was lifting from the high narrow bed. At first, the sensation startled him, but when he realized he was right where he was, not moving at all, not floating away, he began laughing — sceptically at first, then easily, with carefree joy.

The edge of the door was easing open. Brud noticed the movement and was proud of himself, waiting for the show to begin. The lawyer, or a man who looked like him, drifted into his room.

The lawyer spoke, but Brud could not make out the words until his friend was closer and Brud heard, "How are you?"

"Heaven too," Brud said, pointing at the lawyer with an enthusiastic smile. His upper lip rose and he nodded, blinking and blinking. He covered his mouth with his flat palm and laughed with shy eyes.

The lawyer surveyed the room and smiled confidently, realizing what Brud was implying. A little bit of heaven in what he expected to be hell.

"You like this place?"

Brud indicated his approval, becoming serious and observant, "Like this very much."

"You're under sedation now." The lawyer paused and stood by the side of the bed. "Do you feel any different?"

"Very much." His fingers gripped the edges of the bed, his mouth shaping a merry circle, "Whoooo!"

The lawyer could not help but feel happy for Brud. "I've never had a shot like that," he said. "But I bet it's lots of fun."

"Fun." Brud nodded quickly. "Very much fun. Mother too."

"Mother?" Quizzically, the lawyer sat on the edge of the bed.

"Yes. Mother in heaven."

"Oh." He glanced around the room, taking in the atmosphere. "Sooner or later, we all end up here. You know, this place is very much a part of other people's lives."

Brud agreed with great enthusiasm, even though he did not understand the lawyer.

"Everything like in the clouds," he said.

"Yes, very white," said the lawyer, scanning the room.

"White like heaven."

"This is a hospital. We come here when we're sick... not feeling good."

"Yes, feeling good now."

"We have to go soon. Out there." The lawyer pointed toward the door. "My brother is waiting for us in the car. He's a policeman, Brud. He'll take us right to your new home. You can meet Petrina. She's your friend." The lawyer stopped and frowned, realizing his simple tone and the careful way he was speaking. He laid a hand on Brud's arm. "We'll wait a little longer, and then we'll go."

Brud looked down at the hand on his arm, then looked up at the lawyer. The lawyer patted Brud's wrist, then started to move away, but Brud's hand came down on the lawyer's, holding it against his arm.

"You and," Brud placed a finger against his own chest, "Brud, like flowers with God faces. Close together."

"We're friends, Brud." The lawyer swallowed hard, his eyes misting in an uncustomary way.

Brud pointed at the lawyer. "I ask your name."

"I'm Jim. Jim Kelly."

"Mister," Brud said, remembering what he had been taught. "Jim Kelly."

"No, just Jim."

"Oh, Just Jim," Brud appeared discouraged. Regardless, he leaned close to touch Jim's face. "You and Brud. Stars in place, move but stay the same." He firmly webbed his hands together. Making one big fist, he shook it. "Together like."

"Great friends," Jim said. He laughed and coughed, feeling the tears rise. "We'll look out for each other the way friends do. This is a good place to start. In heaven. Yes?" Jim laughed and sniffed, then wiped at his nose. He stood from the bed and mumbled something to himself. He could not believe what was happening to him. The emotion coming so easily was out of the question. He coughed hard to get a grip on himself.

"Yes." Brud chuckled deep in his throat and fell back against the pillow. "Whooo!" His fingers clutched the bed. He waited for a moment, staring straight ahead, face frozen, as if gliding toward something unbelievable, then he laughed again.

"Heavy stuff, huh?"

"No, light stuff."

"Yeah, I see what you mean. It'll wear off in a little while." Jim thought of what would wear off; the sense of liberty that the medication granted Brud, or the confinement that this place inspired. He wondered what Brud's father had accepted as truth and marvelled at the idea of such staunch beliefs. Whispering to himself, he heard the door open and turned to see the nurse enter the room. He was surprised to discover that he was mumbling under his breath, talking to himself. It was not like him to be so distracted.

"How's our little friend doing?" the nurse asked, smiling kindly. Jim felt like shouting at her for speaking in such a condescending manner. But just as he was about to say something, Brud exclaimed, "MOM!" and threw up his arms.

Nothing can touch him, Jim thought. *Brud knows no difference.* The sound of his words startled him. He had not meant to vocalize the thought, yet he heard it in the space around him. The nurse glanced at him.

Jim made certain his mouth was shut before warning himself to be more careful.

chapter five

no land

Brud did not want to leave the hospital. There were too many amazing things to investigate. The sedation was wearing off and he felt slightly tired, but not as confused as when he had first entered.

"Bye," he said to the nurse and doctor and to Jim as well, for he believed that the lawyer was staying in the hospital, remaining in heaven. Brud was being sent away. The people in white had decided to move him elsewhere. Perhaps he was not good enough, or maybe he was going to a better place.

After kissing the nurse on the cheek and generously embracing her, Brud joined Jim beside the elevator doors. He smiled and slapped his friend on the back, making him flinch. When the doors slid open, Jim waited for Brud to step in.

"Let's go," he said.

"Go?" Brud asked.

"In."

Brud stared into the box. He had been in there before, but had no idea what the little room was for. They had put him on a stretcher and wheeled him into the room. He had watched the ceiling and felt a strange rising, then a quick short dropping and the doors had opened again and he had been wheeled out. Staring up, the ceiling moving above him was the same. He could not understand the point of it.

Brud stepped into the room. The doors slid shut and the box quickly sank, lifting Brud's stomach with the sudden downward sensation. Brud pushed both of his hands flat against the walls and backed into the corner.

"This takes us from floor to floor," Jim explained. "See the lights?"

Brud looked where Jim was pointing and saw the numbered circles popping on and off in a row.

The elevator came to a hasty stop. Brud grunted as the doors whisked open, revealing a new place, a wider room with chairs and big glass doors at the far end. Jim bravely stepped out.

"Come on, Brud."

Brud was surprised when the doors began to slide shut. He was even more surprised when Jim thrust his foot against one of them. Fearing that the doors would lop off the lawyer's shoe, Brud sprang forward, shoving his friend away before leaping clear of the box.

Jim tripped backward, but he did not fall.

Brud marvelled at the new look of the room. Someone had changed it around from the time they had stepped into the box until the time the doors opened again. It did not seem like a long time, but it could have been.

45

Brud was amazed. He looked at Jim's confused expression. His large palm patted and mussed up the lawyer's hair in a playful manner. Brud chuckled and glanced down at the tile floor. He stomped on the floor, then jumped up and down, paused with an inquisitive look on his face, and jumped again, waiting for the floor to sink just as the box had.

"What're you doing, Brud? Why'd you push me?" Brud pointed back at the doors and opened his jaws, biting down fiercely.

"That's an elevator," Jim flatly explained.

"Fun!" Brud exclaimed, enthusiastically glancing around the hospital for other wonders.

"We better get going." Jim began walking. Quickly Brud followed, keeping pace, his head looking one way, then the other, like a young, clumsy creature that had stumbled upon unexplored territory.

At the main entrance, Brud stared through the glass doors. He could see the cars parked outside. An elderly couple were moving toward the doors. The woman was limping, the man holding her arm.

"Bye," said Brud, placing a sad, weighted hand upon Jim's head. Brud seemed to tower above his friend, but he was a mere two inches taller, his wide frame setting the illusion of greater height.

"You're coming with me," Jim said, trying his best to mask his feelings of irritable exhaustion.

"Oh." Brud waited.

Jim tilted back his head and sighed, then led the way toward the doors. Brud followed, taking one last look back at the bright waiting area with the many different people watching him.

Outside, the bland air rushed into Brud's lungs. It

seemed to be thicker than the air inside the hospital. This air was heavy. It did not seem proper. Brud could smell things hidden in the air. Metals. He recalled the odour of iron from his axe blade. It reminded him of work.

Brud looked up at the sky. It was late afternoon. The greyness sweeping in to mask the sun seemed to linger in the air as well. The sun was bright despite the unclear sky. Brud had to squint and force his lungs to work harder. The air felt dirty inside of him. He coughed and glanced around the huge parking lot. The cars glistened and were neatly clipped like metal hedges.

Everything was so dull, but shiny. The smoke and the noise... Brud looked around and saw tiny patches of grass framing the parking lot. Only so much was allowed here. The people were being taught a lesson for something they had done. They appeared to be related. All of them. They were close to each other. The houses close, the distant buildings close. Many people were forsaken to this area.

Brud understood. He realized he was in a place much like hell. The same but different. A place of no land.

The car ride through the city was fascinating. Brud's fear had been subdued to shades of hesitance and caution. His mind seemed numbed, made senseless and sterile by his vast, new-found expanse of vision.

Brud watched the windows of the towers where the sunlight was glaring, as if burning against the highest ones. There was orange fiery sunlight, but darkness as well. Quiet dimness was settling on the streets. Light and darkness all at once. It was of interest to Brud. Shadows of buildings masking sunlight, huge shadows like dusk itself settling into night. But this dusk was false and without reason. There were no animals close by to be informed of the coming night. It blanketed the streets. From between the buildings, wide slanting strips of orange sunlight touched the people, setting them aglow as they strode across the asphalt.

The people. They were amazing. Brud had never seen so many people moving at once, rushing in different directions. It hurt his eyes to watch. He rubbed them and continued staring. The zigzag motions confused him. He wondered why they were moving like this, as if working against each other.

The people were different in many ways, but they were also much the same. Many dressed in similar unnatural clothes that looked too tight. Like Jim, many men wore suits. Brud told himself that they must be a special breed of people, like cows who give milk. They looked the same. Others wore the colours of animals, the skins of dead animals wrapped about them with an amazing fit. Among the constant movements, there were flickerings of all shades similar to the arc of colours Brud had sometimes seen in the sky after the rain had fallen.

Brud wondered where the people were going. They were stepping in two main directions. But, occasionally, a person would break away from the crowd to cross the black passageway. Groups of them waited for the cars to stop while the more adventurous ran among the traffic as if planning an ambush. They shouted at the screeching cars in a way that was strange and futile.

Along the ride, Brud noticed the eyes of the policeman watching him in the mirror. There had been a mirror in the farmhouse, but this one was different. This one was smaller with bits and pieces of colour and movement flashing through it. And in front of all of this, the policeman's eyes were there, steady and certain.

Brud did not know if the eyes could see him or if they were only set in the mirror, moving around but seeing nothing. Regardless, he smiled each time the eyes seemed to stare at him. He'd watch them for a while and then they'd sweep away, disappear, then flash again, as if trying to snatch hold of something. It was almost funny, but Brud was careful not to laugh.

"We'll be there soon," Jim said, turning in his seat to face Brud. Brud pointed at the eyes in the mirror. Jim looked there but could not see the eyes. He believed Brud was pointing at a huge building up ahead.

"Amazing, isn't it?" Jim faced the windshield, deciding that Brud was okay now and would continue to gain confidence.

"He doesn't know what amazing is," the policeman said under his breath.

The eyes flashed in the mirror. Brud smiled. The eyes disappeared.

"You have no idea what he's capable of," said Jim. "He could be a million times smarter than either one of us. Who says we're so special? Just because we think we're smart."

"Don't talk philosophy with me, Jimmy."

"Why?"

"You think like that, then maybe he is smarter than you."

"Who's to say? Maybe he sees things that none of us are capable of seeing. Look at him. He's alive, vital."

The policeman thought for a moment, puckering his thin lips. He ran his fingers down over his moustache and made a clicking sound with his tongue.

The eyes watched in the rearview mirror.

"Yeah, but what does he see or hear?" asked the policeman. "What kind of voices are talking to him?"

The car dipped down a concrete slope and they were suddenly gliding underground. The sound through the window became hollow and clear, like the sound in the root cellar.

Brud admired the quietness and leaned forward against the front seat to watch as they rolled toward a concrete wall. He flinched back when the car came to an abrupt stop in a parking space.

"This is..." Jim said, pausing to unfasten his seat belt and push open the door. Stepping out, he swung open Brud's door and leaned in, "This is your new home."

Brud poked his head from the car, then mindfully stepped out, one foot at a time. The concrete was smooth and pressed beneath his feet. He felt perfectly straight and strangely level standing on this new surface.

"Home," he said, surveying the cars, the yellow painted numbers on the ground, and the rough walls. Everything was grey, above, beneath, and around them. Brud did not like the idea of living there.

"No, no," Jim laughed. "Not this. Up." He pointed toward the ceiling. Brud's eyes stared up, fixing on a row of lights protected by wire meshing. His head tilted forward and he curiously regarded his feet, then jumped up and down on the concrete.

"You've got it all wrong." Jim was delighted. "This way." He pointed ahead, then leaned close to the open passenger window. "Thanks, Steve."

"Sure," the policeman flatly remarked, pulling the gear stick down into reverse. "My pleasure." The tires squealed into the silence of the parking garage as the car backed out and stopped, rocking slightly on its springs. The policeman's voice carried through the open window, singing, "I'll be seeing you in all those old familiar places."

The car screeched forward, up the concrete slope and out.

"Steve's my brother," said Jim, staring after the police car. "But sometimes...I don't know. One of us must've been adopted." Jim grimaced and shook his head, walking toward the steel door in the distance. Brud followed close behind, observing the dark sheen on the back of Jim's shoes.

When they reached the doorway, Brud took one final look back at the cars gleaming beneath the subdued lighting.

"Quiet," he whispered, hearing his own voice. "Pretty."

The elevator smoothly glided to a stop in the main lobby and a black man stepped on without looking at either Brud or Jim. Brud had come to realize that this smaller room was not a room at all, but some kind of passageway that led to different places. Brud was enthralled by the black man. He was dressed in a dark suit, and gripped a silver, metallic briefcase tightly in his hand. Where would they be going with such a man? Where else but a dark spooky place where only the eyes glowed? The barn at night. Brud remembered. The eyes of many dead things watching him. Animals. They wanted to tell him something of what they had been through.

A low stream of air slipped from Brud's lungs, "Ooooh!" He stared at the back of the man's neck, at the bristly hair that evenly sloped up. Brud was about to touch the hair when the elevator came to a stop and the man stepped out. Brud was glad they were not following the man into his place. He feared that there was danger. Danger changed everything. He heard the man's cushioned footsteps as the door eased shut. He heard a faraway cough and he knew it was the black man. The sound of the cough seemed to suit him.

"Black man," said Brud, watching himself speak in the reflection of the elevator mirrors. He could see Jim in there, too.

"That's right," Jim replied. He was staring up, studying the double row of numbers as they glowed on, then off, one by one, until the last one was shining and a bell quietly dinged. The elevator came to a delicate halt.

"Your father chose this place for you himself." Pulling a small envelope from the inside pocket of his suit jacket, Jim tore the seal and turned it upside down, shaking loose a key. "You're going to love it." He stepped close to the door and carefully slipped the key into the lock. "Of course, I gave him a little help with the selection." Jim's smile was seasoned with witty pride.

The door swung open and Brud gazed at the lavish stillness. The room was put together strangely. There were many things and they were very different. The lawyer moved aside from the door.

"Go ahead, it's all yours."

Brud grinned at Jim, then glanced down at his cowboy boots. He wiped them on the mat with studied, generous movements.

"Go on in. Don't worry about that."

"Okay." Brud bluntly stepped in; Jim followed.

The apartment was wide-open and tastefully decorated

with the most contemporary furnishings. The living room was sunken, down three carpeted stairs, and framed by a square of brass railing. To the left, a woman had appeared. She was wiping her hands on a cloth as the door behind her swayed to silence. A smile grew wider on her small face with each wipe of her hands. She was a petite woman with striking almond-shaped eyes.

"This is Petrina," Jim said, extending his arm in the woman's direction.

Petrina stepped forward until she was close to Brud. She carefully wiped one hand, then enthusiastically outstretched it.

"I'm very pleased to meet you, Brud," Petrina said with a quick, bright voice.

Brud stared, baffled. This woman was not like his mother at all, and yet she wore an apron and a plain, simple skirt and blouse. This woman was younger with clear-skinned beauty and straight, yellow hair combed over her forehead and hanging down her back.

Jim stepped toward her.

"Nice to see you again, Petrina," he declared, shaking her hand. For Brud's sake, he said, "You see? You shake hands to say hello." Brud slowly nodded, his murky eyes made cheerful by the clarity of Petrina's eyes. He knew about shaking hands. He knew very well about that. It was a simple thing. He felt excited, but too calm to move.

Jim stepped back and Petrina stood with her hand still outstretched, waiting as she coaxed Brud on with a smile and slight nod.

Brud saw a hot summer day in Petrina's hair, the warm air settling out over the tall still fields. He could almost smell the country air. He thought of the crows' caws from the trees. He thought of the silvered moon and its reflection in the lake, but it was Petrina's eyes he was watching. The narrow, good-humoured eyes.

Brud slipped one foot forward, then the other. He touched her hand, then quickly raised his stubby fingers to softly pat her hair.

"Tall fields," he said, pleased with himself. "Petree, Petree." He tried to say her name. It was difficult and he settled for "Pretty."

"Thanks," replied Petrina. "I guess." Shyly laughing, she glanced at Jim, her eyes crinkling at the corners.

Brud said, "Oooooo," at the sight of her teeth. They were white and perfect.

"I'd say that's a compliment." The lawyer noticed the open apartment door. Stepping forward, he reached for the edge of the door and swung it shut.

"I'm sure it is," she said to Jim. Her eyes shifted to Brud. He seemed dazed.

"Can I get you something, Brud?" she asked, the smile still with her.

"Are you hungry, Brud?" Jim asked, glancing around the apartment, admiring each crafted and polished item; the small sculptured figures on the mantlepiece and the pastel abstract paintings. The green paisley-covered sectional couch, and matching chair. The wooden coffee table with ornate hand-carved details.

Brud had begun stroking Petrina's hair. He was enthralled by how the light sheened there.

The lawyer refocussed on his client, "Brud?"

"Uh?" Brud was startled by Jim's voice, but his hand remained on Petrina's head.

"Here," protested Jim. He stepped forward and lifted

away Brud's fingers. "You can't do that. That's Petrina's hair, not yours."

"I don't mind."

"Yes?" Brud stared at Petrina, then cast an irritated look at Jim before quickly resetting his gaze to her.

"Just *look* at the view," Jim exclaimed, turning his attention elsewhere. Stepping down the living room stairs, he strolled toward the huge glass wall. "You can practically see the whole city from here."

"It really is something," Petrina agreed.

Brud turned to see what had captured Petrina's attention. He saw Jim stepping closer to a huge hole in the apartment. The city was far below them and Jim was moving toward danger.

Jim raised his fingers to touch the glass.

"NO!" Brud shouted, stumbling forward. Tripping down the stairs, he regained his footing and rushed Jim, grabbing him in a bear hug. Brud lifted him off his feet and took several awkward steps back. Jim's legs dangled helplessly, his face flushing with embarrassment.

"What're you doing?" Jim groaned.

Petrina could not help but laugh. She flicked her hair back over her shoulders and moved down the steps.

"He's saving you," she explained, pointing at the glass. "It looks like a hole. It's so clear."

"Come off it, Brud. Put me down." Jim did not struggle. He knew it would prove futile. "You don't need to save me. I'm fine, okay?"

Brud carried him over beside the couch and let him down.

"There," he said proudly, watching Jim straighten his cuffs and pant legs, then pull at the crease in his trousers.

"It's just a window," Jim snapped. "You're impossible."

He puffed out a furious breath, holding back other words that were certain to hurt the fool.

The proud smile faded from Brud's face. He hid his four-fingered hands in the pockets on his jeans. Slowly, his eyes crept toward a view of Petrina, hoping she would not punish him.

"It's okay, Brud," she said, nodding, the corners of her eyes lifting with sunny assurance. "You did save him. You were good."

chapter six

urban animals

Passers-by scanned the police car with mild interest. They understood how the vehicle was linked to an excitement that was sure to envigour them, trigger a rush of adrenalin into their bloodlines. But there was no visible sign of action close by, and so they continued on.

The car was parked by itself, a lone officer inside. Dusk was settling and Jim's brother, Sergeant Steven Kelly, watched the apartment lights soften, then grow brighter.

Occasionally, a tenant carrying parcels would enter the main doors. The doorman stationed there, remaining perfectly still in his long burgundy coat with gold thread epaulets and braided cord trim, would then lean into action, mechanically swoop to the door, pull open, hold, nod, release, then return to his position.

Sergeant Kelly heard the distant voice of the doorman offering salutations to the tenants. The replies were brief, one-sided, and noncommittal.

"Country Estates," Sergeant Kelly said scornfully. "What a fraud." He read the fashionable script along the front of the canopy. "They always do it. Pretend it's something more than it is." He mumbled to himself as he pushed opened the car door and stepped out. Checking both ways, he crossed the street with smooth confident strides, heading for the phone booth. He shoved open the narrow, folding door, then quickly closed it. Sliding in a coin, he pressed the numbers and waited impatiently. The connection clicked. Five rings.

"Come on," the policeman urged. "Wake up, scumbag."

Finally, the other end clicked. There was a pause.

A low, hoarse voice answered, "Yeah?" The voice coughed and cursed. "What? What is it?"

Pressing the receiver tight to his mouth and ear, the policeman whispered, "I've got something for you."

"Well, Whispering Steve. How's tricks in the crime game? You come out ahead yet?"

The policeman glanced around him. No one was close to the booth. He huddled around the receiver as if to bury his intentions, force them through the mouthpiece and into the line to connect and be speeded into action.

"You're a funny man," he said. "For such a filthy animal."

"So much for being nice. You're not a very nice man, Whispering Steve. Anyone ever told you that?" The voice trailed off. The policeman heard a tired female voice. The voice came closer, then faded out. "How about a little respect for the filthy animals who keep you in a job."

The policeman heard the lighting of a cigarette. "Cut the crap."

"Yeah." The voice coughed again, a laugh lodged and scraped in its throat.

Staring toward Country Estates, the policeman read the letters, understanding the deceptions that must be set right.

"Is that all you have to say, Whispering Steve? You just call to tell me you love me?" The amused voice wheezed, then growled deeply, "Yes, I'm in need?"

"I've got something for you." The policeman watched a middle-aged couple be admitted by the doorman. The woman could easily have been the policeman's wife. Same build. Same hair colour. But it was impossible. He tossed the thought away, focussing on the issue at hand.

"I've got something that's worth millions," he said, feeling for his holster, fingering the hasp to make certain it was there for him, "Like taking candy from a baby."

The voice gave a ragged half-hearted laugh. "Good old tune."

"The set-up," said Sergeant Kelly, glancing back at his police car, studying the gold insignia on the door. "You have to hold back. Got it? I don't want you going after this one before the right time, like you've done before. Understand? Slow set-up. Bigger dollars."

"Tell me."

The policeman outlined the specifics, certain that the man would not hold back, knowing he would pursue Brud immediately. The policeman was playing with the scumbag. But the scumbag knew it. He got rid of people for the policeman. Money was involved, but smaller sums than indicated. It was an understanding. Even though they spoke of big plans and big money, brisk, violent death was the issue at hand.

Brud reached into the pocket of his loose jeans and felt the tiny seeds from the farm. He forced a seed under his fingernail — a sensation he always liked — then lifted out two tiny spheres and dropped them into a flowerpot. A vine already grew from the pot, hanging down over the glassy black-and-white mantlepiece in the living room.

He dug his fingers deep into the dirt, feeling the fine texture. His face eased close to the soil and he took a deep, satisfying breath. A rush of memories surfaced inside of him like new green thoughts sprouting up through the soil, always fresh, always vibrant.

Jim was sitting on the couch talking with Petrina. Occasionally, he would glance at Brud and nod with a look that signified how well he understood his client.

"Brud, how're you doing?"

Brud quickly spun around, his heavy weight pivoting on his heels. He stared at Jim. He looked at the woman, waiting for instruction.

"Okay," he said. "Jim okay?"

"Yes, I'm fine, pal. Having a good time?"

Brud nodded with his mouth open and turned back to the soil, lowering his head for another rich helping of memories.

"He's great," said Petrina. "Wouldn't you just love to grab him and squeeze him?" She smoothed a wrinkle from her skirt, her eyes quietly studying Brud's actions. "He's awfully interested in the soil."

"Country boy," confirmed Jim. "He's still attached. It'll take a while, you know?"

"It's hard to figure out how much he understands. One minute, he's like a child." She rubbed her lips together. A moment later, she looked at the lawyer. "And the next minute, he has this look of supercontrol. Superintelligence, like he understands everything and can prove it. That look."

Brud poked his finger deeper into the soil, hoping to find something buried there; the smiling face of his mother that he would tenderly wash clean, an image of his father bending in the fields. He dug gently, taking his time, not wanting to damage the treasures should he come upon them.

"I once had a cat that'd never been out of the house." Jim leaned forward to place his cup on the coffee table. Reclining, he spread his arms along the back of the couch. "He lived in the same apartment for three years." Holding up three fingers, he went on, "ever since he was a kitten. When I moved into my new place — just downstairs here, you know — with my wife Andrea, the cat hid in the cupboards for weeks. He just huddled there, terror-struck. Wouldn't come out, only at night when it was dark, and he'd just keep meowing until he almost drove us crazy. We had to get rid of him.

"I was expecting something like that from Brud. I don't know. Maybe I was a little naive."

Petrina smiled politely and got up from the armchair. There was something about the lawyer that she did not care for, but she was unable to put her finger on it. Bending to retrieve the empty cup from the coffee table, she said, "I'm fixing a nice dinner for Brud. Something special as can be." She straightened her back, pausing with the cup held in her small hands. "Will you be staying? I've made enough for four or five. You wrote on your list of foods how much Brud likes leftovers."

"Yes. But no, thank you, Andrea's expecting me." He stood, his expression grateful. "Thanks all the same."

Using both hands, he buttoned his suit jacket as if finishing a long business meeting.

Petrina returned his smile — her red cheeks lifting — before turning away and walking up the carpeted stairs. Her footsteps were silent. *In tune with her manner*, thought the lawyer. *If I wasn't married...* Petrina did not look back as she moved into the kitchen. Jim was mildly disappointed. She was the type of girl who made him question his commitment to his wife. Yes, he loved Andrea and would not leave her for anything, but there was no fault in thinking, exploring the possibilities. It was only harmless speculation. He turned his attention to Brud, then took his time looking over the living room. He was searching for items that would entertain his client. He felt an obligation. His sight fell upon the television. *Perfect*, he thought. Leaning forward to take the remote control from the coffee table, he called out, "Brud?"

Brud flinched, and quickly turned, his fingers still planted in the soil, like roots, connecting him.

"I think you'll get a kick out this. Watch." He aimed the control and pressed the power button. An image popped on. It was a game show.

Brud waited, glancing around, expecting to get a kick at any moment. When the picture on the screen brightened, he fixed his eyes there. "Little people!" he shouted, astoundedly pointing at the television, laughing in spurts.

"It's a television. T.V." Jim pressed the channel selector, leaving each station on for a few seconds. All the while, he watched Brud's face, appreciating each reaction.

Brud moved away from the soil, pulled his fingers free from the depthless memories and treasures, and stood next to the televised images. He smeared his fingers in his jeans, brushing away the dirt as he stepped closer, watching the channels change.

Quickly he bent and touched the curved glass with his fingertips, as if trying to trap something. His fingers lingered there, then flicked against the glass. He listened carefully to the sharp, hollow sound that was almost musical. It would tell him something of what to expect, of what it was made of.

"Ding," he said. "Ding. Ping."

The channels continued changing until a wildlife program flashed on. The lawyer understood that this was the perfect channel for Brud.

A leopard was quickly climbing a tree, scaling toward the camera, its jaws open in preparation, its thick sharp teeth exposed.

"Whoooo!" Brud jilted back, expecting the cat to take a swipe at him. He looked to the lawyer for encouragement. The lawyer was laughing. It was supposed to be a funny thing, but Brud did not see the humour. Hesitantly, he leaned forward and touched the T.V. Looking back at the lawyer, his eyes tried to brighten, but they were charged with disappointment and uncertainty.

"Tiny animals?" Brud offered.

"That's right," said the lawyer, struggling with the smile that teased his lips. "But they're not real. I mean, bigger." He held out his arms to indicate the size. "You know how big they really are." He lowered his arms. "What I meant first was they're not really here."

"No?" Brud returned his gaze to the television and flicked the screen. Straightening, then leaning, he searched behind the set, clumsily running his hands over the box, seeking the entranceway.

"It's just T.V.," the lawyer protested. He sighed, wanting to resolve the situation. "It's not real." He let his head fall back, "Ummm," then he sat on the couch, settled, thinking. "It's television, Brud."

"T.V. not real," said Brud.

"No."

"Make believe? Fairy tale?"

"Yes."

"Ohhhhh." Brud moved around to the front of the television and knelt, face to face with the screen, the light making his skin seem whiter, vaguely greenish.

"Not real," he fervently insisted, flicking the tube with his fingers. "Not real. Not real…"

Brud's attention was drawn from the television by flashes of movement in the corners of his eyes. He turned to see Jim roaming around the apartment and he realized that Jim had said something, but Brud had not heard the meaning of the words, only the sound. He was watching the television. As Brud observed him, Jim opened various doors and gestured to the spaces within.

Brud leaned forward and changed the channel back to the game show, regarding the doors on the screen and listening to the applause. He looked at Jim and tried clapping his hands.

The lawyer dismissed Brud's foolishness with a shake of his head. Other things interested him. He slid open a closet door.

"Lots of space," he called confidently. "We'll have to buy you something to put in here. Tons of empty space. People look for that, you know. It's very important. You need clothes and shoes. Shopping. You'll have a ball at the shopping centers." He slid shut the door. Glancing briefly at Brud, he then strolled across the plush carpet, toward another door.

Brud looked back at the screen. He pressed the button until the animals reappeared.

"This is your room, the master bedroom" came Jim's muddled voice from down the hallway. "You should have a look at this bed. I forgot how huge it was. It's a king, I think. Yeah, it's bigger than a queen."

Brud turned in the direction of the sounds, Jim's words. He smiled in recognition, then glanced back at the T.V. to see a snake swallowing a field mouse. He understood this action, having seen it before. Hunger overpowering the life of another. He could smell food. Mice did not smell like that. The food must be somewhere else in the room. He did not care too strongly. His fascination with the little animals was greater than his hunger. The way the T.V. showed them blankly eating each other. He had seen similar actions in the woods around the farm and had felt this awareness of being devoured on his way into the city. It seemed to be everywhere. The light itself. The glow from buildings and streetlamps ate up the darkness. The noises on the streets fought with each other. Even the people seemed involved in a race of some sort. They moved quickly, pushing by. There was this sense of nature in the city, but it was a man-made nature that spun strangely to master itself, racing in circles like a dog chasing its tail and finally, one day, biting into itself with a yelp. His dog. Brud remembered his dog. It was a long time ago, but close in his mind. The dog was gone now.

"Oh, I almost forgot." Jim stepped out of the bedroom and down the three carpeted stairs into the living room. "Speaking of buying things, I have some money for you." He stood by the coffee table and popped the latches on his briefcase. Inside, a yellow envelope lay atop a stack of long papers. Jim lifted out the envelope and broke the seal with a flick of his fingers.

"There's a thousand dollars here, Brud." Turning the envelope on its side, he slid out the bills and licked his thumb before counting them: five one-hundreds, six fifties, and ten twenties. "Here you go." Jim tapped Brud on the shoulder and held the bills out as an offering. He could not help but glance at Brud's hands, the missing thumbs. His eyes were drawn there. He had to pull them away and force them to stare into the seemingly neutral ground of his client's eyes.

Brud accepted the money without comment. Bending his fingers, he held the neat thickness against his palm, then laid the bills on the ground and spread them out, looking closely at the small pictures of faces. He noticed the different numbers. The pieces of paper were pretty. There was a beauty to the consistency of their design. Brud glanced up at the lawyer, nodding his head.

"Nice," he said.

"Do you know what this is?" asked Jim, sitting on the couch. The briefcase was still open, and from it he lifted out a document.

"Paper," Brud declared. "Worth something."

"It's money, and lots of it. You can buy some clothes or..." He tried to think of the things Brud would like, but only toys came to mind, so he named the simple things that he recalled liking when he was a boy. "You can buy books or a stereo for music, videos for watching movies, magazines...anything."

"Mmmm." Brud took one uninterested glance at the money and turned to face the screen.

"You better put it in your pocket." Jim tapped Brud on the shoulder and handed him a pen and the paper to sign the document. "You have to sign for the money. Just an X, or whatever." He tried not to look at Brud. He did not want to cause embarrassment. Cautiously bending down, he picked up the cash. In the corners of his eyes, he saw Brud lay the paper and pen on the carpet.

"Brud!"

Brud looked up. "Okay, Jim? Forgot my manners." He casually stroked the pen and paper. "Thank you. Nice."

"I want you to sign it," Jim scolded, holding out the money. "Here, put this in your pocket. Money is very valuable. It is very important."

Brud gripped the money between his fingers, glanced at the faces once again, then forced the bills into the loose pocket of his jeans.

"I'll show you how to sign your name later."

"Sign your name." Brud nodded, remembering his father's teachings. For an instant, he felt the touch of his father guiding his hand, helping him hold the pen between his fingers to outline his name, his signature. "My name," Brud whispered, the sound of the words sweet in his mouth as if he were speaking them for his father. He anxiously picked up the pen to show Jim, to make his father proud.

"Go ahead," the lawyer urged, "Right there. I'll hold the paper. Do you need some help?" He moved to put the pen between Brud's fingers and hold it steady, but Brud jerked away and groaned a protest.

His face strained. He sucked his bottom lip into his mouth and painfully shaped the crooked stick-like lines and fat circles that were his name. When he was done, he sheepishly stared at Jim, wide-eyed, his eyebrows rising.

"That's great, Brud. Wonderful."

Brud straightened his head and laughed, squaring off his shoulders.

"Dad teach. See?" He touched the line where he had written his name. Then stared at the T.V., his eyes wet with tears. He wondered how that happened, how the tears always came when he remembered the people who had disappeared.

On the screen, a big white bird was soaring high above the land. The flight of the bird brought to mind his father's laughter. Reaching forward, he pressed his palm against the screen, warming the shallowness of the cold glass.

"Supper," Petrina called from the kitchen. "On the table."

"Okay," Jim shouted back. "Come on, Brud. First I'll show you your bedroom. Quickly." Reaching down, he turned off the television and led Brud up the living room stairs, down the hallway, and into another room.

"Isn't this great?" Jim stepped across the threshold with his arms at his sides. With a funny smile he fell back onto the bed. A pleasurable sigh escaped him. "I could just slip away," he crooned to himself, then strained to raise his head, calling, "Brud, come on in and try this out."

Brud waited in the doorway. He leaned to look back down the hallway at the T.V., but it was blank. Staring down at his socks, he felt that they were damp from being in his boots for so long. He wanted to take them off, to feel the soft carpet against his toes.

"What do you think?" asked Jim, leaning up with his elbows at his sides, pressed back into the mattress.

"Jim. Okay take socks off?"

Jim nodded. "Of course. Do what you want."

Brud studied the room as he pulled off each sock. His eyes traced the details. The furniture was trimmed with brass and coloured grey with tinges of black. The lamp shades matched the carpet and the carpet matched the paint. The bed covering was thick and puffy. Brud wondered where the wood was hidden. It must be buried under all of the grey and black.

Jim pushed himself to his feet, motioning for Brud to sample the comfort.

"Okay." Brud stepped forward and, with a flurry of brash movements, leaped onto the bed, landing on his knees. He waited for several seconds, then fell forward so that he was lying flat, his face pushed into the cool quilt. He smelled the covering, hoping for the fresh scent he was used to savouring in his bed back on the farm. He turned his head to look at Jim, his eyes blinking heavily.

"Petrina has supper ready," said Jim.

Brud yawned sleepily, letting his eyes close in a calming way. It was an easy thing to do, following the commands of his body without challenge.

"Tired," Brud said, his voice coated with the coming of sleep.

"I'll tell Petrina to put your supper in the oven for later."

"Okay, Jim." Brud was soon drifting inside himself, floating back to the fields, hovering, staring down at the animals moving through the moonlit darkness. "Little animals," he mumbled sullenly, a quiet smile on his lips. "Far away. T.V. Feed little animals."

There was a shadow ten times black against the side of the barn. The shadow's huge jagged teeth tilted back, protruding skyward as if to bite a hole through the delicious darkness. There was much noise: mechanical grating and an earth-rumbling threat.

Brud watched the shadow grow larger, fall over the entire barn. He was numbly suspended high above his father's land. Beholding the yard, he squinted to see through the tiny particles of rising dust that swirled as if to blind him. He saw that his house was demolished, reduced to a criss-crossed pile of splintered lumber. In time, the dust began clearing away from itself, opening for the form of a balding man. The ruined face leaned back to stare tauntingly up at the sky, the smile stretching wide, uncovering two gnarled rows of brownish-yellow teeth.

The fallen house lay faultless, and then the barn was struck. The heavy metal pushed easily through wood as if into cardboard, buckling. The structural collapse snipping Brud from the air, one side, then the other. Falling soundlessly, but landing without collision or injury, he found himself on his knees. Someone was trying to take hold of his hand, but the fingers kept slipping through him. He set his palms flat to the ground and felt the grass, its sweet moistness. The lingering pleasantness turning warm, a comforting warmth like temptation, like hunger, like need against his fingers, but then the heat intensifying. Soon, it hurt to hold his fingers there. Scorching red embers roared beneath the ground as the grass was charred black, then given new gleaming life. Red. Brud pulled back his hands. The land was smouldering, smoke curling and streaming into his nostrils. The smoke circling as whirlwinds of flames in his lungs. Fire and smoke and noise possessing him. He raged and screamed the fire into the air. The savage rush of orange and black lightning crackling from his split lips. Staring at his hands, and finding his thumbs in place, he felt admiration. The fire of the Holy Spirit. Or was it the power of something false? Renewing him.

When Brud awoke, he was sightless. The room was black and his clothes were soaked with sweat, stuck to his skin. Tossing his legs over the side of the bed, he breathlessly sat up, needing to find a levelness in the darkness. He wondered for a moment where he was. He wanted to check his hands. Thumbs. Did he have thumbs? Moving his fingers hesitantly, he was aware of his senses scrambling to brace a point of reference. Was he back on the farm? Had this all been a dream? Dreams could move him from place to place. He knew that. Dreams could lead him anywhere.

His mind circled itself in the darkness. Questions jeered and bound at him until he understood that the questions were all meaningless, impossible to answer. He wanted to step away from them, and, by thinking so, realized that he was moving further into himself and subsequently becoming only one thing — alone. The feeling was like a hollow hand gripping the top of his skull. He slumped on the bed as the questions and the confusion of waking cleared off. Everything was still and quiet. He sat in the center of the void, staring at the black floor that gradually, surprisingly, grew lighter.

The bedroom door eased open and a small voice whispered, "Brud?" It was the voice of his mother. "Brud? Are you awake?"

He pleaded sadly through the darkness, "Mom?"

"Brud. It's Petrina."

He saw her silhouette in the doorway and his head

dropped, hung against his chest with the utter weight of disappointment. He wanted his mother. She had been close to him. He had felt her in his dream, leading him. Someone had been trying to hold his hand, but he could not see who.

"Would you like something to eat?"

"Okay," he glumly replied.

"Are you alright?"

"Okay." He tried to come up with her name and thought of how it sounded like "pretty."

"Okay, Pretty" was the best he could do.

"I'll be out in the kitchen."

The door eased shut and the narrow streak of light retracted as if Pretty had taken it with her. In the darkness again, the past easily merged with the present and Brud — defencelessly raising his head — moved backward and forward at once, blindly grasping at all possibilities.

chapter seven

love of…

"I hope you like chicken." Petrina laid the plate on the table. She joined her hands in front of her waist and watched Brud's tired eyes; the way they were squinting under the fluorescent lighting made her feel sleepy. She could not help but yawn.

"Oh, I'm sorry," she quickly apologized.

Brud briefly smiled at her, then studied the food.

"I thought about where you came from, and so I bought a fresh chicken from the market over on Slattery Street." She paused, and then turned for the stove. Speaking with her back to him, she stirred a pot of soup, "I knew you'd like chicken. Did you raise chickens on the farm?"

"Yes, chickens. Eggs." Brud held up his hand and bent his fingers to shape an egg. "Baby chickens. Yellow. Chirp-chirp, chirp-chirp."

Petrina did not see his gestures. She continued stirring the soup, smiling down, watching the vegetables and savoury swirl in the murky broth.

"They're the cutest things, aren't they?" she said, turning and wiping her hands.

Brud nodded and used his middle and index fingers to pull a piece of meat from the quarter chicken. It lay garnished and spiced on his plate of fine china. He slipped the glistening strip into his mouth, savouring it with his tongue before chewing.

"Mmmmmm. Chicken."

"Oh, I'm sorry. I forgot about your fork and knife." Petrina hurried to the drawer and scrambled to deliver the utensils.

"I'm such a clutz," she said, laying the silverware down on either side of Brud's plate. She could not help but look at his fingers, interested in how he would hold the fork.

Brud watched Pretty's hurried movements. She seemed as if she wanted to help him. He looked at the empty seat across from his, asked himself if he should set a place for his father. He wondered why Pretty hadn't laid out an extra setting. He answered that his father was not here. His father was back at the farm. He thought of his father, then he thought of the lawyer, the faces following one another. Jim had come after his father disappeared and they were therefore linked. Certain caring gestures and expressions of genuine concern were evident in Jim's eyes. Brud recognized these symbols of affection. They belonged to his father and he wanted to know how Jim had managed to capture them.

"Jim?" He looked around the kitchen, his heavy jaw working.

"He's downstairs," Petrina said, standing close to the table. "In his apartment. He told me that you should go down later and meet his wife, Andrea."

Brud chewed in silence and swallowed, stabbing a circular slice of potato. He pressed the top end of the fork against his palm, the handle clamped with two fingers on either side of the utensil. He watched Pretty's hands as he sucked each morsel before chewing. He had never tasted food quite like this before. There were hints of other flavours hidden within the basic tastes of the food. It was excellent. Brud looked away from Pretty's hand and stared at his plate, chuckling, shaking his head, amazed.

"I'll let you eat in peace," Petrina said, glad that he had stopped watching her hands. She was nervous enough. "If you need anything just call." Petrina gently touched the top of his head. Before turning away, she smiled encouragingly, then pushed through the door.

Brud looked over his shoulder and saw the door swing to and fro. When it finally stopped, he stared back at his plate and continued eating. All of the food, the spiced chicken, the creamy corn and scalloped potatoes, tasted familiar yet different. His stomach grumbled and he looked down and patted it.

"Shhh," he said to his stomach. "I forgot." He laid down his fork and joined his hands before him in prayer, "God is gracious. God is good. Let us thank him for our food. Amen." He lifted his fork again. "Better. Food good now."

There was not a sound in the kitchen, and the bright lights made everything seem stiller, like the light in the hospital. Brud thought of a picture of heaven he had seen with clouds hanging hugely in the sky. He remembered seeing thick clouds like these hovering above the farm, across the wide open fields that were green and brown and golden. He thought of Pretty walking beneath those clouds through the tall grass, a delicate wind lifting her from her feet, rising and then settling without notice onto the ground again. Her presence was reassuring and he decided that this place was safe. It was a pleasing place, despite the absence of wood. Many tastes, smells, sights, and sounds that had somehow escaped him in the past were now here, as if they had been waiting for years to discover him.

A look in Pretty's eyes had opened something in his stomach. He did not know what it was, and it was not quite in his stomach, but growing in his chest. A warm blanket soothingly folded around his heart. He wondered if Pretty was outside, behind the swinging door, or if she had moved on, gone back to the fields where she must have come from. She had grown there, Brud convinced himself, but then shook his head, remembering the horses having baby horses, the cows doing the same. People were like this too, he insisted. People don't grow from the ground.

His jaw worked quicker. He would finish his supper, then search for Pretty. Hopefully he would find her so he could discover her eyes again, touch the fine warmth of her hair like the fields under sun. He wanted to touch her face, but was unsure if he should. He did not want to harm the surface, to make shame of this Godly creation with his awkward four-fingered touch. He felt a great need to caress her, stroke her skin like he would with his mother. The need was much greater than anything he had ever felt before. It was a soft feeling in his stomach, but it threatened to close in on him if it did not get its way.

The want was new to him. It was a kind of happiness

that he felt in every inch of his body. A happiness that could make him very sad. It was strange and unsettling. He wanted to stand, but if he stood he would not know what to do. The feeling knew no direction. He needed to see Pretty before sleeping, to touch her and to see her. It must be soon. He knew he needed sleep. His body told him. An early rise was understood by his mind and body. It was as certain as the spinning of the world. He would sleep and then wake as he had done all of his life. He would rise from bed and look for the animals in the T.V., make sure they were safely kept. And if they were still inside, he would try to find a way in there, to offer food so they would not be hungry and mad with him.

Jim sat at his desk and glanced around the room. One of the first things he had done after moving into the apartment was convert one of the bedrooms into an office. He took great comfort in knowing that he could work at any time. Everything he needed was in this room. All of the books from his downtown office had been duplicated in his home library. It had cost a great deal of money, but the sense of security was worth it. A gooseneck lamp cast a soft hue upon the book he was reading. He was researching a court case. His mind was tired and the words were beginning to lose their meaning. He read the same sentences over and over, then glanced at the two stacks of books on either side of him.

Andrea called from the living room, "Are you finished?"

He noticed his cheek was numb and raised it away from where it was resting against his palm.

"Soon," he shouted in reply, a touch louder than intended.

"Come on, Jimmy," she whined. "I'm lying out here on the couch all by myself." Pausing, she listened. Nothing. "Forget about the law. What's more important? Hey? What do you want more?"

"You can't just forget about the law," he played along. "It's too ominous and all powerful."

He heard Andrea's warm laughter and he smiled and quietly shut the book. Slowly he pushed himself up from his chair, feeling the tight muscles in his calves and shoulders. He flicked off the light and tried to wag the fatigue from his legs before carefully stepping into the living room.

"Jimmy?" Andrea pleaded, reclined on the couch. She was half-heartedly reading a magazine. She did not see her husband where he silently came up behind the couch.

"Enough for tonight." She wet the tip of her index finger and wiped away an ink mark from the back of her other hand. Trying to recall how her skin had been marked, thinking back over the day, she eventually recalled sitting at her desk, tapping the pen against the back of her hand, her nerves shrinking and expanding against the newspaper deadline. And then Frank had strolled over from his desk across the newsroom to show her a photograph. Just what she needed. Another interruption to further discourage her already uncooperative thoughts.

"You can't just ignore me like this," she continued in a loud voice, "It's...neglect. We've only been married for four months and you're neglecting me all ready."

"BOO!"

"OH MY GOD!" Andrea shrieked, her hands automatically shooting up in fright. The magazine flew from her hands, striking the coffee table on its way to the carpet. Before she realized what she was doing, she had bolted upright to a sitting position and slapped back at Jim. He hopped away, laughing boldly, defiantly.

"You, you, you…"

"You what?" he teased as he hurried around the front of the couch to sit and seize hold of her hands.

Andrea pulled free and shoved him away.

"I hate that," she said, the fright still in her voice.

"I was only playing," Jim said, "Come on. I'm sorry."

Despite his apologetic tone, Andrea would not look at him, "You really scared me."

"Hey, it's okay," said Jim holding her. "I didn't mean it."

Andrea smiled over his shoulder. Carefully lowering her hands, she viciously pinched the flesh around his waist.

"Owwww."

"Ha, ha," she raved triumphantly, pushing him back. "Don't like that, hey?" She flashed a vengeful smile; weakly attempting to hold up the mask of anger that was steadily slipping.

"Yeah, so that's the game, huh?" Jim grabbed both her arms at the elbows. "You want to play rough? I'll show you." He roguishly bit into her neck and growled like a beast.

Andrea shook her head, trying to shield the smile that came freely.

Jim let go of her arms, "I can't hurt you," he protested theatrically, slipping his fingers through her short brown hair. Her bangs were longer than the sides and he brushed them up, away from her eyes. He pinched her small chin before tracing along her lips. Watching her eyes, he was compelled to kiss her.

"I know what you can do," he whispered. "If you want revenge, write a nasty little note about me for the social pages of the paper. No one knows who you are anyway. You write that thing under an assumed name. So, go ahead. There's your weapon."

Andrea closed her eyes and, smiling, coyly tilted back her head as Jim continued to softly peck her lips, then her neck.

"Prominent lawyer batters wife." She spoke sweetly with a luxurious sigh. "Headline."

"Tell me how much you love me," he commanded. "I'm waiting."

She kept her eyes closed, her face beaming with smiling contentment.

"No, I don't love you any more," she insisted, playing at seduction. Her hand slipped behind his neck, stroking his skin the way he liked.

Moaning, "Mmmmm. Well, that's grounds for a divorce, I guess."

"You wouldn't!" Andrea's eyes widened. "I dare you."

Jim watched the greenness of his wife's eyes. The colour seemed to glow as he slowly nodded his head, "Oh, yeah. You bet. I get a real break on lawyer's fees." He felt Andrea's fingers stiffen and pry into his skin.

"OWWWW! Owww! Owww!"

"That's what you get."

"Hey, that hurt." He looked at her, seriously. "That's enough."

"Ooow, I'm sorry, baby."

"Now that's definitely grounds for a divorce." He stood and rubbed the back of his neck, genuinely angry, but trying to reclaim the jovial mood of moments ago. "I'm going to have to look that up in the books. Let's see," he tapped two fingers against his lips, "where would I find it? Subheading: fingernail attacks? Under F, I guess."

"Cut it out." Grabbing her husband's hand, Andrea pulled him down on top of her. Their bodies felt comfortable together. They were aware of how nicely they fit as they studied the details of each other's features.

"I love you so much," Andrea whispered. She squeezed him tightly, holding her breath as emotion overcame and thrilled her. "I just love you, and it feels so good." She shivered.

Jim lifted his head from her shoulder. "I love me too," he said, then gingerly bit the tip of her nose.

"I know you love me," she told him. "Now get off me. I've got to pee." She gave him a quick shove, toward the edge of the couch, and jumped up. Tumbling to the floor, Jim was struck by how the carpet was not as soft or thick as the one in Brud's penthouse. He was mildly offended and made a half-hearted grab for Andrea's ankle as she scrambled away, but his fingers could not get hold. She was gone.

"Not fast enough." She rushed from the living room as Jim leapt to his feet and sprinted after her. Screaming in mock terror, she ran for the bathroom door, crossing the threshold in the nick of time. She shrieked, slammed the door, and thrust her body against it. Her heart was racing as she fumbled for the lock. She had to push the knob in against its spring and turn it. *Come on*, she coaxed herself, *lock*. It stuck. She rattled the brass fixture, until finally it complied. Triumphant, she gave a shout, a delightful rush of nervous energy escaping her.

She could not stop herself from clapping her hands together and punching at the air.

"Yyyesss," she said. "Yes, yes…"

Hearing the sound of the lock clicking into place, Jim shouted, "Forget it," giving up and turning back for the couch, but pausing, he silently stepped to the side, out of view.

Andrea waited, listening. A few moments passed before she felt confident enough to open the door to peek out. Seeing nothing, she opened it wider, deciding to flaunt her victory.

"Hey, loser!" she called out.

As if from nowhere, Jim rushed the door, jamming his foot into the crack and pushing with all his weight. As much as she strained to hold steady, Andrea felt herself slipping back along the tile floor.

"Ha, ha. Who's laughing now? Huh?" He grunted, forcing his arm, then half his torso in through the opening. Andrea scurried backward, the door slamming against the tile wall. Jim watched her. He felt his heart beat in his chest. Andrea was standing still in defeat. She was tense, but then she laughed and freely opened her arms to him.

"Take me," she said, a big smile on her face, her bangs hanging down into her eyes.

She looks adorable, Jim thought.

"So, you give in?" He was pleased. "You're guilty as charged. I always questioned your integrity." Moving closer, he knew what to expect and dodged to catch her as she raced around him and ran for the other bathroom in the main bedroom.

"Fool!" she shouted. "You've been duped. Face the

facts: Women *are* smarter than men. A million times smarter."

"Yeah" the lawyer grumbled, leaning back dejectedly against the bathroom counter and folding his arms. "Smarter, no." He called out after her, "Just more devious."

The policeman waited in the driver's seat. His stomach was churning with hunger, but he told himself he must ignore these mere physical cravings. He must push himself a little further each day, holding back to assure his grip on himself, proving to some unknown presence that he was capable and worthy of occupying his own body.

He was going over the options in his mind, attempting to explore all avenues that would lead from a single action. Completion, he understood, was the purpose of all things. The beginning was only an introduction to what waited on down the line. The dead end claimed nothing, but was a conclusion all the same. Finished and filed away. One more shallow victory. He was trying to complete a picture, confident of his ability to rationalize each action.

Justice was coming into form. The twisted image was taking shape, but the edges were not sharply defined, which made it difficult to piece things together. Justice rarely fit, or fit sloppily. It sometimes needed to be forced.

Then all of his thoughts were scattered as a police car screamed by with lights flashing. Sergeant Kelly switched on his radio and listened. No broadcast call for assistance. He surmised that the car was on its way home, the officer inside late for supper. Perhaps it was only a joy ride. Kelly saw how the windows were rolled down as the car passed. A good way to stir up a breeze and cut through the humidity.

Enough time wasted on these thoughts, the policeman told himself, dismissing the fleeting image of the police car. Once again, he took the dark pleasure of reading the name on the canopy. Sneering, he opened and closed his lips as if the letters had left a bitter taste in his mouth. Spreading thumb and forefinger down over his moustache, he spoke the words aloud and understood that he was waiting for something. *What was it?* he asked himself. *What has been lost here?* He thought of it and turned his back on the discovery of the truth, how it made his insides tighten. His plan, that was the important thing. Tomorrow. So there really was no need to be here now.

The policeman turned the ignition switch. He was simply waiting, making sure that Brud did not leave the building. That was what he was doing there, but it was something else. The look in Brud's eyes. He smiled smugly, his vision glazing over. He was convinced of what must be done. Shutting off the ignition, he eased back into the cushioned seat. Yes, he was convinced. He wiped at his eyes, glancing around to see who might be watching.

It could be a satisfying job. With a little coaxing and planning, the judicial continuum could be maintained. For every criminal set free another would be substituted. The severity of guilt was not a question. One day they would catch up, the in and out line would meet and become one double file line edging toward the noose. Brud was guilty. The simpleton was a criminal. No doubt. He was abnormal. Deviant. Look at his hands, his thumbs.

g in the back seat. The eyes of his wife
turned quickly, but saw nothing. Fac-
ı, he wiped away the sweat that had
ve his moustache. He spread two fin-
own the thick rise of hairs. He venge-
tters on the canopy. The glamour of
ecalled the image of his wife sitting in
oom with a bed and a steel cabinet of
lothes; her thin fingers still, her eyes

hecked the rearview, moved closer, saw
ning into view, and started at the un-
cursing himself, he felt his lips tighten
ignition, his breath turning heavy in
ıg him.

Gone. A [...]
things to [...]
The simp[...]
crime gre[...]
How can [...]
who shou[...]
away, put [...]
retard sho[...]
even-min[...]
would be [...]
tiness insi[...]
on the city[...]
earned mo[...]

There wa[...]
of many c[...]
let them c[...]
run while [...]
spun arou[...]
watching [...]
In the city[...]
spit-shine[...]
Derelicts w[...]
money. D[...]
themselves[...]

Justice w[...]
tate or a br[...]
the body. S[...]
whenever a[...]
when he fo[...]
cell. Justice [...]
guments. [...]
take their o[...]

Searching[...]

something movi[...]
stared at him. H[...]
ing forward agai[...]
beaded loose abo[...]
gers, ran them d[...]
fully eyed the l[...]
such places! He [...]
the corner of a r[...]
drawers for her [...]
gone out.

Sergeant Kelly [...]
his own eyes co[...]
covering. Quietly[...]
as he twisted th[...]
his chest, troubli[...]

chapter eight

flowers for Pretty

Petrina pressed the numbers, then kindly looked up at Brud. He was noticing her fingers, how they carefully pushed each little square. Letting his fingers drop to duplicate Petrina's actions, he jammed the buttons, and the shrill mechanical signals sounded above the click of the line connecting. Petrina moved Brud's hand away. He waited for a moment, then turned and stepped across the living room.

The line rang twice before Andrea answered. She was laughing at something Jim had said.

"Hello?"

"Hi, this is Petrina."

"Hi, Petrina."

"Brud would like to talk to Mr. Kelly, please."

"Sure. Hang on a sec."

Petrina heard Andrea explaining to Jim. He said a few words to complete what they had been discussing and Petrina heard Andrea scolding him before the receiver changed hands.

"Hello, Brud?" Jim's voice was smiling.

"No, this is Petrina. Just one second."

Petrina covered the mouthpiece and called to Brud.

Quickly he turned from studying a painting of a herd of horses. It was a strange, soft painting with light colours. The horses were galloping through a door and there was water flowing beneath their hooves. Brud's eyebrows were wrinkled in confusion.

"It's Jim," said Petrina, holding out the receiver.

Brud walked to her and took hold of the hard plastic in both of his hands. He looked down at it, then nodded suspiciously at Petrina.

"Thank you," he said, smiling as he admired her brown eyes, slanting up at the corners. They were soft and always lingered like the eyes of a newborn animal, delicately seeing for the first time. He remembered the eyes of a barn cat. They gently curved upward at the corners just like Pretty's. He had loved that cat. It was silent and wondrous and always came to him when he stepped into the barn. But the cat had disappeared one day and had not returned. He hoped the same thing would not happen to Pretty. He hoped the same eyes did not mean a mirroring of pattern.

Thinking of the cat, and touching Pretty's hair with his free hand, he pet the warm strands as if stroking the memory.

Petrina glanced down at the receiver. She nodded toward it.

"Hello?" called Jim's static voice.

Brud flinched and dropped the receiver. He watched it tumble, striking the leg of the end table, then landing snugly against the carpet.

"Brud, Jim is on the other end." Almost impatiently,

she took his hand from her hair. She was slightly flushed as she squatted for the receiver. Brud bent at the same time and their heads knocked together. Petrina fell backward, soundlessly sitting on the carpet, but Brud remained crouched. He groaned at his mistake, and then rushed duck-like to her side. Anxiously picking Pretty up, he carried her to the couch where he laid her down and watched her with boyish concern.

"I'm okay, Brud." She touched her forehead and waved him away. "Get the phone."

"Okay? You okay?"

"Yes, fine."

Brud dabbed at her forehead with his fingertips, panic-struck as if checking for damage. He could not stand still. Something must be done.

Petrina sat up. She pointed at the phone, tapping the air with her fingers.

Brud quickly retrieved the receiver and passed it to Petrina.

"Sorry," he said.

"No, it's for you," she indicated, the corner of her eyes narrowing with a weary smile. "He wants to talk to you." She placed the receiver to her ear as an example and then handed it to Brud.

He imitated her movement and heard a voice, "Hello? Brud?"

"Hello," Brud replied, then gave the receiver back to Petrina.

"Mr. Kelly, Brud doesn't know what to do..."

"Just hold it up to his ear and I'll talk."

"Okay." She did as instructed.

"Hello, Brud?"

"Hello!" Brud smiled, noting a familiarity in the voice.

He looked into Petrina's eyes with astonishment.

"This is Jim. Are you there?"

"Here?"

"Brud, I'm going to bed now," Jim explained. "I'll see you tomorrow. In the morning, okay?"

"Jim?"

"Yes, this is Jim. I'm downstairs." Jim sighed, sensing futility. He was tired. It had been a very long day.

"Okay. Tomorrow." Brud understood. "Don't forget your prayers." He remembered his father telling him to say his prayers, and he thought it only appropriate to extend the sentiment.

"Sure," Jim plainly agreed. He thought of explaining his feelings. *I'm not much of a religious man, Brud. You know, faced with constant corruption one tends to lose one's faith after a while.* Instead, he simply said, "I lost the faith a long time ago, Brud."

"Oh. Okay." Brud wondered about losing faith. How was it possible? Where did the lost faith go? Who collected it?

"If you need anything, Petrina will get it for you."

"Yes." He was staring at Petrina. He smiled. "Pretty right here."

"Does he want to speak to me?" Petrina whispered, pointing at her chest. Brud looked at her finger. He blushed.

"Goodnight, Brud." The line clicked and a strange hollowness deadened the earpiece.

Brud listened for a while longer, his eyes glancing around the apartment. He was expecting more. Petrina took the receiver from him and moved it to her ear. Hearing the silence, she set it on its cradle.

"He's gone," she quietly said. "Tomorrow, I guess."

Brud stared down at the telephone. "Gone," he said, lifting the receiver ever so carefully. He turned it over in his fingers, studied the hard plastic, and listened to the buzzing. He was shocked and greatly disappointed by Jim's new appearance.

Petrina was standing in her bra and panties when Brud opened the door wide and stared in. Thrusting both forearms against her chest, her mouth hung open speechlessly. Quickly she sat on the bed, as if trying to lean further away.

"Sorry," Brud said, frowning at the intrusion. Regardless, he stayed right where he was, not knowing where to turn. He continued watching Petrina. The sight of her long blonde hair loose about her shoulders did something to him. It was much like pain but it did not hurt. It was like an ache. Petrina's skin was pale and fine-looking in the dim light of her room. Her arms and shoulders were slightly freckled, and her bare feet were small and perfect.

"This is my bedroom, Brud," she said indignantly.

"Oh." Brud had not realized that Petrina was still in the apartment. She had said goodnight to him earlier and he had repeated the word, but after returning his attention to the soil on the mantelpiece he did not see where she was going. He had heard a door closing and thought that she had left. Now, he came upon her by mistake while he was exploring, opening doors and glancing inside just as Jim had done earlier that night. It all reminded him of the T.V. He paused and waited for applause. Deceived by his own senses, he thought he heard it in his ears.

Petrina seemed frozen with her arms pushed tight to

her chest; the pressure lifted the deep white curves of her breasts.

"You should knock on the door before coming in," she insisted, trying to retain a pleasant tone.

"Okay." He closed the door and Petrina shook her head in disbelief. She reached for the cotton nightdress that lay beside her on the bed. Glancing back at the door, she waited, listening, then stood. The nightdress was long and she searched the bottom of the material to pull it on. Suddenly there was a knock and, before Petrina could settle the nightdress over her head, Brud opened the door again and cautiously peered in.

Petrina dashed the fabric against her body. "Brud!"

"Sorry." He stepped back out and closed the door. She was the most perfect thing that he had seen. Smiling at the image of Pretty, the curves of her body still fresh in his mind, he covered his mouth with the flat of his palm and his shoulders rose with quiet laughter. The door in front of him was made of hand-carved wood. Staring, as if he could see through and into the room, he imagined Pretty's movements. He remembered pictures of the woman called Mary in the Bible. In the picture, she was holding flowers in her hands and her breasts were rounded like Pretty's. He wanted to see Pretty holding flowers. These women belonged together. Pretty should be sitting in his mother's chair with a cat in her lap, stroking it. Kindness in her merciful eyes.

Turning away from the bedroom door, he wandered through the apartment, discovering a vase of flowers beside the main door. The vase was tall and shiny white. Brud moved toward the flowers and bent to grasp them. He would bring them to Pretty as an offering. But when his hand came down, he felt as if he was touching something sharp and lifeless. They did not feel like flowers at all. They had somehow changed into terrible empty things that only *seemed* alive. He stumbled back. The flowers were not flowers at all but something deceitful. He was being tricked again. They felt like the hard thing that Jim had changed into, only these flowers were thinner, slimmer, but equally as misguiding.

How could Pretty survive among such flowers? She could not be like them. She could not feel like them. Brud wondered what she might change into. He hoped that she would stay the same. Tomorrow he would find the proper flowers for her. They would help her to stay as beautiful as she was. They would be a good example to her. He needed flowers like those from the farm. Tomorrow he would leave her and find a way down into all the tiny motion far below them. He had seen it from the window.

Settled on this, he continued with his exploration of the apartment. Moving further down the hallway, he knocked on all the doors before opening them. The rooms were different, but many of them contained beds. One contained a table with a green cloth and coloured balls, another was filled with rows and rows of dark-covered books and fine, comfortable chairs. He tested all the chairs and wondered who had deserted these rooms. Perhaps the occupants had escaped upon realizing where they were. Perhaps they had seen and touched the flowers, and fled. The idea disturbed Brud, but he forced himself to think only of Pretty, and his thoughts soon quieted.

At the end of the hallway, he recognized the room where he had napped. It was huge and he stepped inside and lay on the carpeted ground. Lying there, staring at the ceiling, he thought of his father and how they would lie in the grass and stare up at the night sky, saying nothing. He took a deep breath of country air, but it was only a mechanical coolness in his nostrils, a strange quality of air. He heard his father's voice, low and patient like a clear sound rising in a field at night, "The stars move but stay the same. Like you and me. Even when you can't see them, they're always there."

Brud stood and moved from the room. Stepping down the hallway, he was pleased when it opened up into the living room. He saw the couch. By sleeping on the couch he knew he would be closer to the little animals, closer to fulfilling the wishes of his parents, the chores that Brud completed for his father.

He laid his body down and thought of Pretty. His muscles settled as he imagined her flowing hair like a swaying field coming down to cover him, her warmth, her freckled arms and shoulders, her naked toes, the rises and slopes of her body, fitting the emptiness he felt inside. He loved her like he loved God. It was the same feeling. It led him into sleep.

chapter nine

disappearance

The telephone rang from the night stand beside Jim's bed. Cutting short the second ring, he grabbed for the receiver, fumbling it to his ear with a strained expression. He was still half asleep, weakened and confused by the sudden affront.

Andrea mumbled beneath the blankets and rolled over, away from Jim, avoiding the possibility of waking.

Jim's voice was groggy in the darkness, "Hello?"

"Mr. Kelly." It was a woman, her tone urgent.

Jim felt the cold tingling rush through him when he realized it was Petrina on the other end. Quickly he pushed himself up in bed, expecting the worse, sensing the explicit energy. "What is it?"

"Brud's gone." Petrina burst into tears. "I'm...sorry, Mr. Kelly. He's just — "

"What happened?... Petrina?"

"When I woke this morning to fix breakfast, his bed wasn't slept in, and he was gone."

"Okay, okay, it's okay, Petrina. He's probably in the building somewhere. I'll be up in a second."

"I'm sorry, Mr. Kelly."

"Okay." Jim hung up and lurched from bed. He was amazed to see his wife, lying still, sleeping undisturbed despite the sense of panic that had unleashed itself. He watched the bed as he dressed, wanting to wake his wife, but realizing how hopelessly unnecessary it would be. Things would not change. The situation would remain the same. Then again, it could be nothing. A false alarm. Pulling on his shirt, he thought of the dream he had been having. It was about Brud. They had been on the farm together and he had felt child-like, carefree, yet there was something final about the place, foreboding that troubled him. He was overcome with incidental thoughts, specific details from his dream. However, a feeling of elation and well-being had falsely mastered the ill effects.

He realized it was Saturday, his day to relax, and now this had happened. There was no peace. He stared at the covered form of his wife as he fastened his shirt buttons in haste. Simply lying on the bed would take him back. Strange. The bed was like some sort of time machine that remained still but moved him in a million different directions. His sense of anxiety quickened. He was trying to spook himself, yet these thoughts somehow assured him that Brud was in no danger. The uncertainty was a sign to him. Everything would be okay. Suddenly an idea struck him. He imagined Brud wandering the streets.

Pulling on his shoes, he ran for the door. He thought of kissing his wife. He had done so every morning for as long as they had been intimate. This thought trailed him as he raced from the apartment, past the elevators, heading for the exit sign, and taking the stairs two at a time.

Jim and Petrina searched the corridors on every floor. They checked the elevators and stairways, expecting to see Brud sitting on a metal step or standing by the globes of lights on the walls, fascinated by the brilliance trapped behind the glass. But their efforts proved futile. There was no sign of Brud.

In the lobby, Jim caught sight of the doorman, smiling and tipping his hat to a young girl with a cat in her arms.

"Have you...," Jim paused to catch his breath, "seen a...a, uh, guy..." He set his hand level with his own head. "About this high...with, uh, brown hair...blond in places...round face. Funny looking plain face. Baggy jeans. Plaid shirt. Um, green, and...black, or blue checks."

The doorman nodded, smiling, "Yes, sir, I did."

Jim sighed, the pressure seeping from him. "Thank God."

Petrina was less relieved. She stood beside Jim, feeling powerless and weakened, blaming herself.

"How long ago?" He noticed the young girl staring up at him with the cat over her shoulder. As much as he wanted to, he could not smile at her.

"Hour and a half, two hours." The doorman pointed toward a small strip of grass between the sidewalk and the street. "He was digging up the grass there. Trying to plant some kind of seeds."

"Where'd he go from there. Which way?" Jim frantically searched in both directions.

The doorman let his pointing finger drop to his side. He was puzzled, wondering if he had done the right thing.

"I told him he couldn't be digging up the ground like

that. Not in front of this building...I've got a job to do, sir." He looked at Petrina, saw her devastated expression, then looked back at Jim. "I...told..."

"What?"

"This guy came over to me..."

"Brud," Jim interrupted. "His name is Brud."

"Well," the doorman glanced at Petrina, his eyes shifting nervously. "Brud came over to me and gave me two seeds. Counted them out, one at a time. He told me that's all I needed. Then he wandered off. Big smile on his face. He was laughing, covering his mouth. Crazy." He smiled freely, then the smile gradually drooped into a frown. "Or...was he a friend of yours? Did he do something? I thought he looked kind of weird to be in there. Did he break in somewhere?"

The young girl tugged on Jim's pant leg, "I know who you're talking about?"

"You do?" He bent to her.

The young girl nodded. She held the cat against her shoulder with both hands and pressed against the fur as a means of rubbing it. It stayed where it was and offered no struggle. Jim could hear it purring.

"He gave me this kitten."

"Is that so? It's kind of big to be a kitten, isn't it?"

"He just gave her to me and told me to feed her and water her." She giggled. "You don't water kittens. They drink it." She turned away and wandered into the building.

"Is that your cat?" the doorman asked, returning from opening the door for the girl. "Is that what he stole, or is it worse?"

"No, he's a friend," Jim said, straightening. "Which way?"

"I don't remember. Hang on. No, I watched him going

that way, toward east. I remember I saw the Quagmire Tower — the big Q.T. up there — when I was watching him, so he went down that way."

Jim stared east. It was relatively quiet on the sidewalk. An early Saturday morning. The occasional passer-by walked around him. A police car moved down the street.

Jim spun around, so overcome by a thought that he misjudged his distance and banged into Petrina, the impact needled their already shaky nerves. Petrina began to sob, turning away and covering her face with both hands. Her words were muffled but Jim thought she said, "Dear Lord."

"Sorry," Jim apologized, grimacing.

The doorman watched them, concerned about the couple. He thought, *They look a little crazy themselves this morning. What're they up to?*

Petrina let her hands drop. She took a deep breath, her eyes trying to brighten with a smile.

Okay, she told herself, *that's enough. God give me strength.*

"The police," Jim said, reclaiming the thought that made him spin so haphazardly.

Petrina nodded with assurance, "Yes, of course."

The doorman stepped toward them, cautiously pulling his hand from his pocket. "This is what he gave me." When he held out his opened hand, it was trembling slightly. Two seeds rested in the center of his palm where two lines met. "I thought I'd keep them and plant them back at my place. Give them a try."

Jim studied the seeds, then regarded the doorman's uncertain expression.

"They're okay, aren't they?" asked the doorman. "Not illegal or anything?" He closed his hand into a fist and shoved it away, deep into his pocket.

Petrina laughed, painfully, once.

"No, they're just seeds. Plants," Jim instructed. "From a farm." He glanced at the passing cars, wondering about Brud, thinking about the police, his brother, seeming stuck in a stupor, his feet made of cement. He needed to push himself ahead. Everything was moving away from him. He should step forward to connect, to flow and become a part of it.

"How long has he been missing?" the policeman asked.

"Since early morning."

"You know I can't file anything. Twenty-four hour minimum. Absolutely nothing I can do."

"Come off it, Steve. This is Brud we're talking about."

The policeman took a long draw on his cigarette. He leaned back further in his chair and stretched, yawning, "Yeah, I know Brud. Like I told you before, what harm could ever come to him?"

"Wrong, Steve."

"He wouldn't know it anyway." The policeman nudged his chair forward and set his arms vertical on the desktop, "Harm, I mean."

Jim stood from the chair in front of the policeman's desk. He could not remain still. He knew very well about the twenty-four hour minimum; that was why he came to his brother. For special assistance.

Steve smirked for an instant, taking great pleasure in his brother's discomfort.

"Relax, Jimmy. I'll take care of it."

Jim turned from where he was blankly staring at a framed picture on the wall. "When will you take care of it, Steve?"

"Right away." He settled back in his chair and stroked his moustache with an air of detachment.

"You mean like right away now, or right away next week some time?"

"In a few minutes." One corner of his mouth rose with a smile. "Soon as I finish my smoke. We can't smoke out there any more." He pointed at his closed door. "New rules. Keep it clean. Healthy. You know. Second-hand smoke, all that crap."

"Anything could be happening to him." Jim returned to his chair. He stared down at his shoes. His socks were grey, his shoes brown. The blueness of his pants seemed very bright. He shook his head. *If they could only see me in court. I'd be a laughing stock.*

The policeman chuckled.

Jim glared at him with anger in his eyes, "You're a great help, Steve. A real comfort. Amazing how you just jump to do your duty."

"Listen," the policeman retorted. "Don't tell me about duty, brother Jimmy." He leaned forward, across his desk, the files sliding beneath his elbows, falling and liberally scattering across the floor. "We all know about duty. What's your duty, hey?"

"Nothing, forget it." Jim bent to retrieve the files. He could not bear the sight of them spilled across the tile flooring.

"Leave them alone. Don't touch them."

Jim straightened in his chair. He watched his brother's fingers snub out the cigarette in the glass ashtray. He imagined the cigarette being pushed into his own face, hot words being shoved there. He knew what was coming. He'd heard it from his father and, now, moving down the family line, from his brother.

The policeman drew his eyes away from the pile of butts and glared at Jim. A brooding anger clung to him, the lines in his face etching deeper with a tightness that wanted to lash out at something.

"Duty!" The policeman hurled back his chair, the wooden legs screeching, and bolted to his feet. "Your duty or mine?" He stepped very close, hovering over his brother.

Jim felt trapped. He would not stand, for fear of provoking a physical confrontation. The stillness was charged, like the air before the first far-off crackles of thunder. They listened to each other breathe, sensing the danger that could come from this, then the silence was violated.

"My duty is to catch all the no-good trash, hoping I won't get my brains blown out in the process or some filthy disease from their blood if they're cut open. Wrestle the crazies into this place so they won't be able to kill each other and decent people, too. Stick the nigger junkies in the cages where they belong. The homeless scumbugs stinking up this city. Everybody wants to feed them. What for? So we can feed them forever? Feed them and feed them and — "

"Those are Dad's words, not yours," Jim calmly professed. "You don't even know what you're saying. You're just reciting."

"Shut up, Jimmy. Let me finish what I'm getting at. Just shut up, alright?" The policeman swiped a hand in front of his brother's face. "I'm talking about stopping the pimps from killing their whores. Their property, Jimmy. Slime like a plague, an epidemic. You know what's going on out there? You know how whoever created this mess — god with a small 'g' — is finally coming down on these people, trying to make things right. This disease they're spreading. They'll all be dead soon, which isn't too bad, but, in the meantime, they're infecting other people too. Babies. It's not just what you can see any more. It's a virus that kills, in the blood. Justice in the blood. The pimps and the ones up higher got half of this police force on their payroll. This slime forcing me to ask myself, 'What the hell am I doing here?' Stupid question to be asking, most people would think. Most people would be real high and mighty, and say, 'The police are here to uphold the law.' What law? Whose law? Yeah, whose law? Why not just walk away with a bundle, early retirement. Have the scum feed me with all the cash I want. Head down south. Live a good life in the sun. Not this smoke-filtered heat that we're choking on."

The policeman's eyes searched Jim's, but his brother would not look at him. "Only thing is, Jimmy, I hate the sun. I hate the thought of life down south. I'm here for a purpose and no amount of money is going to screw up that sense of purpose. I just broke a guy's nose yesterday and hauled him in for trying to bribe me. One of the Cartel guys, greasy little latino, but he'll be free, and I'll be reprimanded for assaulting him. You wait and see. I'm fighting my own people here. Fighting against the force. Our father would turn over in his grave if he knew what it'd come to. He was against all of this. His life was all for nothing. Our father's life, Jimmy. Wasted."

Jim sat still, feeling the hot breath stream against his face, his brother's body leaning close to him, hot like a blast furnace.

"Those scumbags only know revenge. They suck in justice whole, like one of those big snakes that eats animals, but this snake spits up the bones. And we try to hold them together, see what matches what, but they don't fit back together. They don't move the same.

They're like the arthritis that's getting worse in my hand from when it was crushed by a sledgehammer. A sledgehammer as a weapon. They use anything. This hand crushed. This kneecap snapped. This ear almost bitten off. I feel like I'm glued back together. Piece by piece. Don't smirk at me, little brother. It's you that gets them out again, puts them back on the street to do this to me. And it's not just me, either. It's anyone and everyone else. Legalities. Petty technicalities. Inconsistencies in testimony. Is that what the law really is?"

The policeman turned and stepped away, quietly sat behind his desk, trying to calm himself. Eyes still set on Jim, he joined his hands and waited for a statement, more words he could rail against.

"What about Brud?" Jim asked, ignoring his brother's outburst, overly familiar with it by now.

"Justice and duty," — the policeman stared at his door, as if expecting someone to walk in. He was thinking of his father. If Jim did not know better, he would have sworn his brother's voice was filled with sentimentality — "they're hollow words now." He studied the framed citations on his wall. His father's awards were up there, too, side by side with his. "You say those words, Jimmy, and people laugh. They laugh now. Can you imagine what the world's come to? The cynicism. They laugh, you know." He looked at his brother, and his tone changed. "But then they come running and screaming bloody murder when the scumbags disrupt their lives. Then are they laughing? No, nothing. They come to us, calling for justice in a way that doesn't sound funny any more. Then it's my turn to laugh." He opened his drawer and searched around, but he was not looking for anything in particular. He slammed the drawer shut. "Because I think of you and I see these terrified faces shouting for justice and I know nobody's going to get it. Nobody any more."

The policeman touched his package of cigarettes, then tapped his fingers against the box. He looked at the clock. "Cops and lawyers don't equal justice. It's like those magnets we used to play with when we were kids. Remember those? They used to push away from each other. They'd stick to everything else, but they'd push away from each other." His eyes locked on his brother's. "You know how that works, Jimmy. You know what justice is made of. The stage show in court. The twisting of words. Using people. You use people all the time. Don't look so offended, so righteous. You're their pal, as long as they've got the fee. So, don't act so high and mighty about saving a stupid idiot. Forget about this retard. He wouldn't know a friend from a groundhog. Forget about him and let's get back to playing the game we take such pride in winning."

"You've got a problem, Steve. I'm trying, okay? At least I'm trying." Jim stood from his chair, his legs weak from being crossed. He turned to leave, but could not resist hitting home a point. "You just don't try hard enough."

"You haven't been listening to me at all, have you? You just haven't been listening." He waved a dismissive hand at his brother, then glanced at the files strewn along the floor beside his desk. "Go on and have a good time. Pretend you're being honourable trying to protect this moron. But what are you really after? Ask yourself that. What're you trying to save? What's so special about someone who has no idea what's happening to him?"

Jim sat in his study, settling in his high-backed leather chair. He recalled his brother's words. They were much stronger than he had heard before and, strangely enough, they made him fear for his brother. It was hardly the first time he had been forced to face questions of ethics. But each time he was confronted by the argument, the resiliency of his pride seemed to dull a little more, allowing compromise, introducing false values. If he could not claim authenticity as one of his virtues, then he would have to refocus his attention, claim other things: a new yellow sportscar, a cottage in Cupid's Compound, a lavish apartment...

Jim questioned the good that he was doing. Pages and pages of documents came to mind. Technicalities. Social inequalities. Integrity. He *must* be doing some good. Several of his clients were genuinely innocent. But what about the criminals he had freed? He thought of the time he devoted to legal aid work, but, even then, the clients were mostly guilty. Images of the people he had defended flooded his thoughts. Specific faces. Helpless because they were trapped, caught, not because they were innocent. He tried to tell himself differently. He could competently argue against himself. But there was only one truth. It was obvious, despite his attempts to cloud it with false reasoning. His brother was right — it all came down to the guilty people he had defended. The not-guilty verdicts were wrong and easily negated the good.

The image of Brud cleared Jim's head, and the balance of guilt and innocence swayed in favour of what he knew was right. It was so simple. He felt insignificant, but alive and clean.

"This is madness," he tensely whispered. Pushing himself to his feet, he stared at the stacks of books on his desk. "Words," he whispered. "Nothing." He felt like swiping them to the floor, but his immaculate sense of restraint and reason cooly prevented a futile outburst.

Sighing, he stepped toward the window and turned the thin shaft that opened the blinds. His mind repeated, *Brud, Brud, Brud.* He would not succumb to the possibility of speaking the name, giving substance to the need he could not understand. He was almost in tears when he finally whispered the name like an admission of guilt. His bones ached. They seemed hollow as he turned from the window to see his wife standing in the doorway.

"You okay?"

He nodded slowly, the heaviness of his thoughts wanting to drag him down, making him speak as plainly as possible. "Yes."

"No word yet." She walked to her husband and pressed her body close, holding on. "He's probably just out there exploring."

"It's the same thing."

"What?" She looked at him.

"I was thinking, he's like a child, like losing a child in a store. When you're a kid and you get lost, wandering. It's like you're blind. You can't see anything unless you can see your parents. Only Brud has no fear of it. He's so amazed by everything. Enthralled. But it'll be dark before we know it, and he doesn't know what danger is."

"Maybe that's what'll keep him safe." Andrea ran her palms up and down, along the front of his shirt. "He'll turn up. Let's just hope."

"Hope." Jim wondered why he smiled when he felt such sadness.

"Here, look at me." Andrea set a finger under his chin, coaxing his eyes to hers. "You tried your best to find him. You looked everywhere. There's nothing more you can do."

"I don't know. I just feel this energy under my skin, like I have to move. I have to move because something's happening now, right this minute, and I have to be there to stop it. Every second counts." Jim searched his wife's green eyes, wanting to find absolution there. "I don't understand why I'm so concerned, so obsessed with him. I wonder, you know."

"You can't understand everything. If you did, you wouldn't be here with me. You'd be running the whole show."

Jim weakly shook his head. His wife did not understand. "It's as if I'm in despair, like someone close to me has died." He had to stop. His voice was quivering. "This is so unlike me. I can't help it. This feeling in my bones, as if I've lost someone."

Andrea moved closer, wrapped her arms around him and pressed her lips to his neck. "He'll be okay," she spoke against his skin. "I know it."

"They'll kill him." He was startled at what he had said. He could not believe the words.

Andrea raised her head. Her husband's face was smooth with sweat. She wiped her fingers along his forehead, then kissed him.

"How about a little faith in human nature. I know, I know. It's hard, Mr. Lawyer. But there must be a little left in you." She tried to smile, but realized she had said something very wrong.

Jim protested with a slight shake of his head. He closed his eyes as if to shut back the tears. Now his wife, too, was claiming he was ruined. A voice — his voice, he assured himself — spoke clearly. *They'll murder him, and, this time, there will be no deliverance. We will all be forgotten.*

He did not know his own voice. For once, he was not controlling it.

chapter ten

the street

"YES, BROTHERS, YES.

"I HAVE SEEN THE HELL FIRE DEVOURING THOSE WHO DEFIED THE WORD. ABOUNDING VISIONS OF DARKNESS. DARKNESS IN DAYLIGHT AND TERRIBLE NOISE. TERRIBLE NOISE FORCED THROUGH AS TRUTH.

"IF YOU'RE NOT SAVED, THEN YOU'RE NOT GOING. ADMIT TO THE HOWLING SQUEAL IN YOU. THE UGLY DENIAL. LISTEN AND LET IT OUT. YES, YOU SIR. YOU. WHAT WILL BE. IS, AND WILL BE.

"READ ABOUT IT, SIR. YOUR CHILDREN AND THEIR CHILDREN YET UNBORN. ALL OF US AS ONE. WE MUST SPIT OUT THE WICKED SEEDS THAT AWAKEN INTO DARK BLOOM. BE ONE FOR THE LORD. BE ONE DIVINE AND SACRED LIGHT TO ENTER AND MERGE WITH THE HOLY SPIRIT. EXTINGUISH THE UNPURE FLAMES. EXTINGUISH THE CORRUPTION. CLEANSE IT OF IMPURITY. DO NOT CONFUSE THE DIVINE LIGHT WITH THE FLAMES OF

WANT. EXTINGUISH THE FIRE OF BURNING BODIES ABLAZE WITH FALSE IDEALS. WEAK SHIVERING BODIES. THE SEETHING NAKEDNESS. DO NOT FAN THE FLAMES. PURIFY THE LIGHT. UNTANGLE THE TONGUES OF FIRE. WHAT THEY SPEAK. THE LIGHT YOU FEEL INSIDE. THE LIGHT THAT DIMS ONCE YOU HAVE SINNED. THE HOLY SPIRIT LASHED BY SATAN'S VICIOUS FIRE. YOU FEEL IT. DO NOT DENY HOW YOU FEEL THE GUILT. CLEANSE THYSELF OF WRETCHEDNESS. SPIT OUT THE BLACKENED CLOT THAT TROUBLES YOU. THE WICKED SEEDS THAT BURN THROUGH THIS EARTH."

Brud sat on the concrete rising and watched the man. The man's face was a strange colour, like beets from the ground. He continued shouting and handing out pieces of paper. Brud's attention had been drawn when he heard the word "HELL." The amazing flowing sights and spectacles of the city had hushed his belief that this place could be hell, until now. The man knew something that the others did not. Brud could see the smartness in those wide eyes.

Why were the people ignoring the man? The man was trying to save them. He seemed good and sincere, although a little angry. He was angry with the people. Perhaps they had done something to him. They seemed ashamed, their eyes were afraid to meet his.

Only a few of the passers-by actually accepted the paper from the man, but they did so without acknowledging his presence. It was as if they were snatching the papers from mid-air. Was it possible that the man was only visible to those who were good? Brud took great joy in this conclusion. It felt reassuring that he was one of the chosen few able to see the man. He was very pleased with himself and pushed off the concrete rising to accept one of the papers.

"YES, MY BROTHER. THIS IS YOUR TICKET TO SALVATION. THESE WORDS ARE THE PURIFIERS OF LIGHT. THE SAVIOUR OF ALL MEN. READ AND BE SAVED. READ BEFORE THE FIRES OF HELL LASH OUT FROM INSIDE YOU TO SINGE OTHERS. READ AND UNDERSTAND THE ACTIONS THAT DEFY YOUR SOUL. YOUR GREED. YOUR WANTON OBSERVANCES. TEAR OPEN THE FLESH. LET THE LIGHT SPILL OUT, UNMUDDIED AND BRILLIANT."

Brud stared into the man's compelling eyes, then took the paper. He was enthralled by the display. The man's devotion made him separate from the crowds. The man's cheeks were slick with tears. He whispered, "I have seen you," and he quickly turned away, shouting as he continued forcing pamphlets into the hands of those who would accept them.

Brud stood perfectly still and looked down at the paper. He did not hear the man's words or the sounds of the people passing close to him. The swishing and honking noises of traffic faded away as he took in the drawing of a man standing in a sea of clouds. Brud smiled and tugged on the man's sleeve.

"YES, BROTHER. YES. THE WORD. THE LORD. DO NOT DISGUISE YOURSELF TO ME."

Brud pointed at the picture. "Heaven."

"HEAVEN AWAITS YOU. HEAVEN IS YOUR SALVATION. PRAISE THE LORD OUR FATHER WHO ART IN HEAVEN. HALLOWED BE HIS NAME. SALVATION." The man firmly squeezed Brud's hand, then shook it. "READ THE WORD, BROTHER. HEAR THE WORD DESCENDING FROM THE HEAVENS. GOD'S CHILDREN DEAF AND BLIND TO THE WORD." The man lowered his voice. "But you, you will be saved, my friend. You are blessed here in the home of my heart. I have seen you before. You walk among us."

Brud disagreed with a flick of his head. He carefully shut one eyelid and touched it. "No read."

The man threw back his head, and wailed toward the sky, "BLESSED ARE THE PEACEMAKERS. BLESSED ARE THE MEEK FOR THEY SHALL INHERIT THE KINGDOM OF HEAVEN. THAT MEANS YOU, BROTHER." He implored to a passing man. "TAKE THE WORD. EAT OF THE WORD. FEEL THE WORD SWEEPING CLEAN YOUR FURY FOR SUCCESS AND WEALTH. YOUR ANXIOUSNESS FOR ACCEPTANCE. WHAT ARE YOU TRYING TO PROVE? GOD WILL ACCEPT YOU AS YOU ARE. DO NOT CHANGE. DO NOT DISGUISE YOURSELF. HE WILL NOT RECOGNIZE YOU."

"Yes?" Brud asked, staring at the drawing.

"YES."

"Mine?"

"YES, BROTHER, YES. YOU ARE ONE WITH THE LORD. I have seen you, what comes from your eyes. You wear no mask."

A hand touched Brud's shoulder and he looked at the man's face to see his eyes running with tears. He licked the fluid from his lips, his words growing more anxious. "Go quickly, before the crowd defies you."

"Thank you," Brud offered, staring at the drawing, wandering off into the flow. His body was jolted as a woman bumped into him. Stumbling, Brud felt the paper slip from his fingers, drifting to the ground where it was kicked by the rush of feet. Bending down to retrieve the pamphlet, he was jostled by a hurried man knocking him to his knees. The paper moved away from him, stuck to the heel of the hurried man's shoe.

"Heaven," Brud called after the man.

"Sir?" a small voice sounded in Brud's ear. "Hey, sir?" Brud turned to see a boy with a stained face.

"Got a quarter, sir?"

Brud smiled and covered his mouth with his hand. He laughed and shrugged his shoulders.

"I need a quarter, sir. I'm starving to death. Just look at me."

Brud studied the boy. The small face was full and flushed with colour. His hair was thick and healthy, shaggy and almost covering his eyes.

Brud rose from his knees and stood. He thought it funny that the boy was wearing two shirts, one over the other. The knees were out of his jeans, but Brud had seen other people with knees out of their pants as well, and they did not seem poor. Brud decided that if the boy was starving, then he was doing it in a secret way. His father had shown him pictures of starving children and explained how lucky Brud was to have food and to thank God. His father explained how they sent money to these children to help them buy food.

"No, you okay," said Brud, patting the boy's unruly crop of hair.

"No, listen," the boy pleaded, savagely grabbing hold of Brud's wrist with both his hands. "I need something to eat. Come on, my mother's dead and my father's a boozer. He beats me all night. I need money to escape." The boy sighted the bulge in Brud's pocket, the fold of bills that the lawyer had given him. "You got money," the boy said, taken aback, stunned by the possibility.

"Very rich man," Brud proudly informed the boy, repeating what the lawyer had told him, knowing the words were somehow linked to money. "Very, very rich man."

The boy let go of Brud's wrist and stepped away. He squinted and laughed, meanly, staring up at the plain face. "You're not rich. You're just a fool. I got on better clothes than you, fool."

"Fool," Brud said, liking the sound of the word. The way it made his lips push forward, the way he had to blow to pronounce the sound.

"Look at me. I got better clothes."

"Yes," Brud agreed. "Nice."

The boy's smile was sly. "But I bet you've got a quarter. Or even a dollar. That much I know."

"Money?"

"Yeah, money," the boy snapped. "If you're so rich, then lend us a hundred dollars." He smirked and stepped backward, off the sidewalk, toward a building. Leaning there, he folded his arms and smiled with ridicule.

"Hundred dollars."

"No," the boy brazenly called, "make it a thousand, fool."

Brud quickly trudged toward the boy, smiling at the sound of the word.

"A thousand?"

"Yeah, a thousand bucks." The boy's bravery waned as Brud came closer. He was uncertain of the danger that could present itself. "You said you were rich, right?"

"Yes."

"Well then, cough up." He held out his hand and wiggled his fingers.

"Cough up."

"Yeah, a thousand."

"Cough up. A thousand." Brud laughed for a while, then seized the boy's hand. "You meet Jimmy."

114

"Hey! Jimmy who? Let go of me." He shoved at Brud's fingers, feeling the smooth space where the thumb should have been. Ducking to check the left hand, he saw that the other thumb was missing, too.

Brud had started walking, forcing the boy to step along with him.

"You're not kidnapping me, are you?" the boy asked desperately, pulling at his arm, using his free hand to try and loosen Brud's grip. "A freak, too," he mumbled, cursing at the vice-like hold that would not release.

"Flowers," Brud announced, continuing his clumsy pace.

"You want flowers for Jimmy?" the boy asked, his voice cracking with fright. He stared up at Brud, and his eyes were scared. "Hey, what're you gonna do to me? I'm gonna scream."

Brud stopped. "Scream."

"Help," he said tentatively, in a low voice, as he nervously watched the people. He did not want to draw attention. He had something else on his mind. Something that could not be interfered with. A plan. "Let go or I'll scream. Help."

"Help," Brud said, smiling at the men and women passing close to them.

The boy yelled low, "Help."

Brud did the same, "Help."

"HELP."

"HELP."

"HELP."

"HELP."

The boy fell quiet, holding back a laugh, "Lay off with that," but it was useless. He saw Brud's smile and the way his fingers came up to cover it, one hand rising and then the other one covering the first, and the feeling was infectious.

"You're nuts," the boy laughed. "Out of your mind. Whacko!"

"Flowers," Brud said, becoming serious. "For Pretty."

"Ahhh, for your woman."

"Woman." Brud nodded, a kind glint in his eyes. "Yes." He shifted on his feet, thinking of seeing Pretty again.

"That way for flowers." The boy pointed with his hand, "Two blocks that way for the flower shop." He thought, *He must have money after all. Everything would work out just fine. Skully was right all along.*

Brud's smile was inspired by thoughts of Pretty. He wanted to see her face turn nice after he gave her the flowers, the way his mother's face would change when he brought flowers in from the field at the edge of the woods. He knew she would be pleased with what he brought for her. She would understand flowers. She was like his mother.

Brud continued walking at a quick pace so that the boy had to struggle to keep up. Half a block ahead, they passed a thin skull-faced man standing in a doorway. The boy winked at the man and the man hesitantly stepped out, checking both ways before carefully following behind.

"You've really got some money?" the boy innocently asked Brud. "Real money?"

"Rich."

"Yeah," the boy said. "But I'll take your word for it." He whispered "fool" under his breath and glanced back to make sure the lanky skull-faced man was keeping a safe distance.

"Store's right there." The boy indicated a shop window ahead and to the left.

"Flowers, then eat," Brud explained, smelling the scents of food cooking nearby. He knew that someone would be kind enough to offer them a meal. After all, they were hungry. The people with food would understand. The abundance of flowers in the plate glass window brought a familiar feeling to his lips. He swiped at them and laughed.

"I'll come in with you," the boy enthused. "Help you pick out the best ones. I know." He jabbed a finger against his own chest and raised his eyebrows. "I know. Me."

The skull-faced man had stopped two doors behind them. The boy caught a glimpse of the wrecked face and the thin limbs, and he flashed a triumphant street smile that skillfully razed the innocence of his years before stepping into the shop.

Brud sensed the fragrant smell of flowers blossom in his lungs as he moved across the threshold. The air changed for him. It became cooler.

The saleslady lifted her eyes from where she was totalling orders on a small pad beside the cash register. When Brud looked her way, she politely smiled and nodded, then briskly finished her addition before stepping from behind the counter.

"What can I do for you?" she asked with her hands clasped together in front of her slim waist.

"Flowers," Brud announced, nodding, his lower lip coming up to cover the top one, his eyes searching the interior.

"Well, yes," the saleslady chuckled. Straightening her

glasses, she glanced at the young boy who unkindly stared up at her, holding his father's hand. "Yes, of course. A special occasion. For your wife?"

The boy turned his gaze on Brud. But Brud was not paying attention. He was preoccupied with the splendour and vibrancy of the living colours. Releasing the boy's hand, he wandered away, reaching for the powdery feel of the petals.

"Those are very nice." The saleslady quickly approved, stepping by his side. "A lovely arrangement of wild flowers. Brilliant and lovely to smell, and on special today. For a lady friend, no doubt." A flush rose in her cheeks. Lips burning with interest, she offered a teasing smile.

Brud turned to her and nodded, distracted, but amazed at how she had known his thoughts. "Lady friend," he confirmed, his eyebrows scrunched together. He firmly nodded his head again.

"Might I suggest a variety of roses?"

Brud watched the woman gleefully turn and hurry toward the large refrigeration unit set into the back wall.

"They're the most expensive," the boy glumly called from where he was leaning against the pine counter, suspiciously eyeing things within reach, small things that could easily be concealed.

The saleslady lifted a crystal vase from the unit. She held it securely with both hands, her eyes filled with admiration. There were yellow, red, and white roses perfectly arranged with ferns and white dots of baby's breath.

Brud was startled by this creation. He had never seen flowers like these before. His fingers stroked the satiny petals as the hairs on the back of his neck began to stir. He wiggled his toes inside his boots. He was happy. He thought of Pretty's face and how her skin must feel.

"It's something I'd absolutely love to receive," the saleslady assured Brud. "I'm sure your wife will be overjoyed. Completely."

"Yes," Brud said, staring at the saleslady's fine thin lips. He liked to watch them. When she spoke, her lips were tight and barely moved. They looked like the lips of a fish. Brud pictured the woman underwater, swimming. It was funny to imagine her holding her breath.

"You'll take these, then?"

"Yes." Brud stared down at the roses and continued caressing their petals.

"Will you be needing the vase as well?"

"Vase," Brud said, admiring the sound of the word.

"Yes, the vase." She flicked the base of the vase with her finger.

Ting.

Brud smiled, still hearing the sound in his head.

"Lead crystal. On special today, as well."

Brud looked where her fingers had miraculously made the sound. He remembered seeing several vases at the apartment, but neither made a sound like this, nor contained flowers of such absolute beauty. The ones at the apartment had felt lifeless and deceptive. Something had been drained from them. They appeared to be fresh, but they were dead. What were they made from? Who controlled them? Were the real flowers trapped inside? A shiver raced up his spine when he remembered how their texture had managed to disturb him.

"Vase?" Brud touched its bevelled surface. It felt thick and made from the worn earth. "Yes."

"Fine." The saleslady's lips pertly curled into a smile. She moved away from Brud, her steps graceful and controlled. Brud's hand hung in the air where the roses had been.

"I'll just wrap these," she called.

The boy watched the woman step behind the counter where she began tearing a wide sheet of coloured paper from a roll. The boy wandered over to Brud and tugged on his sleeve.

"You better have lots of cash," the boy whispered in a threatening tone. "I don't want to be embarrassed, have to run outta here."

Brud glanced down at the boy. "Cash." Another fine word. He said it again, "Cash." Blinking, he chuckled once, as if a blast of air had been pumped out of him. The word sounded like "shhh." Brud held a finger up to his lips.

"Money." The boy sighed.

"Very rich man." Brud was catching on. He patted the wad of bills in his pocket.

"What's that you got stuffed in there?" The boy thought of shoving his hand into the fool's pocket. He doubted that he would be stopped.

"Yes." Brud turned from the boy and slid open the door of the refrigerator unit. Leaning in, he took a deep breath. The air was cool on his face. It surrounded him, and it was refreshing. He forgot everything, felt like staying there forever. He thought of having one of these machines — filled with flowers — brought to his apartment. After all, Jim said he could have whatever he wanted. He wanted this more than anything.

"Is there something else?" the saleslady's voice came to him above the humming of the unit. She had finished wrapping the flowers and now stood behind her customer, anxious to be of further service.

Brud pulled his head out to face her quizzical expression.

"Will there be anything else?" Her tone turned vaguely suspicious, a touch of impatience surfacing, the prospect of this man having no money gaining substance in her mind. He was a bit strange.

"Yes." He touched the cool glass door, but decided he did not know where he lived. He wanted one just like it, but he would wait and tell Jim, and Jim would take care of bringing it to him. "No," Brud said.

"Nothing else?"

Brud shook his head, his brow wrinkled in concentration as he pushed out his bottom lip and glanced around the shop. "More later."

"Yes, sir." She made a sweeping motion with her hand, gesturing toward the counter. "Your flowers are ready."

Brud followed her. At the counter, she motioned toward the wrapped package. It was standing upright and was heavy when he lifted it, pressing it with both hands against his chest.

"There's water in there, so make certain you hold it straight." Brud nodded thanks and quickly turned to leave.

The boy watched the saleslady's eyes tighten. He grabbed Brud's sleeve. "The money," he said. "You forgot." A cute smile was produced for the woman, "He's always forgetting."

"Money. Okay." Brud pulled the wad of bills from his pocket, and dropped it onto the counter, where the dollars folded open.

The saleslady blushed excessively. She was stunned, baffled. It took her a few moments to regain her composure before she could summon the strength to finger through the thick fold, searching for the smallest bills.

Discovering a batch of twenties, she smiled nervously up at Brud.

"Fine," was all she could manage.

"Okay." Brud turned away.

"Sir!" screeched the saleslady. "Your change."

"Hey." The boy stood frozen, his mouth agape. He could not take his eyes off the money.

Brud shifted the vase into the crook of his elbow, pressed it tight against his upper chest, then turned back and grabbed the boy's hand, tugged him along. Making a quick grab for the cash, the boy struggled to stuff it into his shallow pockets.

"Thank you," the saleslady whispered, hearing the bell clang as the door swung open. She heard the stout, plain-faced man laugh and saw him glance up, saying "Mooo" before stepping out and shutting the door. A hundred-dollar bill and three twenties remained on the counter. The woman gingerly picked up the bills as if they were a foreign material and felt them between her fingers. She even brought them to her nose to sniff them. Then she turned in the window to catch sight of this famous, eccentric man, who she thought she recognized now. A movie star! Had she seen his picture somewhere? A corporate tycoon? He was wearing cowboy boots. A string of oil wells responsible for the bulk of his wealth. Yes, she had seen his picture in a magazine. Women in bathing suits surrounding him. He was smoking a cigar, sitting back with his boots up on a rock painted gold. It was him. She was sure of it. A southerner. They were like that. Slow and easygoing.

No question, he was quite gifted in this way. She had watched him while wrapping the flowers. There was no doubt about it. He was a man of supreme and focussed intelligence.

"I've got a friend you should meet," the boy casually remarked.

Brud slowed his pace and looked down at the boy, studied the small hand he was holding, how it fit so neatly between his four bent fingers. The paper-wrapped vase was pressing into the skin along his chest. It was beginning to hurt him. His father always said that he held things too tightly, but he was concentrating on trying not to hurt the boy's hand and his force was unbalanced. He sniffed the air. Despite the obvious smells of food, the new fragrance of roses was plain to him through the wrapper.

The boy searched over his shoulder to see the skull-faced man no more than ten feet behind them. Brud followed the line of the boy's attention, but he saw many people and many sights.

"Just hang here for a second," the boy instructed.

Brud agreed with a smile and lowered his nose to the wrapper.

"Over there." Pointing with his hand, the boy tried to contain his nervous enthusiasm. "Someone for you to meet. A friend of mine who'd really like you. A lot."

Brud regarded the boy and his smile widened. "Friend," he said, as the boy led him to the curb.

"We'll cross right here," the boy indicated, but his voice was low and it seemed as if he was talking to himself. He was thinking of the fool, and he felt something close to pity.

They waited for the light to change and the boy

briskly led Brud across the asphalt. "Come on," he said, wanting to get it over with.

"Right there. Down in the back." The boy showed Brud a narrow space between two buildings, recalling the words he had heard from the skull-faced man: "This is what I like about the city. All these crowds and you can still get quality privacy."

The alleyway led to a grey brick wall with a large blue sanitation bin in the corner. Brud stopped and stared at the bin. He tapped it with his knuckles and chuckled at the hollow sound. He hit it with his fist and the sound boomed above the alleyway. Brud turned to the boy for encouragement, but the boy was staring at the opening where the skull-faced man stood. The small hand pulled clear of Brud's grip, and the boy ran frantically toward the skull-faced man, who languidly checked both ways before strolling into the space. But before reaching him, the boy stopped and fell to the side, bracing himself against a concrete wall.

"Let's have it," spit the skull-faced man, his arms dangling by his sides, his long fingers twitching and curling.

Brud was facing the brick wall, staring up until his eyes saw the blue sky. He did not hear the voice. He was preoccupied with thoughts of the stars, trying to pinpoint them. But the sky was empty of tiny lights. Brud asked himself where they went in the daytime.

"Hey!" screamed the skull-faced man. "I'm talking to you."

Brud shuffled around to face the voice. He extended his free hand as if to greet the man, just as he remembered Jim doing.

The skull-faced man spit and slapped Brud's hand away. He stared at the paper-wrapped parcel and tried to snatch it. But Brud held tightly, one hand against the bottom of the vase, the other toward the top where the petals and stems lifted away from the crystal. He squeezed until he felt a pricking against his fingers and was startled. He glanced at his hand to see the bloody marks along his palm and fingers. The roses must have teeth. He had not seen inside of them, down into their mouths. He had pressed too tightly and they had bitten him. It had happened before with animals on the farm. He was sorry. He was sorry for them, and sorry to feel so hurt.

The skull-faced man tore away the wrapper. Pausing at the sight of what was uncovered, he sneered and leaned close to the roses. He took a deep breath, his severe eyes watching Brud.

"Sometimes you just got to stop and smell the roses," he said, laughing back at the boy. "Ain't that right, Dogger?"

The boy silently forced an uncomfortable smile, hoping the skull-faced man would not notice the bulge of bills stuffed into his pockets. He had earned the money himself. If the fool had any more money, the skull-faced man would get it. But this money was his. It would let him live like a king for a while. He thought of his friends who could use a few dollars. It would be nice to act generous for once. He would buy them stuff: sunglasses, cool sneakers, and warm burgers — not the cold half-eaten ones that they fished from the dumpsters.

The skull-faced man pressed closer to Brud, cleverly withdrawing the smile from his lips. He dashed the roses against the brick wall without looking at them. Crystal shattered and sprinkled against the ground. From this explosion of sound a knife seemed to have been drawn, as if snatched from the air by the nimble fingers of the skull-faced man. He held the tip close to Brud's face.

"The money," he said, his teeth clenched and grinding. "You give it, here." His fingers curled beneath Brud's lips. "Right here, right now, or I make a mess out of you."

Brud stared at the roses scattered on the ground. A liquid warmth welled up inside of him. He coughed as the fluid glazed his eyes, then bubbled over, dribbling down his smooth cheeks.

"What we got here?" the skull-faced man shouted back at the boy. "What you bringing me, Dogger? A retard?"

The boy shook his head, denying any knowledge of the situation. He heard the sobs bucking from Brud's chest and he felt for the money in his pockets, hoping the skull-faced man would not notice, but the skull-faced man was watching the boy's fingers.

"What're you holding, Dogger?"

"Nothing." His hand flinched away.

"I don't know about that." Turning to face his victim, the skull-faced man clamped a hand onto Brud's crumpled shirt collar.

"I got newspapers stuffed in there to keep me warm for the night." The boy forced a laugh. He licked his lips and searched for words. "You know the scene. What it's like. The cold goes right through you."

"Yeah, I know the scene," he said, studying Brud's pitiful expression, then whispering under his breath, "Right through you. I'll check you out later, Dogger."

Brud's meaty lips were big and blue. They were cold, frightened. He saw how the roses were sprinkled with bits of crystal and how they shimmered in the dull light. The tears came quicker from inside of him, spurred by the wounded beauty of this loss.

"Just gimme the money. Cut out that crap and gimme the money." He shook Brud and shoved him against the wall.

"Money," Brud wailed. "Money. Money."

"Yeah." He pulled Brud forward, then slammed him hard into the wall again. "Money. Money."

"Rich man." Brud tried to smile. He swiped at his wet face, a laugh sticking in his throat. He glanced painfully past the skull-faced man's shoulder to see the boy inching toward the opening to the alleyway.

"Don't make me stick this in you."

Brud knew this man was angry by the tone of voice but he did not know why. He shuffled to the side, more and more, until colliding with the edge of the sanitation bin.

The skull-faced man shifted with him, moving closer with each step, pressing the blade deeper against Brud's throat.

Brud raised a hand to his face and clumsily wiped away the tears. His breath was shaky and impossible to control. It stuttered, tightening to a squeaky whimper when he tried to speak.

"It goes in like cutting butter," the skull-faced man dreamily professed, his lips twisting with a sharp-edged smile, his eyes darkening until the tiny spots of light that reflected there, as if from nowhere, deceived Brud into believing they were stars. Terrible stars sharp like the teeth of roses. He would tumble into the sky before him, the utter eternity of what it had to offer. "You wouldn't know it went in at all, until you couldn't breathe no more."

The air was suddenly colder than Brud had ever experienced. The cold was inside of him as if it had started beneath his skin and was trying to push out with each shiver. The tip of the blade forced a deep dent into the flesh along his throat. He knew the world would stop spinning if he was opened in this way. The ground would tilt and he would slip sideways, thrown off balance, like a balloon racing away from what was rushing out of it. He sensed the world spinning faster, attempting to bound away from itself. Animals had been opened in this way and they had fallen, their feet kicking wildly, wanting the lost ground that had been spun out from under them.

The skull-faced man patted Brud's pockets, vigorously searching. His glance darted back at the boy who was almost at the lip of the opening. "Dogger," warned the skull-faced man. "He ain't got nothing. You stay right there or you'll end up like this crazy retard. I'm warning you, Dogger, get back here." The boy paused, realizing the power of the skull-faced man's command. If he ran, he would be found, sooner or later. Helplessness was a small place. The boy dejectedly returned to the wall. Slouching there, he stared at the filthy ground.

Sighting this display of obedience, the skull-faced man felt a soul-shuddering rush of greatness and scowled at Brud, seeing the uninhibited fear in the fool's face. He spit at the ground. "You're nothing but a dolt." He lowered the knife and shifted his jaw to the side, eyeing Brud, wondering why he could not push the blade through the fool's throat, unsure of what was preventing him. His eyes jittered around, searching for an answer in the bland face. *There's no way*, he was thinking, far away in a place he barely heard. *No way of hating what's not there.*

The boy's warning shout came instants before the gunshot violated the alleyway; the blast like a stain spilling throughout the confined air.

"Police officer!" a voice shouted. "Down on the ground!"

Brud threw his weight against the skull-faced man in a fit of panic. The gunshot had startled him, spurred him forward. The sound was like shrill thunder and a flash of light. Thunder and lightning. The danger of things splitting. Trees falling. The sky opening up to unburden its weight, pour its punishment down on them.

The skull-faced man's eyes narrowed with a strained stillness, then brightened for a moment. He remained unmoved, his hands clutched around his belly. The blade of the stiletto had been folded halfway back on its spring, the tip pointing at the skull-faced man. It had slipped in quietly. The man dropped to his knees and fell to one side, his lips awkwardly touching one of Brud's boots. He struggled to speak, but instead made a sloppy kissing sound as his throat gurgled.

Brud stared down, understanding the fall and the position of the body. He knew that the skull-faced man would soon disappear. It was over. The thunder and lightning had taken him. He had been struck by elements well beyond his control.

The policeman hurried into the depths of the alleyway, digging his fingers deeply into the boy's arm and dragging him along. A pistol was gripped in his other hand. He held it steady and level, its barrel aimed at Brud's chest.

"You killed him," the policeman declared, staring down at the body, then glaring at Brud. "You killed him, Brud." His expression slowly changed; an intricate revelation. He appeared pleased in a faraway manner.

Brud could find no words. He knew no reasoning to explain this outburst of action and sound. Even though he recognized the policeman, he felt no sense of relief.

The policeman set the barrel of his pistol against Brud's temple, and pulled back the hammer with his thumb.

"You're no good," said the policeman. "Not what people thought at all. You've disappointed us. Disappointed everyone who believed in you. Fooled my brother. But I knew better. I'm the only one who knows you. I've lived with you for years and years."

The boy could not pull his eyes away from the body on the ground. What remained of the skull-faced man was intriguing, the complete emptying of the body like that. The boy was numbed by confusion. His eyes shifted away, back to the opening of the alleyway where a crowd began gathering. He cursed himself for not running. He cursed the skull-faced man and savagely spit on him.

"I could just kill you for disappointing us." The policeman puckered his lips with thoughts of release, gunfire erasing what would not stop troubling him. "But you didn't disappoint me. Things worked out well." He slid his black shoe to the side and nudged the body. "I didn't expect this at all. But it's a fine ending." Pausing to ponder the situation, he then said to the boy, "Your friend here." He nodded at the body. "Thought it was going to be easy money. Easy. You remember this. How it's never easy."

"Jimmy," Brud whispered, sniffing and dragging his palm up over his nose. He closed his eyes tightly and thought of Pretty. The glass sprinkled among her flowers. He imagined the body at his feet and how the falling of this body would change things for him. He was sure of it. When a body fell, all sorts of things happened to set everything else off course.

"YAAAHHH!" The policeman screamed as the boy's teeth sunk into his wrist, gouging deep and nipping the bones. The boy broke loose, running with his arms and legs working, as the policeman cursed off the assault and steadied himself, bending his knees and levelling his pistol at the boy's back. The trigger. His finger stiffening. Focussing ahead for an instant, he saw the group of people gathered at the head of the alleyway. The policeman knew he was defeated, witnesses always overpowering him by their mere presence. He straightened and casually lowered his gun. Remembering the throb of pain, he flicked his wrist. The purple teeth-marks were there as plain as day. He recalled the boy's frightened face as he slipped his gun away with a displeased sigh.

The boy scrambled through the people, despite the hands that tried to hold him. He kicked and scratched, then tore away, down toward the safety of Slattery West.

The policeman turned to Brud, vengeance eating up his eyes. He sneered until his teeth showed, then spun Brud around and slapped the handcuffs on. *No thumbs*, the policeman thought. *The cuffs might slip off his wrists.* He squeezed them an extra notch tighter.

"Let's go for a ride," he growled, grabbing Brud's shoulder and shoving him ahead. "They are going to put you away for this. Justice for you. A great big example for brother Jimmy. You're a murderer now."

He gave Brud another push, provoking him, wanting a fight. "Let's go. Come on." He punched him low in the back.

Brud's swollen eyes were red and clouded. He felt pain of many kinds. He tried to look back at the body, but all he saw was a dark haziness. The body seemed to be gone. The roses were gone too. Everything in the shadows was a jumble that neatly fit together. The skull-faced man had taken the roses with him. Perhaps they had crawled toward the body, bitten and eaten what was left of it. Brud understood that they were not wasted at all. If this was the truth, then they were of no use to Pretty.

The policeman shoved him again. Ramming him against the brick wall, he cursed into his ear, taunting him, calling him an imbecile, a brainless sack of flesh, a life-size example of the weakness that was bringing down this black-eyed country.

The reporters gathered before the policemen had time to section off the alleyway. They were there before the ambulance arrived, before the police photographer sauntered in to be the umpteenth person to snap a picture of the body. The reporters rallied in an attempt to coax what little information they could from whomever was near. They were told the approximate time of the murder, the method, and the standard information concerning the arrest of the perpetrator.

"Who's the man?" one reporter shouted above the onslaught of questions. "A name?"

"No way can we release information right now. You know that." The impeccably dressed homicide detective motioned for the crowds to make way for the stretcher.

"Please," his nasal voice insisted. He fingered his balding forehead and fluttered a hand at them. "Will you just give us a break? This once?" He stomped his foot indignantly. "Go on, back out of there."

"Why not his name?" the same reporter countered, savagely pushing an elbow out of his face.

The detective gave his best wry smile and adjusted his wire-rimmed spectacles, "Because I do not know the name. Because we do not know the name. When we find out, you will be the first to know. I will call you personally. We'll do lunch."

The reporters laughed and nodded at each other, evidently pleased with the detective's response.

"You'll be laying charges, then?" a female reporter shouted.

"Smart, smart." He dabbed his temple with a stiff middle finger. "Who says there's no such thing as equality? You're just as bright as the rest of the boys, dearie." The detective smirked, turned, and stepped further into the alleyway. Sighing with a hint of inconvenience, he watched the body be lifted.

A voice called from behind him, "Was it a robbery?"

"We're not certain," he casually replied, still regarding the body.

"Is it true there was a boy involved. A boy who escaped?"

"This is no place for little boys." He was speaking more to himself than to the reporters, but the reporters heard him and easily found humour in the statement.

The body was slid into the black bag and the zipper drawn. The sound was mildly raunchy. It never failed to disturb the detective.

"Did the suspect have a police record?"

"We are checking right this instant." The homicide

detective moved aside to let the stretcher pass. The crowd parted, allowing only a narrow walkway.

"Any signs of teeth?" someone shouted.

The detective stared into the crowd, searching for who had spoken. The voices dropped to a simmer. It was an important question and each of them wondered why they had not asked it.

"Teeth?"

"Is this another tooth fairy murder?"

"I absolutely cannot comment."

"Then, it could be."

"Enough. Now, that's it." He held up his hands and stepped away from the crowd. A coy look came over him and he paused to offer, "Need any more answers?" He smiled with his lips puckered, sucking in his cheeks.

A few reporters laughed.

"The minute we know anything, the information will be made available. You all understand how we have a great respect for informing the public. The utmost expediency." He wagged a finger at them. "You all know that."

The reporters laughed again as the homicide detective stepped toward the red light flashing from the roof of his unmarked vehicle, an orange two-door sports car. He tongued the insides of his mouth, swearing he could taste the bitter sting of nicotine, but it had been over a week since his last cigarette. His nerves made him jumpy. He felt vaguely unreal without a cigarette in his hand. But smoking was no longer fashionable these days. He bent into his low seat and shut the door. Fussing, he straightened his silk tie, then unbuttoned his double-breasted jacket. His stomach was troubling him. He found it necessary to take a few deep breaths. The thought of eating struck him. He was hungry. He could do with a bite. A house salad with the creamy dressing at The Emporium of Food Love.

"The tooth fairy murders." He huffed, then flicked his chin to the side to glare back at the reporters. *This tooth fairy thing*, he told himself, *there's absolutely no end to it. But I'll be clear of it soon. Vacation! Paradise.* He twisted the ignition and revved the engine, listening to the harsh sound and smiling appreciatively. *I love this car. I just do.*

The ambulance left before him, its lights and sirens shut down.

chapter eleven

Brud becomes John

Sergeant Kelly watched behind the two-way mirror as Brud was questioned by the homicide detective. Muddled words crackled through the speaker. He had just come from the forensic lab and he stared through the mirror, certain now, holding the plastic baggie between his fingers, the tooth cleaned and preserved inside.

The detective sat on the edge of the long table. He was calm with his hands joined together, resting on his thigh.

"You just have to tell me your name," the detective said in a patient, but slightly strained, voice, "and everything will be much better for you. I'll tell you my name. It's Detective Peach. Now, you tell me yours."

Brud stared down at his hands, feeling as if he would never talk again. The traces of dried blood on his fingers reminded him of the farm, but this blood was more important. It was a person's blood and he feared for himself and the consequences of what would become of him beyond this world. The initial terror of entering the city reintroduced itself. He felt sickened by regret, wavering and tightening unevenly, restlessly stirring in his stark thoughts like shadows of unwelcome creatures cast against the night dirt. He felt tired and drained. A dreamlike trance attempted to lull him toward the darkest sleep, but he held onto himself, starting and gasping to catch his breath as his mind began to shut off.

"I'm going to ask you something," Detective Peach licked his lips, his head tilting slightly, "and I want you to be perfectly honest. I know you can do that for me." He reached out and touched Brud's arm, then moved his tongue around the insides of his mouth, hoping to discover a taste of nicotine. He wished he could smoke again. It would make things so much easier, but there would be pressure and disappointment from his lover and friends. Tut-tutting, he pulled out a chair and sat, straightening his shoulders before leaning an arm over the back and crossing his legs. He thought of the brochures in his car. His airline ticket. Escape. Only a few more days. He glanced at his hand, admiring the tone of his skin. The sessions in the tanning salon were paying off.

Brud's eyes bluntly scanned the man's face. The entire scene was charged with disunity. He had been walking. He had bought flowers. A boy had been his friend. The boy had taken him to a narrow place where a man was mean to him. The policeman had come with the thunder and lightning and the mean man had fallen. And, now this. He wondered what this man wanted. There was nothing for him to give.

"Did you kill that man in the alley? Did you?" Resentfully, Peach fingered his shiny forehead and spoke in a calm voice, but he did not look at Brud. He glanced at the corners of the ceiling. "You have to tell me. There's nothing else for us to do." He simply shrugged his shoulders and held out his hands reasonably.

Thou shalt not kill, Brud thought, staring at the detective. He meshed his fingers together and squeezed. His four-fingered hands had done wrong. Everything wrong. He could do nothing right. Stupid, he called himself. Stupid, you are.

Thou shalt not kill, he shouted inside his head, the slow words hardened by the hatred he felt for himself, but the hatred was actually fear for the thought of how he had killed the man, how the man had dropped and disappeared. It was his fault. He understood how none of this would have happened if it were not for him. He wondered where they would send him from here.

Brud stared at Detective Peach's babylike face. He could not see the thoughts that the detective played with: *A religious nutcase? The tooth fairy? Maybe. What about that tooth the arresting officer claimed he sighted at the scene? Where did that disappear to? Is this man actually capable of such things? Look at him. If only he would just tell me something. I can't figure it. I simply cannot. I need a cigarette. Is that it? Is that what's cramming up my thoughts, or is it something else? This man is more like a boy. The look on his sad face. He's innocent. If I had that tooth, things would be different. But, now, I say he's innocent. The police report. The policeman was a witness.*

A noise burst the silence as Peach quickly pushed back his chair and stood.

Brud flinched, whimpering lightly.

"I'm sorry," said the detective, placing a reassuring hand on Brud's shoulder.

A rumbling sound invaded the bright, bare room. It came from Brud's stomach. He looked down and wondered if he would ever eat again.

"That's it for me," Peach announced as if tossing off a burden. Pacing away, he said, "I will not bear any more. I see no point to it. No point at all." He tilted back his head, rubbing the back of his neck. "We'll have to charge you for the one murder. You'll go to the lockup from here. You'll just go there then. We'll wait for the team to scour the alleyway for that tooth." He secretively glanced at Brud, and something went weak in his knees. *Poor boy.* He leaned forward on the table. "Do you understand all of this?"

Brud nodded, feeling it was the proper thing to do, the signal that this man was waiting for.

"You're going to need a lawyer. Definitely."

"Lawyer," Brud said. He felt the sharp shadows change form, become friendly and less anxious, quieter, the shapes of the lawyer, Pretty, his apartment, food. Images, although insubstantial, completed themselves in his mind. He saw them. What did he have to do to make them real?

"We'll provide you with a lawyer, if it's beyond your means." Detective Peach leaned back slightly, touching his hip. "You'll have a court appearance tomorrow." He groaned joyfully, pressing his fingers deep into the muscles in his lower back, mercilessly punishing himself. *Who's controlling who?* he bitterly thought. Peach licked his lips and nudged up his wire-rimmed spectacles. He coughed, mucus coming up, and he was livid with embarrassment. Cringing, he hurriedly left the room and returned a few minutes later. Brud was sitting in the exact same position.

"Are you presently under a doctor's care?" the detective asked, remembering the question he should have asked. "Medication?"

Brud nodded.

Peach watched him, unconvinced.

"What's your name, my friend? Won't you tell me your name?"

Brud knew that a killer was not entitled to a name. His name was lost with the life he had forced out of this world.

"No name." He shook his head and lowered his eyes. In seconds, he was crying remorseful tears. He thought of his mother. Her kind words of instruction. Her patience with him. She had taught him the good things and how to hold them dear to his heart. He had betrayed her. He had hurt his mother. He sobbed as if he had lost everything, his wide chest bucking.

Detective Peach stood still. He bit his lower lip and touched Brud's shoulder.

Behind the two-way mirror, the policeman held the plastic baggie up to the glass and shook it. He heard the detective's voice through the hazy speaker: "I'll just have to file you under John Doe. I know. I know, don't tell me. 'How tacky.' Am I right?" He chuckled and offered a comforting smile.

The policeman thought, *Perseverance. That's what this job is all about, finding the clues, the evidence. I told you there was a tooth. I just happened to find it somewhere else. It just happened to be downstairs, in a dead man's mouth.*

But here it is now. He shook the tooth around inside the plastic baggie. *It came out so easily. The evidence.*

The cage was dark. It was quiet and surprisingly peaceful after the confusion of the ordeal. The smell reminded him of the odours in the barn. The sting of ammonia. The sloppy floors that made him skid if he was not careful.

From the next cell, a man grumbled, coughed and coughed until the sound unpeeled toward a horrible squeal before its shrill pitch climaxed, wiping itself out.

Brud brought his fingers up close to his eyes, barely able to see them, but he could smell the spots of blood and the smudges of blue ink on his fingertips. He remembered how they had pressed his fingertips onto the paper, the strange sensation of someone else guiding his fingers and applying pressure. How a woman in a uniform had reached for his thumbs and her fingers had slipped over the smooth space of his skin and she had blushed, briskly skipping the spaces on the paper for the thumbprints.

Brud had seen the strange swirling design when they lifted his fingers away. The swirls reminded him of the small pond behind the farm, how the ducks would come waddling toward him as he approached. The ducks' and ducklings' beaks — shiny and hard, like shells — would nip at his fingers once the food was gone. It reminded him of when feeding time was over, how he would toss stones into the lake, watch the ripples that expanded when the stones moved through the surface. The curves on his fingertips had provoked these memories; thoughts moving out from the center, like the rippling circles after the stone falls. He was pleased at the memory of the water, but in his recollections of pitching the stone he could not disconnect himself. His hand would stick to the hard edges of the dropping stone and he would fly away as well. He was sinking, slowly, steadily wavering in liquid descent with the anticipation of lodging in the murky bottom.

Brud closed his eyes against the darkness, discovering bright light behind his lids. A bright light that had been flashed into his face. The glow still lingered there, only now it was inside his eyes. He knew of a similar sensation from looking into the sun. These people — displaying their powers and the completeness of their control — had flashed the sun at him. The woman in the uniform had moved him to face the other way and they had flashed the sun at him again. It was a blinding strobe of light, but, unlike the sun, it was not warm. It was sterile and empty of heat. It did nothing for him. No comfort or growth, only a vague indication of capture.

There had been much confusion and noise. But now it was quiet, except for the occasional introduction of a new person who arrived after the light came on in the compound and was put in a cage just like Brud. Then the man who showed these people where to go would leave and the light would be taken away again.

Silence was the thing. Even when the visitors came, they did not speak. They were guided soundlessly to their places and the doors were closed as if they belonged there all along and had finally found their way back. The silence was greater than any noise. The silence was like a fabric; one heavy quilt over another, and another, pressing around him with the shapeless, yet skintight, form of darkness.

Brud stepped close to the bare bars. He touched the steel and felt that it was cold. It was reassuring, the cool touch of the bars. He had expected them to be hot, charged with fire. Because they were cold he held onto them and pressed his face between the steel rungs. His thoughts wandered back to the country. The smell of air after dark, the cold chill of the breeze stroking each moonlit tip of grass, brushing along the field until it touched him where he stood on the steps of the farmhouse with his mother and father sleeping upstairs. He would stand this way late at night, watching for something that always seemed to linger across the fields for him, linger in the barn where the animals stirred, along the dim rails of the corral. A sweetness. A perfection that he wanted to hold close to him in hopes of forcing it into his heart, but it was something he could not touch. He could not hold it in his hands. Was it because his hands were wrong, or simply because this thing could not be held at all? Regardless, he felt the beautiful mystery of it reassuring him.

A cool night lived in the prison bars. He sensed it there, and understood how he would never fully hold this perfection. He thought, eight, ten.

He quietly said, "Eight, ten. Never ten," to the darkness, remembering his mother and his father. He pushed his lips together, holding back a sob, his eager love punishing him.

"You know his father was hoping Brud would die first?" Staring at the blank ceiling, Jim spoke into the darkness. His voice was colourless and far away. His right arm lay heavily across his forehead, but the weight of it felt comforting. He left it there. "I know it sounds cruel, but it's the proper choice when you think, huh?"

"Maybe he should have killed Brud before he died," his wife suggested.

"Come on now. It's too late to get into that. I need the sleep."

Andrea pulled the sheets up close to her chin. The fabric was cool and smelled lovely. She savoured the fragrance, secretively sniffing and cradling lavish memories of her youth.

"Okay, then. Let's do that," she agreed, but knowing different. Her husband would not be so easily silenced. "Let's just get some sleep, Jim."

"He always said to me, 'If I die before Brud, then he's going to need all the help he can get.' The thought of murdering Brud never even entered his mind. It just wouldn't. Issues like that never touch them out there. They're fundamental people. Simple. The way we all used to be before we got so pompous. They wouldn't think of prematurely ending another person's life. Brud's father said, 'If Brud dies first, at least I'd know where he was. He'd be safe in the arms of Jesus.' That was a kind thought, but it would stop right there. He wouldn't go beyond that, cross the line from kindness into cruelty."

Andrea moved her hand beneath the sheets and rested it against Jim's warm thigh.

"Well," she said plainly, "if I'm ever slobbering and drooling all over myself, convulsing, in constant pain, I certainly hope you'd do the favour of putting me out."

"Let's not talk about that."

"You're supposed to be the practical one. But I'm on to you. I know you've got a real soft spot." She nuzzled close to him, a satisfied smile resting comfortably on her lips.

"Right," he said.

"Right," she said.

The room was silent. Jim saw the three red digits of the clock change at once. It was a new hour.

He closed his eyes and the darkness became darker, terrifying, logical. The thought of death. The finality.

"I can almost feel you thinking," Andrea whispered. "It's like an energy. Strange, hey, how we can feel that, know when the other's not asleep? I think that's amazing."

"It's just your perception. That's all. Biology."

"Oh, yeah. Okay, goodnight." She sighed and rolled away from him. A few moments later, she rolled back, settling in place. "That's enough of thinking like that."

"I'm paid to think that way."

"Just close your eyes and think of me."

Jim opened his eyes. He looked at his wife, the faint outline of her face, her eyes calmly watching him.

"I always think of you," he said, a wounded look softening his expression.

Andrea's laugh was tired. "Sure," she said, holding the smile for him. "Don't look so tragic."

"But if I close my eyes now all I see is Brud wandering the streets like a zombie. That's how I see him. Isn't that strange?"

"You always see the terrible things. Now, let's stop. Okay? Come on, go to sleep."

"Brud's scared. There's something wrong about frightening the innocent. I think that's what I'm thinking, what bothers me."

"Melodrama, Jimmy," Andrea pleaded. "Let's sleep, okay?" Her fingers caressed Jim's thigh. "Relax, baby. Shhhh."

Jim closed his eyes, savouring the intimate caress. He saw Brud and he kept his lids shut as a means of punishing himself for his negligence. Brud's face and the hollow of his mouth, widening, the scream, "HELL!"

Stupid. Unreasonable.

"Why do we have to threaten people?" he asked.

"Hmmm?" Andrea mumbled, half-asleep.

"With images of hell. We have to put such fear into people. Can't they just be good without the threat? In this life, I mean. Forget about what happens after. Why can't people be good without the threat of damnation? What's the matter with us? Are we supposed to be good, or is that all just a lie? A fraud. It's only religion that tells us we're supposed to be good, but people say they don't believe in God and still they act with kindness, goodness. Why? They must believe in something. Why would they act good, want to act good at all?"

He looked over at his wife. She rolled away, offering her back to him. He accepted the invitation, pressing in close to her warm body, subdued by the naturalness of how he fit against her.

"Sleep," he whispered, forgetting his struggle. "You remember that quote, 'Sweet, clean sleep of childhood — where has it gone?' Remember that?" He gently nudged his wife but there was no reply. "Who wrote that? Was it a Russian?"

Andrea gave a satisfactory, "mmmmm."

Jim strained to look back over his shoulder, toward the place where he knew that window was. He wished that the deep blue curtains were open more than a crack. He wanted to see the lights of the city. From a distance, looking down, they would appear magical. So much light in an area that would be lost without it. He thought of the threats of hell again. The idea of instilling these images in children made his pulse quicken, his heart speed unnaturally. It seemed utterly wrong. Brud had perceived this place as hell. It was far from that. *How off the mark he had been*, Jim thought, secretly pitying Brud for having faith in all the lies he had been taught.

"You know something?" The voice was restrained, fragile, as if delicately held away from itself.

Brud quickly sat up, listening. His eyes strained as if to view the sound, but there was no definition. No indications of life, nothing similar to how the wind could sometimes be seen as it carried the snow in its sweeping design. No breeze. No elements to outline the invisible. Just the strong stench that he remembered from the barn, and the darkness, full now, facing him.

There was silence for a while, then the voice came again, weak and uncertain, "I don't know where I..." A nervous burst of words. "Where am I? Where?"

Brud stood from his bunk and stepped through the blackness, his body seeming to glide. Without thinking, he was drawn toward the voice.

"Alive?" the voice gasped anxiously, shrivelling with dread. "Please. Someone? Answer. Am I alive?"

Brud blindly listened.

"Oh God! Don't do this to me. Please God! You're hiding here. It's a trick. Is that you huddled in the corner? I think..."

Brud inched forward until he was as close as possible to the voice. The bars pressed against his chest. His hands gripped them. Their coolness. Their resistance.

"Jesus Christ!" the voice screamed, pleading. "If there's

a God. I know there is. Now. There has to be. Is this the end, the way it happens? I'm here, but there's nothing. No, don't tell me. I promise. I promise. I promise. Just...I promise."

Brud's lips parted. He wondered who this man could be. Why he needed God so desperately.

"Hello," Brud pledged.

"Who's that?" the voice recoiled, jutting back into its body.

Brud thought of his name, his new name. He was no longer certain who he was. They had made him into somebody else.

"No one," he said.

"Oh, my God, please. Am I alive? Tell me."

Brud did not understand the question. He waited in silence for the voice to speak.

"It must be..." There was a pause, and Brud heard the slow shifting sound of movement, feet touching, whispering against the concrete floor. "These are...I'm in a cell...prison," the voice ecstatically announced. "I'm alive. Tell me I am. You. Who are you? You, No One." The voice became angry, confused, and savage, "NO ONE!"

Brud ran his hands up and down the bars. The voice within the darkness bewildered him with such resolve that he could almost understand what it was trying to say. The feeling was in the air, but, shamefully, he could not hold it.

"Tell me I am, No One," pleaded the voice. "I am and only you can tell me. Must be." A sharp scream, the sound sparkling in the air, "SOMEBODY! PLEASE SOMEBODY. TELL ME THIS ISN'T HOW IT ENDS. GET UP." Brud heard the sound of a foot kicking into another body. "GET UP. GET UP. WHOEVER YOU ARE."

A grumbling assembly of voices laboured from sleep. Grunts and curses rose, then roughly settled, back toward the silent tread of unconsciousness.

Someone called, "Shut up!"

The voice laughed. "Thank God. Thank God. Thank you for your guidance. Your threat. I will shut up. I knew it. I'm here, was here all along. It's just the darkness does it sometimes. Okay. It's okay. It's okay. We're here, No One."

The silence carefully sealed itself and became whole again. Brud said goodnight. He said it the way he had said it to his mother and father. At first, he was glad he had said it. A nostalgic smile reinstating heartfelt sentiments. But then the certain distance of those sentiments delivered brutal sadness.

The voice spoke to him, "Goodnight, No One. Everything's okay now. It doesn't end this way. It doesn't."

Jim was holding the refrigerator door open, staring at the side of a milk carton when he heard the telephone ring. The sound made him flinch. He turned to go for it, but Andrea called from the other room, "I've got it."

Listening for a moment, he then stepped toward the kitchen door and leaned out, staring across the living room where Andrea sat on the couch. She lifted the receiver, awkwardly trying to set it against her ear. Her burgundy terry-cloth bathrobe was loosely tied at the waist and she was holding a towel in one hand, attempting to dry her hair.

Jim thought, *Who could it be this early? On Monday?*

Andrea looked toward the kitchen. She was listening,

but when she saw her husband standing there, she said, "Just a minute, please," and held the receiver in the air.

"Who is it?" he quietly called, pushing through the swinging door, hearing it flap behind him.

Andrea shrugged her shoulders.

"I'll get your breakfast," she said, letting the receiver change hands. She smiled at her husband and kissed him on the cheek, but she did not leave his side. She stood there, slowly towelling her damp hair, watching her husband's lips, then the receiver.

"Yes?" Jim inspected his wife's eyes.

The voice on the other end explained the situation. A lawyer was needed to handle a legal aid case. The case in question involved defending a man charged with murder. The crime was committed two nights ago. The man was a John Doe, possibly psychotic.

"Who'd he murder?" Jim asked, automatically thinking what he had been dreading for days now: that Brud had been killed. He kept calm, always calm. He was taught not to worry, believing himself to be gifted in emotional avoidance and self-control. He covered the receiver and mouthed the word "business." Andrea nodded and wandered toward the kitchen.

The voice explained, "A guy with a criminal record the length of both your arms. Jake Skully. You hear of him?"

"No." Jim licked his lips. He thought of his brother's words. He thought of the charge: murder. He wanted to take the case if only to spite his brother, to flaunt it in his face, but he knew the foolishness of the gesture and the state of exhaustion that made him think this way. Presently, he could not trust his judgement and so he understood it would be wrong to accept.

"I'd like to handle it, really. If it was any other time I'd take the case without question, but my plate is full. I should say, very full, overflowing."

"Can't persuade you?"

"Seriously, I would — "

"This guy's going to need a good attorney. They're thinking he could be the tooth fairy murderer. He's a real creepy character. Momma's boy. Crybaby type. I met with him. Not a word. Wouldn't open his mouth. Crazy."

"Crazy, huh?" Jim mused. "I know crazy."

"You wouldn't believe it."

"Oh, yes I would. Believe me, I've seen them." Jim watched his wife turn and push the kitchen door open with her behind. She paused, staring at him, listening. Then she turned around, the towel around her shoulders now, her short hair looking slick. The door swung closed, concealing her.

"Okay," said the voice, "thanks anyway."

"Listen, did you try Rowe?"

"Who?"

"Give Rowe a try. Toby Rowe. I'm sure he'd be willing."

"Your office?"

"Right. But don't say I mentioned his name. I don't want him feeling pressured. He's new and he's ambitious and he could use the experience. He'll do a good job."

"Okay, later."

"Yeah." Jim hung up. He stood still, thinking about the possibilities of the case, then he lifted the telephone and turned it over, clicking the volume control up to high.

"Andrea," he called, setting the telephone back on the side table. He looked up, seeing his wife leaning out of the kitchen.

"Yeah?"

Jim smiled appreciatively at her, "Did you see my cellular?"

"It's in the bathroom."

The bathroom, he thought. *Good. I'll hear it in the shower.*

"Breakfast is ready."

"Breakfast," he whispered. He heard the kettle whistling and looked down at his feet. They were bare and the carpet pressed between his toes. *What luxury*, he thought, feeling the guilt trying to correct him, make him a better person. He thought it seemed that way.

"I should have taken the case," he said on his way to the kitchen. Andrea watched him step toward her. She held the towel with both hands. Her skin was fresh and pink as if it had been scrubbed.

"I don't like myself much these days," he said to her.

The morning was blistered with uncertainty. Brud felt vaguely reassured to see the light again, but he did not know what was to become of him, having no idea who would visit next. Two people had come early in the morning. They had asked questions, then left. He answered nothing. He did not know these people. Why should he speak with them? They asked questions that his parents had told him never to answer. Strangers. Then he was pleased to see the detective appear outside his cell. Brud smiled and pressed close to the bars. He nodded, covering his eyes and sadly peeking through his fingers.

Detective Peach was with another man who was also wearing a suit. The man was tall with whitish-blond hair and a very fair complexion. A man in a uniform opened the door and motioned for Brud to step outside. When he did, the man in the uniform placed a set of metal rings around his wrists, then bent to fasten a set of shackles and chains around his ankles.

"Good morning," the detective said, patting Brud's shoulder.

"Good morning," Brud replied, smiling as he looked down at the chains. There was no harm in being friendly, even if there was a possibility he had been damned.

"This is Detective Lilly." Peach tilted his head toward the other man. "He's going to tag along. Regulations." Detective Lilly did not smile. He glanced at the row of cells, rubbing his index finger against his thumb. He reached into his pocket and took out three jellybeans.

"You want the black one?" he asked Brud.

Brud nodded, his eyes glistening with relief, sensing the wonderful kindness in the words.

Detective Lilly placed the jellybean in Brud's open mouth, then lowered his fingers. Brud chewed instantly, his wide jaw fiercely working, his eyes wet with appreciation.

"How about me?" piped Detective Peach. "What do I get?" He held out his hand, wiggling his fingers and smiling with a flush in his high, round cheekbones.

The man in the uniform chuckled and gripped Brud's arm, and led him down the corridor. The two detectives followed behind, exchanging comments about their favourite colours of jellybeans — red, no black, green if it's spearmint, not the other green — and asking polite questions about each other's articles of clothing. They calmly swapped information on various suit sales around the city. A deal on Slattery East. Two for one. Tacky!

Outside the building, the air was humid and unreasonable. A crowd of reporters was waiting. They appeared listless or bored, but when they saw Brud appearing through the high wooden doorway they alertly straightened on their feet and began to swell closer.

The questions were a jumble of male and female voices. Numerous pitches and tones rallied for dominance. One reporter shouted, "Is it true that you're charging this man with the tooth fairy murders?" She clutched a microphone and pushed it so close to Peach's face that he was obliged to slap it away. Microphones and mini-cassettes were blindly held high, reporters stretching up on their tiptoes. Cameras flashed and whirred. Television cameramen stepped backward, carefully feeling their way.

"Please!" the homicide detective protested, pushing a clear path through the bodies, pressing harder, furiously slapping as he advanced. The crowd, seeming denser, shoved back upon itself.

"Is it true this man is a vigilante?" one reporter called out, then tripped and fell down the stairs. Both detectives smiled and cameras flashed brighter, a furious volley.

"Out of the way," Peach demanded, straightening his spectacles. "This must stop." Someone stepped on his foot and he winced with pain. "Mother Mary!"

Brud saw only a whirl of colours, as if he had been spinning and spinning with his arms held out and had stopped to face this. A buzzing of sound, like the disturbed hum of wasps, only louder and uneven. He felt dizzy, overcome. His stomach turned against him. He did not know where he was stepping, how they were moving toward the car. They seemed to be inching through a crowd that wanted him in some way, needed to touch him to be fulfilled. Their need was severe and he wondered what they were lacking, why he was called upon and brought here to appear before them. Their numbers seemed to be endless, but he could not place the image of a single face. The movement was too erratic. He could not actually see them or hear what they were saying. He did not see the boy standing across the street, watching the chaotic display.

The boy caught a glimpse of Brud. He hoped the poor fool was okay. He thought of telling the police that they were wrong. He'd like to do that, but he wondered why he should and felt uneasy. It was nothing to him. He was free, so why bother? Why encourage his fear that the police would take him, lock him up, and find a place for him with a fake family? He could not bear to be penned up. The abandoned buildings that he lived in were wide-open and uncluttered, except for the litter and rubble. The structures offered shelter for as long as their walls were standing. And when they were struck by the demolition ball or levelled by a dynamite blast, the boy would move to another building, not realizing the blunt range of his trail; how progress left many things behind, places to be occupied by the people it also left in its wake.

The boy watched the police car pull away from the crowd. Then he stepped from the curb, bracing enough courage to relay the truth to the reporters. They would not hold him. They had no right. But, when he stepped closer, they dispersed instantly, answering their beeping pagers or speaking into wireless telephones.

The policeman from the alleyway stepped out onto the rise of concrete stairs. He watched the patrol car roll down the long main street and take a turn to avoid the traffic on Slattery. Walking with lazy self-important strides, his face was held by a smug smile. He had given the tooth to the duty officer, claiming he had first found it in the alleyway, but then had lost it. It was later recovered on the floor of his car, he insisted. It must've been knocked there during a scuffle. The suspect had given him a rough time.

The boy was not afraid of the policeman. He was certain he could outrun him. He watched as the cop wandered into the square parking lot alongside the station and paused by his car. It was not the law that frightened the boy. It was something much more potent. The idea of admitting the truth troubled him. The lies he told himself and others were what kept him alive, convinced him that he was special and important. He knew that the truth would bring him down, make nothing of him, reveal the emptiness that he turned away from every day. Lies kept the pain at bay. And the truth was pain. The truth would make him soft. He struggled not to see it, never to face it, deny it always. To be strong with lies allowed him to believe in himself, to be confident of his worth. But he felt it adding up now, how the fool had forced him to question the false understandings he had built up over the years, how the fool and he were so much the same. Frustration needled him, but he would not cry. He knew how tears were the ultimate show of weakness. Tears would take his strength away, make him hollow. So instead he cursed, showing them all how right and brave he truly was.

part two

judgement

chapter one

the mystery

The reporters were waiting on the courthouse steps, chatting among themselves or jotting notes: the time, the day, key features of their surroundings. The patrol car ambled closer, hesitantly approaching the scene. The detectives stepped out first, then Brud followed, and the questions began again as if the situation had been put on pause and then the pause button suddenly released, liberating the action.

Brud studied the steps as he was hustled forward. Detectives Peach and Lilly held his arms tightly and it was difficult to make his legs work in sync. The chains cut short a natural stride. His hands were bound in front of him. He thought it would be easier to lie on the ground and let the men roll him forward, but there was no room at his feet, and so he shuffled awkwardly ahead, tripping, but held up by the men on either side of him.

The crowd seemed angrier than the last time he had

walked through them. Their voices were more demanding, as if someone owed them an explanation. Brud stiffened his body so the detectives could not force him forward. He was frightened by this crowd. Where were they leading him? What were they going to do?

"Come on, come on," said Detective Peach. "The quicker, the better, my friend." He pressed his palm against Brud's back, pushing with uncharacteristic force.

Brud stumbled up the steps, all the while watching the grey wash of concrete. He thought it best to keep his eyes focussed on the ground. Avoid looking at the crowd. He had seen awful things in their eyes; the same strained sense of anticipation he had seen in the eyes of dying animals struggling to kick free from what held and kept them down. He hoped these people were not dying. He had heard of plagues from his father, sicknesses that struck down lots and lots of people at one time. He hoped these people were not afflicted. If they were, he hoped — despite their desire to harm him — they would be delivered swiftly, mercifully taken out of pain.

The court session lasted only minutes. During the brisk proceedings, Brud stared at the judge, stupefied. It was true, what he had thought. The crowd had indeed been afflicted with a plague and they were all here now awaiting word from the man who was seated on the throne above everyone else, his face expressionless. Others spoke to this man as if trying to find favour. This man controlled their souls. This great holy man would bestow his eternal gifts upon the people of his choosing. Could it be Saint Peter? Where were the gates?

The man sitting beside Brud rose to his feet and said a few words. Another man, across the room, spoke enthusiastically and seemed to be referring to Brud, calling him by a loud name he did not recognize. Perhaps it was his true name, the name that only the Lord and those closest to him were aware of. They called him "The Defendant." It sounded mighty and special.

The judge regarded Brud with a strict question in his eyes, as if deciding whether Brud could possibly be worthy of what was in store for him.

Brud cried out, "Yes," but the judge hammered against a piece of wood and the man sitting beside Brud took his elbow and guided him back down onto his seat. Brud called out, "I love you" the way his father had taught him to love the Lord, and the crowd roared with laughter. He turned and saw that people were drawing his picture. They were worshipping him. He was their idol, but false. He wanted to assure them of their mistake.

The judge hammered his desk. Perhaps something was loose, something coming undone up there.

He heard his father's words through the laughter. "One day we shall all be judged. The good will go to heaven — that's you, Brud. You're a good boy. The best. But the bad, well, the bible says they will be tormented in hell. Do you understand hell, Brud? I don't think you have to worry about that. I don't want you to worry. Think only of the good things and the good things will stay with you. Your smile, Brud. It's one of the very best things."

He smiled now, remembering and holding a palm over his crooked teeth. Looking up, he saw that the judge was gone. The two detectives stepped from behind the low railing of the gallery and guided Brud to his feet. He felt the metal rings cutting into his sore flesh, the skin around his ankles being rubbed by the curved metal edges.

The man beside him, who had said his name was Toby

Rowe, touched Brud's arm for an instant, then looked at the detectives.

"There's no way," he told them.

Detective Peach shook his head. He tutted and tilted his chin up, blowing out a disgusted puff of breath.

"Just look at him," said Toby Rowe.

"I know. I know."

They looked at Brud. Brud had no idea of how to react. He raised his cuffed hands and scratched his nose.

"If he's crazy, then I'm the Queen of England," Peach stubbornly maintained. Then he thought, *He's not crazy. And he's not guilty either.*

"They still have a queen?" asked Detective Lilly, popping a jellybean into his mouth.

"Anyone with a grain of common sense can take one look at this man and know he's innocent." Toby Rowe shut his case. He shook his curly-haired head and frowned.

"Good?" Brud asked. "Heaven?"

They all studied him.

"Thirty day psychiatric observation," Toby Rowe informed Brud, clicking shut the latches on his briefcase.

Brud blinked. He carefully searched from face to face. Perhaps he could find something there that would explain things better than these words he did not understand.

"Heaven?" asked Brud.

Detective Peach smiled, but drew his lips in and pressed them together. He raised his shoulders, then let them fall. Glancing at the ceiling, he said to himself, *Pity, pity, pity.*

"What's he talking about?" asked Detective Lilly, popping another jellybean between his lips. He handed one to Brud. It was black. Brud held it between his fingers and stared at it, remembering the dark sting of its taste.

"Hell?" Brud asked, his voice unsteady at the sight of the jellybean.

Detective Peach imagined the psychiatric hospital. He was about to jokingly confirm Brud's suspicions, but then realized who he was dealing with and bit his tongue.

"You'll be okay, sweetie," he said, leading Brud across the courtroom's wooden flooring. "Don't you worry about a thing. They'll look after you for a while."

"Don't you worry is right," Detective Lilly assured him, confidently walking by his side.

"If you're the tooth fairy murderer, then I'm the King of Spain." Detective Peach glanced back at the lawyer, "They still have one of those over there, too? Yeah." He shook his head and muttered, "Kings and queens. What's that all about?"

Outside the courtroom, the reporters' cries carried through the high-ceilinged hallway. "Psychiatric assessment? Evaluation? The Bin?"

Peach nodded bitterly, but would not look at the crowd. In his earlier years on the force, he had detested the sight of reporters, but eventually he had accepted them as a cornerstone of the process, to be ignored or acknowledged according to the circumstances. They were as much a part of the legal system as the law itself. Too much a part of it. He held tightly onto Brud's arm and stared straight ahead. He was not in the mood for this. Reaching into Detective Lilly's pocket, he swiped three jellybeans.

"No sweat," Lilly obliged.

"Noise," Brud indicated, his bottom lip quivering as he was rushed down two flights of dark wooden steps and out into the bright street. The patrol car was waiting beyond the crowd. Brud was shoved forward. Detective Peach hurled open the rear door of the car and quickly pushed Brud into the back seat.

"Very bad," Brud said, sniffing and rubbing his nose.

"Very bad. Me. Man fall and goodbye."

Detective Peach slid in beside Brud.

"What?"

"Very bad boy."

Peach smirked, sucking in his cheeks and pulling shut the door. He touched the thin hair at the side of his head, then leaned over the front seat.

"He says he's a bad boy, Lilly."

"Yeah?"

"No go to heaven now," Brud admitted.

Eyes flashed in the rearview mirror. Brud feared for who was watching him. He began to sob, lifting his cuffed hands to his face. Detective Peach sighed, losing his humour. He leaned close to Brud and whispered, "You'll go to heaven, okay. Don't you worry, sweetie."

Brud dried his eyes. He tried to smile, but his lips felt heavy and tight, swollen from sobbing.

"Okay," Brud said, patting the detective's knee with his hands. "Okay, okay." But he saw the eyes in the mirror, watching him, and he wondered about the words. Why did one person tell him something and then another person insist that different words were what mattered? Why did the words sometimes seem to mean one thing, but, by the way they were said, hint at meaning the complete opposite? He did not want to live in a place that tried so dutifully to trick him. He was saddened by the prospect of heaven being this way. Or was he being led in the opposite direction? Was this the middle ground? If so, then it was possible that he would find himself in a horrible place. They were trying to fool him. It seemed to be their one true purpose. Regardless of what people said, frightening things were certain to happen.

Andrea's morning schedule was thrown out of whack, subsequently making her late for work. In consideration of her husband's dilemma, she had decided that a little extra attention should be directed his way. So she had gone about preparing his breakfast: a hand-selected combination of multi-grain cereals, and a mixture of carrot and parsley juice that was easily processed through the juicer. She had also taken the time to iron his shirt and tie (chores that Jim usually took care of himself). She believed these acts would grant Jim a greater sense of security and command. He seemed preoccupied. Tired. Perhaps this display of domestic devotion would bring him back to earth.

In her office, Andrea scrambled to meet a deadline. Sitting at her typewriter with her fingertips stroking the shallows of the key facings, she blankly stared across the newsroom, feeling the thoughts swirling to come together, but the words jumbling beyond the lurch of a mis-start. Milk prices were rising again and she was putting together a story on the seemingly corrupt judgements of the milk marketing board.

Her editor, Mr. Sparkes, paused behind her chair, remaining silent as he stared down.

"Work harder," he finally said.

Without looking back, she playfully snapped, "Pay me more." It was her standard response to his standard gruff statement.

Sparkes wandered off, only to pause at another desk, attempting to spur the process. By inciting his journalists, he meant to scatter their huddle of speculations, forcing them to latch onto one fleeting word, a starting point. From there, they would creep toward a coherent stream of words that forms the opening line.

"Clarify!" she heard him shout.

Andrea began typing. She surveyed the pages of notes beside her typewriter. Finished with the top sheet, she slid it aside, paused and read the second sheet. In fifteen minutes, she had the rough version together. It was only a matter of closing off, using the remaining details to reach the 600-word length she had been assigned. Perhaps one more quote. She rifled through her notes with one hand, lifting her mug with the other. The coffee was cold when it touched her lips. She grimaced and spit it back into the bottom.

"Andrea," Sparkes appeared behind her once again, breaking her train of thought.

She turned on her swivel chair, obviously irritated, but also slightly grateful to disconnect for a moment.

"This guy accused of the tooth fairy murders, you hear about him?" Sparkes held out a black-and-white photograph of the man.

"I've seen the stories," she said, glancing at the picture.

"Good girl. You actually read our paper. One of the few working here."

Andrea smiled and reached back for her coffee mug, raising it halfway to her lips before remembering it was cold. She carefully lowered the mug and rested it against her lap.

"Tell me what you know."

"He was arrested, something to do with the tooth fairy murders."

"Something?"

Oh no, Andrea thought. She hoped he would not harass her the way he always did when she did not know the exact details of a story. The absolute facts. The proper words. She glanced at his overweight frame, his opened suit jacket and wide-waisted trousers rounding out.

"Well, obviously you're not as on top of things as I

thought." He blew out air and glanced around the news-room, as if searching for a more worthy recipient of his gifts. He continued speaking, but he did not look at her. "He was arrested at the scene of a murder. Thirty day psychiatric observation. Standard procedure up to this point. But there are rumours. Things not right. Something about the guy that's making people wonder. You get it?" He looked at her, his curly eyebrows rising. "You with me?"

She nodded and leaned back to set her coffee mug on the desk.

"This John Doe's under heavy police protection. They're afraid someone might take a shot at him. The families of the victims are looking for revenge. It's a hot situation. Leo's got all the details. You get what I'm saying? You figure it out? Suspicion. The possibilities."

"You want me to cover the story?"

"Yes." Sparkes stared out across the room. Someone waved at him and held up a telephone. Raising his hand, he jabbed a thumb toward his office and tossed the photo onto her desk. "You're a good girl," he said, striding off, labouring sideways to squeeze between the desks.

"Crime," she said, happily picking up the photograph and holding it in her hands. It showed a large man in chains and handcuffs being led down a set of concrete steps. The man was looking at the ground. He seemed to be crying.

Andrea turned and lifted a fresh pad from her drawer. Staring at the photo, she jotted down the details that Sparkes had told her. At the top of the page she wrote "Tooth Fairy Murders" and circled the words several times.

Glancing up, she saw Sparkes heading back toward her.

"Okay," he called, standing in front of her desk, his back almost touching the chair of another reporter's desk.

"Crime," she said, smiling.

"Don't complain," he said, noticing someone and shouting to them. "Ten minutes." He held up one thick arm and furiously tapped the facing of his watch. Andrea could hear him breathing.

"I wasn't complaining," she said.

"You always wanted this." Sparkes leaned with both hands on her desk. He sighed and closed his eyes, his forehead glazed with sweat. "Just do it," he snapped, his eyes opening wide. "Yes."

Andrea nodded and thought, *The man is going to have a heart attack if he doesn't slow down.*

Sparkes' breathing was fast and raspy. He wiped at his mouth, using one hand, then the other.

"I want a human side. I don't think he's the tooth fairy. I'm telling you. My opinion. You know what an opinion is? It's not the facts. Right?"

"Right."

"They don't know this guy's name. That's something right there. Right there." Slamming his palm against her desk, his tight smile jerked. "You see that. The connection. You invent a name. But be careful with the name. It can't be judgemental. You see what you're up against? You're dealing with a mystery. You like mystery novels?"

"I don't know."

"There's a mystery right there. Everything's a mystery. Always. That's what the news is. Mystery. That's why people read. They want to know what happens next. It's the closest thing to having an eye in the future. That's what gossip is. The society pages. Who's banging who, and how long will it last? Books, plots. Everywhere. Conflict is mystery. Give me some conflict, Andrea. Make this guy into something, but make sure it's what he really is.

Just look at him." He jabbed his pudgy finger against the photograph, his white face charged with splotches of red. "He's got the looks, the manner, the face. It's a contradiction. It's not a murderer's face. The people will love it. There's a mystery right there. You see what I mean? Contradiction is a mystery. Can you understand what I'm getting at, or do I have to do this myself? I wish." He straightened up and pulled at the waist of his trousers, shouting around him, "FIVE MINUTES."

"If I could do everything myself." He rolled his eyes. "Bliss. Oh, what heavenly bliss!"

"Keep the photo?" she asked.

"Yes. See Leo. Teach us all a lesson. Teach everyone a lesson about this man. Show Leo how to do his job. You're a woman. Prove it. You think this John Doe did it?"

"I don't know." Andrea stared at the photograph.

"But you see the possibilities? Tell me you do. Please tell me."

She smiled up at him, "Yes."

"You know what this means, don't you?" He dug a roll of tablets from his pocket and popped three into his mouth, chewing and shifting the powdery pieces around with his tongue. "What is it?"

"A test?"

"Exactly." Turning, he waddled off, shouting back at Andrea, "Who's being tested? Tell me that?" He laughed in his throat and snatched several yellow pages from a raised hand.

Andrea's head was reeling from the pace of the confrontation. She did not know if she was happy or confused. It would take a little time to sort things out. She stared at the photograph. *He's innocent*, she said to herself. *No, guilty.*

chapter two

the right place

Brud was glad when they opened the metal rings and lifted them from his wrists and legs. They were like the snares that his father hung from the lower branches of the trees, only they did not grow tighter when he tried to pull away. His father had caught many rabbits using snares. But the rings on Brud's wrists were made from heavier metal and did no harm. They were only used to hold. For what purpose, Brud could not decide. He wondered if he was to be eaten.

The place where he was now appeared familiar. It was white and bare and smelled just like the white place he had visited when he first came into the city.

Two men dressed in white led him down a corridor. Brud smiled with recognition. This was a good place, a place where he had seen the woman much like his mother, a place where they gave him things to make him happy. It was the quiet, clear, and peaceful place. His body gradually relaxed and he sensed how his muscles had been ravaged by fear. They ached. He remembered the happiness that had come over him the last time he was in a place like this. He waited and hoped for that feeling to visit him again.

Quiet, clear, and peaceful. Brud sensed it with each level step across the shiny flooring. He looked from side to side, smiling at the two men. He glanced at their hands, the way their fingers securely pressed into the sleeves covering his arms, rumpling the fabric of his plaid shirt. They were leading him through doors. At each door they passed a person who watched over the barrier and then shut it again. Guardians. It seemed like a special place where only special people were permitted. Everyone must be trying to get in here. Brud chuckled, covering his mouth with his hand, hiding his teeth. He was happy. He understood that they would soon come to a final door. The woman much like his mother would be waiting and she would sting his arm to give him the feeling like he was floating. It was the sight of this woman, the great joy and familiarity, that seemed to lift him from the ground and make him extra happy.

Brud was encouraged to discover he had been directed to the right place, despite the mismatched words and intentions. This place, though different on the outside, seemed to lead to the same inner area. The buildings acted as entranceways and were magically connected. He wondered why he had been taken out of here in the first place. Walking in stride with the two men, he decided that it was all part of the judgement. Perhaps they were uncertain if he was right for the place, if he was deserving. So, they had put him through a test. He laughed. He knew that he belonged here.

171

It was just as his father had said. His body bathed in the peaceful lull. He felt his eyelids wanting to rest, growing weighted with contentment. A secure smile found its place on his fleshy lips. The sense of ease and acceptance was like a delicate porcelain sculpture revolving inside him. It brought to mind the orbit of earth, a graceful match. Nothing would ever disturb him again. He would not listen. Nothing would trouble the deliberateness of rotation, the day and the night, everlasting inside of him. He was convinced. Absolutely. There was no doubt. They had kindly confirmed all of this for him.

But then, his thoughts were shattered. A scream, erupting from behind a door, was cut with frenzied laughter. It was shrill and choppy, snapping loose the orbit of the earth. The delicate white sculpture cracked within his veins, sending splinters throughout the courses that guided all paths and waterways toward belief and sustenance. He could not interpret the reasoning for such screaming laughter. Was the person happy or in pain? He knew only to step away, to save himself, and so he ducked to the side, pinning one of the orderlies against the farthest wall before dropping to the floor. The sound was everywhere. It was, indeed, a screech of pain. He must shrink into himself, but draw the noise close to him as well, hug it with hopes of quieting its panic and want of flight. He would be its friend. The sound could be calmed. He was certain of that.

The facts were scrawled across two pages of Andrea's notepad. She had studied the words, trying to extract a name for the man by the joining of obvious words and letters. She had called her husband's brother for assistance. Leo had informed her that Sergeant Steve Kelly was the arresting officer. Regardless, the policeman was curt over the telephone and had very little to say about the proceedings. He simply reiterated the basic information, emphasizing the discovery of the tooth. No question. It was cut and dried now. Andrea had no idea about the tooth. It was a new piece of evidence. She scribbled the fact along the yellow notepad. Although trying to remain neutral, she was noticeably disappointed with the news.

The policeman had not even asked about his brother. Andrea often wondered why they were so distant. Jim had told her what had happened to the policeman's wife. There was cause for frustration and regret and she assumed that self-pity had embittered the policeman, causing him to avoid his brother, to distance them. The Sergeant told her that he would be in touch should any new information come to light. He had said, "I'll keep my ears open for the scoop," then had laughed mildly. "They still use words like that?" Andrea had told him no and thanked him for his help. "Jimmy sends his best," she had added, against her better judgement as a professional, taking it upon herself — no matter how much she disliked him — to encourage a reunion. After all, they were family, and that seemed important.

The policeman merely grunted and hung up.

Andrea stared at her notepad. Detective Peach's name was underlined. She had called him earlier, only to be told that he could not discuss the case with reporters. When she informed him about the discovery of the tooth, he seemed surprised, but quickly tempered his tone. Neatly clearing his throat, he told her he had to go to another call and briskly hung up. Then she had taken Leo's advice and contacted a detective who was good for inside information, but he knew very little, other than to offer his views on the growing speculation that the guy was inno-cent. He made no mention of the tooth, and Andrea did not bring it up, realizing she had stumbled upon some-thing valuable, sensing the blood-rush of discovery.

It was after two and she had not eaten lunch. She stopped thinking for a moment, veering away from all speculation, to localize the insistent nagging sensation that had been troubling her. Pausing, listening to sounds inside of her, she realized the sensation was hunger.

Andrea glanced to the right of her typewriter. Monday's newspaper was open on her desk. Page three: the picture of the accused. It was the same photograph Sparkes had left with her. She was struck by how different it appeared in print, the grainy starkness of the ink malignantly im-plying guilt.

MYSTERY MAN ACCUSED OF STABBING. And then the kicker: Tooth Fairy Murders Possible Link.

Implication. The words were printed on cheap paper and smudged easily. Andrea rubbed her fingers over the text and watched the words smear into each other. She inspected her fingers. It was a silly thing to do and she scolded herself. The ink was well into the grooves of her fingerprints. *Who is guilty?* she asked herself. *This man's assumed media guilt.* The thought was fleeting; an old and tired preoccupation that was sometimes brought on by hunger, but was quickly dismissed like a senile elderly patient being guided back to her reasonable room.

Andrea looked up and across the huge office and saw the desks, most of them empty; people were on their lunch breaks. But several journalists remained tapping the computer keyboards that had recently been installed. The luxury was for senior reporters and desk editors only. The words never stopped. Someone was always typing out the news. A need had to be filled and people were willing to pay for it. The newest news. They wanted the freshest, the quickest, the briefest news. The fix. Word from the world around them giving scope and dimension to their own lives. Sparkes was correct. He was a smart man. She wondered about him: What was his wife like? Were there any children? Did he truly care for them? Or was this everything for him? Was this all that was important?

Andrea found herself stuck in a daze, her mind like a marble lodged in wet clay. She jerked her head and sat up, thinking of herself as something less than honourable. That feeling clung to her — not a dirty feeling, but one of being mildly dispirited. *Close enough*, she thought. Anxiety was doing this to her. She understood. Stress. Exhaustion. She rolled her shoulders and wondered where all the stress had suddenly come from. No one ever heard of such things until a few years ago. Now, everyone was stung by the bug. It was like a reply to the heap of demands that could not be met; too much to consider and perform. All the unattained aspirations rotting inside of everyone, stewing until they transform into a virus-like toxin. A flu of sorts. People moaned to each other and sniffled about their wounded psyches. She told herself she must be tired to be thinking this way. A dark blue mass began moving in the corner of her eyes. Blinking, she gazed that way. It was Sparkes in his navy blue suit, and he was heading toward her. She set the tip of her pen against her pad, poised, pretending.

"That's the bastard. Him." The loud man stabbed a knife through the picture on page three. "That's him, right there." Frantically, he snapped his arm up and down, shredding the newsprint held in his other hand. "He's a dead man."

The boy was watching from above, lying on the thick concrete floor, staring down through a ragged hole to the next floor. He liked to lie this way, seeing things from high up as if hanging in the sky. Below him were the remnants of the concrete room: the brown table with the metal legs, the grey-and-white striped mattress pushed into the corner, tins crushed and scattered around the floor, and the woman in bright, tight clothing. He could see where the roots of her blonde hair were growing out black. Lines of black were also streaked through the length of it. The woman was sitting still, but the loud man was whirling around the room, slashing the newspaper and hurling tattered pieces against the graffiti-covered walls.

The woman began crying. She mumbled a man's name, but her tears made the word soft and pulpy between her wet lips.

The boy rose away from the hole. He stood still and gazed down, saw the man swirl into sight, then disappear. The concrete was loose around the edges, and he kicked at it, as if attacking the man. Bits crumbled and sprinkled down. The loud man was suddenly silent. Moments later, he appeared beneath the hole, his head tilted back.

"Dogger." He winked. "What's up?" His sharp smile did not change as he ripped out a handful of paper. He wore a plain white T-shirt with the sleeves torn off and green army pants with black slogans thickly drawn into the fabric with a marker. His arms were bare and thin.

The boy pointed at his chest, "I'm up."

"Yeah." The loud man spit against a wall. "You're up, alright, but not as up as me."

Heading for the concrete stairway in the corner, the boy raced down the two flights and spun out into the room he had been watching.

"What you know about this?" the loud man demanded, lifting another newspaper and pointing to an unshredded version of the picture. A third copy of the photograph was pinned to the wall with a red upside-down cross painted across the face.

"He's a demon," cursed the loud man. "Like in those movies."

"I was there," the boy bragged. "I saw it. The cop."

The woman cried louder. She had to look away from the picture. Burying her head in her arms, her shoulders rocked with sobs.

"You saw it?" the man asked, intrigued, stepping closer, folding away his knife and dropping it into the deep pocket of his army pants. "You saw Skully get stuck? You were really there?"

"Yeah," the boy said indignantly. "Why? What's it —"

"And you never killed this creepy-looking guy?" The loud man shot an arm out, pointing at the picture on the wall.

"That creepy-looking guy's just a fool, Tumbles. He never did it. Skully fell on the knife. A cop fired a gun, and..." The boy demonstrated. "Bang. The cop's fault." He pushed an imaginary knife into his stomach and gagged, letting his tongue hang out the side of his mouth and his eyes roll up into his head.

Tumbles struck the boy with a blow that sent him crashing back against the wall.

"No," Tumbles screamed. "That creep did Skully in. He looks like the type that'd want Jake outta the way." He sped his knife from his pocket and flashed it open. "The type," he said, rushing for the wall, slashing the picture, forcing the knife through to the concrete so that sparks scratched loose, leaping into the air.

The boy held his face. His knees were shaky. He watched Tumbles slashing the picture, the sparks arcing away, seeming to sizzle, but it was only Tumbles's growling through the spit held in his mouth.

"This guy," Tumbles shouted above the scissory sounds. "This guy, this guy."

The boy numbly stared at the woman. She was watching Tumbles. He had expected to see her crying, but she was smiling and cheering in rhythm with Tumbles's actions, clapping her hands, her knees jerking under the table. She laughed and looked at the boy, but the boy was not smiling. Nervously wiping at her eyes, she continued clapping her hands, glancing at the boy again, uncertain.

The boy sat in the chair across from her. "This cop shot a gun and when the fool pushed off the knife went into Skully. It went in just like that." The throbbing in his face was easing, but he felt the skin tightening as it swelled hot. He stared at the loud man and hated him. *Why did he always have to hit me? It doesn't change anything. The truth's still there all the same. I know*, the boy told himself, *what's underneath, what people pretend is real*.

The woman began stomping her feet. But her vigour did not last long and, soon, she started sobbing, crying with her mouth weakly held open, looking at the boy and clapping, as the last of the picture fell in thin shreds against the floor. Tumbles kept slashing the walls, maniacally moving around the room as he scraped the blade into the concrete, kicking the concrete, spitting at it, until he wore himself down and returned to the table, gasping for breath.

"Pigeon here's...upset," Tumbles gulped, wiping at his

forehead with his bare arm. His fist pounded the table. Pigeon flinched as the table bucked closer. She pushed her chair back from it. "Ya know, Dogger." Tumbles pounded the tabletop again and again, shouting and pounding, "Skully...was...Pigeon's...man."

The boy nodded, staying quiet, knowing not to cross Tumbles. There was truth and then there was the violence that came with what was all dishonest. Resistance. The violence was there all around them like a tension, as if the air itself knew that the loud man was dishonest. You needed to use force to cram what was wrong into place.

Tumbles lifted his fist and stared at the bruised side.

"Understand?" he asked his hand.

Pigeon laughed, struggling to wipe the smudged mascara from under her eyes. She looked at her long fingernails, then at her fingers, sighting the blackness. She licked the mascara away, her tongue turning charcoal, then wiped her fingertips against her shiny blue pants. Seeing the dark grey marks left there, she seemed offended, her mouth agape.

"The cop's guilty, then," proclaimed Tumbles. "That's the way it is, Dogger? Is that it? Lock away a cop. Bang, Boom." He spun in circles, swooping his arms through the air, punching the space with his words, "Clang, Bing, Dang." He leapt high and kicked a wooden beam that was splintered and hanging from the ceiling. His bare feet landed on the floor with a soft sound. He crouched low and looked down at his toes.

"Lock away a cop." He leapt again, kicking, pretending to crack the air. "HAH!" The sound carried through the hollow building. He landed. "That's like breaking the arms off that statue."

"What statue?" Pigeon asked, desperately wiping at her

face, wanting to be pretty now, to match the sculpted perfection of what they were speaking of. "You know how I love statues."

"You know that statue, Pigeon. The one with the woman holding them scales. Blindfolded, waiting for it. Good and ready. You know that statue. That real cool lady. Hard as a rock."

Pigeon nodded, chasing away the tears, "I know it. I like that one, too."

"NO," Tumbles shouted, pausing, listening with a smile as his voice coursed throughout the building. "I'm everywhere," he whispered. "Listen." A rush of power made him spin in a tight circle. He ran for a wall, raced up the side, and somersaulted backward, landing perfectly upright with his hands held out at his sides.

"Even," he said, balancing himself, "the score."

"Do that again?" the boy asked, inspired and intrigued. "Wow! That's something!"

Tumbles wagged his finger at the boy. "You have to learn that justice don't come to no cop. Justice comes between us, like I told you before. People don't screw with us because we even things. Bang, clang, boom, landing on our feet. No cops taking care of us. Word gets around that creepy boy stiffed Skully and if we don't take care of him, then next thing you know they'll be stiffing us all over the place. Can't walk down the street like the honest folk we are without some lame cracker putting the jump on us. Blam, zap, crash." His foot jerked up, kicking the bottom of the table. It lifted and scraped noisily against the wall before dropping back into place. When the silence settled, Tumbles spoke in a whisper, "Show me a man with a dead dog in his arms and I'll show you a man with the worst kind of need."

chapter three

according to the plan

When she heard the apartment door unlocking, Andrea hurried to the couch and quickly sat, trying to appear perfectly casual. She crossed her legs, then uncrossed them, draping an arm along the back of the couch. She sat up straight, leaned forward, picked up a magazine.

When the door opened, she glanced across the living room to see her husband stepping in, his occupied gaze cast toward the floor. It was close to eight o'clock. Jim had not called or left a message on their answering service. Andrea knew that he was looking for Brud. She tried to understand and came very close to understanding completely, but she could not help but feel let down by his neglect, his selfishness. She wondered if selfishness was the correct word. It seemed a touch extreme considering the circumstances. Self-centered maybe.

"Any luck?" she asked, vying for nonchalance. She

stood and walked toward him, being drawn, not realizing she was moving at all, her sense of concern directing her. Standing close, she felt like kissing him, but he appeared detached and prone to aggravation.

"Nothing," Jim dully informed her. He took off his suit jacket and flashed a brief smile her way, leaning to kiss her on the cheek. His face went stern again when he stepped away, his eyes not wanting to linger.

"You okay?" Andrea called, watching as he moved down into the living room.

He turned and paused, staring back at her. He stared for a moment before he realized what he was doing. With a tired nod, he loosened his tie, then undid his top button.

"I'm sorry," he said, turning for the couch, explaining as easily as that. He tossed his jacket over the back of the chair across from him and dropped onto the couch. Sitting there, exhausted, he stared off, barely noticing Andrea as she stepped in front of him.

"Can I get you something?" she asked, restraining the impulse to accuse him, to demand an apology for his tardiness and lack of regard.

"No, fine," he said, offering another brief smile. "Thanks."

She sat next to her husband. "I guess it would be the wrong thing to ask how your day was."

Jim chuckled with his lips shut, one corner of his mouth rising in a gesture of resignation.

"My day was pretty bad, too," Andrea hinted.

"Good," her husband mumbled.

"Jimmy!" Andrea shoved his arm. He looked at her, squinting.

"What?"

"Are you with us?"

"Yes." He stood and walked across to the easy chair, turned, and sat staring at Andrea.

Andrea stared back at him.

"I'm tired," he said.

"Me too. It's eight o'clock."

"Yes, it's getting late." He looked toward the window, where the sky was darkening and the lights in the towers were growing sharper and brighter, the edges of the buildings beginning to lose their clear definition, the orange shadows waning off, dragging closer to the horizon and over, abandoning the city to a calm luscious dusk.

Andrea stood and went to him. She kneeled by the side of his chair and reached up, slipping her fingers through his hair. *I love him. That's all that matters*, she told herself, and she believed it, dismissing the opposition that, strangely enough, wanted to drive a wedge between them. *Why?* she asked herself, looking at her husband's handsome face. *Why would I want to do that?*

Jim tilted back his head and shut his eyes. He sighed, sensing the weariness in his body, the strain as if he had been tossing concrete slabs all day. He remembered the feeling from his days as a teenager. He had worked part-time in the construction business, working for the same man who was now buying Brud's land. He thought of his old boss, Mr. Quagmire. His soft courteous eyes, his yellow-stained teeth, which always flashed with enthusiasm for a good deal, the legalities, the arguments of uncontestable ownership. He remembered Quagmire's tall frame, how the man had put on pounds over the years. He lived the good life, but his hunger and insistence had remained unchanged. And those teeth, why hadn't he had them polished or replaced? They were repulsive and gave him a jaded appearance, even though Jim realized that Quagmire was simply an investor — a smart business-man, sharp as a tack, and cleverly in tune with the ever-changing financial marketplace.

Jim opened his eyes, "I'm sorry tired — so tired, I mean." He wiped his face, then held his chin, feeling the stubble and appreciating the sound of it beneath his fingers as he rubbed. "I checked the morgues, hospitals. As many streets as I could cover. I spent some time at the station."

"Let's go to bed," Andrea whispered in his ear.

"Did you talk to Petrina?" He focussed on his wife's face, then glanced at the newspaper on the coffee table. He was too tired to read it. He glumly wondered what he was missing. *Nothing extreme*, he assured himself. *The world is still here, in front of my eyes*.

"Oh, I forgot. You won't believe this. I called her looking for you and she said it was all her fault and she was joining the Sisters of…something or other. I don't remember the name." Andrea shivered and felt goose flesh rise along her arms. "She blamed everything on herself and started crying, said she wasn't worthy of the job. Can you believe it? Joining a convent, that's what she was talking about. Do people still do that sort of thing?"

"I don't know," Jim said.

"I went up to see her, but there was no talking to her. She'd been thinking about it for a long while. A long while is what she said. She's only a young thing. It was too much. Hard to take. She barely knew Brud. She was packing then. I walked her to the elevator. She wouldn't listen. Gone. What do you think? Maybe she has a screw loose. Huh?"

Jim slowly shook his head, "Unbelievable."

Andrea stood and walked behind the chair. She sunk her fingers into her husband's shoulders and squeezed.

"Oh, God!" he sighed, his shoulders drooping. "Mmmm, great."

"You want something to eat?" Andrea asked, wanting to change the subject. "Chicken on pita?"

"No," he groaned appreciatively.

"I called around, too. When I could get a free moment. They gave me a crime story. This murder case. The tooth fairy thing." She tilted slightly to the side to glimpse her husband's expression. He was smiling, stupidly.

"Great," he said.

Continuing to massage his shoulders, Andrea stared up at the ceiling, then out over the city. The days were getting shorter. She was sure of it. They were getting shorter, earlier. Year by year and even shorter now. She took a heavy breath and forced her fingers deep into Jim's muscles, pushing against despair.

"Oww!" He flinched away from her.

"Sorry," she said, thinking, *See, that's not so hard to say. Sorry.*

Jim strained to glance back at her, with a cross expression. "What're you doing?"

"Nothing." She shrugged and stepped away, sat across from him on the couch and folded her arms. She offered a brief, almost saucy, smile, having discovered the sodden irritability of his mood. *I despise what all of this is doing to us. I wish that it was over. That this Brud character would turn up and go away. He's become nothing more than a complication, a pest. Why did Jimmy take this case? Why did he agree to look after a simpleton? Because I don't want to have children? Did Jimmy think he was adopting Brud?* She thought of confronting him with this argument. Staring at his dopey eyes, she thought it wise to leave well enough alone. He looked pitiful.

"Forget it," she whispered.

Jim did not respond. Sleep had taken him. He saw Brud's face painted like a clown's on an inflatable punching bag that pivoted back with each smack. No matter how vigorous the force of his punch, the bag continued to right itself, the painted smile more harrowing each time it bobbed up to face the challenge.

The policeman admired the feel of the shot glass against his fingers; the nimble smoothness set against the savage sting of the bourbon in its hollow made him smile. He slowly raised the edge to his lips, but then paused, holding it away for a moment as if trying to divine something in the liquid. Smiling with satisfaction, he tossed back the bourbon, savouring the velvet burning. Fire and ice at once. The perfect hypocrisy. He smiled and looked into the thick glass, puckered his lips, licked his moustache, then tentatively put the glass on the bar.

"Back in a sec," he called to the bartender. "Same again." He fingered the glass, then slammed a bill down next to it.

The bartender watched the policeman leave. He said something to one of drinkers and shook his head, then glanced at the money on the bar.

Outside, the night air was fresh and alive with the sounds and lights of cruising traffic. Huge maple trees lined either side of the street. The policeman could hear the leaves moving up high, rustling in the breeze. He watched the cars passing, their windows down, faces talking to each other or leaning out, calling to the people strolling on the sidewalks. He recalled similar experiences from when he was young, but stopped himself. It meant nothing now. What was the sense of remembering? The past was nothing. It was far away. He could not touch it, even though it continued to occupy him.

The policeman stepped further out onto the concrete fronting — occupied by café tables and chairs in the daytime — to get a better look down the street. He had a clear view of the hospital. The large brick building was two blocks west. Curtains could be seen in the windows, and behind many curtains there was light.

The policeman wondered about life inside. He knew the layout of the sparse lobby, the smell of the old elevators, the wide white corridors of that building. During visiting hours, he came to feel as if he was gradually blending with the pallor of those walls. He had watched the woman fade into that timeless place. She was a woman, no longer his wife, barely recognizable. The beauty had been drawn from her by the same cruel and precise power that had bonded her flesh tighter to her bones. Her body seemed to be emptying itself, her skin clinging so tightly toward the end that it acquired an elastic sheen.

Then, for no apparent reason, there had been hope. The woman had begun eating food again. Her smile, although distant and vague, was a smile nonetheless. Soon she began to resemble herself, the stirrings of light returned as if by magic, the individual gestures that had made her what she was found their place in her fingers and across her face. There was hope that she had resolved her contest against herself and would find the way back into the space in life she had once occupied.

"A useful productive life," the doctor told the policeman.

Exhausted from a silent visit, sitting in the chair, the

policeman had asked the doctor what that meant — "a useful productive life" — but the doctor had merely offered a kind smile and reassuringly squeezed his shoulder.

And the woman was fine. Gradually she reinvented herself as his wife. *She was fine*, he told himself over and over. She was eating meals with him, eating at lunch when he came back to their three-room apartment. A tarnished look still lingered in her eyes, the look wanting to set her eyes with something immobile, something hard and soft at the same time, denial and acceptance, something not like eyes at all but resembling the shell and the underbelly of some lower-caste silent creature that pulls itself in and out of life.

Every day they would eat lunch together. A few stray bits of conversation concerning the morning's activities would pass between them. He would watch his wife, trying to see past the dullness to what was hardening in her eyes, what he understood she was fighting to see beyond. On the day when her eyes turned dense and still — the desperate putty fixing — he remembered looking at his watch.

He saw himself staring at his watch, always, and the time: 12:20. Then he turned in his seat, glancing over the back of his chair to see the round wall clock, which gave him the exact same time. His eyes wandered to the arm chair below the clock where he hung his holster. The empty holster. When he faced the table, his wife was not sitting in her chair. He could feel it now, the weakening rush in his legs as he stood. And the sound that stopped him, the explosion ripping at something behind his own eyes as he heard the body fall, slapping the cool tile behind the bathroom door.

He wondered how she had left the table without him

noticing, how she had taken his gun. Where was he? What was he thinking of? Had he seen her stand and step across the small room to the chair? Had he realized that the dullness had settled with his wife and she had welcomed it, accepting the impenetrable rigidity that was her own death?

She was better off dead. He told himself this and he would lose his breath when he did, realizing the crushing truthfulness of it, hating himself for admitting what he believed. Had he allowed it all to happen? Had he wanted this?

"She's better off," he whispered now, standing still, watching the hospital, feeling the air against his skin. He was alive and he despised the sense of it. He wiped at the corners of his moustache, remembering how she used to trim it. Her smiling eyes so close to him. Youth. Nimble fingers. Such profound easiness. He dreamed of the numbers 1, 2, 2, 0. His empty holster that his hand fit into, drawing clear again, empty. His hand gone. The clock.

0, 1, 2, 2.

1, 0, 2, 2.

1, 2, 2, 0.

He would not go into the bathroom. He stood from his chair and listened. She would be dead or dying and the shudder of relief repelled him, tore from his bones so that he felt he was turning weightless and would drift away. He telephoned an ambulance. But when they answered he realized he had called the station by mistake. Why? No, it did not matter.

He thought of every single word and action that could have saved her, and still she was gone.

The policeman knew Brud was in that hospital. He was glad that the fool was in his place. He felt vindicated. Justice. Personal justice inspiring his dismal form of joy. He was punishing Brud because he had seen that same look in the idiot's eyes; the distracted softness he first witnessed in his wife's eyes before they turned hard with resignation. He was punishing his wife for what she had done to him, the grief she had blasted into his head when she pulled the trigger.

The feeble-minded losers, the policeman assured himself. *Weak ones lacking the strength to carry them through periods of uncertainty. The frail and the crippled and the weak and the traumatized. Useless. Christ, have them. Take them all. The meek. The blessed. What unholy hypocrisy!* He spit onto the ground and turned for the bar, yanked open the door, and stepped inside. The smell and dim feel of the place welcomed him. He glanced at his watch: 9:15. "The time," he said, smiling at the shot glass waiting to fit into his hand. He raised it to his lips. This time the bourbon stung more fiercely, as if a wound had been reopened in his throat. He coughed twice before getting a grip on himself, then called for another.

Again, he thought of Brud and he imagined his brother.

"Christ, have them," he said. He liked the sound of it. He nodded at the bartender when the drink was delivered. His family was finished. He was alone. The bourbon made a sad sound going down. A loud gulp inside his head. He yearned for something — the return of his wife or the disassembling of hate. He could not localize the need that clawed at his belly, in that place of longing connecting heart to gut. He would drown it. Kill it. Kill again.

Visiting hours are almost over, he reminded himself. He would have to hurry.

The farm was dark, peacefully stilled by night. The moonlit shadow of a man crept along the worn path leading to the farmhouse. The man stopped, his feet pressed firmly against the ground. He listened to the silence, secretly abhorring its presence. There were no sounds of animals. No bellows, neighings, or bleatings. The beasts had been sold off, auctioned, and slaughtered. It was a shame. He would have cared to butcher them himself. Regardless, their odours still lingered on the grounds. The smell was like a melancholic vacancy, expressing itself only through its absence.

The man glanced back up the path. He saw the soft-hued image of the company truck. The vague logo on the door, the words and the letter "Q" for Quagmire Construction. The canvas length of the man's black coat flapped as he swung the fabric back and pulled out the long cardboard tube. Uncapping it, he coaxed out the blueprint.

Kneeling on the ground, the man's balding head was flatly polished by moonlight. Only a few lengths of hair remained, strategically combed across the top. The yellow-toothed man unrolled the plan and stared down, offering a stained smile as his fingers held the curled corners in place.

Another acquisition for Quagmire Construction. The deal would soon be finalized. Only one minor legality flitted anxiously across his thoughts: the lawyer. He had telephoned and faxed Jim Kelly for the closing signature, but there was no reply. One final signature from the simpleton. *Tomorrow*, he assured himself. "I believe in myself," he whispered, smiling ambitiously as he raised his head, allowing the moonlight to cast shadows across his sallow face. "Go ahead," he said to the dim light, "your best shot."

Reaching into his pocket, Quagmire lifted out a black

glass candy that smelled of licorice and gently slid it between his lips, quietly provoking the flavour with his tongue. He admired the appearance of the land in darkness. At this time of night he could best envision his plan. He searched his pocket for a lighter, extracted and sparked it, and, holding the flame above the wide paper, imagined what was to come. A shopping mall here. He guided the flame through the air. Rows of identical houses. Bland airless office buildings. A medical center occupied by mock healers. A self-contained suburban community. Nothing will be far from their reach. They will have everything and thus feel purposeless. He could smell the dumptrucks of asphalt. Black, even pavement would soon be covering the fields. He lusted for the odour. The tarry heat of it in his nostrils. The mounting roar of the dozers. The jackhammer, its merciless persistence. A penetrating grind of noise. The torn earth, opening for him. Fresh red clay glistening with worms. Its ragged sod replaced by a thick black crust. The final seal.

Quagmire's thumb slipped from the lighter and his yellow-toothed smile vanished. The world was darker now. He waited, his piercing eyes adjusting. Vague outlines gradually reappeared. He cracked his knuckles, one at a time, bones snapping elsewhere.

"First we burn the place," he whispered accusingly, glancing up at the stars, as if mocking their petty attempt at brilliance. "A pathetic display." Standing, he wandered around the land, one moment in the field, an instant later in the dark front window of the house, staring out, then looking up to see himself on the roof of the barn, spinning like a dark weather vane, laughing to kill himself.

chapter four

heaven becomes hell

It was quiet, clear, and peaceful, yes, but Brud believed there must be something more to heaven than this. He stood and looked out of his window. The courtyard below was submerged in darkness. In the distance, the building towers were straight and solid with light. He wondered about distances. How could heaven be so close to what was beyond the glass? How could heaven be so small? Perhaps the number of people granted entry was very limited.

He had waited to see his mother and father, certain that they had found their way in here. He had sat on the edge of the bed in the room chosen for him. Settling one hand over the other, he waited for the beginning of the things that were to be done in heaven. After arriving through the main doors and being left there by the two men in black uniforms, he listened to the woman behind the desk and believed he would soon see his parents. The woman was dressed in white and smiled reassuringly as if everything would be fine. He had made it to heaven and nothing could harm him now. He had passed the test. Then a man in a long white coat had joined the woman. The man had two other men with him and they were all dressed in white. The man had told Brud they'd be seeing a lot of each other. The man had smiled like the woman, but the other two men did not smile right away. They smiled later, as if their smile belonged to a different part of the plan. They smiled when the man in the white coat nodded at them to take Brud to his room.

"Just put your complete trust in us," the man had said. "We're like family here."

Brud nodded and smiled, understanding the word "family," confident he would soon see his parents.

It was not much of a welcome to heaven. His father had told him there would be special music and golden gates. He had seen the gates but they were not golden. They were tall and made of iron and looked like the bars from the cage he had been in. They were hard and appeared as if something was trapped inside of them.

Brud assured himself the screams he heard beyond his walls could, indeed, be joyous. The screams ran toward laughter. Laughing and screaming together. Perhaps it was the purest happiness of heaven that made people scream this way. It was hard to divide the two. It seemed as if heaven was okay, though, and now he was waiting for his parents.

Brud faithfully watched the door. Once or twice, eyes appeared in the round glass window. They looked straight at Brud as if expecting something more of him. He wondered if he was acting properly, if he was supposed to be doing other things that would confirm his goodness. Was this still part of the test? He sat up straight. He smiled, and the eyes disappeared.

Looking at his fingers, he picked a line of dirt from beneath one fingernail and ran his tongue along the cavities in his teeth. He could feel the pain in there. He could feel it in the tiny places where his tongue touched. The pain spread as if fire had been spilled across dry grass. Then the lights in the room went out and it was dark. The pain in his teeth got worse as he breathed in the air.

Brud stood and moved for the window. There were no people in the courtyard. There was only the familiar darkness in the trees and their branches gently swaying. The trees were sparse in heaven. He wanted to open his window, to hear the reassuring sound of the leaves with the wind in them, but the window had no handle. When he touched the pane with his fingers, he knew that it was thick. It was not like glass. It was more like glass and rubber combined. The image was deceitful, and it troubled Brud.

The leaves. They were trying to break free. Brud could sense the wind in the veins of the leaves, the exciting prospect of tumbling free. The chattering as the leaves were stirred against each other by the wind. The speculation as to when they would free themselves. But they were green, not yet orange and gold, the colours of their final escape. Autumn. This is when their strength was greatest. All year — seemingly endless — with the breeze in their veins, pushing, giving strength, until the fall when they claimed their true vibrancy. Breaking loose, they would dazzle Brud with their sweeping, drifting, gliding descent to the ground. He would run and catch them, clapping his palms together with the laughter bucking in his solid chest. They were falling especially for him.

On the ground, the leaves would be incited by the

breeze, and they would mingle freely; the final thrill of sensation, of great triumph before they were gone, wilted and crumbled by their exhaustive march toward complete independence.

But there were no leaves, no trees, no animals inside the walls of heaven. If this place was heaven, then where was the eternal light? He looked back into the dark room. Eyes lingered in the door's round window. Light was shining out there. What had he done to be kept away, to be sent to the fringes of heaven?

Brud was saddened. Why did God make him feel so alone? Where were the animals? Their familiar touch and smell? The great beasts of heaven? Where were the leaves and the trees and the vast uncluttered land? Where was it all? There should be no need for walls here.

He dared not say what he thought. The idea of a false heaven was unspeakable. It was quiet, yes. He understood that much. It was calm and clear. Yes. He wanted to see his mother and his father. He was promised that he would see his family. His father's words: "Patience is a virtue." And virtue meant something fine. A man always waited if he had good reason.

Sitting on the bed, Brud listened. The silence was complete and unto itself. But a strangeness was lingering in the air, filtering through. He sniffed and was alarmed by the odour.

Bells began clanging. Cow bells clattered fast and loud like a stampeding herd racing down a distant corridor. The air in the room was growing faintly thicker. Stained. The smell of cooled ashes in the fireplace. It had all been wrong. Ashes. Dust. Yes, he had been led astray. Fire.

Two firetrucks wailed down the street as the policeman

stepped from the comfort of the bar. The sound stopped him dead in his tracks. He watched the trucks and saw how they were slowing. Stepping further toward the curb, he leaned to see the trucks swing past the gates and into the hospital's parking lot.

The policeman stepped in that direction, his pace increasing as several other people joined him, curiously chattering to each other. The policeman could see thick grey smoke urgently billowing from a few windows in the lower levels of the east wings. He searched for flames. Nothing. Then several windows blew away and he could hear the roaring surge of flames and see them licking out.

A group of firemen were pulling hoses from the trucks. One of them shouted orders and pointed, but the others seemed not to be listening, merely acting by intuition. The brilliant light of the flames was full on the policeman's face as he stepped into the hospital grounds. He could sense the rage gently pressing against him, the persistence of the tantalizing heat warming his skin. He felt lulled and soothed, the flames stepping for him, guiding his trance.

Patients were rushing from the entranceway to join the others already gathered on the grounds. They were dressed in pajamas and gowns, coughing and shrieking, hands in the air, snatching as if at flames, sounds snapping around their heads.

The policeman's eyes discovered his surroundings. The red-and-black wash of light melded everything. He vaguely recalled the image of a man he was searching for. Brud. The soft look hardening. He scanned the crowd, freely stepping among their terror and ambivalence. A tall, still woman was watching the fire, her face without concern, only the insistent opening and closing of her lips and the sounds like a baby's. Another woman held both hands over her face, squeezing her skin as if furiously pressing a mask into place, then throwing her arms away, unsatisfied as she glanced around for reaction. She covered her face again, pressing harder. A man pointed at the flames, stood sideways, and pointed, hiccupping and laughing. A short man, stretching up on his tiptoes, whispered into a woman's ear. She stared at him with panicky eyes, snarling, "Untrue, Jesus knows, untrue..." Several men and women were pawing at the firemen. They were angry and reciting what appeared to be rehearsed speeches regarding the Lord Jesus Christ. His fiery wrath. Nurses and orderlies hurried across the grounds, guiding patients back into place, only to have them wander off immediately.

In the corner of the policeman's eye, he saw that the entrance had emptied. There was no sight of his wife. No sight of the look that he must rescue. His obligation was to his wife. He must stop her from perishing again.

The air grew denser with heat. He wandered closer. It was difficult to breathe and his skin felt as if it would dissolve and be washed away with the sweat that glazed every inch of him. A fireman snatched hold of his arm and another pushed him back, but the policeman flashed his badge and the fireman shouted above the crackling of flames, "I don't care. Get back."

He stepped in reverse, his lungs craving cool air. He remembered the entranceway at the back of the hospital and was encouraged to find that it was unguarded. The metal felt warm when he touched the handle. The stairwell was relatively smokeless, but he knew he would not last long, and sprang up the stairs, gasping, aware of where the criminals were detained. Opening the door to the sixth floor, he saw two orderlies rushing from a room. There was no sign of fire on this floor, but the air was hazy, vaguely grey and dim. The policeman could feel the heat as if the furnace had been cranked up to bust. The soles of his feet were hot. He could sense the floor. Glancing down, he saw steam rising from the edges of the tiles. The flames would burst through at any moment. He anticipated the sound, a synchronized volley of cannon blasts.

The orderlies had overtaken him.

"Get going," they shouted, jostling him toward the stairwell.

"Hands off." He shoved them away, shouting. "I'm a police officer."

"There's a guy who won't come out," one of the orderlies exclaimed, his mouth dangling open as he covered it and coughed. He pointed, then ran into the stairwell. One of them paused to shout back, "We couldn't move him."

And the metal door closed.

The policeman rushed toward the room with the open doorway. He knew that something was not right. He would not see his wife at all. Everything had been a mistake. Arriving at the opening, he squinted and stared. It was familiar, but somehow very different. A tinge of amusement toyed with him. Who was torturing him now with this charade? Whose game was this?

Brud was sitting on the edge of the bed, sweat streaming down his face onto the front of his shirt. The policeman saw him and shivered. "I get it," he said to himself and laughed bitterly, "Save the fool...save myself. Easy."

Brud licked his lips and stared down at his hands, watching them move over each other, feeling the sweaty smoothness. He coughed and sniffed, then glanced out the window, sadly shaking his head.

The policeman stepped in and coughed as if the sound had suddenly become the strange language of this place. Brud glanced over with mild curiosity and felt his sadness lift a little. He even tried to smile at Jimmy's brother, but he could not muster the confidence. He remembered. Steve was the man's name. Brud saw now that the man was close.

"The place is burning," Steve calmly informed Brud.

Brud nodded, ashamed, "Judgement wrong."

"Judgement?" Bending close to him, Steve stared into his eyes.

"Heaven, no heaven." Brud coughed several times, quick and clean, his throat so dry his words squeaked. "Hell."

Steve gripped Brud's arm and straightened, but only Brud's heavy arm lifted. He would not move.

"I should've done this before. I should've taken you out of here, forced you to appreciate what was around us." Steve's words came rushing out like a blast of water onto the fire. "I should've been more alive for you."

"I'm sorry," Brud said, knowing that he had disappointed Jimmy's brother.

"Let's go before it's too late for you."

Brud shook his head, having accepted the certainty of his demise. Steve saw the defeat curdling in the fool's eyes. The fool. Yes, she was a fool and he was a fool, too.

"GET UP!" he shouted at her. "It's your last chance. Our last chance to leave here."

Brud's face was impassive.

"To get out."

"In fire. You're going put me in fire."

Steve's heart felt as if it would burst. His bones ached with impossible longing.

"I didn't," he assured her. "I won't."

"Don't want go to fire."

"I'll help you out of here." There was a thunderous sound as the roar of flames splintered a wooden column below them. Steve stared into his wife's eyes and saw the resolve softening, a shimmering of recognition brightening her look. Merciful hope.

"Leave?" Brud coughed. "No burn in hell?"

"Hurry." Steve wondered about the tears in his eyes. They were hot. They could not be tears. The smoke had thickened to a cloudy grey, sifting through the air. It was difficult to breathe, the air full and scalding, touching his skin, and sticking. It was almost whole. "Come on." He tugged Brud from the bed. Brud followed without protest, happy now with the belief that he could leave and was not to be tossed into the flames to burn for all eternity. There was pardon after all. It did not have to end this way. Change was possible beyond the fact. Inside of Steve, the fire cleared everything.

Brud followed his rescuer to the stairwell, then glanced back to see the glass explode in the window as the stairwell door was shoved open further. Fire, almost invisible, crept up the walls, then raged freely, punching loose, cackling and tossing its amber hair. Steve whispered his wife's name. She seemed to call hello to him, racing to lash against his face with consumptive words.

Brud covered his mouth with his shirt, just like Steve. He tore his gaze away from the flames and the water that streamed through the window, rushing along the floor and soaking their feet in an instant. Steve yanked Brud into the stairwell and slammed shut the metal door. The sound made him gasp.

Brud gave in to the tugging on his arm, turned, and clumsily followed Steve down over the stairs, practically clipping the policeman's heels. He was delighted to have seen that they were fighting against the fire, the water coming from outside to subdue the flames. He thought of baptism and the conversion of hell. A force was following him, something good, always helping, always teaching him. He would know some day. It would be plain to him.

"Out," Steve shouted, holding the back door open, leaning against the metal bar, and feeling the heat of it against his clothes.

They both stepped from the building, the cooler night air punishing their lungs. They coughed violently as the clean air assaulted them. Steve fell forward with his hands on the ground. Brud felt his stomach churn. A rancid surge of fluid burned in his throat. He leaned with his hand against the brick as the thick liquid spilled from his mouth onto the grass.

Steve struggled to swallow. He stared up at Brud, seeing the simpleton, watching the fool regain his own breath, no longer resembling his wife, becoming Brud, breathing out the unity, the air of tragic resemblance. Steve settled on the fact: he must go back into the building, find his wife, find himself. He knew that a part of him was already in there, waiting for the deliverance of the rest of his body.

A fireman and a nurse were suddenly by their sides. Steve weakly flashed his badge, coughing and insisting that they were fine, "This...patient's in...my...custody."

There was no argument. The couple hurried off, searching the back yard for other casualties.

Brud wiped his mouth and stood straight, staring at the policeman who had taken him from the alleyway and made him face the judgement. But now the policeman had saved him from the flames. He was deserving of his name. He had done a good thing. Brud tried to understand what Steve was doing, stepping back toward the building. Brud could sense the feeling in Steve's eyes, the sadness of how he must return, the dwindling hope of other accomplishments.

"Go on," Steve called, nodding toward the fence. "Get out of here."

Brud stumbled back, frightened by the harsh force of the policeman's command. "You?" He pointed at the man he thought was his friend.

"There's someone else in there." Steve gestured toward the opening. Within the stairwell, flames had burned through the framing of the fire doors and were rushing sideways along the stairs.

"GET THE HELL OUT OF HERE."

Brud stumbled backward, turning, but watching Steve standing in the doorway. Steve was frightened by the promise of what had been accepted. Brud raised his hand, waving his stubby fingers. He thought, *eight, ten. Eight but never ten. Is all. Goodbye.*

Steve did not wave. The flames were roaring behind him. He smiled at Brud and watched until the fool had reached the fence and climbed over the iron spikes to reclaim his freedom. Once on the other side, Brud held the bars and watched. He saw Steve turn to face the flames and begin to advance through the doorway. Slow steps toward the immortalizing heat.

Steve smelled the hairs of his moustache burning, guilt undoing in an instant. He heard his wife's voice sizzling into his skin. Licking. A blazing big-lipped kiss. The colours were so beautiful, such beautiful light burning his eyes, flames thickening like clots, tangling, dragging him down, through his burning clothes. He heard screams from outside of himself. It seemed too loud to be his own voice, even though his eardrums had popped moments ago. He had never heard it before. No, it was not his voice. He did not recognize himself, nor any of the others.

Who were these people with their skins in their hands?

The Quagmire company truck pulled to the side of the road. Rolling down his window, the yellow-toothed man watched the fire, dark orange flames languidly reflecting in the innermost spheres of his intent eyes. The sight intrigued him and he offered a smile and a curious nod. Reaching for the radio dial, his long fingers switched off the volume. Sweet clarity. The fury of fire and voices called to him from across the street, coaxing his smile to an unnatural width, thick lines etching into his skin, like plastic being warmed out of shape. The sparks leapt and bound until his eyes were completely orange and swished with spikes of black.

The building began to crumble, the roof snapping, a crashing of beams giving way, and then the rushing boom of great weight pounding down through the floors. The patients — held at the edge of the grounds, against the wrought-iron fence — shrieked and jutted back, scrambling in tight circles, some of them holding chests or squeezing their heads and spinning, others pointing and yelping with great pleasure. A barricade was being set up outside the gate. A stretcher moved through the crowd toward one of several ambulances parked with their red lights sweeping. A fireman lay flat on the stretcher, his face a smear of black, his eyes white and open.

Quagmire watched with great amusement. He envisioned the new structure that would replace this burned-out shell. Down with the old and up with the new. Without the certainty of such tragedies, his business would never survive. His company (through bribing the appropriate officials years ago) had built the hospital, and he was certain the same routine would be adhered to, settling the construction contract for the new institution.

Quagmire stared away from the building. His fiery eyes shot further up the street to see Brud stumbling out into traffic. Cars screeched to a stop, allowing the stout, seemingly drunk, black-faced man to cross the road.

"Ah-hah!" Quagmire exclaimed, recognizing the jest and leaning out his window to wag a finger at the sky. "Naughty, naughty," he teased, a favourite joke of his. "Don't make it so easy."

Brud shuffled toward the truck. He could not stop coughing. Something seemed to be stuck in his throat and it was impossible to expel. He paused and set his hand against the hood of the pickup.

"Hey?" called Quagmire. "Friend."

Brud stared through the windshield. Coughing, he shuffled closer and bent toward Quagmire's face. He blinked and tried to cough away the burning itchiness in his throat.

"Closer," Quagmire whispered, unflinching.

Brud leaned forward into the truck, the sounds around him growing muffled. He kept his mouth closed, trapping the coughs that punched behind his lips. His breath pulsed heavily through his nose with a noticeable wheeze.

"This city air," said Quagmire. "Fills your lungs with cancer."

Brud looked back toward the building. He pointed plainly as if to explain.

"What happens if they see you?"

Brud shrugged.

"They'll take you back. Lock you away. They shouldn't do that to crazy people. Crazy people see the clearest, recognize the urgency of the task. They have superior powers of concentration, attention to detail. Compulsion. They commit themselves entirely to their beliefs." Quagmire closed his left hand into a fist and covered it with his right palm, squeezing. A knuckle cracked. "It doesn't seem fair."

Brud straightened swiftly, his head striking the metal rim of the window. Wincing, his eyes pushed closer, dipping at the ends, his brows knitting together. He delicately rubbed the top of his head.

"I'll give you a ride." Quagmire indicated the empty seat beside him. "You do me a little favour." He thought of the signature, of how he required a witness to make it all legal, but he could arrange that later, pay a man to pretend he had been there. The simpleton would not deny he had signed the legal paper. He was an honest sort. Quagmire was certain of this. He had known the fool's father, but had failed in his efforts to buy the land. The fool's father did not know the value of money. He was an honest fool as well.

"Ride?" he asked. "Take you where you want to go. Drive."

Quagmire moved his hands along the steering wheel, imitating the act of driving.

Brud chuckled, then laughed aloud, pressing his palm over his mouth to hold in a cough. His shoulders stooped as he nodded with appreciation. Reaching in, he mussed up the few strands of hair slicked across Quagmire's head.

"Listen, get in," Quagmire said with annoyance, rapidly plastering his hair back in place.

"No go back in." Brud turned to the building. "Saved."

Quagmire stared at the flames, the humour returning to him, only now resembling sarcasm, his sense of displeasure tainting his high spirits.

"Must've been hell in there," he said, showing Brud his teeth.

Brud turned to look at the yellow-toothed man, a startled expression on his face.

"Yes," he said, nodding. "Yes, hell you can leave."

Quagmire burst with laughter. He tried to speak between the spasms. "Hell...you can...leave." He roared, growling and lashing the steering wheel with his fists.

Brud could not help but smile, but he remained slightly concerned.

"Yes," he insisted, pointing toward the building. But the laughter was too infectious. He sensed it tickling inside of him and felt the tension lift from his face, a tiny laugh jutting through his thick purplish lips. Soon he was laughing with as much gusto as Quagmire.

The yellow-toothed man was disheartened by the accompaniment. He did not care for the idea of laughing along with someone. The whole idea was to make a joke out of Brud, laugh at his stupidity, not in unison with him. Why don't people ever understand the true value of ridicule? Instantly he became cheerless and serious.

"Get in the truck, fool," he demanded, losing his temper. He shouted, "GET IN!" Brud's laughter was cut short, and Quagmire realized his mistake. He cursed under his breath for losing his patience.

I have to learn to control that, he lectured himself. He saw the scowl that now mastered Brud's face, the eyebrows drawing down and the big bottom lip coming up to cover the top.

"Bad," Brud said, stepping back, hearing the screeching of tires and the whirling sounds of horns as cars swerved to avoid him.

Quagmire smiled, speaking through his brownish-yellow teeth, "Sorry, friend. Really, jump right in." He playfully patted the seat. "It's nice."

Brud pointed at the man, feeling his face burn red with anger and frustration, the confusion of the night mounting to hurt him, to be unkind to him.

"No like," he called, walking away, but still pointing and looking at the man.

Quagmire kept smiling. His smile was undefeatable. He held it for the crowds who curiously glanced at him as they passed by, wondering about the situation. Quagmire waved a hand at them, wiggling his fingers. He showed them the black glass candy on his tongue, then blew them kisses, stinging each and every one of them. "My people," he said behind his teeth. How well he understood the power of public relations.

chapter five

invisibility

"Spare a quarter, sir?" asked the boy. He slowly walked backward, keeping pace with the approach of a thin elderly man. The old ones were the easiest to con. The boy could follow them because they only inched along. It was not a struggle and they usually gave in after a while, broke down. But this man was ignoring what was right before his eyes. No matter how many times the boy crossed in front of the old man, the old man would not see him.

Finally the boy gave up, calling, "What are you — blind?" The old man glanced back and stared, the lines on his face explaining everything. Always that look, but never help.

The boy enjoyed begging, the possibility of obtaining money from people for doing absolutely nothing. He thought it was the best idea ever. Even though he still had a pocketful of Brud's cash, he knew the money would not last forever. He needed to horde his funds. He had even thought of setting up a bank account, but those shirts-and-ties were sure to nab him if he went in there with a big load of dollars. They'd want all sorts of things from him, identification and crap like that. And the questions! That's what they really took joy in getting on with. Asking all their questions. Why did they always need to know so much stuff about everyone else? The boy had seen them in the big windows, sitting behind their desks with forms in their hands. The shirts-and-ties wanted all this information before they'd do you a real favour by taking your money. That was stupid. What was the matter with them? They had no idea about anything.

Hand steadily outstretched, the boy pleaded with a woman dressed in an expensive mauve-coloured dress and overcoat. But she ignored him too and he spit after her, almost hitting the heels of her flat-soled designer shoes.

The boy was becoming tired and irritable. He only noticed now, after the spitting episode. He rarely acted that way. It was hunger that changed him. His young will was not impenetrable. He found weakness in the faces he constantly confronted and cursed these people under his breath. Standing still on the sidewalk, he tried to forget them. He thought of Brud's money and the night ahead and he was vaguely refreshed. He knew he could sleep in a clean comfortable place again tonight, one of the medium-priced hotels on Slattery East that didn't ask questions and kept a clean house. He smiled at the thought and, taking a deep breath, continued begging. He was hooked, compelled by the only relief that could come with ease. It was his preoccupation; the possibility of free cash was foremost in his mind.

Brud spotted the boy before the boy saw him. He stood across the street, in front of a restaurant window, looking much like a man who had just stepped from a fire. He listened to the sweet, tiny voice imploring the passers-by.

Brud coughed and smiled, his memory of the yellow-toothed man and his anger breaking away like a hard dead bird dropping to the ground. The boy was good to him. He had saved him from being hurt in the alleyway. He was a good omen, and seeing him again reversed his thoughts, sent him backward to think of the flowers for Pretty, Jim, back further along the course to the farm.

Brud considered the momentum of the cars cruising along the street. People were looking at him, others were making kissing sounds at the women who strolled close by. The women were dressed in bright colours like the lights that flashed around them. Brud offered smiles and a few of them were returned. At sights such as this, his heart would stir as if something was coming to life inside of him, a baby animal bending and struggling, delicately straightening its legs, attempting to find its footing. A pure and ignorant sense of bravado. He would reach for them, but the women would quickly lean away.

Brud looked up at the carnival of neon colours. The lights were flashing, imploring, like the voice of the boy. There was an eagerness in the colours, an urge wanting to be satisfied. The insistent flashing was like a broken, dotted line that strove for connection. But what would make the colours flow steadily? Was it something in him that had to be offered, a gesture necessary to connect the empty spaces of the pulse?

It seemed as if everyone was in need. People were calling to others to give them things, to come to their assistance. But few were listening. Strange as it seemed, the majority of men and women were ignoring each other. They had no time to waste, everything was so alive. They had to move quickly before the sights escaped them. The light and the energy in the air gifted people with a sense of confidence, as if they did not need companionship. A breathless energy overcharged Brud's surroundings, even bringing still objects to life. The buildings, the sidewalks, and the parked cars throbbed and swayed beneath the light. The air cascaded with fresh sound, crackling with the chatter of conversations.

The boy turned and spat onto the sidewalk. Lifting his eyes, he saw the blackened figure standing across the street. The man was filthy. At first, the boy did not realize that it was Brud, but the sight of this soot-stained man with his hair sticking up in the back was amusing. The boy wondered why the man was staring at him, why the man was waving, and then he recognized the shape of the body and its hesitant movements and was jostled by a rush of memory.

"Hey," the boy nervously shouted, thinking of running, but finding himself frozen. Moments passed before he felt reassured by the sight of the fool's white smile.

Brud waved and flatly shouted, "Hey?"

The boy glanced toward a doorway, then up ahead, just in case of trouble. He thought of the fool's money and feared for its safety.

Look at him, the boy told himself. *He's totally harmless.*

The vague ominous shapes of uncertainty shifted inside of the boy, fading toward what he welcomed as a reasonable thought, the idea of more money.

"Come over," he called, quickly motioning with his hands.

Brud moved to the curb and watched the shiny cars pass, the animated faces behind the windows, the lights reflecting off of shifting steel. He waited for an open pathway.

The boy stepped close to the traffic. He studied the flow as if guessing the strength of a river's current, then darted forward with agility, easily weaving between the automobiles.

"How ya doing?" asked the boy, shoving his hands into his pockets and watching Brud, cautiously searching for a bad sign that would spur him to turn and run.

"Okay." Brud shrugged his shoulders.

"Okay?" the boy laughed nervously, catching his breath. "What happened to you? Look at you!"

"Hell," Brud said, "got me for little while."

The boy looked him over.

"Wow, you were in a fire or something!"

Brud pointed back up the street. "Fire."

"Where to?"

"Heaven burn." Brud nodded, his nose twitching until he sneezed, his body lashing forward.

The boy flinched back. He waited, cautiously, then shook his head and laughed. "Must've got ashes up your nose."

Brud sneezed again, his thin bangs flicking down across his face, hanging in front of his narrow eyes.

"Bend down," the boy said, motioning with his hand. When Brud complied, the boy gently swept Brud's bangs back into place.

Brud stared at the boy, staying bent forward with his hands braced against his knees. He smiled and his eyes filled up with the pleasure he felt at finding his little friend. Reaching forward, he took hold of the boy's shoulders, shook them, and laughed.

"Nice to see you," said Brud, remembering the name that the skull-faced man had called the boy, "Dogger." Brud stopped shaking the boy because the boy was looking uncomfortable.

"Hey, nice to see you, too, man." He hesitantly shook Brud's hand. "But you gotta get them tears out of your eyes. It's not right." He glanced around, licking his lips.

Brud stood straight, still shaking Dogger's hand. He chuckled and wiped at his eyes, streaking the soot.

"Good," he said, his smile giving way to a frown.

"What's the matter?" Dogger felt the fool's hand go weak in his.

"Good," Brud said, his lips quivering.

"If it's good, then why're you sad?"

Brud shrugged, his eyes waiting for an answer. He remembered the screaming laughter that he heard in the false heaven. He thought he felt that way now.

Dogger took a deep breath. "You're too much."

"A lot." Brud confidently nodded his head.

"We better get you cleaned up. Check out a washroom."

Brud dragged the back of his arm along his nose. The movement left a clean strip above his top lip and across his cheek. He glanced down at his pants and saw how black they were.

"What hell did," he said, pointing at the blackened fabric.

"Nice fashion. Maybe it'll catch on." Dogger walked ahead, turning to make sure Brud was close behind. "Come on. There's a washroom in that shopping mall up there. Don't think it's closed yet. What time is it?"

"Two o'clock," Brud said automatically, remembering the different numbers his father would say whenever he was asked the same question. The numbers would change all the time and so he guessed at two, although it might have been four.

"It's not two o'clock," Dogger said, "Where'd you get that?"

"Four o'clock," Brud said, nodding hopefully, the corners of his mouth dipping down with stern assurance. "Four o'clock. Yes. Uh-huh."

"It's not four o'clock either. Give it up. You just don't know, do you?"

Brud fell silent, the hurt creasing between his brows. He looked at his hands, put them in his pockets.

"Naw, you're right," Dogger lied, slapping Brud's arm. "I just wasn't thinking of the right kind of time, I guess."

Brud smiled with his lips closed, but soon his teeth were revealed and he slapped Dogger on the back. He liked the boy. Dogger made him feel important, made him feel he could say the right words that sounded so special, placing him above all others.

"Rich," he exclaimed, his eyebrows lifting as he tapped a finger against his chest.

Amusement drained from Dogger's face. "I don't have your money," he carefully said. "I lost it."

"Rich," Brud assured him, standing tall.

"Maybe you can lend me a dollar or two?"

Brud laughed, flashing his crooked teeth. He nodded and said, "Yes." He felt the action would make the boy happy. Yes was always much easier than no. It meant something better.

"Great. Come on." Dogger sprinted ahead, then ran back to Brud. "We can get anything we want, right?"

Brud laughed louder. He clapped his palms together.

"Right?" Dogger turned around. He squealed and drummed his feet against the sidewalk. "You're the best."

"Yes. The best." Brud winked enthusiastically, dipping his chin close to his chest and eyeing the boy.

"Come on. We'll get you cleaned up, then celebrate. Get some booze. Okay?"

Brud did not answer. His attention was drawn else-where. He watched the lights flash off and on, then stared up at the sky, viewing the scarce stars, the quieter, muted twinkling. The sky seemed bright, but not from starlight. Perhaps the stars were closer in the city, down on top of them with all their lights turned brilliant and intense. He saw a light sweeping across the sky. A moment later the line of light swept around again. Brud looked down at Dogger.

The boy was smiling up at him, beaming as if ev-erything was perfect. Dogger had never felt such an unconditional sense of security. The feeling left him light-headed. He could not form a thought, only treasure the sensations that lightened his entire body. He was aware that this man was good, and they were friends, and that was all that mattered at this moment. He would hold onto this pleasure, walk quietly, and hope its delicateness would not splinter and stick him; happiness easily turn-ing to pain. Dogger had memories of how they often crossed boundaries, running together.

But this man was good. This man would not even know how to hurt another person. No one could ever be harmed by a fool. Even the boy knew that.

"Use this," Dogger instructed, lifting a handful of paper towels from under the stream of water.

Brud took the pulpy clump and regarded himself in the mirror. Wiping a clean space across his cheek, a laugh escaped him, his eyes blinking. They were white and obvious.

"What a mess," Dogger declared, leaning against the sink. Taking a skinny cigar from a thin metal case, he sparked his lighter. Brud flinched at the sight of fire.

"Sorry." Dogger closed the top of the lighter. "Fire, hey?" He opened the case and replaced the cigar beside the others.

Brud looked at the lighter, making sure it was no longer alive. Confidence restored, he returned his attention to the mirror. He wiped his face clean, then dipped his cupped hands into the cold running water. The water was so cold it stung his fingers. Lifting his hands to his face, he made a whooping sound when the water splashed him.

Done with his face, he scrubbed the black from his hands, but could not cleanse the black arcs of dirt from beneath his fingernails. He worked furiously, understanding the need for cleanliness, remembering how his mother had scrubbed his skin in the big tub on the farm. "Pink and perfect," she would always say. "Pink must be God's favourite colour. He makes all the beautiful things that colour. Roses and sunset skies and baby's new skin. What do you think of it, Brud?" Brud would nod and splash water at her, laughing with his head lolling back.

Brud coughed and sneezed, dashing the memory far back into its secret place. He felt ashamed for not having washed in a long time. His mother would look at him silently and he would know that she was not happy. He could see her watching him now.

When he turned to look, Dogger had disappeared. Brud stood straight by the sink, waiting for instruction. Then he knocked on the row of doors, but there was no answer. Some of them swung open and he saw that they were empty. He looked around, uncertain of what to do, where to go.

He glanced at himself in the mirror. Perhaps he was lost somewhere. Perhaps his memories of his mother had moved him to another place. He turned on the taps and watched the water gush loose. Cupping his hands, he tossed water on the top of his head, repeating the exercise until his hair was dripping wet. He pushed it flat to his head like the hair he had seen in a picture in one of the store windows along the street. He turned his face to the side and forced a smile, attempting to duplicate the smooth smile he had seen. But, surprisingly, it would not match. His hair was thinner and his face rounder. The man in the picture had black hair and a handsome face with dark eyes. He was wearing a tie and a suit. Brud wondered why he could not be like this man, why he could not look the same. It was disheartening and he showed himself a look of regret. He sadly said, "Eight, ten. Go so far, then make up two. Can't make up."

Brud shut off the water. He turned away from his reflection and headed for the door. Pulling it open, he saw Dogger quickly coming his way, a shopping bag dangling from one of his hands. He was wearing a dark pair of sunglasses that were much too large for his face.

"I bought you stuff," Dogger said, glancing back before stepping close, past Brud. "I got big sizes. Extra large. Should fit." Dogger poked in the bag then looked at Brud, who was still holding open the door. "Close that." He glanced down at Brud's boots, thinking, *We'll have to wash them off, shine them up nice and spiffy.*

Brud moved his fingers away from the door and watched it slowly ease shut.

"I got a pair of sunglasses for you, too. Super cool."

With a curious expression, Brud watched as Dogger pulled brightly coloured clothes from the shopping bag.

"Hawaiian shirt. You like that? True fashion. And these." He yanked out a pair of white rugby pants. "These are excellent. Slick. Here." He laid the bag on the floor and set the clothes over the rim of the sink. Reaching into the bottom of the bag, he extracted a big pair of sunglasses, identical to his own, only with pink ear stems instead of orange.

Dogger opened the sunglasses and held them toward Brud's face, nodding for his friend to lean close. Brud bent forward and the sunglasses were slipped into place. Everything turned darker, with a deep blue shade.

"Have a look." Dogger walked close to the mirror.

Brud turned and studied himself. He seemed different without eyes, invisible to himself.

"You'll look sharp with these new clothes. Cost a fortune and I didn't even steal them. I bought every single thing. Look, here's the receipt. I had some money put away. It wasn't yours, though. Really. It wasn't. You like them?" he proudly asked, holding up the Hawaiian shirt so Brud could see it in the mirror.

Brud's smile was loose and big. "Yes. Like very much."

"Great colours, hey?" Dogger examined the fabric, rubbed his hand over the shades of red, orange, and yellow. "Wild."

"Colours," Brud mumbled, seeing his lips move. He opened and closed his mouth. It was like he was asleep, like no one could see or touch him even though he was walking and moving through the air. Only he could see himself in the dark blue tint. It was strange and he felt out of sorts. If he was sleeping now, strange things were sure to happen to him. His eyes were gone. He twitched his nose from side to side. He could see all of this in his reflection, but he could not see his eyes. How was this possible? What had made him turn invisible?

"I know a place," Dogger enthused, walking backward

along the dark street so he could watch his cool new friend, "where they don't worry about age or any of that stuff."

Brud stepped gingerly. His arms felt heavier than usual, anticipating something. He could scarcely see where he was going and was listening to the sounds of Dogger's words.

"That's a great act," Dogger said, falling in alongside Brud. "They'd never think of looking for a blind man. Yeah, I know what you're up to. You're not so stupid. I saw your picture in the paper. I can read, you know. You probably never even thought that. You were locked away somewhere. I know and you burned the place down, right? To get out. Is that what you did?"

Brud did not answer. He was preoccupied with feeling his way through the air.

"Don't worry, I'll keep it quiet. No sweat. You're wild. Here, let me take your hand and lead you. That'll really make it look good." Dogger slipped his hand around Brud's thick palm.

A warm calm settled over Brud as he sensed the boy's small fingers touching his hand. He felt his other arm lighten a little, relax, fall in closer to his body. Dogger would make sure no harm came to him. He understood this by the feel of how Dogger held his hand.

"Like I was saying before, I know this place where they don't worry about age as long as you got the cash. A bootlegging hole in the wall. Booze is more expensive, and it's not open to just anyone, but I know the guy on the door so it's okay. It's not a classy place. You heard me, right? That's not what I meant. You know? You'll see."

"Dark."

"Must be real dark with those glasses on. They're the darkest ones I could find, because I knew you'd be hiding. No one'd ever recognize you in those. Oh, listen." Dogger stopped and Brud stopped with him. "One thing about this place I forgot to tell you." Dogger glanced at the passing people. No one was paying attention. No one seemed to see the two of them.

Brud looked straight forward, his head perfectly level, waiting for Dogger to continue, to give him sight.

"These murders they were trying to pin on you, I know you didn't do them. You're not the guy, but I know the guy they're looking for. That's all. Okay. Let's go." He continued on, but stopped again. "I'm just telling you. I wanted to let you know that I was going to get you out, tell the cops, but you got out. Okay? So don't blame me."

Brud nodded. He saw the vague shadows of people moving around him, the muted shadows and signs.

"The real guy's not far from here. He's a bit whacko." Dogger made a quick motion of circles with his finger, but he looked slightly troubled as if he was dishonouring someone. "Real whacko. I know because I know him." Dogger stared off. The words he had spoken were better kept to himself. He waited for a moment, his small face tightening with concern as he glanced down at the sidewalk. He said, "He's my father," so low that Brud could not hear.

"Dark." Brud said, still staring straight ahead.

"The guy who killed all these people," Dogger said, as if it was so obvious now, "He's my father."

"Killed," Brud said, remembering how his father butchered the cows and how it was not the same as murder. Killed and murder were when people killed other people.

People in God's image. The difference. Brud shivered, remembering what he had done, feeling hollow and lost, not like himself at all.

"Sometimes he's at this place we're going to. You'll see. I'll show you, so you'll know and can tell the cops to get yourself off the hook. He's my father, okay? So don't say nothing if he tells you. He's a bragger."

Dogger continued walking, distraught by the fact that the fool did not seem to appreciate this information, his betrayal of his own flesh and blood in favour of Brud.

Led briskly by Dogger, Brud offered no resistance. The boy increased his pace and Brud wondered about this. Why were they hurrying? Were they being pursued? He thought of taking off his sunglasses but he remembered how Dogger had said that people would never find him with the shades on. He was safe with the world gone darker. No one could make him out now. They would be looking for him. Bad spirits are never discouraged. Once they leap from the flames, they never rest until they take what should have been theirs. Once you murder another man, they come looking to capture your soul. But Brud did not know what would be removed if they took his soul. Was it like an arm or a leg? Were his thumbs his soul? They were already gone. Maybe his soul had been taken away a long time ago. He blinked and moved his tongue around in his mouth. What did a soul taste like?

Brud was cold and scared. The short-sleeved shirt was not enough. Dogger was not enough. He wondered where he was being led.

chapter six

the rush of realization

Andrea had gone off to bed hours ago. Jim had promised to join her, but he did not feel tired. He sat on the couch, his overworked mind labouring to clear itself, to uncover an avenue not previously explored. He remembered the symbol from the karate lessons of his youth. The two halves of a design, swirling after each other. Black and white. He thought of accuracy, the need to pinpoint the facts, to separate them. Extremes could not be constant and forever merging. Thoughts of his brother. The division. Who was black and who was white? The symbol became his own thoughts. Notions languidly curling to chase one another, then slowing until they were still, like the yin and yang. *Split them*, he told himself. *Once and for all. Pry them apart from each other.*

The small wooden clock on the mantlepiece mocked him as it ticked away, the movements offering no hope of division, only a distrustful sense of eventuality that guided all matters. Despite his fatigue, he pushed himself from the couch and moved toward the clock. Instead of smashing it, he turned and looked across the living room. The apartment had been so familiar, but now, in the late hours, it appeared vivid and alien. He felt his breath turn shallow, his heart speed. The room was too still, charged with an impregnable clarity that wanted to snap through his skin.

Slowly he moved for the couch and sat, fearing he would whiteout. Lack of sleep and constant thought had led him to the brink of an anxiety attack. He was no stranger to them. Years ago, at law school, he had woken in the night, not knowing where he was, struggling to catch his breath while his heart hammered in his chest, punched in his throat. Words working through him, taking control. Arguments. Accuracy. Division. Integrity. Admission.

Jim laid back on the couch and closed his eyes. He inhaled deeply, holding the air in his lungs for a count of five, before slowly releasing to a further count of five. Repeating this several times, he felt his body and thoughts lull. He opened his eyes to view the off-white ceiling above him. Turning his head, he saw the coffee table, the newspaper resting there. Reading would take his mind off Brud. Attempting to move casually, he sat up and leaned for the paper, felt the grimy touch of the pages. He scanned the front page — nothing of major interest there. He opened the wide sheet to page three and let his eyes skim the broadsheet. Up and down. News of the arrest of a murderer. His eyes took in the photograph and the buzzing whiteness rushed from where he thought he had tamed it. The whiteness attempting to shrink his scope of vision. The whiteness sizzling in his ears. Nothing seemed familiar. His hands. The newspaper. He had the impression that he was settling sideways, tilting off at an angle. The black-and-white photograph defied him. The man looked like Brud. He brought his face closer to the newspaper, obeying his need to see. The similarity was striking, astonishing. He blinked his hollow eyes and took several deep breaths. He read how the man had been unnamed, how he had been linked to other murders. It was impossible. The likeness. It was Brud. But how had he killed these people? It could not be Brud. If it was Brud, then he was innocent. How could he have killed all of these people that were named? It wasn't Brud. He looked closer. It was Brud. It could be no other.

Andrea heard her name vaguely. She rolled over and listened inside herself, then, discovering silence, raised her head to look through the darkness. Once more, her name was spoken. She glanced toward the door and saw the outline of a figure standing there.

Sleep had hold of her. She was struggling to cross over into a state of knowing. A murkiness weighed on her body. Her head seemed outlandishly heavy, her limbs equally cumbersome.

Suddenly, the light was blasted on and she flinched, shutting her eyes against the assault. Even though her eyes were closed, she felt the intensity. She pulled her numb arm from under the blanket and laid it across her eyes. Falling back onto her pillow, she heard the rustling of a newspaper.

"Do you know who this is?" Jim demanded. The newspaper crackling above her, the sound so loud and disturbing.

She tried to open her eyes and saw that the light was

dim, the newspaper practically touching her face. Observing the picture of the murderer, a far-off realization made her stomach turn queasy. Her eyes squinted to get a closer look. She shook her head, even though she felt the dread of revelation splicing together.

"It's Brud." Jim yanked back the newspaper.

Andrea covered her eyes and moaned, "Jimmy," half a protest, half an apology.

The lawyer stared at the picture, still unbelieving. The brilliant overhead light washed clean his tired face, giving it a sickly pallor.

"Is this the man you were writing about? Is this him? Your new assignment? I don't see your by-line. Where is it?"

Andrea rubbed her face and nodded.

"I can't believe it. Andrea!" Jim turned and left the room, slapping off the light as he left.

Andrea lay in darkness. She was wide-awake and her nerves were sparking from the sudden abrupt summoning from sleep.

"Jimmy?" She made a plea, her voice raspy and barely audible. She coughed and called his name into the strange void that had settled between them. Her husband did not answer her call. She knew that she should get out of bed, but felt somewhat threatened knowing what she would have to face. Her husband's anger was complete. No, it was not anger. It was indignation. *How was I supposed to know?* she wondered as she pushed herself from the sheets and trod toward the bedroom door.

Standing there, she heard her husband's voice, his tone subdued and even. He sounded strangely defeated, speaking into the telephone receiver with his back to her. It was difficult to make out his words, but she knew that he was trying to contact his brother. After all, Steve had met Brud. He would have known everything about the entire fiasco.

She whispered a soft curse and stepped from the room, feeling the carpet against her feet. She felt cold and vulnerable standing in her underwear, barely able to hold her eyes open. Jim spoke clearly, staring at the ground. Andrea heard him asking where his brother was. He mustn't have been on duty. She went back into the bedroom and pulled the quilt from the bed, sloppily wrapped it around her body, and returned to the living room. Yawning, she covered her mouth, not wanting her husband to see, to mistake her yawning for disinterest.

Jim asked for another policeman, an acquaintance. He waited, then spoke again, low and reserved, professional. He asked, "Where is he being assessed?"

Andrea watched his impassive body, the way he gently moved his socked feet over the carpet, making wide strokes in the plush pile. His foot stopped in midmotion. His back straightened.

"What do you mean, fire?"

chapter seven

Brud sees the light

Heads turned glumly, with mild interest, as the occupants of the large square room watched Brud and Dogger step in from the alleyway. Behind them, the door was briskly pulled shut by the bouncer. A handful of customers peered through the smoke before focussing back on their tables, coughing, or resuming where they had left off, arguing a point. Brud's brightly coloured clothing held the attention of a few others. They studied his new pants and his cowboy boots. It was a sign of money, the rewards of a recent crime.

A few chairs scraped along the wooden flooring as a pathway was made for the two newcomers. The round-headed man with thin hair and sunglasses looked important by the way he hesitantly moved among them. The boy was walking triumphantly by the man's side as if the man was the legendary power behind some sinister underworld.

Brud accidently kicked the leg of a chair (a sign of dominance) and the crowd hushed and straightened in their seats. The man sitting in the chair glanced over his shoulder, saw Brud's dark glasses and expressionless face, then stared back at his drink, studying the glass, taking hold of it, hoping the man would not provoke him further.

A gang of teenagers all dressed in black sat on the floor in the corner with their backs slouched against a painted mural of torn clouds in a scarlet red sky.

"They're The Crows," Dogger informed Brud.

"Crows," Brud repeated, staring at the vague image of the teenagers. He squinted and stood in front of them, gazing down at their disinterested forms. "No wings."

"That's the truth," Dogger laughed, tugging Brud away from them. "One of them tried to fly once, but it ended on the street. All kinds of crazy stories. They're all screwed up. Something really weird about every one of them."

A few more heads turned to appraise Brud and Dogger. Newcomers or intruders? A hand waved in the air and Dogger heard his name being called in greeting.

Waving briefly, Dogger smiled at a man sitting with his wife and daughter at a table by the bar.

"They're a wild family," the boy declared, moving in front of Brud so the family could not see him speaking. "They drink together and everything. The girl's my age and she follows them around. They try to lose her but she keeps tailing them, so they come here sometimes as a treat so they can all sit down together and have a drink. Then they try losing her again. I've seen it. Followed them. It's the funniest thing."

"Smoke," Brud said, sniffing the air and remembering the fire, feeling the same discomfort in his throat. He coughed and looked around the room, sighting the overflowing tin ashtrays on every table.

"Smoky alright." Dogger strayed toward the back of the room and dropped into a chair. "Hey," he called. "Here." Dogger patted the empty seat beside him. Leaning sideways, he pushed it out for Brud.

Brud carefully sat — his hands braced against the arm rests — and watched Dogger. But the boy was not interested in Brud. He was interested in inspecting the crowd, wondering how many of them had noticed him, had seen him come into the room with the rich fool. He winked at two separate tables. The men there nodded distractedly with filmy eyes or shook their heads, letting them hang loosely, close to their chests. He liked to look at the faces. They always amazed him, the young and the old. He knew some of their backgrounds, but others he liked to speculate about, just by seeing their faces. The drawn, taut expressions. The young ones turning dark-eyed and pale-skinned, something eating them up inside. The young girls with makeup and jeans and the raunchy things they told him and laughed about. And the man with one eye missing, only the empty hole in his face and a deep scar running from behind his ear all the way down the side of his neck to his shoulder. The man's head had almost been torn off when he was run over by a truck and dragged three blocks at the age of three. A block for each of his years, he took pride in telling everyone. His eye had been gouged out when he was a young man. Drunk one night, he fell face first onto the stem of a beer bottle. Bullseye, they called him.

Dogger was enthralled by the scars. Skully had told him once that you earned your scars. They gave you character and he wished he had a scar like that one; a serious thick scar that showed he had fought against whatever was trying to snatch him out of his body. Had fought and had won, living to talk about it. Better than everyone. All the frightened people he saw hurrying to work every morning. Afraid of being late, afraid of missing lunch, afraid of meeting someone, afraid of breathing... They needed to tangle with something that would tear them up, make them know that they were real again. Flesh and blood.

Brud was still watching his special friend. Dogger's small face was alive with the thoughts racing behind his child eyes.

"Hey, kid," a big man snapped, standing next to the table, his huge bowling pin arms hanging away from his sides. They looked stuffed and heavy, Brud thought. On the back of his right hand there was a tattoo that looked like two Z's crossing over. His hair was greased to his head and his sleeveless T-shirt was imprinted with the image of a red-eyed skull.

"You just want to stare, get the hell out."

"Who's staring?" the boy scoffed, proudly pulling a fifty from his pocket. "Two beers. I got cash, Mono. See?"

"Good for you." Mono swaggered off, pausing when the boy called, "No, make it two each. Four beers. Me and my friend here moving for Big Zero Land."

Mono listened with his back to them, then turned and stepped up to their table again.

"Big Zero Land," he said, resting his arms on the table-top and leaning on them. His swastika hand gripped the boy's arm.

"I got something take you there a lot faster."

Dogger stared at the symbol.

"That's pretty neat."

"Right hand for the right." He laughed with his teeth clamped shut, his cheeks rounding out. Then he looked at Brud. "What's your problem?"

"Nothing," said Dogger. "No problem with him."

Brud stared blankly at the big tall man.

"Just the four beers for now, okay?" Dogger maintained.

"Unfriendly bastard," Mono cursed, straightening on his legs and gladly releasing Dogger's hand. He looked at Brud and jerked his head. "Hey."

"Hey," Brud said, staring at Mono.

"Where you coming from, man?"

"Coming from?"

"Yeah. Where you stand? Where've you been?"

"Been from hell," Brud insisted.

Mono glanced at Dogger, then looked at Brud. "Funny," he said. He even laughed to show he was a good sport.

"No," Brud flatly replied. "Burn you."

"You don't burn me, man."

Brud nodded and curiously scanned the room.

"Your friend here blind?" Mono tossed a thumb toward the pale round face wearing sunglasses.

Dogger smiled at Brud. "Maybe."

"Maybe? What kind of crap is that?"

"Crap," said Brud, an interesting word. "Maybe, crap." He watched two women come in through the door. They were wearing very little clothing, and Brud blushed at the sight of them.

"Just recently," Dogger insisted, "gone all blind."

Mono snickered, wiping his hands in the front of his T-shirt. "Yeah? Well, get him unblind. What's he smiling about?"

"Crap," said Brud.

"Blind people can be happy, too, you know. You're not prejudiced are you? You got a law against blind people or something?"

One of The Crows starting cawing from where he was

sitting on the floor. Another joined in, and soon they were all mimicking the sound. Sharp bird music filled the air. Brud's mouth dropped open. He stared up, searching overhead.

"Crows," Mono sneered. Spinning toward them, he shouted, "SHUT UP!"

The Crows' sounds were jolted into silence, dislocated in mid-caw. The entire room went quiet until someone laughed and the conversations picked up again.

"We understand," one of The Crows called, "the absolute necessity for human order. We live on what's left of it." There was a pause. Then another Crow added, "Order becomes disorder always."

No one said a word. They waited for more, knowing there was truth in the statement. When The Crows spoke, it usually sparked a glimmer of enlightenment for those within earshot.

"Two beers it is," Mono said. Turning away from the newcomers, he shot one final look at The Crows before heading for the bar. Several people stood waiting to be served and carefully watched his approach.

"Four," Dogger corrected him, comically holding up four fingers as he glanced across the faces in the room.

Brud did the same. He lifted his hand in the air, "Four," he shouted, letting everyone know. "Four, four. Eight, ten. Eight only. Never ten." For the convenience of others, he laughed at himself, sensing this was what they wanted, making a fool of himself for the very first time.

From the distance, Mono growled, "That's what I said, two beers each."

One of The Crows turned where he was sitting and shouted at the torn clouds and scarlet red sky, "We accept what's left to us. We'll take anything, the scraps that fall

233

from your mouths." The rest of The Crows cawed and cawed. Aware only of their own sounds, they did not hear the applause, but they saw it in front of them, a mute clashing of action through a haze of smoke.

In the middle of drinking his fourth beer, Brud reached across the table and touched the boy's hand. He felt funny, happy, and in need of contact. Holding up his beer bottle, he let his loose smile work its way toward laughter.

"Good," he said, a loud belch flowing naturally from his mouth. Quickly he covered his lips with his fingers, and his eyes turned apologetic.

"Excuse me," he said.

"You like that," Dogger laughed, acting more drunk than he actually was, allowing the alcohol to take sloppy control of him, helping it to do so.

Brud grimaced and blinked. He twisted his mouth to one side, swaying his head to look at the people in the room. His eyelids felt as if they were slackening, but he was not tired. He saw the dark image of one of The Crows — a girl. The girl reminded Brud of the woman in the apartment. Pretty. Her hair was black instead of golden, but it was shiny and tied back in a sleek ponytail. Her skin was very white. The girl was silent, not saying a word, only staring straight ahead.

Brud stood, needing to pause for a moment to steady himself. His hands quickly gripped the rim of the table.

"What?" Dogger asked, gazing to where Brud was looking and seeing the girl. He glanced back at Brud with a seriousness in his eyes.

"Trouble, man," he warned, waving a loose, joyless finger.

Brud did not hear Dogger's words. His foggy senses tunnelled in on the girl. He wanted to touch the girl even more than he had wanted to touch Dogger's hand. A tender nostalgia troubled his bones. He was sad and happy at once, just as he had been the first time he saw Pretty. Moving away from the table, he walked slowly, unsure of his footing.

The Crow girl ignored Brud as he stood in front of her. Her eyes were quiet and motionless. They were stuck, in need of dislodging. Brud squatted next to where she was sitting with her back against the wall and placed his hand on top of her head. She looked up at him, her large watchful eyes seeming lazy and dull. A gleam of recognition sparked through Brud, as if he recalled seeing her before. There was something in her eyes that he had witnessed in his own reflection. But that look was gone from his eyes now, covered by the invisibility he had easily slipped on. The Crow girl had found his look and claimed it as hers. It was wonderful to see it on a female face.

"Like crow feathers," Brud said, stroking her hair. A feather fell from where it was tucked behind her ear, and she blankly looked down as if it were a part of her that had been cut away and there was little hope for refitting. Brud took it between his four fingers and carefully slipped it back into place. He took his time studying the short white marks along her face. They were thick and rose from her skin, as if she had been taken apart and put together again.

The girl stared while the others sitting to either side of her laughed cynically at Brud's gestures.

One of them snapped, "She's not for sale, pal. Hands off."

A teenager sitting next to the girl declared, "Leave her alone." His voice was unsteady and his eyes flitted to stare at Brud's hand, about to slap it away.

The Crow girl looked toward the table that Brud had come from. Dogger shouted, "He won't hurt anyone. He's okay."

Brud sat cross-legged in front of the girl. The Crows stared at him. He smiled for a while, then pulled his legs up to his chest, clasping his stubby fingers around his knees.

"You hear me?" the teenager threatened. "Get away from her."

Brud watched the girl. The girl's eyes would not leave him, as if she was spellbound. She tried to see past his sunglasses, to see into his eyes, to recognize the unassuming expression that seemed to be present in the mere shape of his face.

The teenager slid forward. "Listen, leave my sister alone. Is he bothering you?"

The Crow girl shook her head.

"She doesn't say anything, so no wisecracks. You got it?"

Brud looked at the teenager.

"You got that?"

"Got what?" asked Brud.

"Got what I'm saying. You hear me?"

Brud nodded. He heard the voice. Definitely.

The teenager glared at Brud, his expression tightening with bitterness. "Don't you touch her. She's already been touched bad. You see those scars on her face. You see them. Understand? You got it? She's been touched and touched and touched. And the guy who touched her took her tongue. She doesn't say anything, so I don't want to see you laughing. You got that?"

"What?"

"You got what I'm saying."

"No." Brud was being honest. He shook his head, and

thought of checking his pockets. He knew they were empty, except for a few small seeds from the farm. He had checked them before, but he felt obliged by the boy's command and searched the area around his feet.

"No," he said, "No got it."

The Crow girl laughed with tears in her eyes. She reached forward and gently slapped at Brud's knee, pushing him slightly. The Crow boy settled back, cautiously keeping his eyes on the couple.

Brud rocked back and forth. Each time he swayed back, his body struck the chair behind him, nudging it forward. The man in the chair looked behind and down. He saw the rear of Brud's round head and studied the broad back striking his chair. The man waited until Brud rocked forward, then shifted his chair out of the way. Brud flopped to the floor, his hands slipping from their hold around his knees, his back booming against the wooden floor.

The room quieted, except for the disoriented mumblings from a table in the corner. Laughter then burst forth, gaining momentum, crackling and roaring. The crowd believed that the man behind the sunglasses had passed out. He had dropped and lost himself. The sight was affirmation that the rest of them were alright, they had not fallen, they were still present. They applauded themselves for their durability.

Brud stared up at the ceiling. He saw the brown-edged stains and cracks in the plaster. It was an old place. This place. It had many memories in it. He began chuckling to himself. Great guttural rushes of laughter. He sat up and beamed at the Crow girl. She was not laughing. Her eyes showed concern. During his fall, Brud's sunglasses had flown from his face and now everything was clear and fresh and uncovered. The light was purer despite the cigarette smoke. Brud glanced around the room and saw that everyone was smiling. He laughed along with them, the coolness of their manner breezing over him, sending a shiver up his spine. The Crow girl reached and touched him again, and he saw by her eyes that he should stop laughing for her sake.

Warmth was waiting for him. The girl's eyes were brown and quiet. What they lacked in expression, they made up for in concern and sullen elegance.

The Crow girl's hand was resting on his knee. The laughter had lost its impact, derailed and weakened by this gentle act of kindness. The rest of The Crows appeared blank and noble. They seemed to understand what was moving between Brud and the girl and they showed respect.

The man with the scars offered a charitable mumble, a weary blessing of good will on them and the walls and the ground beneath his feet.

The family of drinkers bowed their heads. Perhaps they were searching for dropped coins.

Dogger saluted, remembering an old black-and-white movie he had seen.

Even Mono was silent, but he was no fool. He waited only a moment, then coughed to break up the tension.

The Crow girl took Brud's hand in both of hers and placed it on top of her head. The Crows resumed cawing in appreciation. They tilted back their heads and opened their throats, punching out the sounds.

Brud's bottom lip rose to cover the top one. He saw the tears well in the girl's eyes as her lips curved with an understanding smile. Two heavy tears burst along her eyelids and found their erratic course down her cheeks. They screamed Forgiveness. Leaning forward, she searched deeply into Brud's eyes. Up close like this, she saw her own eyes reflected in his. The placidness and tired compliance.

She could not stop herself from laying her fingers against Brud's fleshy lips. She wanted to make them settle. The steadying of his lips would benefit them both. Observing this act of intimacy, the people in the room glanced at the walls or into their beer bottles, unsure of what to do, how to react to the clumsy inner silence that suddenly held them. The cawing of The Crows now filled the room. Not even the shouts and threats from Mono could silence their defiant calls for sustenance and discovery.

chapter eight

barricades

"Listen," Andrea pleaded. "I'm sorry, okay?" Light from the red strobes up ahead pulsed through the windshield, washing across her face. She watched the distant fire spark high into the night, giving the black sky infinite dimension.

"Just forget it." Jim increased the volume on the car radio, listening to the report of the fire as he chewed the thick skin on the side of his thumb. Then he snapped his hand away and flicked off the radio. "This is just great."

"I'm sorry," Andrea whispered, confoundedly shaking her head. "I didn't know."

Jim rolled down his window and stuck out his head, straining to see beyond the congested traffic.

"Nowhere," he said, ducking back in. "Let's get out. Walk."

Andrea gazed back at another red light flashing behind them. A firetruck was stuck in two lanes of traffic. There was no way to clear a path.

Jim slammed his palm against the steering wheel and opened his door, bolting from the car, moving away from Andrea. She felt useless; the image of the trapped firetruck had intensified her feelings of helplessness. Throwing open her door, she almost struck the fender of a car in the next lane. Threatening eyes flashed at her from the window on the driver's side. Startled by the closeness of the image, she stumbled away, hurrying to catch up with her husband.

Weaving among the cars, they had to move sideways to squeeze through. People shouted from their windows. Horns blared to clear the road. When the couple finally reached the roadblock, one of two policemen raised his hands to them.

"My client," Jim gasped, "is a patient...in there."

"I'm sorry, sir. No one's permitted through."

"I'm his lawyer."

"I don't see how that matters right now, sir."

"What about them?" Jim cast a glance at two people moving between the policemen.

"Reporters."

"She's a reporter," Jim blurted out, maniacally pointing at his wife, as if denouncing her.

"That's fine," said the policeman, but he did not move.

Jim looked at his wife, dumbfounded, "Where's your press pass?"

Andrea's eye turned meek, her forehead wrinkling as she grimaced. "At home, in my purse."

Jim cursed. He felt like tearing off his skin, bursting out of himself if he only could.

Andrea glanced away, toward the car, and saw a familiar face moving toward them.

"Frank!" she cried.

Turning to face Frank, Jim noticed the sounds of mayhem backed up for two blocks. He saw that Frank was wearing a camera around his neck. The man seemed out of sorts, as if he had been called from a deep sleep.

The policeman glanced at Frank. The photographer stopped suddenly, hesitant.

"What?" Frank asked. "What's the matter?" He stared ahead, through the barricade.

"I work with this man," Andrea said, grabbing her co-worker's arm and yanking him toward the policeman. Frank stumbled, one smooth sole slipping along the asphalt. "This is Frank."

The policeman studied Frank, took in his clothes, the camera around his neck. Both of the policemen looked at his shoes. Then they leaned to the side as if inspecting the cut of his suit.

"Your press pass, please," the policeman indicated.

"Right here." He lifted the laminated card from where it hung on a string around his neck. "I've got to get by."

"Okay." The policeman stepped aside. Rushing through the barricade, Frank called back, "She works with me. She's the new crime reporter. No ID yet." And he was gone, toward the noise of the crumbling building.

"Okay," the policeman said, staring back to face the line of traffic. "Go on."

Andrea and Jim rushed through, but Jim was jolted, the policeman's hand rammed against his chest.

"You're a lawyer," the policeman noted, still watching the traffic.

"Yeah, right." Jim frowned and shook his head.

"You're not a reporter."

Grumbling a savage curse, Jim then apologized briefly. He stepped back in a daze, staring at the policeman's uniform. A thought struck him. It hit him so hard, his knees felt shaky.

"My brother's on the force," Jim nervously announced, then gave them his brother's name.

The policeman took notice of the lawyer, glimpsing at his eyes for the first time.

"Yeah," the policeman said, his face showing interest. "I see the resemblance. Your brother."

Jim nodded, growing concerned by the uncertainty in the policeman's manner, the hesitation, and sudden softening of character.

One policeman nudged the other and whispered a few words. They both stared at Jim.

"What?" he asked.

"We're sorry," they said at once.

"What?" Jim demanded. "Sorry, what?"

Andrea stepped from behind the barricade, witnessing the shock on her husband's face. She heard the policeman's words: "...from the fire."

Jim felt himself receding inward, gliding back inside his body as if what must be his soul was on wheels, veering away from him.

"I'm sorry," the policeman said again. He stepped out of the way as if Jim had been graciously accepted by default. "Go ahead. I never saw you."

Stumbling forward, Jim regarded the expansive view of the flames, the clear wide-open ground before him. He saw firemen on ladders wrestling with lengths of hoses that spouted out swaying torrents of white water. He felt as if he was drowning in a mist, as if the air was mostly liquid.

The firemen were battling with the flames, just as he was struggling for breath. He was aware of the resemblance. It matched, and he felt shaken for having braced and internalized the similarity. No matter how hard he tried he could not draw his concentration away from the flames. Without warning he felt hands touch his face. It was Andrea. She was watching him. Her eyes were close to his.

"What was he doing?" Jim asked her. "Here?" He leaned back, away from his wife, and stepped along the littered street leading to the gates. He felt confined by the heat enclosing him. He heard the clicking steps of his wife through the erratic sounds of turmoil. She was following him.

Jim glanced back at the roadblock. He saw the faces leering, held in check, studying him and his grief. They were pressing close to the barricades, their faces wavering deceptively by the light of the blaze.

Jim paused at the gates, hearing the confused voices of the patients, like frightened animal sounds, as they were led into mini-buses and vans. He contemplated the hospital, saw the flames lapping the structure. Again, he turned toward the stretch of roadblock, as if he had crossed a line. He seemed cut adrift in this buffer zone; his wife watching him, the shock on her face, the faultless uncertainty. He asked himself, *How could she possibly offer comfort to anyone*? The air itself pressed against him from every direction, implying that he move all ways at once.

The crowd was hypnotized by the prospect of catching a glimpse of unbearable tragedy. He had never seen it so obvious before; the command that the flames held over them, the flames somehow tempering their need. They would torture themselves in this manner, with all the horrible sights that were possible. It was their contrition, their need to be forgiven for their petty lives. The madness — overcoming as it was — would show them how fortunate they actually were, absolving them of their insignificant fears.

Jim stepped closer toward the building, holding the crowd's obsession at bay. His stupor was twofold. Already stunned by the word of his brother's death, he was now finding seduction in the lashing, rumbling vigour of the flames.

The red glow was everywhere. He numbly surveyed the grounds and saw that Andrea was no longer by his side. She was standing off, by the wrought-iron fence, her hands covering her face, her body seeming to tremble. Was it only the swaying of light? The red-and-black shadows that made her waver?

"What happened?" he asked himself, but was he speaking to her, or speaking to the very voice that spoke the words, the voice that continued to speed away from him, but deep into him? He would need a pair of tweezers to pull it free. It would be stuck. He shuddered at the disturbing complexity of these thoughts.

Andrea was usually stronger than this. What could have happened? He went to her and took her hands, trying to move them from her face, but she would not comply. She held tight. Afraid of him. Afraid of how he would look at her.

"Andrea?" Jim asked, setting his hands on her shoulders. "What is it?"

His wife fitfully shook her head.

"What?"

"It's like one long bad dream," she called into her hands. Her voice revealed that she had been crying, and Jim was further weakened, cut down another notch, the reasonableness of his voice burrowing deeper.

He struggled to pull the thick air into his lungs, his discomfort impelling him beyond the threshold of grief. Futility crossing over to anger. After all, it was he who had lost his brother. What was the matter with Andrea? Why was she acting this way? He was the one in need of attention. He was the one who should be offered comfort.

Jim stepped away, knowing the impossibility of consoling his wife. Forsaking her to her shallow grief, he wandered through the gates toward a group of patients waiting for the vehicle that would transfer them to an affiliated institution. The faces were appealing to him. Oddly enough, he felt at absolute peace among their incoherent expressions. He admired the way the patients' hands brushed against his body, wanting to snatch hold of the piece of him that was not whole and complete. Fingers pressed against his clothes, snapped away, then came again, against his hips and waist, swiping at his groin, caressing his back. He slowly stepped through them, closing his eyes and allowing their hands to explore his body. Moving blindly, he soon felt the hands lift away and, opening his eyes, he discovered that he was standing at the edge of the group. The faces marvelled at him. A few of them nodded and sucked on their tongues, chewed on their fingers, or stared up with bowed heads. Jim turned away, pivoted to confront the startling face of Mr. Quagmire, the willingness in his leering expression as his lips peeled back to offer his yellow-teeth, displaying how the grandeur of fire had kindly shadowed them darker.

the man who would be me

Brud led the Crow girl to his table and pulled out a chair for her, the same way he remembered doing for his mother. It was a sign of respect, his father had told him. Women were special and deserved to be treated with courtesy. They were to be adored. From them comes creation. Always treat them gently. They hold everything inside their bodies. Only through their selfless acts of submission are we able to continue on.

"Hi," Dogger said, happy to have company. He spread his arms along the table and leaned toward the girl. "What's your name?" he asked with a foolish grin.

The girl moved her tired eyes away from Brud and glanced at the smallness of Dogger's hands. They were stained with dirt and the fingernails were bitten down, desperately in need of an even clipping. Her expression appeared distant as she raised her right hand and stroked the neckpiece of her black turtleneck. Wetting the tip of her finger against her bottom lip, she spelled her name in the coating of ashes on the table.

Dogger took a drink from his beer bottle, watching the letters being spelled out. When the name was completed, he quickly said, "J...O...Y. Joy. Nice."

"Joy," Brud said.

Tilting the bottle back again, further and further until he was facing the ceiling, Dogger soon realized the liquid was gone, and his hand came down hard, the bottle slamming the tabletop.

Joy flinched, and Brud pried the bottle from the boy's hand. He looked at the girl and nodded, indicating that everything was okay now.

"I don't even know your name," Dogger said, pointing an accusing finger at Brud, and saying to himself, *Fool, fool, fool*.

Brud smiled and pointed a finger at Dogger.

Dogger laughed, his head dropping forward as if suspended on a loose spring. Raising his chin, he saw a man step into the room. Dogger's mouth opened, and his face changed, becoming both serious and mischievous.

"Hey," Dogger called, then sat up straighter to shout, "HEY!" He pointed at the man, and said to Brud, "That's him."

Brud smiled, agreeing, "Okay. That's him."

"Hey, killer," Dogger shouted, trying to stand in his chair, but the chair would not co-operate and he fell back, sitting. Cupping his hands around his mouth, he repeated his call.

The noise in the room levelled out. Eyes watched the killer, then quickly shifted in Dogger's direction. The man with one eye cowered and squinted from his table. The mother of the drinking family lifted a brown paper bag from the floor and staggered to her feet, banging into a chair. Undisturbed, she shoved on, staring depthlessly toward the exit. The husband and daughter followed course, past the killer and through the door that was held open by the muscle-bound bouncer. The Crows began cawing, but the sound was silenced by a dark stiff look from the killer. All faces watched him move for the bar. The customers would not look at Dogger, hoping the killer would ignore him as well.

"KILLER. HEY, NO GOOD KILLER. COME OVER, KILLER. COME HERE AND MEET THE MAN THEY THOUGHT WAS YOU."

Glancing over his shoulder, the killer scanned the room: looking briefly at the man with the scars, then shifting to catch the smile of an old lady, her face painted with brilliant colours. He could ignore the calls no longer. His eyes tilted off, signalling to Dogger. Picking up his drink, the killer walked with restraint, as if he was gearing up for a run, but holding back until the last moment, tightening the inner coils.

A hushed silence cleared the air. Bottles clinked behind the bar. One of The Crows began cawing again, sensing the coming of danger, the possible reward, the spoils. The killer shot a glance at The Crows, offering a sarcastic smile as he exposed the black holes of his missing teeth. His long chin curved forward and up as he smiled elaborately, his eyes seeming to creep back into their black rims.

The killer paused beside Dogger and rested his hand along the back of an empty chair.

"Anyone *sitting* here?" he casually asked.

"No killer," Dogger laughed, but the laugh was hollow and forced, a gesture made silly by its absolute lack of humour.

The killer looked Dogger squarely in the eyes, then stared at The Crows and let his lips curl open to reveal the holes again. He sat in the chair, straightening his back.

"If you weren't my boy," the killer said, his eyes still fixed on The Crows, "I'd do something that you'd *never* be able to remember." Sucking his gums, his eyes darted at Dogger. "Lucky for you, you'll be able to *remember*."

Dogger frowned dejectedly, "Yeah, real lucky." He picked the label from his empty bottle, his carefree disposition suddenly, completely crushed.

The killer looked at Brud, "So, this is you. The innocent man I saw guilty in the papers. They must have realized how *wrong* they were." Coughing bitterly, the killer swallowed the intentions of a laugh to anxiously continue with his thought. "Realized their mistake and let you go. They're genuine like that. *Generous*. Once, free, not again. The man who would be me. I've got puzzles in here that you'd never fit into." He tapped the side of his head.

A beer bottle was swiftly set in front of the killer. The hand with the swastika pulled back, and the killer looked up.

"Compliments of the management," Mono generously announced, slapping the killer on the back. "Take it easy, okay?"

"Yeah," the killer stared up. "Easy, easy." He glanced, frozen-eyed, around the room and raised his new bottle to everyone. Conversations resumed, and Mono hesitantly returned to his station.

"They can't hold people like us, can they?" the killer asked, nodding exclusively for Brud's benefit. "The *spirit* won't have it. We just take a deep breath, close our eyes, and force between the bars. I've dreamed I've *dreamed* it. When you got seven spirits moving around with you, seven souls that I stole from other people, then it's all the harder to keep us down. One of us'll get out and open the doors for the rest of us. Most times we get along. We're a *happy* bunch." The killer lifted a finger to trace the raised veins in the back of his left hand. "Streaming in there. You *feel* those spirits pushing the blood through me."

His hand flew away, seizing the bottle and swooping it to his mouth. Eyes glued on Brud, the killer pushed the stem deep into his throat, gagging and coughing, but swallowing against the strain. In a split second he was talking again, the bottle reset on the table. "Excuse me, darling," he apologized to Joy. Noticing the scars on her face, his eyes lingered here and there. "Nice work, but *heartless* all the same." He clapped his hands together and threw back his head. "Tragedy! Tragedy! Tragedy!" Jerking his body to the side, he reconnected with Brud, "And here *you* are as *proof* of what we do to each other. How we try to free ourselves. You were me and now look at you. Here. Sitting here. Out. Out of me. Is that it? What does that tell you?" The killer laughed a scratchy laugh that seemed to trouble his mood. He glanced at the faces to either side of him. "Nothing, right? Nothing tells you *everything*. I believe in it."

a perfectly ferocious harmony

"Sorry about your brother," the yellow-toothed man said preciously, tilting back his head for Jim, allowing a view of the flames, of the charmful way they danced around in his eyes.

"Quagmire," Jim whispered for the third time, as if unable to grasp the meaning of this discovery.

"Another new site." Quagmire locked onto Jim's gaze as if laying claim to what was his. "I was out earlier, checking the farmland. Beautiful space. I will redesign it, of course." A devious smile flickered on his lips. "Most people would think it a shame to cut into such wondrous land, but they're just neutered bumpkins. Ecological crybabies with recycled lives. They have no bravery. They only have shame, that's all. Ashamed of themselves — an entire race — for what they're doing to the land. What absolute rubbish. We have to keep changing to stay abreast. Continual evolution." Quagmire paused, mulling over the idea of shame — the extremes that must be summoned to produce it. "But that's progress. We know progress, don't we, Jimmy?"

A covered stretcher wheeled across the pavement behind Quagmire. He grinned as if he could feel it moving through him, thrilling his insides. He watched Jim's eyes following the stretcher.

"Your brother's already gone. They took what was left of him a few minutes ago. Off. Gone. That's the body of the man who tried to save him. Went in after your brother, and they both went up. Poof. Pretty fast. But this one..." Quagmire turned to catch a quick admiring glimpse of the stretcher. "This one made so much noise. Not like your brother. Your brother took it silently, stepped into the blaze like he was going home."

"You...saw?" Jim asked, baffled.

"I wasn't there, Jimmy. A young girl from the street told me, from behind the fence. She was still alive, you know. She watched your brother go in, but she was helpless to do anything. Poor girl, locked out, the fence too high for a young girl to climb. Imagine the torment for the rest of her life. The nightmares. Fences keep people out, too. That's what they're for, separating the good from the bad, keeping wishes in, or out. It's horrific, my friend. I know. Horror lives in fire. It wavers around like the flames themselves. You can never put your finger on what it is that offers you that hypnotic feeling. You think you sense something in there, but it's just the mirage of fire, sometimes quiet, seemingly not there at all, but then it flares up, and you have to catch your breath because of what it's doing to you."

Jim remembered his wife, dismissing this crazy man's nonsense. Without comment, he stepped away from

Quagmire, moving toward where he had left Andrea leaning against the outer side of the high iron fence.

"It's peculiar how the disparity is there," called Quagmire, anxiously side-stepping to follow Jim. "The fire sounds so comforting. Fire is the voice of a strange harmony. Like all the flames want to join together with the flame that is your soul." Quagmire gently touched his own chest. "My soul. The flames sing so well they enter each other. And sing for you, in you. A perfectly ferocious harmony. Listen to it."

Quagmire's eyes were ablaze. He showed his yellow teeth. Smoke wafted around his long coat, apparently clinging to his skin.

Jim stumbled over a pile of sooty rags on the asphalt. Turning for the gates, he stepped out, searching for Andrea. He was genuinely frightened, well beyond being merely disturbed or unsettled. What he was seeing was without logical explanation. He did not want to understand, fearing that the understanding of such things would place him in a hospital much like the one now burning behind him.

"She's gone back to the car," Quagmire informed him. "I saw her wander off that way. A little bit of a casualty herself."

"Yes," Jim whispered, moving off, but numbly entranced by Quagmire.

"No. Not a casualty, rather more at ease with herself, with what she's made of, with the uneasiness of what we actually are. She's close to something very terrible, very beautiful. Essence is like that, when you squeeze in close enough to yourself."

"You're crazy," Jim finally insisted, breaking away and hurrying off toward the barricades.

"Something very terrible." Quagmire turned his head and watched Andrea step from behind one of the ambulances. "Something very beautiful." Andrea was searching for her husband after fainting, overcome by heat and confusion. She had been carried off by two paramedics. They had revived her with oxygen and offered a plastic cup of water.

"Your husband's gone back to the car," Quagmire called to her.

Andrea stopped, then wandered over to the yellow-toothed man. The close proximity of her body made his fingers ache. He took one hand in the other and snapped a knuckle, his tongue flitting around inside his mouth.

"My husband," she said, her tone faraway and defeated, her mind still clouded from the fainting spell. She pointed back at the stretcher. "I thought that was his brother. But they told me he's…already…" Her gaze shifted beyond Quagmire toward the fire and the smoke that billowed grey into the black sky.

"The sounds," she said.

"Yes." Quagmire nodded. "Priceless, aren't they?" He bit down on his tongue, holding back the words that he knew would frighten her away. He did not want to prevent her from going where she was expected, moving further into the distressing inevitability that had suddenly become her life.

"I better find Jimmy," she said, squinting at the image of the yellow-toothed man. "You're a friend of Jim's, aren't you?"

"Yes."

"Did you know his brother?" She wiped her hands in her skirt as if she had been handling thoughts half perished.

"No. But I know him now. We're pals." He believed his smile was a wonderful thing. He treasured it.

"Oh." A puzzled look changed her face. "I better find Jim."

"What I meant was, I feel like I know him. From what Jimmy has told me."

"Yes." Andrea backed away and finally turned, straying toward the barricade, toward the car that was stuck two or three blocks back among countless other cars, trapped in the congestion.

"I'll see you later, alligator," Quagmire said in a breathy singsong. "I'll see you later, alligator," holding his hands together, swaying, and crooning romantically. "Make all your dreams come true."

chapter eleven

the beat makes us one

"He's a blind man," Dogger said, proudly pointing at Brud. "My disguise."

"Blinder than you think, but no blinder than *you* or *me*. Blinder than a blade shoved into the dirt. It feels *nothing*." The killer gulped another quick mouthful of beer, watching Brud over the stem of the bottle. He tensely mumbled, "Umm-hhh," while he swallowed, then reset his bottle on the table.

Dogger squinted, trying to discover the meaning of the killer's words. He watched as the corners of his father's lips curved sharply upward, revealing the holes between his teeth.

Dogger pointed, "You lost another tooth."

Ignoring this observation, the killer watched Joy slide the pair of sunglasses back onto Brud's face. She had seen the need to retrieve them from the floor and cover the eyes that peered heavily, vulnerably around the room.

The killer leaned forward, observing the reflection of his face rounding out in Brud's sunglasses. He took delight in seeing the holes in his mouth expand and deepen.

"Nice," he noted, fingering an empty space. "You're right. But that tooth was there yesterday." Turning in his chair, he shouted, "Check the papers! That tooth must've turned up somewhere. Who's got the hotline?" He faced Dogger with a generous pointed smile, "It was loose, I remember. *Loose*, you know." He leaned back in his chair and took another sudden drink. "That's eight missing now. Used to be seven. Seven missing, seven little white bodies, dead. Torn from their roots. Lying there. Ahhh, so *cute*. Now, it must be eight." He shouted over his shoulder, "Check the papers! Get me the President!"

"Eight," Dogger meanly pronounced. "Soon, you'll have none."

"Sure," he said spitefully. "And soon every little white body will be dead."

"Dead," Brud said, paying attention.

"You know what I mean?" he asked the sunglasses. "An eye for an eye, a tooth for a tooth." The killer pulled back his lips with both sets of fingers, displaying his blackish-pink gums. "What could be more simple than instruction from the Bible? Biblical revelation, but who's paying attention these days? Eyes gone *shallow*, T.V. tube, only cozy thoughtless depths now."

Joy lifted both hands from her lap and placed them on the table, entwining her fingers. The killer watched the movements, his tongue running over and savouring the empty spaces in his mouth.

"You two must be related," he concluded. Glancing at Joy, then at Brud. "She your *sister*?"

Joy looked carefully at the kind man who had led her

to the table. She blushed and smiled to herself. Edging her chair closer to Brud's, she took his hand, placing it in her hair.

"Ahhh," the killer sighed. "Love. *Kiss* me, Marquis de Sade." He snapped his fingers high in the air and stared at the dilapidated ceiling as if observing a lover's moon. "Romance is such a simple thing, in a simple mind. But in a mind like mine — tortured by genius — love *busts* up all the cute stuff. Painful delusions. I am *not* inspired." He slammed his fist against the tabletop. "I am not having *fun*. Love tears me to pieces. Since way back, when I was a child, doctor." He smirked at Brud. "I have no problem with calling myself a martyr." Cheerfully he shrugged his shoulders and searched from face to face. "The sledge-hammer of love has cracked me in the knees. Please do not disturb me while I wallow in my own *oh-so-intelligent* self-pity. We're a sorry, sick lot. We love ourselves too much. One big problem: we possess the *brains* to think of all the other alternatives. All the love we're missing when we're devoted to one woman. The brain wants to make strays of us." The killer jabbed at the side of his head as if to poke a hole through and let the scalding accuracy of reasoning flood out.

"This love thing." He leaned across the table, speaking exclusively to Brud. "Of course, I'm happy and I'm sad for you. That's the kind of man I am, Doctor Freud." Turning to include the girl, he continued, "You can't realize how love is the end and the beginning. A baby's born and we've *done* it, wrestled it through the hole, into this *stinking hollow* world. Love that's done it, that's made this baby. The feeling. The *feeling* anyway. If love hangs around or not is another thing, but it's got to be there somewhere in the first place, *fooling* us, so we'll make this little baby. *Perfect*." He motioned to Dogger. "Love's just a trick to keep us pumping them out. What'd you think of that? That's something new. Just came to me. And now we're killing people too, sick people, old people, wanting them to die because we *love* them and don't want to see them in pain." He screamed, "WELL I LOVE EVERYONE A WHOLE LOT AND I WANT TO PUT THEM OUT OF THEIR PAIN NOW. RIGHT NOW. I DON'T WANT THEM TO SUFFER AN-OTHER MINUTE. I LOVE EVERYONE SO MUCH!"

Joy cuddled closer to Brud. She was frightened.

A shy apologetic laugh slipped from the killer's throat. He whispered, "Why wait? Why waste time? Who knows what might happen?" Glancing at Dogger, he saw that the boy was asleep with his head resting on his folded arms.

Brud and Joy stared at Dogger. They both wished that the killer would go away and leave them alone. The killer was a man they did not understand.

"He's the only one I've ever loved. Tears me up. His mother came and sold me this *love thing*, then disappeared like the worthless ghost she was, dragging love like a chain around her ankle, kicking it in the door, then dragging off again. Some shackled she-beast with a warped sense of humour." The killer touched Dogger's small face with the backs of his fingers. "She left a note, Dogger. Never told you. It said 'He's yours. Kill him or keep him.' Was in your little crib, on your *tiny* chest. She didn't even sign her *name*. She had no name. I knew who she was, though. I knew what she was trying to do. *Ignorance*. She was. Vicious with ignorance. Stinking with greed, her insides *rotting* out. Time came I could smell her, wondered what the stench was." The killer frowned for the first time. He slid his hand along his son's hair, letting his fingers rest against the reassuring warmth of the boy's back.

"You're all that's left of me now, Dogger. I do *you*, I do *myself.*"

Joy held the seat of her chair and pressed it as close as possible to Brud. She stared off at her brother slouched against the far wall. She wanted his protection, but he would not challenge the killer. He simply nodded at Joy, indicating with his eyes that she should just wait, bear it out. He was there if something should happen.

"All these years, and look. So much like your mother. Growing towards her, *away* from me. Who are you? I thought you left me once? You left a part behind. A little corner of your *soul*, torn away like the corner of a page so it's not *perfect* anymore. Impossible. It's not whole and even. Not *ever* again. WHO ARE YOU? WHO ARE YOU?"

Brud and Joy shut their eyes against the shouting. When it stopped, they peeked out from behind their lids. The killer's chair was empty. Dogger was still sleeping, or so it seemed. On the table, beside the boy's head, a tooth lay on its side, the jagged bottom stained with blood.

A bloody outline of a small heart was drawn against the skin on Dogger's forehead. Brud smiled at the sight and nudged Joy, pointing at the symbol that he understood. It was red. It was a heart. His mother had placed his hand against her breast so he could feel the warm beating. She had drawn that symbol on a piece of paper. "That's what keeps us all together," she had told him. "It connects all living things. The beat makes us one. Always respect the sound of it."

chapter twelve

the grievous ditch

Jim stared through the windshield. No matter how much he believed in the impossibility of changing the past, he could not keep from harping on thoughts of recovering his brother. The more he flashed back on their last meeting, the greater the pain of separation became. He realized all too clearly that they were family. Only death could positively show him this, fill him with an unsufferable longing to reaffirm the bond. Their arguments had lasted for years, their choice of occupations dividing them. The need to survive, the basic need to put food on the table, drove a wedge between their lives. He grappled with the absurdity. The survival of their relationship now seeming paramount, like a profoundly insatiable hunger itself.

Andrea sat beside her husband. She was staring at her hands, wanting to move them toward Jimmy, but there was hostility in the air and she did not want to take the brunt of it. She understood that he was in pain, confused and choking with regret, and there was nothing she could do to change that.

"Jimmy," Andrea hesitantly whispered. Tears came to her eyes at the sound of his name. She wiped them away and bit her bottom lip, then cleared her throat and straightened her back against the plush seat.

Jim ignored her, listening only to himself as he repeated his brother's name over and over in his head. The sound was gouging the grievous ditch deeper and deeper. He wanted to crawl into it, accept its darkness, and lie there, smothered and cushioned against the despair that sluggishly hounded him.

Andrea kissed her husband's cheek and, with nervous fingers, touched the hair along his temple. Jim glanced at Andrea, witnessing the pain in her eyes as she traced each of his features. He did not like the look on her face; her weakness further inspiring his. Clutching hold of the rearview mirror, he tilted it down, staring accusingly at his reflection. He saw the pink lines in his eyes. He held back his sorrow, bit down on it. *What was the point of crying?* he asked himself. *I will not cry. What will that do to correct matters?*

"What was Steve doing?" he asked under his breath, something cringing inside of him at the sound of his brother's name. He asked Andrea, "He was off duty?"

"I don't know," she said, overly aware of the closeness of objects in the car. The windows were steamed and the air stale. They could not move the car or leave it there. It would be towed away when the clutter of traffic eventually cleared off. They simply had to wait for release.

"He was at the hospital." Jim returned his weary gaze to the mirror. "Brud," he said. "It was Brud."

"Did you find him? Did you see Brud?"

"No. Brud's not there." Jim shook his head, speaking away from himself. "I looked. My brother was there." His eyes jammed shut, battling back the tears. Weakly leaning forward, he held his breath with his hands joined into one fist, squeezing as if to force the pain away.

"I'm sorry," Andrea cried, knowing intimately the mercilessness of her husband's anguish, feeling it ripping at her heart.

Jim turned for Andrea and fell against her, burying his face in her hair. Opening his eyes, he saw nothing. He did not want to see a single thing that would make this more real to him. He would not cry. If he did, he would have to punish himself for his uncharacteristic feebleness. It was unbecoming.

"We'll find Brud," Andrea whispered into his ear, but Jim found no sense of reassurance in her words. He could not help speculating about Brud. Questions. Suspicions. What unpleasant twist of fate had delivered Brud to him? Jim told himself, *Look at what he's done to my life.*

Dogger trailed behind Brud and Joy. They strolled carelessly along the deserted night sidewalk. At this hour, the neon seemed so lonely, detached from the energy of the crowds. The huge digital clock on the distant Quagmire Tower blinked from time to temperature. It was almost six in the morning and a comforting warmth hung like a lull in the air.

"The streets are so neat," Dogger blankly said, "in the morning like this." His voice sounded clear between the empty buildings. "Everything's strange."

People with unconcerned faces stood on the street corners selling the early editions of the newspapers. Folded broadsheets were clipped to the sides of newsstands or laid out on a wooden ledge with rocks pinning them down. But the news would have to wait for the people to wake and find their places back on the streets.

Occasional wanderers purchased one of the papers, glanced at it with disinterest, then, discovering that the world was, in fact, still spinning, shoved the paper under their arms, and wandered off.

"Hey," Dogger said, wiping at his eyes. "Let's see if you're in the paper." He jaunted ahead, feeling the dryness on his forehead and scratching at the blood outline of the heart. He had been awake for only twenty minutes and the alcohol was still in his system, only now it seemed to have turned into a kind of sludge that attempted to send him back to sleep. His body felt exhausted and he thought of crawling on his hands and knees, then laughed at the idea.

Brud stopped and looked at the old woman selling newspapers. The skin on her face was wrinkled and streaked with thin blue lines, like the surface of a shell. Her face seemed to be closing in on itself, attempting to settle shut like a clam. She extended a prune-like hand and shabby sleeve toward the boy. The boy handed her the bill, then lifted a paper from beneath the rock.

When the woman offered the boy his change, she saw that he had turned away.

"Keep it," he called, kneeling on the sidewalk.

The clam-faced woman dipped the coins back into her grey pocket without a word, without a change of face. She stared at Brud, her eyes buried behind folds of wrinkles.

Brud's stubby fingers slipped the sunglasses from his face and moved them to the eyes of the old woman. He believed that they would help her disappear. He could tell that this was what she wanted most, to move on. She was tired. Joy smiled as Brud proudly regarded his new creation.

Offering no protest, the clam-faced woman simply stood within her booth and straightened the jars of candies and chewing gum that lined the ledge. Then she paused for a moment and gestured to Brud.

"Is good," she said in a crackling voice.

Brud smiled with his lips shut. He felt Joy stepping past him, close to the clam-faced woman to set her fingers against the woman's face, discovering the depths of the lines, listening.

Dogger was oblivious to the whole scene. He was reading a story on the front page of the newspaper that he held flat against the concrete.

"You guys," he announced, still reading. "They got a tooth. They got a tooth on you."

Brud looked down. Dogger was pointing at a story, his finger pressed into the newsprint. Brud saw the building and the black-and-white fire. He stepped closer. He agreed. "Heaven in hell," he said for the benefit of those around him, repeating what he had heard from Jim when they were in the first hospital. He gladly offered instruction, passing on what he knew, remembering the friendly expression on Jim's face when the lawyer had said those words. Now Brud felt the same way and the words came naturally. He even laughed at the thought. But no one else was laughing, so he was shortly discouraged.

"Not the picture. That's not it," said Dogger. "The story down here." He jabbed his finger against the newspaper. "The cops found a tooth in that alleyway where Skully got stuck."

Brud nodded and shifted on his feet.

"You know already?"

Brud nodded, again, "Teeth," he said, showing Dogger his teeth and tapping them.

"You got all yours."

"Teeth," he insisted, speaking through them. "Not too bad."

Joy stared at the bronze-coloured hairclip that the clam-faced woman held out in the cup of her hands. The woman motioned for Joy to turn around and, when she complied, the old woman gathered the girl's long hair in one hand and fastened the clip in place. Joy's feather tumbled from behind her ear, landing on the newspaper ledge. The clam-faced woman took it and, motioning for Joy to turn around, slipped it back into her hair, then approvingly held Joy's cheeks.

"Angel look," the woman said, the big sunglasses occupying most of her small face. She motioned with both sets of fingers, as if brushing hair away from her lips. "Back. Los Santos Inocentes. Angel, look in your face." Her sunken lips shrivelled up, showing off her bald gums, sheening like new wet skin. "Los Santos Inocentes." Still smiling, she handed the girl a lollypop and humbly nodded twice.

chapter thirteen

if only...why?

ACCUSED KILLER ESCAPES.
Andrea held up the newspaper for her husband to see.
Her heart was pounding after returning from the deli,
pacing in the elevator and madly pressing the buttons,
watching the numbers change.

"All the afternoon papers have the same headline." She
told him.

Jim was sitting on the couch. He reached up for the
paper and held it level with his chest. Studying the photograph, he wondered how Brud had deceived him. He
had seen elaborate frauds before. In law school, he had
studied all the great cases. Bruff versus CM Publications.
Adams versus Adams.

"I should've went to work after all." Andrea sat on the
edge of the coffee table, shoving her hands between her
knees and watching the carpet. "Think of the story I could
break."

The rustle of paper startled her. Looking up, she saw Jim's vicious stare ready and able to extend itself.

"What story?" he demanded.

"About Brud. They obviously have the wrong guy."

Jim huffed and raised the paper, covering his face. He could not hold his attention long enough to read. Directing his concentration inward, his gaze slipped out of focus. He asked himself, *If only...why? Why did his brother walk into the fire? To save Brud? Or had Brud led him in there, fought with him to escape?* Onlookers confessed they had seen a rotund man talking with his brother, and then the large man had run away, leaving the policeman to walk into the fire. Others had claimed that the rotund man led the policeman toward the blaze or perhaps shoved him into the fire before fleeing over the fence.

"What're you thinking, Jimmy?"

"Nothing."

Andrea stared at him. She could not take many more of his curt replies. "Do you know what I'm supposed to do? My job, I mean?"

"I don't care what you do," he snapped.

"Listen." Andrea stood. "I understand that you're grieving for your brother, but don't take it out on me. It's not my fault."

Jim threw the newspaper onto the floor. He kicked it away.

"I don't want to talk about it." The heat was rising in his face, his heartbeat feeling as if it would undo him. He leaned forward, staring at the coffee table.

"Just remember who I am, that's all," Andrea warned. "I'm your wife, the one closest to you. Don't take it out on me just because I'm within reach. Because I'm convenient."

Jim stared away, his eyes burning into the mantlepiece and the red brick hearth beneath it.

"What do you know about Brud, anyway?" he said, tossing the words at her.

"I know what you told me. I realize now how he changed you. How he made you feel when you were taking care of him, looking after him. I see that now. It changed you. You were nicer. Remember? Think about it. Now, look at yourself. You're bitter. You're a lawyer again." She was sorry the instant she said the words.

"Brud has escaped," Jim said. "What does that tell you about someone's guilt? If I'm a lawyer — which I am — then I know what that tells me."

"I wouldn't call it escape," Andrea said. "He was probably frightened. He ran away."

"Well, that's what it is now." He shot a glance down at the headline. "That's what he is now. He's guilty." The blurry photograph of Brud on the courthouse steps further taunted him. It was the same one he had seen yesterday, only now the photo was enlarged and cropped to concentrate on Brud's face. Jim's eyes slipped out of focus and the grainy, expressionless features appeared criminally distorted, vague, graceless, and smutty.

"You know about guilt," Jim droned. "You're a journalist. All you have to do is infer guilt and the damage is done. Presto. Instant judgement." In the corner of his eyes, he saw Andrea move away from the coffee table.

"So, it's my fault," Andrea retorted, pacing into the bedroom and slamming the door.

Jim sat up straight. He assured himself that he was being reasonable. Leaning forward to retrieve the newspaper, he used both hands to toss the folded broadsheet onto the table, then settled back with his eyes glued on the photograph. He could not look away from it. He was in a daze as he kicked off his slippers. The sound of Andrea's crying touched him from behind the door. He wondered, *Why does emotion do this to us? This complex baggage we lug around in our hearts and minds only clouds our abilities. Emotions wrongly distort our capacity for rational thought.*

He pleaded with whoever was in charge, but found no comfort in believing. And so he pleaded with himself instead.

Why can't we simply see the truth?

What is the matter with our eyes?

chapter fourteen

rumbling in for the sacrifice

Brud watched the long smooth snake machine glide from the tunnel, slowing to a stop in the space before him. The doors slid open and people stepped out, while other people hurried in to seat themselves. It was a feeding of some sort. A rejecting and accepting of prey by the predator. The people would enter freely, without struggle, and then be eaten up by the snake machine. Brud watched the people who had been cast out from the belly. He strained to see sores on their skins or signs of the illness that had made them impossible to digest.

Dogger was asleep on the platform seat with his head resting against Brud's lap. After reading the headlines, Dogger had insisted that they hide in a place that would be safe, but Brud did not want to hide. He saw no need. Why should he hide, and from whom? So Dogger had taken them down into the subway, understanding how people did not really look at each other down there. It was a place of avoidance. They would be safe.

Joy was sitting on the other side of Brud, her head resting against his arm, but she could not sleep. Her watchful eyes would flicker shut and she would catch herself, veer away from the chaotic images inside of her head, and glimpse at Brud. She liked the way Brud observed the people as if their presence here was perfectly natural.

Brud viewed this place as a hunting ground. But he was not certain if he was an observer, or if he was to be part of the ceremony. He understood that there were people looking for him. They would find him in time. Something would be proven. He would be tested again. But why couldn't they find him now? Without his sunglasses, he was no longer invisible to himself and therefore totally visible to others. His thoughts were made soft and imprecise by exhaustion and alcohol fatigue. His nervous uncertainty mounted toward an unavoidable conclusion. This was an evil place. A sanctuary of false order. There was no doubt in Brud's mind. He should wake Dogger and take them out of there. He would do it. But he was frightened for what was in store for them. If he moved, would that be a signal to the others that he was ready to accept his part in the ceremony?

Glancing to the side, he stared down a dark tunnel that fell away into the earth. Two eyes of a snake machine were furiously glowing from the distance.

Brud saw that there was a man standing in the head of the snake machine, and he realized that within all animals there must be the image of people. The foreboding presence of people in the heads of all animals constantly reminding them to beware.

The man in the head of the snake machine was trapped

there as a sample of what the snake machine was searching for. When the snake machine rolled in and stopped, another man toward the back of the machine leaned out a tiny window and shouted something, no doubt, a plea for help or a warning. But the people ignored him and blankly stepped into the belly of the snake machine, freely giving themselves up. It must be a sacrifice like in the picture books he had seen, where a man or woman was thrown into a hole to satisfy an angry god. Brud knew that these gods were false. His father had explained. Perhaps these people were offering themselves in order to appease the underground colony, to keep the serpents content so they would remain underground and not harm the crowds above the ground. The ceremony had been mistaught. The people were deceived by this place of falsehoods.

Joy noticed Brud's brow creasing. He was staring at his boots with a worried expression.

He felt that he would be sacrificed in some way. Not this way. It would be for no good. The air in the tunnel pressed against him, implying that there was danger here. He would have to give in to it. He would have to offer himself as a sign of faith, as an act of kindness toward the people above the earth. He did not know what to believe, but he knew how his time was coming and, looking down at the small face sleeping in his lap, he wondered why Dogger had led him here.

Brud regarded the snake machine as it slid off into its cave. He saw the eyes of another serpent, gleaming from the same tunnel, rumbling in for the sacrifice.

Watching it slow and then stop, Brud saw the belly open and the people being sadly rejected. He saw two men on the platform. They were dressed identically —

wearing the same clothes as the man in the head of the snake machine — and staring at him. They watched with dark eyes, the shiny buttons on their jackets sparking in the light, glaring like the eyes of the snake machine that moved in behind them. They were its keepers. There was no doubt. The men had given in to these idols. They worshipped them and freely professed their devotion through their style of dress.

Breezing by, the snake machine forced a rush of warm air against Brud's hands and face. He began to shiver with empty wrongful thoughts, ideas of coming to his end.

Joy passively stared up as the two men stepped in front of Brud. One of the keepers had a newspaper in his hand and pointed at a grainy photograph.

He said, "You see. Who's right and who's wrong now?"

The other keeper glanced down the track, a look of disgust on his face. He shook his head and blew air between his teeth.

The first keeper stared at Brud. Then they moved quickly. In an instant, their fingers were on him, wrestling him to his feet. Their hands were heavy and pressed with great force.

Dogger's head dropped to the plastic seat, but he did not wake. There was nothing that Joy could do. She sat with her fingertips tucked away into her armpits, a scream shivering quietly inside her throat.

Brud stared back as he was hustled away. He called out with a deep wordless cry. A dry sob. From the harshness of this cry, an equally disturbing thought formed. Perhaps Dogger and Joy were to be part of the sacrifice. He stopped in his tracks, his body turning solid so that the keepers jerked in their steps and could not move him. He found no fault with the idea of being sacrificed. If it would help, then he would gladly comply. But he feared for his friends. He would not let such things happen to them. Brud struggled to free himself, to rush back and take Dogger and Joy with him, to save them from the underground, so they could rise, out from this heavy air that spurred such bullying thoughts. But as he twisted and turned to rush back, the two keepers tripped him and slammed his body to the ground. One of them quickly spoke into a black rectangular box that he held in his hand. A voice soon replied, crackling with static.

Brud felt the side of his face flattening against the cold tile. A sharp knee was pressed into his back. He saw feet stopping, black and coloured shoes gathering to stare down at him.

"We've got the tooth fairy murderer," the first keeper announced into the box. He shouted loudly so the crowd could hear. His voice was nervous but triumphant, as if pleased with itself. Then he was scared and his words were uneven, riddled with dots, "We need assistance."

Brud lay perfectly still, flat on the floor with the weight of two men pressing down on him. It was a great heaviness, much like the bales of hay that had fallen from the barn's loft, pinning him when he was a boy. He thought he must look like a baby having to be held down like this, needing to be forced to the sacrifice. He hated to think that deep down he was a coward. He was ashamed of himself. These people needed him to protect them. He told himself that he should go willingly, stop his lips from quivering, and be strong for them. Yes, he told himself. I will be a good boy. A brave boy. Then I will be very special.

He saw the shoes and heard someone laugh. A small laugh. He felt warm and damp around his legs. With great difficulty, he shifted his head and strained to look down at the puddle spreading easily across the tile. He saw the wet stain widening against the fabric of his trousers. An upside-down head came into his field of vision. Hair hung down and he saw that it was Joy. She watched him like this, holding her head out of order, her face looking all wrong, her chin becoming the tiny top of her head, her forehead becoming the bottom. She opened her lips and it was funny. Brud laughed. Then he saw another upside-down face. Dogger. His small mouth was saying something, but the words were upside down too. Brud could not make them out. He chuckled at Dogger and Joy. He could not hold his laughter. It blurted from behind his lips when all the other faces turned upside down to glean a better look at him.

part three

denial

chapter one

staring into the sun

"Look, you have to decide," Andrea told her husband. She checked the leather chair behind her, then slowly sat. Jim glanced at her from where he was standing by the window in his office. The fourteenth floor. The morning haze was hanging over the city, lingering like fog. Even though it was past noon, the haze had not burned off. Jim's mind seemed filled with a similar vagueness, stubborn and congestive.

"I've made my decision," he said, regarding the window.

"You have to ask yourself a question," Andrea insisted, slowly running her hands over the chair's leather armrests. "You know the question. Be fair."

"I've defended lots of people the exact same way."

"What way?"

"What way?" Jim cast his sight up at the glass, finding his wife's thin reflection. She and the chair were small and seemed suspended there.

"Wake up, Jimmy."

"I'm awake," he called. "You know what way. People who were guilty, that's what I'm saying." Jim shifted, turning his head slightly to catch a glimpse of Andrea. "This isn't any different. I'll do my job."

"You see." Andrea leaned forward in her chair, her hands soundly joined and resting on her knees. "You do think he's guilty."

"I didn't say that."

"Come off it, Jimmy. You think I just met you yesterday? You just said you've defended guilty people before. You think Brud killed these people." She used her fingers to brush her bangs away from her eyes.

"What difference does it make what he's guilty of?" Jim protested, gazing down at the tiny cars and the tiny people, feeling like a giant about to tumble on them. "It's something. He's misleading us in some way. I know. I can see that now."

"You know the difference it makes. You're thinking about your brother and you're blaming his death on Brud."

"When I'm in court, I leave my emotions outside. Absolutely." Jim paused to check his thoughts and heard his breath coming hotly through his nostrils. "You know how I operate. It's the law and nothing else. A matter of words, of being alert and swaying judgement, disproving even the truth if necessary. Accuracy. Questions of inconsistencies. Motivation. Speculation. Complete accuracy. Adhering to our facts. I can do that. I know the words. I know the people who sit in the jury, how they think, how their little minds operate. I just lead them. That's how I was taught. Remember? Lead the jury toward the indisputable truth, the counsel's truth, the flavour of the day."

Neither one of them would speak, feeling the tension rising between them. Jim turned around to watch his wife and saw how her eyes gently shifted as she stared beyond him, out the window. Glancing there, he saw a jet moving through the sky, gradually descending toward the airport.

"I just came here to take you to lunch," Andrea casually informed him. "I don't know how we got into this. I just wish it was over."

"We're into this."

Andrea stood from her chair, "Let's give it up for a little while, okay?"

"Listen, Andrea." Jim paused to consider the depth of his love for her. His wife was a beautiful woman, slim and short-haired with fine features, and he loved her fiercely. He sighed, giving in. "I really don't know if he's guilty or not, Andrea. I ask him, 'Brud, did you stab that man?' But he won't answer me."

"How do you ask it?"

"I ask it flatly. I know how to ask."

"You don't ask in a threatening way? That prodding tone of yours? The coercive hints in your voice? You know how that works, what it implies. You're a lawyer."

"I know what I am, Andrea," he said patiently, "and, no, I don't ask in a threatening way." Returning to his desk, he sat in his high-backed leather chair, shuffling a pile of papers from one side of his desk to the other.

"You know Brud won't answer if he thinks you're angry."

"What are you, suddenly a psychologist? You don't even know the man."

"I know him. I've seen him."

"What is it with people these days? Everyone thinks

they can get inside each other's heads. Easy as that." He snapped his fingers without looking at her.

"I'm no psychologist, but I did spend three years studying psychology at UFL. I do know just a tiny bit about it. More than you, Mr. Cut and Dry."

Jim stared up from his desk. His face was set and he watched his wife for a moment. He would not move his hands.

"Let me explain something to you, Ms. Psychologist." He caught sight of another jet, its reflection moving in the glass frame of one of his legal certificates across the room. He followed the descent of the metallic speck and wished he was on that plane, detached, away, knowing nothing of Brud or his wife. He simply wanted to be alone. Watching the jet's reflection, his train of thought calmed and slipped away.

"Explain what?" Andrea asked, dropping back into her chair with resolve.

Jim shifted his gaze, his eyes unfocussed so that he had to make an effort to see her.

"Wake up, Jimmy. What's the matter with you?"

"I'll tell you what." Jim licked his lips. He glanced at his calendar and saw the list of appointments for the afternoon. Moving his hands, he flipped the small squares of paper. One court date. "When Brud gets up there on the stand, I know he won't respond to any of the questions. It's like you said, he won't answer to that kind of tone. And you know what the D.A. is like. Brud won't utter a word. He won't deny anything." Jim pulled open a deep drawer, poked around, and stared down into it. He was not interested in what lay in there. He was not looking for anything in particular.

"What about the plea?"

"Not guilty by reason of insanity." His hand moved into the drawer, senselessly searching.

Andrea scoffed at the idea.

"We've all seen the assessment. It'll work in our favour."

"What assessment? He wasn't in there long enough."

"A doctor friend of mine provided an assessment."

"Jimmy!"

"That's enough." He slammed the drawer. "Enough now, you hear?"

"But he's not guilty by reason of being not guilty."

Jim smiled. Slipping his fingers beneath a long legal document, he raised it slightly from his desk.

"Just let me do my job." He smirked. "Okay? They have that tooth now. Things have changed. It doesn't look good for him."

"A tooth! So what. It could be from anywhere. There are more drunks falling down in alleyways in this city. There must be teeth all over the place."

"Real funny."

"Not funny. The truth. You're not being fair, Jimmy. This isn't like you. I think you should turn the case over to someone else. There are fifteen or twenty lawyers in your firm alone."

Jim's face became serious, darkening, "Don't interfere, okay? Or I'll start questioning some other things."

"What?" Tears rushed into Andrea's eyes. It was as if someone had slapped her. She knew by his insinuating tone that he was referring to their marriage. "I'm leaving," she said, glancing at her watch to hide the blurriness in her eyes. "Lunch is almost over now anyway." Turning and stepping for the door, she halted there, having to dab at her cheeks. "I have to cover the trial."

"Can you honestly tell me that you're going to report

on the trial in an unbiased way? Those biases show up in printed words, too. Feelings turn into phrases leaning a certain way. Feelings slip in there, so don't tell me there's no such thing as unbiased journalism. It's impossible."

"I'm a professional," she snapped, pinning him with a furious glance. "And I've had enough of you for today."

"It's you who should turn it over to someone else."

A groan shivered in her throat as she pulled open the door. Stepping out, she tried to slam it, but the door was heavy and connected to a brass hydraulic mechanism that smoothly eased it shut.

Watching the door close and hearing it click, Jim spun around in his chair, taking in the sky and buildings once again. He stood and moved to the window, hoping to see his wife walking away from the building. In a few minutes, he saw her down on the sidewalk. She appeared inconsequential, mingling among the tiny crowds, the cars, the minute shifting of colours that inspired in him a sense of utter despair. Unconsciously, he took a quick deep breath as if he was drowning. The air conditioner hummed quietly in his ears. Shutting his eyes, he felt the sun against his face. He saw a clear expanse of green, the rolling farmland and the farmhouse where he remembered seeing Brud standing on the steps in the morning heat, waving to him, welcoming him, accepting the fresh sunlight against his face and the quietude that made him stop and stand perfectly still in appreciation.

Jim opened his eyes and wondered, *What do I appreciate here?* He contemplated the street, bracing the disunity of height and power. He set his palms against the glass, a fear drawing outward inside of him. Awareness. It seemed unnatural to be up so high.

"Work, work, work," chirped Quagmire, his smooth skin bleached a ghastly white beneath the country sun. "But work is never done. Idle hands, you know what I mean?"

"How's the survey going, Mr. Quagmire?" asked the foreman. He was a man of medium build who walked with a limp, favouring his right side. It was his first project with his new employer. Faithfully, he followed Quagmire into the dense shadow along the side of the barn.

"Done," said Quagmire.

"When're the dozers starting in?"

"This trial." Quagmire shook his head, then craned it back, lazily panning the scorched white sky. "The fool who owned this land is on trial for murder. You know the man. The tooth fairy affair. So there you have it. Complications."

"Right, I see."

"You never know what the courts will do." Quagmire gave up on the sky, unable to find what he was searching for, and locked eyes with the foreman. "The courts could seize this land. Compensation for the families of the victims. You know the sort of rubbish they get on with."

"Yes." The foreman smiled, vying for Quagmire's good grace. He limped closer to the barn and gave it a shove with one hand; the other held a clipboard. "Solid," he observed.

"We just want him out of our way so we can get on with what needs to be done."

Gazing up at the eave of the barn, the foreman shaded his eyes, tilting his head. Then he took a pencil from his pocket to jot a quick note on his clipboard.

"This is pretty sturdy," he informed his boss. "Won't come down too easy."

"Oh, it'll be easy. I just need the final signature from the previous owner. One simple signature from a fool. Tooth fairy fool take a big bite out of you."

"How'd he manage all those killings, I wonder."

Quagmire shot a penetrating look at his employee. "How do you mean?"

"Didn't he just leave the farm a little while ago?" The foreman limped back out of the shade and glanced across the land. "Isn't that what you told me? Hadn't been off this land all his life?"

"That doesn't mean anything. He could've slipped away at night, snuffed a few people, and slipped back here." Raising a finger, he wagged it at the foreman. "You never know what people are capable of. You have to be more intuitive." Quagmire took pleasure in correcting the foreman. "It doesn't take long to kill someone." As if to prove his point, he elaborately cracked a knuckle.

"Sure, I can understand that. But he doesn't look the part. I saw his picture in the papers. He was on the television, coming out of court. He was on one of those talk shows, too, with his lawyer. Didn't say much though. People were calling in with questions. They say he can't talk."

"Don't need a tongue to kill someone. You don't use your tongue, unless you're looking to lick a person to death."

"I don't know." The foreman laughed, glancing at the empty corral. "I guess."

"You know what?" asked Quagmire.

"What?"

"You're right. You don't know, so stop straining what little brains the Lord gave you. What was He thinking of, you figure, when He held back the brains on so many people? What's that all about? A good question, n'est-ce pas?"

"What?" the foreman asked, offering Quagmire an obedient, but slightly troubled, smile.

"Nothing."

"Oh."

"Nothing, you get it?" Quagmire held the sides of his skull and shook it, roaring with laughter.

The foreman squinted, confused, but soon gave in to Quagmire's smile and chuckled, wiping his sleeve across his face and surveying the dampness of the fabric.

"This heat is something else." He blew out a breath of air. "Whew."

"This is nothing." Again, Quagmire looked up at the sky, staring straight into the sun. "It's a million times hotter where I come from."

"Yeah, the guys said you were from down south somewhere."

"Way down south. Way, way down there."

The foreman's eyes skimmed over his boss's hands and face.

"Not much of a tan, hey?" mused Quagmire. "I hang out in the shade."

"I've got a cousin from down that way. Works for one of those big oil companies. You probably know him."

"Of course, of course. It's a small world."

"Name's Tom Jenson."

"Alive, is he?" Quagmire enquired, his face clean and sweatless, his eyes burning pinholes through the sun.

"Sure he's alive." The foreman kindly laughed.

"I wouldn't know him then."

"How's that?" Shading his eyes, the foreman took a look at what was interesting Quagmire, but his eyes could not bear the scorching radiance.

"Just joking," Quagmire beamed at the sun. "Forget it."

The foreman shut his eyes, then regarded the ground, the image of the sun still burning in his retinas. Glancing back at his boss, he saw how Quagmire seemed washed out around the edges.

The foreman shut his eyes again, waiting for them to settle. All he saw was pinkness and tiny black dots that seemed to sizzle along with Quagmire's voice. He vigorously rubbed his eyes and opened them. Quagmire was still staring into the sun. Flabbergasted, the foreman caught sight of the ground at his boss's feet; an uneven circle of wilted yellow and brown grass surrounded him.

"Must've been a big rock there, or something." The foreman pointed at the ground, tracing his finger along the air. "Right there where you're standing. A burnt-up circle."

"Or something," confirmed the yellow-toothed man, his eyes fixed on the sun, seeming at perfect peace. Finally, he lowered his head, his eyes appearing handsome, paler and bluer. He looked at the foreman. "Something that would block it from the light."

chapter two

oath of the single thought

Brud stepped from inside the machine. It was much like a pickup truck, only covered all around with steel and hollow in the back. He was passed wordlessly from one man to another. The men were dressed in suits similar to those worn by the keepers of the snake machine, but the colours of the men's clothes were of a different shade; a dark grey like the steady blandness of an overcast sky.

Brud moved from one man to the next, watching the changing faces until he saw a man who seemed to be good. The man's face was deep brown and he walked loosely and slowly, unlike the others. The man offered a gentle, closed-lip smile.

Steel doors were unlocked and slid aside. After the man led Brud through, the doors would slide shut and be locked again. Brud thought they must be returning to the underground, but his body told him that they were not descending.

The men took Brud's clothes — the ones Dogger had given him — and presented him with rock-coloured clothes, like those that the other men were wearing. The people in these clothes all seemed to belong to a special group. They dressed the same and moved the same, each of them a single thought that carried itself throughout the pale chambers. Together, they made up one dull thought, as if their clothes had somehow changed the colours inside of them as well, stripping away the greens and blues and reds that could be felt. The single thoughts moved together and breathed together, but had terrible secrets in their eyes.

Brud was led to a cage much smaller than the one he had first occupied. However, the overall size of the place was massive. The cages were stacked, rows and rows on top of each other, and ran in straight lines for as far as the eye could see. Perhaps these were holding pens for the people to be sacrificed to the snake machines. That was the look in the single thoughts' eyes, that similar underground look of confinement and anticipation, restraint spurring the need for action.

Brud shivered, aware of what had been taken from him.

The man watched Brud step into the cage. Brud understood what was expected. He had done this before. The men did not come inside with him. They stood outside, away, as if there were things in the cage that would harm them. The man expected very little from him and this was one of the things. It was simple enough, but it was troublesome.

Brud turned and nodded to the man. The man nodded back, offering his closed-lip smile before he shut the door and walked away, his noiseless shoes moving along the worn concrete walkway.

Brud watched the man until he could no longer see him, then he stepped back toward the bed and sat down. This place was a hard thing to understand, and he gave up trying to do so. He placed his hands on his lap and studied the lifeless walls. They were clean, freshly painted, but there were images beneath the paint that could be detected. Standing, he moved closer and stared at these ghost images: big thick letters made up small words, drawings of long things and holes with hair. Images were under there, trying to get to him, to tell him something of the hatred that lurked here. He shuffled back, sensing the devastating capabilities of these omens, and sat on his bed. Looking up at the window and the vertical bars, he then turned his head to glance at the longer bars across the cell. Through them, he could see the rows of cages far away from him. It was hard to understand. Had he lost something, he wondered? Had someone robbed him of a part of his body that made him normal and able to walk freely? He thought of his soul. His thumbs. The men in uniforms had spotted him and taken him. Something must have fallen off. He looked at his fingers and his legs. He touched his chest and searched the features of his face. Everything was in its place. What could it have been that now made him so different from those outside of this place? Why was he made to be a single thought?

Brud was led to a place to eat with the others. His stomach noisily declared its want. He could smell the tempting odours as the line moved closer. The food tasted fine, but strangely false. Brud detected traces of something that seemed unfamiliar. All of the dinner contained inklings of a similar taste. Perhaps this was because Brud had become a single thought. The natural tastes of the food were plainly there, but they seemed tainted by the same strange blandness that shaded his clothes. The blandness settled in his stomach like hardening cement, reminding him of the images behind the painted walls of his cage.

Brud's hunger slowly dissipated. He noticed how the other single thoughts were glimpsing at him through the corners of their eyes. They wanted to make sure that Brud was keeping faithful to the oath of the single thought. They wanted to make certain that Brud would fit into their thorough oneness.

Whenever Brud mustered enough courage to meet the glance of one of the men, he would smile in the man's direction, nod, and laugh into his hand. But the eyes would flit away, as if they had been disappointed in what they had seen. Only one person returned Brud's smile. He was a small man who continuously stirred in his seat, moving and glancing around, straightening himself. He picked up his fork, then laid it down, poked at his food with his fingers, wiped his mouth, lifted his fork again, laid it down.

Brud recognized the look in this man's eyes. He had seen it in the heaven that had turned into hell. Brud wondered why this man was not back in heaven. Perhaps this was where men were sent when heaven turned to hell.

The small man caught Brud's attention. The small man winked and blinked. Eating, they watched each other. The small man showed Brud his tongue and laughed quick, then laughed again as if he remembered Brud from heaven too. The man laughed and the smile whipped cleanly from his face. He became deadly serious, convinced of where he was and how the single thought did not permit laughter. The small man nervously glanced around, making certain that no one had seen him. He shook his fist at Brud, but the man sitting beside the small man slammed a hand over his fist, driving and pinning it to the table.

Not a word was spoken, only the peculiar harmony of forks and knives striking plates. It tried to be music in Brud's ears, but fell hopelessly short. Brud thought the harmony was out of order. It was in need of tuning. Where was the quiet man who visited the farm to fix their piano? He should be brought to this place. Why didn't these people know of the quiet man who made the music follow itself properly?

vigilante

The faithful crowd had gathered on the courthouse steps, awaiting Brud's arrival. Mingling among the reporters were many hostile family members of those who had been murdered. They stared impatiently, anticipating a view of the man who had taken their loved ones away from them, hoping they would see something vile in his character that would coax them closer to revelation and thus relieve their torment.

Across the street, Dogger straddled a fire hydrant, watching the anxious crowd. He glanced over his shoulder to see Joy sitting with her back against a building. She was not watching the crowd, but rather fingering and rolling a number of seeds around in her hand. Brud had given her the seeds in the late-night bar, and she had understood the simplicity of them. Her long black hair sheened in the sun as she leaned sideways, bracing one hand against a small patch of grass that trimmed the building. She pushed her finger past the blades into the dirt, feeling the cool clay and the sweetness of it. Then she dropped a seed into the hole, covered it, and moved the remaining seeds along the creases in her palm.

Further down the street, Tumbles and Pigeon were reading magazines at a corner stand. Pigeon was fervently studying a photograph of the Statue of Liberty. She was pleased with its look of permanence. Statues never moved, never left, always remained in their place. She liked to circle them, walk around and stare, amazed at how they stayed the same when she went back to visit them.

Tumbles's eyes speared a glimpse at the restless crowd. He too was waiting for Brud. Nudging Pigeon, he wordlessly indicated that they should move toward the courthouse, then pushed his hands into his pockets, confidently clutching the tools of justice: the sharp steely tip of revenge that sliced through human disorder and the explosion of reform that penetrated with greater force. He would select one over the other at the last minute, his timid impulsiveness fitting of a legal decision.

Brud had stabbed Skully and now it was time to even the score, balance those scales, find favour with the blindfolded lady. Once Brud stepped beyond the courthouse doors, Tumbles knew that justice would be bought with words, and Tumbles — despite his vocal bravado — put little faith in words. Why else would he always shout when he spoke, if not to draw attention to the obviously fraudulent gaps that divided each syllable? Despite the presence of these gaps, the words all flowed together in an untrustworthy way.

Tumbles strolled clear of the magazine stand. Pigeon, returning her magazine to its place, also drifted away from the stand. She too was armed with the virtuous implements of justice.

The couple stepped in unison, four feet apart. Tumbles considered the use of the knife, thinking of the smoothness of it as it went in and came out with the red juice of reward washed across the glimmering steel.

Pigeon favoured the gun as her choice, her heart always racing at the sound of its explosion, her knees jerking to the thrill. She would jump a tiny jump and feel the heat rushing to her face, the fired metal warming her fingers. The lingering crackle of a gunblast resembled the popping of fireworks after a statue is unveiled. *Death is a statue, too,* she told herself. *A body staying where it was put. A grave stone is the ultimate accomplishment, the final and absolute sense of security. The fireworks will turn Brud into a statue, a memorial to my poor Skully. All better now. Forever immortalized.*

"Test. One, two, three." Andrea clicked off her mini-recorder, then played back her voice to make certain the batteries were charged. Stepping down two stairs, away from the other reporters, she leaned out to look up and down the street. There was no sign of a patrol or unmarked car in either direction. Absent-mindedly turning back toward the steps, she collided with an anxious, mean-looking man.

"Oh, I'm sorry," Andrea said, flustered, her fingers tightly gripping the mini-recorder.

The man flashed a sarcastic smile and glanced at the recorder. He chalked up the price it was worth on the street, but quickly dismissed the idea, favouring instead the necessity and reward of revenge. Grimacing at Andrea, his shoulders jerked before· he continued on, his disgruntled hands shoved tightly into the pockets of his brown leather jacket.

Andrea was not watching him. She tested her recorder one more time, afraid that the machine would not function and she would miss the perfect quote. She knew that she would forget the words, repeating them over and over in her head while searching for a pen until the words became terribly jumbled and meaningless. She relied totally on her recorder, despite the extra work it entailed, transcribing conversations, pages and pages of notes.

Tumbles waited at the edge of the crowd. Carefully turning his head, he smiled at his accomplice. "Come on, Pigeon," he tightly whispered, seeing that she was watching him with anxious eyes, eyes that mirrored the same treacherous expectations, the same desolate beliefs they held as gospel.

Tumbles rocked on his feet, flexing his muscles beneath his clothing, delighting in the nervous tingle that coursed throughout his skin. An itchiness plagued him. He could barely contain himself, thrilled to the point where he felt like screaming and falling to his knees, grunting and howling, washing himself in the garbage and filth that lingered on the sidewalks, scrubbing himself clean with it.

His lips twitched. He licked them. Shoulders jittering, he pushed his jaw forward in contemplation, then spat into the street. He felt the need to leap and tumble backward, to somersault along the asphalt. His feet did not feel at home on the ground, unless landing, confirming his position. Pow, solid, here I am! Now listen!

Andrea's attention was focussed on the flow of traffic. In the corners of her eyes, she noticed a boy sitting on a fire hydrant across the street. A dark-haired girl with a strange face was leaning against a building behind the boy. They seemed to be waiting as well, their stances and fixed expressions much too contrived for them to be mere onlookers.

Andrea set her complete attention on the boy. She watched as the boy caught sight of something that obviously upset him. He drifted back from the fire hydrant and went immediately to the dark-haired girl. Andrea glanced where the boy was looking, following his line of vision across the street to see the man who had bumped into her only minutes ago. The man's severe eyes were set on the approaching cars. He moved from foot to foot and glanced — with an obviously collaborative smile — at a woman further up the steps.

The man noticed Andrea's stare and, gritting his teeth at her, his eyes stewed with a warning that entailed the promise of violation. He stared and then side-stepped into the people, his cold eyes flashing in and out of sight — watching her — between the varied faces of the crowd.

"The D.A.'s office won't be indicting you for those other murders," Jim blankly informed Brud. "Not right now, anyway. They know they don't have enough evidence. I just got the call." He patted his briefcase, indicating the wireless telephone he had just put away. Glancing through his window to watch the buildings sweep by, he thought of Andrea. They were in trouble; serious doubts were coming between them. They had not spoken in days. Silence at the kitchen table. Silence in the car. Silence at his brother's funeral. Silence in bed. Only essential words passed between them: the answering of telephone calls, the asking of vital questions, money matters, food needs, announcements of comings and goings.

The car stopped at a red light and Jim leaned slightly forward, addressing the plain-clothes policeman sitting to the other side of Brud. "Thanks, by the way, for the mass card."

The policeman nodded, but did not look at Jim. "Steve was a good cop. We all knew that, despite everything." The policeman turned his face to stare accusingly at Brud, then pressed closer, bringing his lips to the prisoner's ear, and mumbling between his clenched teeth.

Leaning back, Jim studied his client's vacant face. His features seemed to have hardened, were not as soft as he remembered. There were lines around Brud's eyes and a slenderness that gave definition to his cheekbones. He was losing weight. It seemed he had lost quite a bit.

"Don't say anything when we get there. Nothing to the reporters. Okay, Brud? Same as before."

Brud raised his handcuffed hands and picked a flake of sleep from the edge of his eye. He liked the feel of it coming loose, enjoyed peeling things away from his body. The feeling of freshness, when he lifted away the scabs that had formed around his wrists from the chafing of the handcuffs was his only sensation of refreshment since he found himself in the place of the single thought. Done with picking the sleep away, he rubbed the crusty particles between his fingers. It reminded him of the fine grains of feed he would deliver to the animals as part of his chores. He was exhausted, confused. He ate the particles, grinding them between his teeth, then laughed at his act, showing everyone his blackening teeth.

"Okay?" asked Jim. "Brud?"

Brud turned his head toward the voice. Jim had said something, but Brud had learned that it was best to block all sound from his mind. The sounds from the darkness in the place of the single thought had frightened him. He had tried to listen closely to the sounds, to the whisperings and the rubbings of flesh. The sounds came from a single feeling. The place of the single thought and feeling. He did not want to hear the sounds. They made nothing of him. They made him smaller than small.

"Did you hear me?" Jim asked, his voice deepening.

"No," Brud said. "Single thought. Single feeling. Jim's voice like that now."

"Forget it." Jim sighed in disgust and stared at the street, every scrap of enthusiasm purged from his body.

The plain-clothes policeman grinned at Jim's defeated sigh and said, "Life's tough."

The driver glanced in the rearview, smiling to match his amusement with whatever he could see.

Brud had learned that the eyes in the mirror were always owned by the person driving. The sight no longer moved him. He remembered the first time he had seen such eyes. They belonged to the policeman who had stepped into the fire. The policeman had been bad, and then good, and then bad again. Always bad in the end. Eight, ten. Eight and never ten. Never ten. He cracked himself on the forehead with his knuckles.

"Hey," warned the plain-clothes policeman. "Come on now. Enough of that."

"What'd he do?" asked the driver.

"Whacked himself in the head with his fist."

"Oh." The driver could think of nothing more to say, so he shook his head skeptically.

Jim watched the street. He was not interested. These displays were nothing new to him. Brud's shifting character, his outbursts of violence, each unlikely action neatly confirmed Jim's growing suspicions of guilt.

"Do you remember me telling you that I'm changing our plea?" Jim glanced briefly at Brud. "In case you're interested, I'll go over it again."

The plain-clothes policeman snickered. "Good idea."

"I'm dropping the not guilty by reason of insanity. We'll enter a self-defence plea. Okay? Remember what I said, this guy had a record that would choke a horse."

Brud imagined choking a horse. It would be a difficult thing to do. His eyes turned sad, sloping deeper at the ends. He did not want to see them choke a horse, but he expected such things now. Perhaps that was where they were going, to make him watch the slaughter. Again, he cracked himself on the forehead.

"Stop that, Brud," Jim demanded, holding down Brud's hand. "Don't do that in court. Okay? When we get there. It won't do us any good."

"Appearances are everything," said the plain-clothes policeman.

Jim tried to be reasonable. Taking a deep breath he added, "I want to portray you as a vigilante. Ignore other possible charges. Try to make a hero out of you. Our only hope. No judge in his right mind will convict you if we can get the media on our side."

The driver glanced back in the rearview mirror. This time he was not smiling. "You've got it down, don't you?"

Turning to Jim, Brud raised his handcuffed hands. Jim could not help flinching, but Brud simply ran his fingers through the lawyer's hair, then mussed it up, chuckling with tired eyes.

"Fool," Brud said, remembering the sound of the word, thinking it to be a good thing.

"Come off it," Jim protested. He cursed under his breath, quickly smoothing his hair back into place, not wanting to arrive in a state of disarray. The expert management of image was a key factor in all of this. Jim inspected Brud's suit and tie. Andrea had picked it out for him. She had been seeing a great deal of Brud, visiting him often. Jim thought, *God only knows what they're up to*.

"Watch those hands," warned the plain-clothes policeman. He reached for Brud's hands and shoved them down, his face turning hard, his eyes narrowing to seal the threat.

Brud had done something wrong. His hands were not to be used. Now everyone wanted to control his hands. He stared down at them and slowly, defiantly wiggled his fingers.

"Sorry," he said to the man. He did not want to upset this person who was of great power and influence.

Jim was angry, the heat burned in his cheeks and throat. It was becoming more and more difficult to divide his self, to segregate his thoughts from his feelings. All of this, and now Brud was stealing his wife away from him.

The plain-clothes policeman leaned forward as they took the final corner, the crowd and the courthouse steps in sight.

"This guy burned your brother," the policeman blankly informed Jim. "What the hell are you doing with him?"

chapter four

the stop colour

Quagmire fiddled with the dials on his radio. Tiny blasts of voice and music jutted into the cab of the pickup truck. His fingers paused as the needle collided with the smooth, haunting sound of a religious choir.

"Nice music," he said to the foreman.

Nodding impassively, the foreman watched the sunlight in the trees and how the stretches of evergreens were thinning as they moved closer toward the boundaries of the suburbs. He laid his palm on the dashboard, sensing the hot air gushing through the vents.

"Haven't heard church music since I was a kid," the foreman cautiously indicated, his throat troubling him. He swallowed with difficulty, straining against the parchness.

"Such a graceful display." Quagmire glanced at the seat beside him. "Like the soul streaming out of the mouth. That consoling blast of authenticity identifying us. Human beings."

The foreman nodded slightly and stared straight ahead.

"Are you a man of faith?"

"I don't know."

"Religion," pried the yellow-toothed man.

"It's hard to say," said the foreman, remembering his sister, how he had lost her to cancer, the disease eating away at her body, doing the same to his faith. The funeral settled a decision, Christian certainty drawn out of him with the unfathomable descent of the casket. The final service seemed very easy, but it was far from that. The foreman watched the hospital as they rolled alongside of it, sighting the familiar entrance and recalling his past schedule of visits. He explained to Quagmire that he had been a patient in that hospital as well.

"A beam of steel snapped loose of the iron ropes. Came down on me." Regarding the cross above the name of the hospital, he felt the sweat rise to his skin. "Knocked my brain out of whack. I was in a coma, then I was okay. But I was gone for a while. Didn't remember anything, like I was dead. Just blankness. Could've been an instant or fifty years. But it was almost two weeks. Out of my body. Gone into the black. When I came out of it the doctors asked me if I saw a big light at the end of a tunnel or something. They were hoping I got a peek at what was out there. No chance." The foreman smiled regretfully at Quagmire. "Where was my soul then? I keep wondering where I was during all that time. How I got back in. Weird, hey?" The hospital was far behind them now. The foreman watched the road speeding under them. "The worst headache of my life. I thought my skull was split in two. I thought I could feel the two halves, and an opening. I would've sworn to it."

"Indecision," Quagmire accusingly whispered to himself. "Inconsistency."

"So I prayed for the pain to stop. Promised I'd go to church every Sunday, work with the sick, save the whales, the whole thing." He laughed under his breath. "But you know how it is. I didn't die and...other things too." An image of his sister's face returned to him, her lips speaking wordlessly among the confusion, the final sight of her bony body in the hospital bed. It was the only way he remembered her, dying. He offered a stray boyish smile.

"I know how it is. Promises, promises. We're a fickle bunch."

"Funny how you remember things." The foreman pointed at the radio. "As soon as I heard the music, I remembered just like that." Gloomily shaking his head, he appeared defeated by his own thoughts. He swallowed hard against the hot air and sighed deeply, forcing out the inner strain of failure. "Mind if I crack the window?"

Quagmire looked at him apologetically, "I get a chill." He crinkled his nose and shrugged cutely. "I'm very delicate, you know."

"Oh." The foreman stared through the windshield, wondering about Quagmire. He tried to recall conversations with his workers, what they had said about his new boss. His personal politics.

Quagmire leaned forward to change the station, his eyes flitting a quick glance at the road as he playfully fingered the dial, as if tickling it.

With his eyes set on the stream of houses moving past them, the foreman undid the second button on his green work shirt. He could barely breathe. As he strained to carry on the conversation, he grew weaker, nauseous. Trying to take his mind off the discomfort he was feeling, his thoughts alighted on the most obvious topic of interest. The murderer.

"This murderer who owned the farm?"

Quagmire gave up on the dial and briskly twisted off the volume with a look of irritability.

"What about him?" he asked, glumly leaning back in his seat.

"When's he going to court?"

"Today." The prospect brought good humour to Quagmire's eyes. He imagined the sequence of coming events, much like a child watching a present being carried into the room.

"You think he's guilty?"

"Oh yes, he's guilty. He's done quite a number on us. This soft-hearted simpleton nonsense he gets on with. I know the difference. I know what he's really up to. People have no idea what he's actually capable of. If they only knew. If they only realized what he has up his sleeve."

"Oh yeah, what's that?"

"He left too many doors ajar, nothing's black and white. He tried to fool us with philosophy. Use us as pliable little pieces in his grandiose game. Theology — he left it wide open to interpretation. Gave everyone more credit than they deserved. Then he handed out brains incapable of processing the gaps between all the information. What a sham! Who's he think he's kidding? I know he secretly wants me to win. Ever since he questioned his conviction; his first major error. Bad idea. It threw a monkey wrench into the whole plan. You think he wanted to die, just to hoodwink us into believing that we get the same deal with a capital 'D'? You think he wanted to die? Who does? It's not a pretty picture. It's nothing like what you're all expecting. Boy, are you in for a surprise when the time comes. A real hair-raiser."

The foreman thought Quagmire must be talking about

someone else. Either that, or the foreman had drifted off and lost the flow of conversation. His expression easily revealed the sense of discouragement that was gaining on him, his sickly lack of enthusiasm.

"You see what I mean," said Quagmire, gesturing toward the foreman. "You're a prime example. Grade A prime, number one meat."

The foreman answered apathetically. "Right," he said, staring out the window.

Quagmire shook his head, scolding himself and deciding on simpler words, speaking slowly and clearly, "I am heading for the courthouse now, in order to catch the festivities."

"I was reading in one of those papers." The foreman licked his chapped lips. Blowing out air, he wiped his face, then glanced at the heat switches on the dash panel. "They said he was some kind of simpleton. That maybe he didn't know what he was doing, had five or six personalities." The foreman wanted to reach for the switch, click it to low, and slide the control lever over to cool. A trickle of perspiration ran into his eye. He wiped it away, becoming familiar with the dampness of his shirt. The hairs on his arms were sleek and sheened from the sweat.

"Personalities galore." Quagmire snapped his fingers, taking joy in the foreman's sudden insight, giving him more credit than he deserved. "Exactly. Take a look around you, all the people. All in his image. Personality disorder is only a joke."

The truck eased to a stop and Quagmire scowled disapprovingly at the red light.

"Funny how red is the stop colour." Smirking at the foreman, his thoughts raced ahead. "You ever think about that? I question everything that comes to mind. I like to suppose. Overactive imagination. Tormented type, you know. Artist. Landscape impressionist."

"Ignorance is bliss," the foreman claimed, wanting to vomit. He drearily wiped his mouth.

"Right," said Quagmire, his voice dripping with sarcasm. "A profound statement. Anyway, where was I? Red. Red is the colour that races through our veins. It keeps us alive, but someone figured it should be the stop colour. Alarm. Fire, maybe. How do you figure that?"

"Isn't blood blue in our veins, then turns red when the oxygen hits it?" The foreman could barely get the words out.

"Maybe some day you'll see my point. I wasn't talking about red. I was talking about an idea. A concept. Abstractions. Hyper-illusions."

"Oh."

"Red as an idea." The light had switched to green and the truck eased into the intersection, Quagmire still staring at the foreman.

"Watch it!" the foreman started, pointing ahead, then squeezing his brow. "We're rolling."

"Relax," Quagmire insisted, allowing the truck to drive itself. "Listen. Red is the perfect colour. They shouldn't use it that way, upsetting people with it; the thought, I mean. They should welcome it. The communists were red, remember that. Red's been given a bum rap. Look at the sky, sunset, sunrise. Red. They don't take this into account. You listening? I am attempting to have an artsy conversation with you and all you can do is appear uncomfortable. Show a little respect. Okay, I realize that people are uncomfortable with abstract ideas. I realize that. They put stress on the brain, but how can you ever expect to exercise the soul if you do not think this way?" The truck sped up, automatically racing forward in a perfectly straight line. The foreman laid his hand on the door handle, his eyes wide and white as the speedometer needle arced over the top.

Quagmire leaned on the steering wheel, as if casually leaning on a window sill, but his look defied all notions of carelesness. His concentration on the foreman was severe.

"Okay, I'll take your earlier point of argument into consideration. I'm not totally unreasonable. I can understand — just an eentsy-weentsy bit — why they might use red as the stop colour. When the blood comes out of you — your point — that's the reddest there is and that means stop. You see, I am open to alternative ideas. That's what being an artist is."

The foreman wished that Quagmire would stop talking. The scene was wavering across a nightmarish threshold, the air growing heavier and unreal. The foreman's eyes were fixed on the car up ahead. They were practically touching its bumper. He darted a glance at Quagmire's accommodating — almost angelic — smile.

"How...d'you...," he stammered, holding the dashboard with both hands, his sweaty fingers slipping. He gripped it again.

"I understand flow; the notion of sustaining even rhythm. How would you rate my work on a scale of nine-and-a-half to ten?"

"What?"

"Momentum, my friend." Quagmire sweetly closed his eyes and breathed deeply, evenly. "Feel it. The gracefulness."

"What is it?" The foreman pressed his back deep into the springs, bracing himself. His eyes bolted toward the speedometer, the needle wavering past seventy-eight miles per hour. The truck weaved around cars, crossing the center lines, over and in. The screeching of tires. The unpeeling of sound.

The yellow-toothed man opened his eyes. Shaking his head from side to side, he raised his hands in protest. "No, thank you. No please, thank you so much but I don't deserve it." He humbly bowed his head, seeming embarrassed to continue. "The life of a prodigy is a lonely one. The fool saw that, and he kicked me out. Couldn't bear the competition so close to home." Leaning back in his seat, Quagmire gripped the wheel and sighed, as if wasting his talent on the boring chore of having to watch the road.

The foreman smelled something burning, the scorched odour of vinyl melting against heat.

Quagmire glanced aside tragically. "Lonely, lonely, lonely." He touched his chin, a look of wounded innocence. "It has always been this way. Too much intelligence equals too few friends."

The killer stood on the street corner, one block west of the courthouse. Shoving two fingers around in his mouth, he admired the smooth spaces, the fleshly pulpiness where his teeth once were. Then the sharpness; his fingertips scraping over the cracked edges of the few remaining dark brown teeth. He spotted his boy on the other side of the street, and he was thrilled by the rush of condemnation that convinced him of his continuance. His genetic pool. He smiled at the connecting thought. *A pool of blood, but inside of us, spilling forever.*

Dogger kept his nervousness in check, appearing cautious as he spoke with Joy. Saying a few words, he would then quickly glance across the street. It was a dead giveaway. The killer looked at the courthouse, then spat into the street. His recessed eyes fixed on the trail of saliva as it struck the curb. Confirming that the spit was mingled with blood, he nodded several times, huffing meanly as he stared at his boy.

He's a smart one, thought the killer. *A survivor just like me. But he doesn't have the life-taking instinct. There's something different in him, something far away at the other end.* As if sensing the killer's concern, Dogger turned his head and noticed his father standing alone. Quickly he waved for the killer to join them. Dogger always knew when his father was close. Intuition. The blood pool reflecting familiar images.

The killer dodged traffic. Vehicles whizzed inches from his waist as he made his way across the street.

"Listen," Dogger raved, pulling the killer close and speaking secretively, looking down at the sidewalk, "You remember the guy I was with at the bar? Remember that?"

"Sure. The man who *would* be me." The killer raised his eyebrows at Joy, but she did not return his attention. Disappointed, he poked two fingers inside his mouth, the dark stains along the edges of his fingers lightening to red, smearing fluid along his bottom lip.

Joy stepped back. She touched the scars on her face, lightly pressing them, one at a time, as if completing the sequence of a code.

The killer, embarrassed, hurriedly wiped at his lips, "Sorry," he said to her, smiling modestly. "I have a very *harrowing* dental history."

"Listen." Dogger tugged on the killer's sleeve. "Listen, will you? The guy'll be here soon for the trial."

"Yeah, okay, Dogger. *Relax*. I hear you. Not just here. I *hear* you all around. Everything speaks to me with your voice." He laughed and touched Dogger's shoulder for a brief moment.

"And there's a guy over on the stairs. Don't look, don't look…" The boy cringed, his eyes jamming shut as if expecting a blow. "He'll know something's up."

"Then how will I see him?"

"Okay, slowly." Dogger peeked at the courthouse. "He's got on a brown leather jacket, thin guy, nervous, see him? Wearing army pants. Do you see him?"

"Yes, yes, yes."

"He told me he was going to kill the fool. I was there. He told me."

The killer frowned. "Take it easy. What's with you and this guy? What's the *matter* with you?"

"Nothing."

"Who is he, anyway? He got inside of you? Got a *hold*? This attraction is *instinctual*. Something to do with survival. Tell me. I need to know this one."

Dogger, unable to find words for what he felt, settled on what he had learned to be the most important commodity of all. "He's got tons of money."

"Money's not everything. Listen to your father with his mouth full of *holy wisdom*." He smiled at the Joy, winked at her. "Neat joke."

She backed away, all fingertips reading the raised white nicks on her face.

"I know he's going before the eyes. The eyes like to *watch*, pass judgement over elaborate performances. *Raise* their scores to rate the lives, give *meaning* to the meaningless, order out of chaos. It's always extra interesting when you *know* the scripts all wrong. You laugh. I laugh."

"Can you stop that and just listen?" Dogger was practically yelling.

"Drop your tone, boy. Remember *who* you're talking to, okay?" He saw how Dogger looked at him disapprovingly, and relented, "*Okay*, forget it. I don't lay any claim to respect. Check that off your shopping list." His dark-mouthed smile was nervous as he studied Joy's troubled eyes. She was anxiously watching the courthouse. Silent and watching, but something flinching beneath the skin of her face, something severed and faintly kicking.

"You've got to stop that guy from killing the fool."

"I've seen him. I *know* him. They call him Tumbles."

"I know that," Dogger ranted. "I know."

"What do you figure he's holding?" The killer's finger-tips scraped along the stubble on his narrow jawline. He liked the sound. He rubbed it fiercely with the butt of his palm, wagging his head to the rhythm.

Dogger waited impatiently until the killer had calmed. "I don't know, could be anything. He's got his hands in his pockets. He's holding... He used to keep a gun and a couple of knives stashed in a hole in the wall."

"Whisper, okay, lower."

"Okay."

"I've *seen* the uniforms," the killer quietly professed. "Any plain-clothes handy?"

"I saw a few. One in a grey suit up by the doors. Another in a raglan, sunglasses, bottom of the steps, looking round."

"I see what you're saying. You've got my eyes. They go on and on, way back into your head. Good *range*."

"Can you take out Tumbles? He's with a girl, too. Skully's girlfriend. They call her Pigeon."

The killer spoke blankly. "Skully? How can you not like the name? Brings *tears* to my eyes."

"He's the guy that was stabbed by the fool." Dogger sighed, his face flushed with frustration.

"Yeah," the killer mumbled.

"I can distract her," said the boy. Slice the spots behind

315

her knees. I've seen Tumbles do that before. A person just drops."

"Good boy. Now you're talking, speaking *my* language." The killer's pride was obvious as he studied Dogger's face. Although he wanted better for his son, he also felt the need to share the personal horror of his life with the only one who was close to him. "You really care for this fool, don't you?" he asked, vaguely disheartened.

"The cash, I told you. Are you listening, or what?"

"Don't con me, Dogger. It's okay. You can let your heart *beat* out a tune to people, too. There's nothing too much the matter with that. Just don't let it get out of hand... Don't let it *tear* you up, or you'll find out. Speaking of that, did you find the tooth I left for you?"

"Right here." Dogger quickly pulled the tooth from his pocket. He sniffed and wiped at his nose. The tooth was hidden in tissue paper. Unwrapping it, he showed it to the killer, smiled for a moment, then rewrapped it and shoved it back into his pocket, more interested in keeping his eye on the crowd across the street.

"That's good," said the killer. "You keep that tooth. That's number *nine* and there's no body to go with it. I broke the line for you, the equation that I've set up, my *measly* doctrine. You got that tooth now, so you're the gap in what I thought was an otherwise solid *divinity*. Snap, crackle, with no pop. You're right in the center of it, making me think. I put *you* there."

Dogger nodded swiftly, as he often did when he could not understand the killer. "So, you're going to help me? Right?"

"You're my boy, aren't you?" The killer's voice changed, softened by fabricated regret. He raised his hands to stroke an invisible violin. "I could never give you much. Living on the streets like this. This is the *least* I can do for you, son of mine. For you and the man who would be me. In a sense, I'll be saving *myself*. You grasp the connection, *clamp* your mental teeth around it?"

Joy turned her head away from the courthouse, the motion smooth as she regarded the killer. Touching her belly, she pushed in as if shoving something out from inside of her. A defeated smile graced her still lips. Raising her hand, she slid a black feather from her hair and placed it behind the killer's ear.

She pointed at the sky, looked up there, shifting her eyes as if following the flight of the most elaborate bird.

"Too *melodramatic* for me," the killer scoffed, throwing the feather to the ground and turning away from her, turning away from the boy, but remembering them as clearly as if he was in their presence. He belonged to them, a live wire in the force charging vileness from this world. He felt the hypocrisy, but it was this feeling he would cast from his body. No, he was lying to himself. He admitted it with a slight chuckle. He could deceive anyone, knowing perfectly well why he was doing this, who had really sent him. He fixed his eyes on Tumbles as he stepped across the street.

Moments later, Dogger and Joy casually followed, walking down to the intersection to use the crosswalk. They stepped together, holding hands. Dogger stared at Pigeon. She was standing in the crowd, stiff as a board, held by the tense prospects of movement.

Joy was dazed by the squall of the crowd. She whimpered as she stepped among them, frightened to be so close, but needing to be lost, to accept the lustreless grace of anonymity.

chapter five

uncovered and marked

Brud became increasingly captivated by the sight of his handcuffed hands. Slowly, he bent and straightened his fingers, remembering the stirrings of insects beneath overturned rocks. He had found them many times. And now he had been uncovered himself. He had been discovered. They lifted the rock away and Brud was there, squinting at everyone around him. He felt this way, matters too bright, too loud for him. He traced the coil of the steel cuffs, thought of a rabbit snared in a trap with its limbs kicking to get loose, the fur stripped away. He thought of stew. He was hungry, but denied his hunger. By not eating, he would punish whoever had condemned him to this.

Jim looked down at Brud's hands and saw the blood-raw welts.

Brud was moving his wrists back and forth, pushing against the edges of the steel. The pain was cool and distracting. Brud knew if his hands came off then the rest of him would be free. No more eight, ten. Never ten. Only zero. If he could push the steel through his flesh and bones, he would be able to move his arms again, lessen the weight of entrapment that kept his elbows pinned close to his sides. Tiny trails of blood trickled down his wrists, staining his cupped palms and dribbling down onto the beige vinyl of the seat.

"Brud," Jim winced, touching his client's hands to steady them, a startling wave of insignificance radiating from his stomach, making him fear for himself.

The car slowed and pulled flush to the curb.

Brud stared into Jim's eyes and saw the pity resting there. He smiled and tasted the salty fluid of tears that clung to his lips. Brud had not realized that he was crying. Had he been crying all along? For days? Weeks? The tears clung to his lips before breaking loose. Swimming for his chin, they hung momentarily, then dropped against his wrists, diluting the formality of the blood.

"Can't you do something about this?" Jim mumbled, leaning to look at the plain-clothes policeman. "He's cutting his wrists to pieces."

The policeman glanced at the handcuffs. "Better his wrists than us," he said, opening his door. "Come on."

"What's he doing?" asked the driver, turning in his seat.

"Cutting his wrists up with the cuffs." The policeman said, stepping from the car, then leaning back in. "Pulling a getaway." He smiled for Jim's benefit.

"Hold his hands apart if you have to," instructed the driver. "Throw a coat over them when we're going up the steps."

The policeman reached for Brud. Brud felt strong fingers move against his hands, bracing them away from each other. His wrists stung, and he remembered how the horses were held before the brand was burned into their hides. A mark that would make them someone's property. The scorching smell filled his nostrils. He understood the fullness that forced behind the horse's eyes as the brand sunk through the surface. He belonged to someone now. He had been uncovered and marked.

What a mess, Jim thought dismally. He waited for the policeman to guide Brud out, then slid across the seat, leaving by the same door. On his feet, he heard and saw the crowds, the mounting fervour as heads strained for a view, the spite seething and buzzing in the air: harsh grumblings, shrieks of recognition. The families and friends of the victims shook their fists and lashed out with words. They were uncontainable, like addicts withdrawing further into their own images of loss. They were coming down and Brud was the cure, the hit, the forever-after fix of spine-straightening hatefulness.

The killer walked among them, his staunchly silent body moving like a ghost, haunting, invisible to the crowd's shattered eyes. The people shoved in tight to one another, their limbs seeming clotted and tangled. The killer pressed on, savouring the private, intimate sensations of pressure against particular parts of his body.

A second patrol car sped up and stopped in front of the courthouse. Four police officers leapt out to join the others, to contain the crowd that swelled behind the weakening arms of the policemen already stationed there. Swiftly positioned, the new officers felt how the crowd pushed harder, fuelled by the accused's arrival, rebelling against the forces trying to temper their rage. They demanded to act this way. No one would deny their explicit right to collectively express themselves.

It was difficult for the boy to edge through the restless

sea of waists and arms. Reporters battled family members for standing room, and Dogger was fiercely elbowed in the shoulders and head on several occasions. He was searching for the killer. His grip tightening on Joy's hand, he led her through the contorted gestures of the crowd. One thought was in his mind, expanding and compelling him like an hypnotic wave. He must find Pigeon. She had wormed into the people and was lost. Dogger searched for colours, for the fabric of clothes and the blonde hair streaked black. He caught a flash of what he believed to be her body. And then a glimpse of her face, stonelike and drained, set in her belief that permanence meant vacancy. Dogger moved toward her, but then she was gone, ploughing forward.

Furiously shoving at the bodies with his free hand, he made his way closer, sighting her waist, the thick leather belt strapped around her jeans, a flash of the buckle shaped like the liberty bell, the crack. Then turning, disappearing, she was gone, the bodies filling in the hole she was moving through, blocking her from sight.

Joy began to whimper loudly and groan. The crowd was too compulsive. They would turn on her if they saw her eyes, how vulnerable she was, what had been taken away from her. She could not show them she was strong. It was not possible. Mouths shouted close to her ears. She felt a hand touch her in the place where harm lived, down beneath her waist. They would do it again. She tugged backward, trying to free herself. The hands. Her body. It was not hers. They would take it completely.

"Hey," Dogger called back to her. "It's okay," he shouted. But Joy could not hear him. Her eyes were fixed on the faces that swayed around her, watching them change, their skin tightening against the raw curves of bone, resentment, anger, their eyes bleaching grey as if the light inside of them was being clouded by the shallowest of shadows. The malice that had loomed above her, pressing down, shredding what covered her, grabbing and cutting out her tongue. The blade and the unending pricks against her face, nicking and nicking… She whimpered loudly. Savagely tearing free from Dogger's hand, she was drawn backward into the crowd, consumed as her eyes pleaded against memories of violation. Seeing Dogger calling to her, his small face, a child, she touched her belly. Why had they done what they had done to the place where things could no longer live inside of her? She was gone, touched and touched again, until her skin turned rigid and impenetrable.

Dogger knew that it was useless. He had lost her. Turning to glimpse the flitting partial images of Pigeon, he saw how the woman had made it to the edge of the crowd, the steps now before her, her fingers coming out of her pockets, rising, steadying themselves around the sculpted metal, cocking the revolver, her hands joined together in the grimmest form of prayer.

"Then, of course, red is the colour we see when extreme rage overcomes us. And… Hey, I'm not boring you am I? Hey, your full attention, please." Quagmire tapped his fingers against the dashboard. "Listening? Okay, like I was saying, this is the time when we move the fastest, when overcome by rage. We are powerful. Unstoppable. So why a stop colour? Why that?" He flashed his yellow teeth as if to garnish his claim. "Breath mint?" he asked the foreman, offering a roll from his pocket.

"No…I'd appreciate…if…you could drop me…that building there." The foreman sluggishly brushed his hand against the window, smearing the mist. His face had turned a greenish-white. He could barely swallow, his throat feeling as if it was clogged with a wad of sawdust, his fingers weakly pressing against the window lever, but it was jammed.

"Not feeling too good, hey? Stomach problems? How about an antacid tablet?"

"It's the heat." The foreman used the drenched cuff of his sleeve to wipe at his lips, but the salt stung the cracks. "Can you...turn that down a bit?" His eyes lagged toward the heating switch. He appeared as if he had just been woken, rumpled, his hair out of place.

"Of course, why didn't you say so? You're looking a mite bit overheated, a little green around the gills. Forgive me, not quite the time for an evolutionary pun. How about a touch cooked, medium-rare, not crisp enough?"

The foreman allowed his eyelids to slip shut, his chest rising with laboured breaths. But the air remained un-changed, the cab sealed. Fever gripped him, his stomach feeling peculiarly delicate, as if the heat had infected the lining.

"I don't feel too good," he moaned, wavering weakly. He reached for the door handle, but his fingers were wet and slipped, dropping with a thump onto his seat.

"How about a cocktail? A trip for two to the Bahamas? Johnny, tell our friend here all about it." Quagmire smiled steadily, leaning on the steering wheel, ignoring the road, and rocking with the zooming speed of the truck. "Some-times, things just take care of themselves. That's human nature. The way your body feels now, it's taking care of its equilibrium, trying to make itself well, but your mind doesn't like this. It's getting the short end of the stick. It wants out. Sooner or later the mind gets its wish. It says,

'I've had enough of this. I want a divorce.' So they call in the negotiators, like lawyers, and that's me or the other guy. The honest fool. Honest, see. So he has no bargaining power. None of the hot items. No valuables to offer. I'm set up with all the charming stuff. Lust. Greed. Power. He's only got goody-goody tokens. Worthless intangibles that get you nothing. Loyalty. Kindness. Modesty. Good will. So you have to be careful who you sign on with. Our rates are a touch outlandish, sure, okay. I'll accept that. But we provide good service. A lifetime warranty. The eternal plan. In case you haven't already figured, that means forever."

"Can you please…just stop…for a second?" The foreman's eyes fluttered open, then shut. He felt that if he kept them open his stomach would surely open too.

"I'll just pull over," Quagmire announced, treason spicing his smile.

The truck swerved to the side of the road and came to an abrupt stop.

Quagmire watched with glee, his elbows still firmly settled against the rim of the steering wheel.

"Don't take it all too seriously." He winked and slapped the foreman on the back. "This is nothing. Absolutely nothing compared to what's in store for you. It's funny how much importance people place on what they do. If they only knew what life really meant. What it was for. They're proving all the wrong things. What a bunch of incompetents, hey, wild and crazy. Save the earth! Recycle! All that nonsense. Save the earth for what? It's all over soon enough. Nothing's going to last much longer. The game is playing itself out. It makes no difference what they do. They make me laugh. Ha ha."

Leaning back in his seat, Quagmire pushed, with all his

might, against the steering wheel as if to split it open, reveal what was inside. It slowly bent against the strain, a horrendous noise languidly emitting a series of harsh cracking sounds splintering in the foreman's eardrums. Strangely enough the foreman felt the nausea leave him. The colour began to wash into his face. Sweet clarity swept over him as the tendons in Quagmire's neck jittered convulsively, straining to lash away from him.

"I'm...tearing...your soul away," groaned Quagmire.

"What...are...you okay?" the foreman asked, his hand blindly scrambling for the door handle.

"If you push..." Quagmire's voice quivered through his gritted teeth, "...hard. Hard as you can, you'll...feel it." The sounds splintered and snapped faster, as if a tree would soon fall, a forest toppling all at once.

"What?" The foreman found the handle, his sickness now expelled completely, replaced by panic, sharp and disturbing. He punched down the handle.

"You can...almost feel your...soul...tearing...away." Quagmire's face shrunk and crinkled against the strain. "Like...when you scream, you can...almost feel...your ...soul rising...above... When you scream...loud as you... can from...the...inside...from deep...inside... Throw it out. Throw it out. Go on, throw it out of you. Throw it out of you." Quagmire laughed, his lips splitting, his ears cracking and peeling off to plop onto the seat to either side of him and squirm away.

The foreman flung open the door. Leaping clear, he hurried for the sidewalk, scrambling away without look- ing back.

The yellow-toothed man relaxed his grip on the bent wheel. Glancing at the empty seat beside him, a smile rounded his features, filling his face back in. He liked what he saw. Bodies leaving him in a state of turmoil. Humorously picking up his ears, he pressed them back onto the sides of his head.

"Another one scared out of his wits," he chuckled, "by mere party tricks." Leaning toward the open door, he shouted, "Hey, I was only joking." Then he sat back and smiled dismally at the sloppiness of the affair. "No one can take a joke anymore. It's all just doom and gloom."

As always, he found humour in his words. "A good foreman is hard to find," he blurted out between the gasps of laughter. Viciously clicking his teeth shut, he snapped off the cheer. "Sometimes it seems like such a waste. All my special words and the lovely way I weave them all together. No one listening, only wanting. That part they understand. The 'want' part."

The passenger door slammed shut of its own accord and the truck swerved back out into traffic. Quagmire smiled appreciatively at the lovely music, tires screeching and horns blaring incessantly behind him.

"People get angry over the silliest incidents." Quagmire flicked on the heat switch and drew a glorifying fill of stale air into his lungs. "That's what I like to see. Waste. Waste your energy. Dance around. Hoorah, hoorah, siss-boom-bah. This little piggy went to market, this little piggy stayed home, this little piggy ate roast beef, and this little piggy read Jean-Paul Sartre and killed them all."

chapter six

the sound of the wind dying

The killer found his place behind Tumbles. It would be simple; a faultless series of movements would correct the issues at hand. He watched Tumbles's head turn to scan the crowd, his ears pricking up when he saw the car pull up, the people move from inside, the car door slam.

The sun had slipped behind the buildings, turning the air cool and crisp, as if autumn had introduced itself prematurely for a brief visit, its early orange light stretching across the streets.

The killer was amused as he watched Tumbles's hands move into his pockets. He knew what Tumbles's fingers were running over, how his fingertips were stroking the smooth steel like a tempered master calming an anxious pet.

A few quick shots of air pumped from Tumbles's mouth. He shifted on his feet, thinking of leaping and somersaulting forward, landing on the steps and firing the gun instead. Breath snarled out of him, the shells of angry mumblings wanting to be fitted with words, words fusing intention to pulse, thus provoking action. Tumbles smiled courteously at the policeman positioned beside him. He would put a bullet in the cop's head first and then shoot the fool, leap and tumble clear, and be his true self again — silent and gone.

The crowd pushed in tight against his back. The sensation was supportive. They wanted what he wanted. They were with him. Their agitation fuelled his temper, and his eyes flashed wider as the fool took the first step. But, disturbingly enough, the fool hesitated, leaning back from the shrill static of the crowd.

Tumbles's mouth opened to shout, to scream an accusation. His body jerked with the essence of a movement, but the movement and the words were unexpectedly aborted. His eyes blossomed with enlightenment, overcome by an inner sighting, a revelation of true command stiffly focussing his eyes so he could see the sweetly infinite nothing before him, the raging darkness swiftly bounding toward him to snatch him in its jaws. His throat loosened its hold on the words he had wanted to shout and his hands slipped from his pockets, dangling lifelessly as something silvery dropped onto the concrete, scraping and sliding away, leaving him.

The killer stepped from behind Tumbles, yanking out the bloody knife and folding it shut. He turned and shoved away, jostling the crowd that grudgingly opened, then closed to conceal him.

Tumbles dropped to his knees.

"Jesus," he heartlessly whispered, falling sideways.

In moments, the killer was around the corner, striding

with wide certain steps. He dug his fingers along the smooth spaces in his mouth, exploring the holes, reasoning with himself, repeating his pledge. His blood raced freely through his body, his thoughts whirled. He had found greatness, performed a truly marvellous feat. It was good and bad at once. It was perfection. He felt light-headed, walking on clouds. Nothing could stop him. The compelling energy. Another spirit into his hands, claimed, of no other body. His.

Brud took the second step, his body gone rigid, before he was hustled forward by the two policemen. A cool breeze lapped at his skin and he welcomed it and the secret of a promise it contained.

The crowd. He saw how the chilly vengeance splintered in their eyes. The simple mechanics of the single relentless thought.

The policemen shoved at Brud, but he would not move.

"Brud," Jim insisted. "Let's go. Come on, move."

Brud noticed a policeman up on the steps. He was bent on one knee, studying a man's fallen body. The officer turned and shouted words at another policeman, and the crowd pushed harder, screeching, realizing that death was already with them, accepting the new blood and finding immediate fault with Brud. The voices surged, crossing a threshold of sound and containment, graduating into a steady roar.

Brud saw the farm. The cries coming all at once. The animals and the mouths he had looked into. He saw a woman spring through his memory of the farm. Rushing forward onto the steps, unannounced like a scary thought, she raised her hands, joined as if holding something away from herself, wanting to cast it off. Brud saw

Dogger rush to her, grab her stonelike arm. No reaction. The scene clearly played itself out. Brud seemed not to be a part of it at all. It went on without him. The world had taken itself over. He searched for Joy, but she was not there. Brud's chest heaved with regret. It was all his fault. He should have taken care of her long ago. She was gone, crushed further by the crowd. He searched, scanning across the street, and saw her close to a building, her stiff fingers covering her face. Sensing his eyes upon her, his clean compassionate want, her hands dropped away, allowing him to see the blackness of her eyes, the way they had gone out completely. She spit awkwardly onto the street and laughed, showing him her teeth. She punched herself and spit once more, beating off what they had done to her, and done again. Brud said a word. It made no sense, but it seemed to calm her. She stared at him, needing more, but when he lurched in her direction, he was held in check.

Pigeon hurled Dogger away, then levelled her arms again, her hands working, clutching the black steel. The sound of explosion ricochetted through the streets, veering off the buildings and rising. A flash of fire lapped out. Fire, smoke, and noise. There was no time for courage, no time for the policeman to shield Brud's shifting body. Brud simply looked away from Joy, stared down to see what tiny hot things had punched him in the chest, the burning of it growing desperate. His sorry smile was lost in the strange, slow confusion of worry for himself. Another explosion crackled in the air, and his hand was blown by fire, straight through the center, snapped back by something he could not see. The air alive and biting. He spun around and heard the third noise, felt the sharpness of another fiery wad thud into his back.

There was much screeching. Gulls. Brud checked the sky. It went on forever, but it was empty. Perfect silence held everyone as if a brief hurricane of fire had swept through the crowd, leaving their bodies standing there, unoccupied, their wishes frustrated, their spirits blown round and bare like glass. An instant of pity, perhaps, before they rushed for him, snapping loose, kicking and punching, fingers prying as if laying claim to what he had been accused of taking.

Brud stumbled and fell backward onto the steps. Hands were against him. Faces flashed in his eyes, but all in silence. He saw Dogger, the eyeless laughing face of Joy, Jim's mouth opening, shouting silently back over his shoulder. Brud carefully puckered his lips and whistled. He heard the sound, felt the heat of the late sun on his skin, a caribou moving through the trees, the branches and trunks blocking it, but the caribou's bulk there all the same, the heavy antlers delicately balanced on its small fine head, never tipping. The twig snapping sound of its progression through the faltering light made it seem more real than ever. The threat of darkness bringing it to obvious life. Death was a lovely wish.

Brud's whistle was dry, toneless. He blinked and licked his lips. Nothing would come to him in silence like this. Nothing would dare to recognize him.

Then the noise of the traffic rushed into his ears as if someone had cranked up the volume of an enormous radio. Instants later, the sound was readjusted, lower, lower again. Slowly laying down to sleep, hushing the earth, he said, "Shhhhh." The sound of the wind dying.

Quagmire found difficulty in letting go the laughter once it spurred him. His insight into the future made it even more difficult to subdue the humour of how things continuously came apart.

He saw the red light up ahead and eased his foot onto the brake, bringing the truck to a stop at the intersection. The courthouse was only four buildings beyond the traffic lights. A siren wailed abruptly. Red strobes flashed, their tone reflecting onto his face from the rearview mirror.

"The stop colour gone berserk," he observed, nodding with assurance. He glanced at the ambulance three cars back. "I'm confused. You can see why." Studying his eyes in the mirror, he questioned himself. "You see, Mr. Quagmire?" "Yes," he answered. "I thought I was someone special." "Forget it." "I believed that what I did mattered." "Don't be an imbecile." "I wanted to make the world a better place to live in." "Yes!"

He took a deep breath, then gave voice to the perpetually conflicting thoughts that had driven him from good grace and into his present line of work. "Then walk on your knees in prayer for five miles, swim in the arms of the beggar children who die with their stomachs bloated by hunger clawing inside like rats' teeth lashing in a blur, sleep with the battered woman who huddles her three infants on the streets that flow with whores, junkies coughing up and stricken by a country with its head stuck in the brightly packaged greed box of depthless satisfaction, each of them shivering for what they do not understand. Death is the only limb of the true one-armed law. It holds the weapon, and righteousness makes it swing its cruel sword." He wagged a finger at his reflection. "Don't be such a hypocrite young man, buy your car, fill your house with extravagant shapes of nothingness, swallow your gold-plated stereos, and inhale your fast food, and

die and die and die. You eat the steaming flesh of the famished and the damned each time you raise your fork. Remember that, always. Recall the meaty taste. Each bite,
and the suck-hole of a baby shuts forever. The guilty
weight of apathy shifts in your soul. I am alive because of
you, and when the time comes I will chew you along your
throat until your head drops off, suck on the luscious jelly
of your brains, and pride myself in your careless, self-centered work, because you have made me so positively
happy."

Rolling through the intersection, Quagmire was thrilled
by how closely the ambulance sped by his side. Sound
and colour flaring. Up ahead, the vehicle bucked to a stop.
Both doors swung open and two paramedics leapt out.

Quagmire sneered and defiantly shook his head. "What
for?" he whispered. "Why waste all that energy? Sooner
or later it leaks out of you. Why this narcissistic buffer
zone called medicine? Why not end the charade?"

A horn blared behind him, signalling to speed up. He
glanced back in the rearview mirror with a sharp censur-
ing stare, and the sound of the horn died off like a cry
being strangled, hoarsely shivering, until it squawked.

Quagmire saw his target up ahead; the woman he had
seen during the fire at the hospital. The wife of the lawyer. He recalled the promise he had made to her, knowing then that he would see her later. Her death would
crush her husband's resolve, make it easier for Quagmire
to secure the land. Then the lawyer would be less likely to
interfere. He would gladly provide the necessary signature, urge the fool to sign over the property. He would be
disillusioned, finally, and why not? Only those pumped-
up with a sense of false worth deny the inevitable. The
lawyer would see it his way. Quagmire knew that Brud

had been shot. It had been an eventuality, part of the plan, the pandemonium confirming his suspicions. And if the fool was finally dead, (dead and dead again), then the final signature would be provided by the lawyer. Clean and without dispute.

Andrea stood in the center of the street, cocooned in a dreamlike trance as she watched the stretcher and her husband following alongside as Brud was wheeled away. She spoke into her recorder, numbly describing what was happening, referring to her husband as "the accused's lawyer," then as "Jimmy," fear slurring fact with emotion.

The stretcher made its way across the asphalt and was lifted into the ambulance. Jim jumped in, and the doors were slammed shut. The paramedics raced toward the front of the vehicle.

Andrea remained in the center of the street. She could not find the words as the ambulance raced off. Below the fading wail of the sirens, she could hear a tiny squeaky wheel turning inside her recorder. She should say something, find an ending. Her mind raced like the ambulance, but, unlike the vehicle, her thoughts lacked purpose and direction. Her legs felt rigid as if her skin was stitched around lead.

The pickup truck raced toward her. She saw the presence gorging closer in the corner of her eye. The yellow-toothed man roared behind the windshield, welcoming the quickening future, pairing it perfectly with the images he had imagined. Symmetry coming to fruition. His hands pressed fiercely against the wheel, his foot stomping harder, pinning the accelerator.

"See you later, alligator." The lights on the dashboard flared red. Oil light. Temperature. Gas. All functions overheated, mercilessly drained. "Go," he said.

The metal sledged against Andrea's knees, then crushed her waist, driving her hands into the sky, her head lifting higher, sideways, her body tumbling, a sightless blur of noise and smeared flashes of colour, until her open hands aimed for the earth again, slapping the pavement first, quickly followed by the rumpled air-popping thud of heavier flesh landing.

The pickup swerved toward the side of the road, crashing into an empty patrol car with the easy bending and grating sound of metal collapsing as glass popped like the jingling of a rammed chandelier.

A policeman rushed for Andrea. Another ran toward the pickup. Pulling at the door with both hands, the policeman found that it was stuck. A second officer joined him and they both tugged vigorously, one getting in the way of the other. The driver's window was shattered, like a web simply hanging in place. A fireman arrived with an axe, chopping at the handle until the steel could be pried open with a crowbar.

One of the policemen leaned into the empty cab, checking the floor, then searching down into the space behind the seat. He glanced back at his partner. "There's no one in here," he said. "Where the hell did he go?" Coughing to clear his throat, he instructed the fireman, "Check around here. Maybe he was thrown from the vehicle."

The fireman and the second officer stared at the windshield. It was hanging loose, but still intact. The fireman moved around to the passenger side and checked the window. It was unshattered.

"Thrown through where?" called the fireman.

Quagmire inhaled the deliciously fragrant mist of the woman's pain. With a shivering, euphoric breath, he blew out what was left and closed his eyes. His face cringed soothingly beneath the woman's perishing skin. He urged her bloodstream to slow. The blood thickening like a churned up river, the sediment rising. Sludge. A stick in the mud. Quagmire smiled marvellously. This was a serious thing. *A little respect, please*, he insisted, lying there, breathing against the ground, enjoying the gritty smell of asphalt until each twitch and flickering nerve expired and he had supped upon the absolute pleasure of her pain. He felt himself rising as Andrea was turned and lifted onto a stretcher. "The party's over," he whispered, using her lips. A good joke on the paramedic watching the woman's face. Another unexplained phenomenon for the tabloids. Keep their minds cheap and flabby and they will believe anything. They will be easily swayed by falsehoods. The paramedic flinched at the sight of the moving lips that growled out several words. His skin turned pale. He almost slid the stretcher into a parked car.

Among the crowd, a man appeared, stepping freely and handing out business cards. Quagmire Construction. *A magnificent opportunity*, he assured himself. A gathering of potential customers. His smile was warm and welcoming, but the yellow teeth betrayed him. One indignant man tore the business card into shreds and threw it back at Quagmire.

"Lousy scavenger," the man shouted roughly.

Quagmire turned on the man, his smile unpeeling, ripping back from his face. Something was coming. Boiling in his mouth. He hawked and worked the spittle with his tongue, shaping it into a black glass candy. Crunching it between his teeth, he then spit the slivers into the man's eyes.

The man screamed harshly, covering his face as blood seeped from between his fingers.

"Yes," Quagmire confirmed, nodding clinically at the man's screams, "Um-hmm. We handle renovation work. Reconstruction. Deconstruction. That sort of thing. Plastic surgery. Get it. Plastic. Anything from that invincible plastic. Lasts even longer than the flesh. Not a worry in the world. My workers are well trained in such projects." Dropping to his knees as if in demonstration, he closed his hands into fists and pressed all knuckles against the asphalt, his voice rising from the melodious stream of bone-snappings, melding like a vibrating belch, "You have my word."

chapter seven

a lovely insane evening

The random punch of bullets popping through Brud's clothes replayed itself in Dogger's mind. The memory was fresh and would not leave him. He noticed the dusk slowly shading the streets and shivered at his lost sense of security. The future. Support. Streetlamps began to flicker on. Dogger stared up at one and let the light slip out of focus. He was thinking, moving away from himself, wondering what was happening in the back of the ambulance.

Joy stood away from Dogger. She understood the sorrow, the cutting ache, as if something black and wet had been spliced inside. She heard the cawing in her head, remembering The Crows, their need to belong inappropriately coupled with their birthright to be unique. The youthful disparity. And now this. Brud. Her emotions changing again. She laughed sadly and slapped herself across the face. She had been deeply affected by the crowd's gnashing and nattering of teeth. She understood now the necessity for flight from these people, flight from the world. Her disappearance. The only things keeping her from falling away were Dogger's kindness and her hopes of being one with Brud. She forced herself to laugh again, but the sound was quiet. Thinking of Brud, her eyes depthlessly reflected vague glimmerings of trust.

A tall policeman stood at Dogger's side, flipping shut his large hardcovered note pad and leaning against the door of his patrol car. Offering a sympathetic smile, he said, "You did more than anyone else. That's good to see for a change. Why don't you take this as a starting point and stay off the streets, Dogger?"

"He's not a murderer," Dogger said, the anger of his tone tightening the muscles in his small body. His stomach was swelling with wrongful thoughts, tempting the tears that threatened to rise. "I saw what happened. He's innocent and...look, look at him. It wasn't his fault. They did him."

The policeman tossed his notepad in through the open window. "Innocent how?"

"I was there," he shouted. "Didn't you hear?"

The policeman crouched, eye to eye with Dogger, "Take it easy, okay. Pipe down." Then he nodded. "Go on."

"I led him into an alley." The boy was forced to stop. His teeth were chattering, his lips turning blue with the chill of dreadful truth. Heavy tears rolled down his cheeks. For the first time, he felt truly abandoned.

"It's okay, go on, Dogger."

Dogger opened his mouth. A sob broke loose. He took a deep breath, not looking at the policeman. "If I didn't take him there, then Skully would've hurt me, like he always did when I wouldn't go along with his scams. I just

339

like bumming money." His small back bent forward, and he continued staring at the ground. "And what was I supposed to do?" Finally he glared, with wet eyes, at the policeman. "Who looks after me? Hey?" Shoving the officer, he shouted, "Get away from me." The policeman rocked back on his heels, bracing one hand against the asphalt.

"Dogger!" he warned. "Calm, alright. Just cut it out. I know what Skully's like. Who'd you think you're talking to?"

"Yeah, you know alright. Nothing about it."

The policeman stood straight and tall on his feet. He knew Dogger was right and did not like the feel of it. "You'll have to come for a ride. We'll need a statement."

The boy wiped at his eyes, drawing a deep quivering breath, facing himself.

"Okay," he said, compromising. "Just this once though."

"Then I'll take you over to the hospital to see your pal."

"Take me to the hospital first," Dogger demanded. "Or I'm not saying another word. I mean it."

"Yeah, yeah. Okay. Come on."

Joy slipped her hands into the back pockets of her black denims and turned to follow Dogger into the car. From far away, she could hear the sound of the ambulance. It faded past her ears like the percussions from a dream, still lingering there. She closed her eyes, opened them. It was the same. She found no division between herself and the world. She was not sure if she wanted to.

I am awake, she told herself, her voice too loud inside her head, a thousand tongues flapping. *No, I only think I am.*

"My goodness! What has been happening here?" Detective Peach watched a covered stretcher rolling along the pavement, a blanket strapped over the body. "It's just a mess. Look, that one there. What happened to that one?" Indignantly he flared his nostrils and pointed with his fingers.

"Hit by a truck. Journalist," confirmed the rookie police officer. He gestured toward the pickup, its front end being hoisted by a tow truck. "There was no one inside when we opened the door." The rookie straightened his hat. It looked too big for his small head.

Detective Peach coughed and tilted his head as he swallowed. He glanced at the rookie, then pulled a handkerchief from his back pocket and carefully dabbed at his mouth. Finished with the handkerchief, he folded it into a succession of smaller and smaller squares, then slipped it into the front pocket of his suit jacket. He turned around to gaze up the steps of the courthouse.

"And what about that gentleman up there?" the detective asked. "I know that gentleman. I can recognize him from way down here."

The rookie shrugged his shoulders.

Inspecting the rookie's hands, Peach saw that the sleeves of the man's uniform jacket were too long. The detective decided that he detested the officer's sloppy manner.

"What happened with that one?" Pointing to make it as plain as possible for the rookie, the detective snapped, "Up, up. Look. Up there."

"He was stabbed. No witnesses. The crowd was going crazy." The rookie used his hands and arms to make elaborate swirls in the air. Watching the movements, Peach squinted, thinking. The rookie continued, "We had our hands full just trying to keep them from rioting."

Detective Peach smiled sarcastically. "Is that so? Your hands were full. I bet they were."

The rookie shrugged, the big shoulders of his jacket moving loosely.

The detective thought he would scream. "Do you have a problem with your shoulders? Do they pain you in some way? Are they stiff?"

"No."

"Hmmm." Peach stared at the rookie's shirt, then at his plain tie, dismissing what he was about to say. He turned and walked up the steps toward the man's body. The ambulance attendants stepped back, clearing a space for the detective to inspect the scene. Kneeling, he carefully searched the open eyes.

"Hello, Tumbles," he said. He spoke to himself, saying a brief prayer, before he stood, meticulously brushing the dust from his trousers with the backs of his fingers.

The rookie took the steps slowly, pausing on each one, uncertain if he should join his superior.

"Okay," Peach informed the attendants. "That's fine."

"You know him?" the rookie called, one foot up on a higher step.

The detective rolled his eyes. "Yes," he said, stepping down. "Do you have to shout, always?"

"Sorry, sir," he whispered. "You know him?"

"Yes, I do know him. And you should know him as well." Fingering his receding hairline, Peach shook his head and strolled past the rookie. He thought, *Relief, relief. It won't be long now. The sunny beach. Hard, tanned bodies*.

The young officer watched the body being sealed in the black rubber bag. He felt the clammy sweat tickling his palms and wiped them against his pant legs, then turned to follow the detective.

"I apologize for not recognizing the body, sir."

"Oh, please," said Peach waving a hand in the air. He

sneezed and stopped, casting an irritated glance at the rookie. "I do believe I am allergic to you."

Standing shorter than his superior, the rookie walked closely behind and studied the detective's thinning hair, noticing how the blond was turning grey.

The detective, sensing the proximity, came to an abrupt stop and spun around.

"Why are you following me?" he snapped, needing to straighten his glasses. "Are you lonely or something?"

The rookie was petrified, leaning awkwardly in a lurch. He had been walking so near that when the detective stopped he had to hold himself in order to avoid collision.

"I thought you might require my services, sir."

Peach looked him up and down. He tried to be serious, but the smirk came regardless. He sucked in his cheeks and forced himself to look at the Quagmire tow truck moving off with the pickup secured behind.

"Let me ask you a practical question."

"Yes, sir."

"Do you have a make on those licence plates yet?"

"They're not registered, sir."

"Not registered? Just fine."

"There's nothing on file for that sequence. The file comes up blank on the computer. They told me over the radio."

"Hmmm." Peach searched the area, his fingers meshed together and hanging in front of his waist. "What are we into here?"

The rookie shrugged his shoulders.

"You better stop that," the detective warned, pointing at the rookie's chest. "I will not tell you again. I will not." Peach squinted meanly at the rookie's eager form. He had to bite hard into his lower lip to hold back a smile. "Do you hear me?" he asked, his high cheekbones rounding out and rising higher with amusement. He coughed and covered his mouth, flicking his head away.

"Sorry, sir."

Regaining his composure, Detective Peach set out the obvious instructions. "I want that car stripped down. Completely. Anything we find, matchbooks, bar wrappers... Analyze dirt samples. This is important. Very, very important. I am convinced, absolutely, that this is something much bigger than meets the eye."

"I see, sir."

"I have this feeling."

"I've heard, sir." The rookie nodded.

"What?"

"About your intuition, sir?" Blushing terribly, the young officer scrambled for words. "I meant nothing."

"And what about this woman who fired the gun? Wounded the accused?"

"She's been brought to the station for questioning, sir." The rookie would not meet eyes with the detective now. He stared straight ahead, his head perfectly level. "We think that the dead man up there and the woman might've been partners in crime, sir."

"Really, partners in crime?" Peach bit his lip again, but this time only the corner. He fingered his scalp, then joined his hands, holding them in front of himself as he rocked slightly on his heels. "How so?"

"The guy on the steps had a gun and a knife in his pockets, too, sir. Maybe they were there to do the same job."

"You just may be right, and proudly so. But let me give you a little lesson in the history of this big bad city of ours. The dead gentleman who they just lifted from those steps goes by the name Tumbles. A very good friend of his, an associate, or, let's say, a partner in crime for many years, was a man who went by the name of Skully. Skully was stabbed not too many moons ago in an alleyway. Any recollections? Tooth fairy murders, et cetera."

The rookie nodded distinctly. "Yes, sir. Very much."

"The man going to trial here today was the man accused of killing Skully." The detective held his arms out and turned over his hands, neatly displaying his palms. Bending slightly at the knees, he said, "You see. It's so simple." He cleverly clapped his hands together, and squealed with mock delight.

"Revenge, sir."

"Ahhhh, yes." Peach patted the rookie's arm in a reassuring manner. "Very good."

"But what about the girl?"

"I have not seen the girl, if you recall."

"Yes, sir."

"I came after all the festivities. But I am fairly certain she is Tumbles's sister and Skully's girlfriend. Skinny woman? Blonde hair like straw? Mean eyes? Scowl mark down the center of her forehead? Sloppy dresser? Jeans, that sort of ludicrous past tense outfit."

"Yes, sir."

"But that could be anyone these days." He smiled at the rookie, humouring him. "Am I right? A crass person is a crass person."

"Yes, sir."

"So there." Peach walked away, wondering about the truck, the dead journalist, and another thing. He was about to name it when the rookie called after him.

"But, sir?"

"Yes?" He turned on his heels. "Who killed this Tumbles character?"

"Now," The detective licked his lips and tilted his head slightly up to the side. Gently touching his cheek, he paused, certain to make his point, "That's a fine question. And what about that mystery pickup truck and the dead journalist?" He left the young officer hanging. Turning away, he headed for his low orange sports car. With his back to the rookie, he called, "Figure that out for me, if you will. That's your very own little mystery to keep you up at night." He spun around and offered a tempting smile. "I'll be on the beach by tomorrow afternoon. Lovely drinks with little umbrellas in them. Far, far away. Wish me bon voyage." He wiggled his fingers, then blew the rookie a kiss.

Quagmire stood up on a set of concrete stairs two blocks from the scene watching a second ambulance whiz past. The lights were on inside and he saw that the stretcher was covered, the woman's face barely visible, scraped and torn down the side. A flash of movement, a picture in his head. He smiled at how he held the images. Magic. That was his invention. Each person's vast capacity for memories. Anguish. Regret.

"Must've been a chain reaction," the killer commented, speaking up from the sidewalk. "*Who's* killing whom?"

"Without question," confirmed Quagmire. "We should write the book. A who's who on the topic." He took his time moving down the steps. "No doubt, it would be a bestseller."

Cheerily coming face to face, they studied each other's mouths, then quickly laughed in unison. Passers-by on the street glanced at them with plain curiosity, before hurrying their pace. A sour odour lingered around them, the mingling scent of damp, rotting wood and sun-dried meat.

"What a lovely insane evening," Quagmire commented breezily. "Can I offer you a lift? My coach is just ahead."

"I'm not *going* anywhere," said the killer, pressing his fingers into the flesh along his own arm, feeling for what was concealed beneath the surface, the bony framework. "I won't be tricked by this."

"Neither will I," announced Quagmire, taking the disgruntled cue. "So join me."

The killer agreed, relishing the idea of companionship, and they stepped around the corner. The light from the streetlamp shone against the new pickup truck, softening its appearance. The doors opened soundlessly and they climbed in.

"How's business? *These* days, I mean?"

"Non-stop." Quagmire flicked on the heat switch. "Every day, more and more contracts. It is a time of great renovations, the doing up of the old. Phenomenal money there. I'm waiting on one of the biggest contracts now."

"What's that? More towers poking holes through the sky? Show them who's boss. *Show* them."

"This one, what all of this was about tonight. The simpleton's farm. The big hole that needs filling."

"The man who *would* be me."

"Yes, a fine job. You took perfect care of that Tumbles fellow, but that girl. I hadn't taken her into account. What was her motive? No, don't tell me. Let me guess. Ah, yes. Love. That's right. It keeps sticking its ugly little head into my lovely portrait, just before the flash goes off. I keep forgetting about that one, what it does to people."

"You'll get your signature," the killer greedily professed.

"No doubt. Doubt is *nothing*. I chew it. The man who would be me is alive. I saw him go by in the first ambulance. He was *awake*. I saw him." Pinching his temples, he breathed evenly, deeply, filling himself with the will to live.

"One little signature," Quagmire commented, becoming gravely serious. "If the simpleton dies, the property is transferred to the lawyer. That lawyer's the sensitive type. I know about him, dealt with him before, other projects. That's why I destroyed his wife. That will weaken him, crush him, make it easier to secure the signature. There'll be nothing left of him but subservience." Quagmire's face washed grey and gloomy with the thought. "The man has my down payment. What more does he want? Doesn't a down payment mean anything any more? I know the economy's a little shaky. Inflation. Recession. Always one or the other, and don't get me wrong — all wonderful stuff indeed — but what's happening to people's values? Morals? It makes a person think twice about feeling at peace with oneself." Viciously slapping the killer's leg, he whooped with laughter. But the killer was not smiling. He was remembering the blood. Its wealth. Its black-red richness and how it stuck to his hands, how it bonded him to such sinister beliefs in division. Another body dead, but the killer so alive and savouring this confirmation.

"You did your job well," said Quagmire. "But I was counting on Dogger to stop the woman. Yes, I did think of it. I was just fooling you about the 'love' part. I know how you feel about it. No hard feelings, though. I'm completely in line with your thinking. Don't get me wrong. Love's everything you always speak of. A festering little brew of trickery."

"Feeding off the *good* of others?" the killer scolded with a hunger in his voice. "That's just like you. Almost truly *you*, in fact."

"That's the elite, most delicious, variety of manipulation." Quagmire leaned on the steering wheel. His eyes shadowed black, rounding out like tarry shells. He opened his mouth to show how his whorish tongue aroused the words, "No doubt — and I claim this as truth — it is quite conceivable to successfully employ goodness as a means of prompting the accomplishment of evil."

chapter eight

a batch of shy red roses

Brud was flying again, gliding through the hospital as if held by the stream of a powerful, soundless current. A surface beneath him softly sustained his body, and he thought of how Joy's body would feel like this. Lying atop her, and Joy flying, taking Brud up above the streets, into the sky that opened for them. He knew how she would soon leave the ground. The decision was in her eyes.

The front of the gurney hit two swinging doors and Brud was through, the doors flapping closed behind all the people who moved with him. Quickly, faster, and he was stopped in the big room beneath a cluster of bright lights. The people wore light-green masks and moved swiftly around large pieces of equipment. They surrounded Brud, seeming anxious to uncover the things that they had lost, things that seemed to be inside of

Brud. They spoke fast, abrupt words, and tools were passed from hand to hand. Dipping down, they came back coloured red.

Shards of metal gleamed in the surgical lamps like sunlight glistening off the feathers of a great metallic bird, hovering high, flesh beneath the armour, a man in there, bargaining with appearance. The beak opened, and a beeping sound filled the room. Brud looked toward the sound to see a machine chirping. An uneven line rose and fell on the screen. It was a small television — like the one back at the apartment — tracing the crazy flight of the uncloaked bird.

One of the masked people pulled a tube from Brud's hand and fastened another. Brud opened his mouth to try and tell them that he did not like to have things put inside of him, to be changed, but his jaw was weakened as a crystal rush of whiteness frosted over his vision like frozen rain tapping his skin in one quick rush.

The masked people dug inside. He wondered what they were looking for, what they would leave there. Perhaps they were checking him, inspecting his insides for signs of goodness. Perhaps this was part of the judgement, too. It seemed to go on and on. He was confident. He would prove himself. His colour was good, but he was concerned as to when the judgement would finally end. White plastic hands moved through sharpening air. Nothing shattered. Unconsciousness slipped its sparkling white blanket on top of, and then through, Brud's skin. He could not feel how the knives were cutting him, how his skin was opening everywhere. He thought of the flowers for Pretty. He had watched them open when they hit the ground, unfolding as if sighing. His skin felt that way now, his wounds yawning gorgeously, like a batch of shy red roses.

"Elevators give *me* the creeps," the killer announced, stepping out onto the hospital floor. He glanced back into the lift, waiting for Quagmire to follow. "Moving you around like that. I have dreams. Moving the wrong way. Sideways instead of up and down."

"Forget your dreams," scowled Quagmire. "Don't be such a baby."

"*Hospitals* give me the creeps," the killer further disclosed. "Moving the wrong way, everything shifting against the *obvious*. That's how tragedy is. It may not be so obvious, but it's hyper-real. Nothing's as real as this place. It's the limbo. Here and now. *This* place. *This* planet. Right where I stand." He pointed at his feet.

The elevator doors slid shut behind Quagmire.

"Nonsense," he said dismissively. "Just think of it as an expensive hotel. Room service. A limb here, an organ there. A few bags of blood, water, and sugar. Medication. Pain killers." He flicked the killer's chest with the back of his fingers. "You should know about that, being one yourself."

The killer laughed and wiped at his mouth, "Pain killer."

"The basics. The very essence of room service. Keeping you going for a while longer, sustaining you. These people are the truly famished."

"You've got a way with words, you know that?"

"Only one way."

"*Many* ways." The killer winked one eye, then the other. Reaching into his mouth, he wiggled a loose tooth.

"It's the words that sway people. An adequate command of the English language ensures monumental conquests."

The killer went over to the waste bin hanging from the wall of the reception area. Secretly reaching into his pocket, he dumped the blood-stained knife through the hole. He had forgotten about the blade, but upon entering the building was spurred by the weight and memory of its presence.

"A proper place to rid oneself of surgical instruments. A wise choice, my friend. You piece it together nicely."

The killer's eyes darted around the reception area. Several people blankly stared at the floors and walls, while others wept openly. Two nurses at the main station appeared preoccupied, discussing patient charts. The killer caught sight of Dogger and the tall policeman sitting at the other end of the high-ceilinged room. His fingers jerked into his mouth, searching the empty spaces, attempting to discover solutions. He felt nervous when he saw Joy. She was standing against the wall, hands joined behind her back as if anticipating the blindfold, her executioner.

"I have *arrived*." The killer smiled. He sucked on a finger, then pulled it from his mouth with a wet popping sound. "I have it for you," he whispered, longing for Joy to hear.

"The kid looks so worried," observed Quagmire, eyes narrowing jealously at the sight of Dogger's concern.

"That's my boy," said the killer.

"A shame he doesn't follow in your footsteps."

Pushing his lower jaw forward, the killer frowned and glared with his sunken eyes.

"You think you would have taught him better."

"What's *better*?" the killer bluntly asked. "What's that? Which way?"

"You know what I mean. Better meaning worse."

Quagmire grinned as he gripped the killer's arm. Tightening his hold, he was pleased by how the killer's fingers shot back to his mouth, finding comfort in probing the empty spaces. *Like a spring*, thought Quagmire. *So automatic*.

"Do cops give you the creeps, too?"

"No," the killer firmly mumbled, shaking his head in quick denial. "They are the creeps that creep around under my skin."

"Then let's go say hello to your boy. You can keep them distracted while I do my job."

The doctor tapped a pen against the side of his thumb. "I'm sorry," he said. The charge of lightness that filled Jim's body paralysed him with a swelling sense of dislocation. His knees went weak and his stomach ached as if someone had bitten into it. It appeared to be so. He could sense the throbbing, the bruise of teeth marks. Claiming the floor with his eyes, not wanting to face the words, he snubbed this most horrible intimacy. Death.

The doctor watched, unconsciously tapping the pen and studying the grief on Jim's face as if ranking it on a clinical scale.

"She was dead on arrival. There was nothing we could do." Glancing overhead, he listened to the name of a doctor paged to I.C.U., then the corridors were silent again. He noticed the pen in his hand, and slid it away, into the pocket of his green O.R. fatigues. "She didn't suffer. If that's any consolation. I'm very sorry."

Jim thought, *She was right behind us, in the other ambulance, and I didn't even realize*. Before he knew what he was doing, he was sitting back on a padded chair. Emotionally, he felt ravaged and ashamed that he could not find tears for his wife. *My wife*, he told himself, but he could not cry. Jim thought, *They rolled her right past me. My wife. My dead wife*. The pain was confounding, but the tears remained distant.

"I'm sorry," the doctor said helplessly. "Do you want us to call someone?"

"No." Jim continued watching the floor. He could look no other place. He shook his head, his bones feeling as if they would collapse to dust, leaving only his empty, unsupported skin to flop sideways. "I'm fine," he numbly insisted, hearing his own voice. Hating it.

"You're welcome to lie down on one of our beds."

"No." A wave of angry dejection introduced itself, mounting frustration filling him with hatred for this doctor. If anyone was to blame, it was this man, this mock healer, this bearer of bad news. "Just leave me alone," he snapped.

The doctor blankly watched Jim. He had seen such reactions before, yet he could not help but feel slightly offended. Absent-mindedly wetting his lips, he thought of the counsellor on duty. He would call her. No, this man needed a male counsellor. The doctor turned and silently walked away to make the outside call.

For an instant, Jim thought that Andrea was there. Her voice. He heard it talking to him. Glancing up, he sighted a nurse speaking, but she was not speaking. She had finished. The nurse spoke again, and he listened to her voice, so much like Andrea's, the unnerving quality of it. He was uninterested in the words. And she was smiling kindly. How could she? He despised the presence of this woman more than anything.

It was impossible to tell if it was day or night; the reception area of the hospital was windowless, and the sterile brightness of the lights remained constant. The clock seemed stripped completely of meaning. It simply went around.

The tall policeman had taken Dogger's statement in the reception area and had left the building, having been called away on duty. He knew where to find Dogger should he need the boy again. Lives on the streets were connected by word of mouth. It formed its own community, a network of eyes that saw everything, and remembered.

Before the policeman had left, the killer stepped forward, announcing his relationship to Dogger. The policeman knew of the connection. It was the only thing that had kept him from taking Dogger off the streets and setting him up in a foster home. The father would never fail to appear at the hearings, seeming composed and responsible. He was not an alcoholic or violent toward the boy. It was what Dogger wanted, and so his father helped him this way. Dogger feared what he thought would be a fake family. He did not realize how a family was something a boy grew into, fitting into the love that the parents held for him, until the child was conceived again, from inside, from the heart.

Jim stood at the reception desk, buried in the air, deadened and forced back into a daze. He was distressed by the sight of Quagmire's presence in the waiting area. There was something inappropriate about that man. He was out of place, yet appearing casual and completely at home.

"Mr. Kelly," Quagmire called, standing from his seat to stroll across the tile. He offered his condolences, loud enough for everyone to hear. "Sorry about your wife."

Jim could not find words, the confirmation of his wife's

death by another person further consuming him. He wondered who had informed Quagmire. How did he know?

"Word travels fast," said Quagmire, sensing the baffled indignation in Jim's face. He smiled, and the smile was ugly and vile, slick with obvious want. "I can understand your remorse. I truly can."

"What're you doing here?" Jim was overcome by the outrageous thought of Quagmire venturing to the hospital for the purpose of business.

"I've lost many people who were close to me. I think of it as my duty to come to those who need assistance. To help out. Offer a hand. I have a police radio in my vehicle. I listen. This woman just happened to be your wife. A lucky coincidence."

Lucky! thought Jim, turning away to wander back to his seat. He needed to get off his feet. Quagmire's presence had made everything seem intensely unreal. He felt faint as he sat, forcing himself to think of leaving the hospital, but he could not imagine where he would go. *My wife is here. She is here,* he told himself. *Forever.* The idea of returning to the empty apartment inspired feelings of nausea and isolation. He stared at his hands. They did not seem to be his at all. They were so plain, so starkly disconnected from his eyes, from his thoughts. Observing his fingers, he remembered Brud, another person he was sure to lose.

Quagmire leaned forward to pat Jim's shoulder. "It'll be alright. You'll be with her one day. That's the only reward for your pain." Bending closer, Quagmire reached into his pocket for the killer's knife he had recovered from the garbage bin, knowing it would be put to use. He felt its leaden weight with his fingers, and held it concealed in his hand. Stooping closer to smile compassionately, he casually dropped the knife into Jim's suit pocket. "There, there," he professed, patting Jim's arm.

"What're you really doing here, Quagmire?"

"Hey, Mr. Kelly." Quagmire straightened and took a disappointed step back, his voice filled with fabricated hurt. "Is that any way to talk to an old business associate?"

"Business. Just leave me alone, okay?" Jim stared at the floor again. *Why did this have to happen*? he asked himself. *Why did this happen to me? What have I done to deserve it*?

Quagmire smiled. "I saw the whole thing. I saw the circus. The fool getting shot. Your wife. Because of him. Because she was there. That's why she died. For the fool."

Jim glared up and sprang to his feet, grossly aware of his stiffening limbs.

"Hit and run."

"What about my wife?" Jim warned, taking a step closer, face to face with Quagmire. "You tell me. Now." Snatching hold of Quagmire's coat, he savagely shook the man. "Tell me."

"Relax, okay, Jimmy. Your hands, get them off me."

Jim flicked his hands away.

"I saw the man in the truck. I know who he is. A foreman of mine. He was drunk. A mean pitiful cripple of a man. Sadistic type. Did it for a laugh. Can you imagine? I have his address. He's probably home now, treasuring his memory of the way your wife flew into the air. He's a bad man. Not crazy, just bad."

Jim's face flushed red. "Who is he?"

"A little business first."

"What business?"

"One tiny signature. You're the fool's lawyer. You have power of attorney. Am I right? In a situation such as this."

Jim fumed away from Quagmire. Further up the corridor, he then turned and looked back. He felt his jaw clamping tighter, his teeth grinding. Quagmire's lone dark figure disturbed the clarity of the air, somehow staining it, as if the blackness of his long coat was leaking away.

"I have the papers. Here," he called, pulling them from his pocket and waving them above his head. "One little signature." Quagmire thought of the knife in the lawyer's pocket. The address of his foreman. It would work out wonderfully, each injustice coming together to conclude in flawless confusion. After he killed the foreman, the lawyer would be charged with two murders. He had been at the scene of the first and possessed the murder weapon. Possession. Evidence. Motive. Being an honourable sort, with an ethical code of conduct, the lawyer would turn himself in. *Of course he would*, Quagmire assured himself. The lawyer was that disgustingly virtuous type.

Jim could not remember moving. He only recalled snatching the papers from Quagmire's hands. Rushing his body to get where he was standing, he called to a nurse who politely handed him a pen. Jim signed the paper with great bravado, and when Quagmire lifted it away, beaming and searching for the signature, he was not amused by the vulgar words of dismissal scrawled across the page.

"That's what I think of you," Jim announced, giving Quagmire a shove that sent him stumbling back.

Joy stood with her hands against the window, gazing down into the operating room. The descending space between her and the doctors was strained by the pull of gravity. Behind her, rows of empty observation seats lifted on an incline, leaving her with an impression of bareness against her back. Below the large window, the masked people diligently moved their limbs and bodies. Brud was open and red, and Joy saw his insides. She wanted to fit him back together, make him well. Her attention was drawn toward the screen with the fluttering line that seemed so unsure of itself.

She could see Brud's uncovered heart. It was full and beating, the grouping of overhead lights blaring down on its jerking, glistening movements.

Sliding her hands in slow circles across the glass, she remembered when her body had lain in such a room, when they had sewn up the place where her tongue had been. The memory of the steady excruciating pain made her mouth salivate, as if she had bitten into her tongue with all of her teeth and was still biting through as hard as possible. There was nothing left to move around in her mouth. Her mouth was hollow. Words were of no use to her now. They were only spoken as a means of manipulation. She would not use them again.

Brud's blood was such a pretty colour. Joy had never seen blood like this before. It looked sweet and thick as syrup. She remembered and watched, seeing herself down there on the table, aware of the scars on her body where she had been cut, the needles sewing up her face, but the face gone now. *Forget*, she tried to say, the stub of her tongue twitching with the trite recklessness of the word.

A masked face glanced harshly to the side, and the surgeon opened his hand for a surgical instrument. The green fabric of the mask crinkled along a horizontal line with the movement of the surgeon's mouth. The O.R. nurse had hesitated. The instrument was large and appeared to be the wrong choice, but it was offered regardless. Accepting the tool, the masked face smiled behind the fabric, the smile stretching, the mask sucking in against the teeth that made it wet.

Joy's hands continued circling the glass, the rhythm quickening, stirred by uncertainty, by the impression that certain matters were out of order. She somehow accepted the familiarity of this man: the yellowish-white eyes dotted black in the centers, the twisted yellowish-white face that once loomed above her, spitting savage words down at her body. She collided with the memory, a word bursting through, quivering from the stub of her tongue, as if splitting from an already crackled shell, one tiny terrified leg kicking out: HELP. She glanced at the screen, saw the line lose its erraticness, flow in a smooth rising and falling pattern. It was the stream of good fortune. A stable strong heart. Light-headed and encouraged, Joy told herself, *He will be fine.*

The hands quickly stitched Brud's wounds shut, drawing the long thread up into the air, then down, piercing the flesh, sealing life back into its casing. The final sutures completed, the O.R. nurse snipped the thread. Everyone left the room, except for two nurses who remained to wheel the gurney out. The operating room now empty, Joy turned to leave, but something caught her eye. Turning back she saw that the surgeon had returned. He was staring up at the observation window, brashly beholding the girl. Tugging down his mask, he showed her the smile. The violation. She shivered as if shoved inside a dark, deep freeze. And then the smile and the yellow teeth faded, the features slowly relaxing to reveal a younger, kinder face, the bright eyes of the surgeon narrowing with a question as if asking himself what he was doing here, staring up at the observation window. He gave an uncertain smile and even waved, nervously, thinking he should. His brow was webbed as he turned away and pushed out through the doors, with one tentative glance back.

Joy tried to determine what had happened. Why had the hurtful man with the yellow teeth saved her friend? And where had he gone? She questioned the things that she saw. They were sometimes actual, often times unreal. Strange new sights frequently exposed themselves since the time of losing her tongue.

chapter nine

the thin blank line

Brud discovered himself lying flat on his back. The light was as clear and bright as the pain that rushed at him when he tried to move his fingers, his legs, or any part of his body.

His head was turned against the pillow, and he saw a person lying beside him on a separate bed. A thick, plastic tube coiled from the person's mouth, and red liquid was draining through it.

Brud could not move his head to see where the fluid was flowing. His head was heavy. Closing his eyes, he hoped the frightening image would not be there when he opened them again. But his hopes were dashed. His vision was sharper, his eyes meeting the blank expression above the draining mouth, and he could offer nothing. The eyes were fixed on Brud. They blinked slowly. They said everything.

The pain flooded more freely. He needn't even move. It

came on its own, blitzing and pricking every inch of his body as it bit its way to life. He tightened up and could not let go. Absolute weight was pressing down on him. The pain was unbearable. It would snap something. Who would turn off the sound that made his mouth open, forcing out the booming groan that rushed harshly from Brud's terror-stricken face? He looked away from the bloody mouth, shamefully turning his head, and the pain clobbered him, breaking things up inside his body. He gasped, quietly, strangled with distress.

A nurse hurried to his side and tapped a syringe.

"Okay," she assured Brud. "Okay. Shhh. It's alright, sweetheart."

Brud felt the tiny sting against his leg. He wanted to swat the bug away, but his hands were heavy and stuffed with the astonishing weight. His fierce cringing hold on himself began to loosen. The pressure that had been pushing down on him began to lighten. Happy clarity swept through his head. Prefabricated flight.

"Okay?" The nurse nodded cheerfully. "You're doing fine, my love."

Brud smiled and chuckled with a slight nod. He tried to say something, but he laughed instead and wiped a rubbery hand across his face.

The nurse patted his arm before briskly walking away. Brud heard the summery chirping. Turning his head, he watched the screen, the line pulsing, and he understood that he was a part of that line. He was convinced that this was what his father had called his soul. He had been instructed with regards to what would harm its good nature and what would make it strong. It was up there on the television, smaller than usual, just like the little animals he had seen.

He stopped breathing for a short time and waited for the line to change. It did, just a tiny bit. Brud believed. This time, he took a deep breath, but the pain made him wince and shut his eyes. He waited for the razors to leave his insides, calling them away. Calling, "Happiness," in his head. "Hello. Hello."

Go, he shouted to himself. Go, go. And the pain went away shortly, speeding off like a toy car, its tiny horn honk-honking, a clown, with a plastic hat that fell off, sitting in the driver's seat, its yellowish smiling face spinning constantly, in faster and faster circles.

"His condition's stable, but he'll be with us in I.C.U. for a while longer." The surgeon sat beside Jim, his joined hands hanging between his knees. He glanced to his side and saw a boy standing there. He offered a reserved smile, but the boy remained serious.

"Is he okay?" Dogger asked.

"He's okay," The surgeon nodded practically, "for now. It seems promising."

Dogger's smile was grim. He looked around for Joy, but she was nowhere to be seen.

"This your son?" the surgeon asked Jim, hoping for a positive connection to focus on.

Jim stared at the boy, thinking of his wife, their impossible future.

"No," he said.

"Oh." The surgeon straightened in his seat. He squeezed his knees. They felt battered. All of his joints pained terribly, as if he had just awoken from a timeless sleep. He thought of the operation, then looked at Jim. "It could've gone either way. It was a tricky operation. Through the heart." The surgeon paused. He remembered starting the surgery, reaching the infinite complexity of a virtually hopeless procedure, and then his mind had shut off. He caught himself staring at the floor. "We almost lost him." He studied the side of Jim's face, as if something there would reinvent his memory of the operation.

The killer sat in a cushioned chair against the farthest wall. He was leafing through a magazine, pausing to carefully study the diagrams and photographs. Occasionally, he glanced over the top to see Dogger standing beside the surgeon. He wished that he was a surgeon. *The truth*, he convinced himself. He wished he was a surgeon saving people, with his boy and wife safely at home, his wife who had left him, torn the love like a rotten organ from his belly, and tossed it in the nearest dumpster. He wanted all of this, and he was enraged. He felt the urge. The pictures of the charred bodies in the newsmagazine inspired him. It was all ugly and it was perfect, unbelievably appealing, a cure for what he could not possess.

"It's still touch and go." The surgeon stood, being flatly reasonable. He moved his closed lips with a gesture of resignation. "Could be complications. Infection. I just want to make it clear to you."

Wandering from around the corner, Joy walked right up to stare at the surgeon's face. Her fingers rose to touch his lips, but she caught herself and held them back.

The surgeon's brief smile was cautious.

Joy chewed on her bottom lip. She heard the cawing inside of her, the need for the wrenching burst from the body, her soul so terrified.

Dogger walked away, sat by himself on an empty row of seats. He took the killer's tooth from his pocket, unwrapped it from the tissue paper, and tightly held it in his hand, making a wish.

Joy could not tear her gaze from the surgeon's face. He was a kind man with a smooth complexion that was refined and caring. It intrigued her. The clean possibilities. She waited for it to speak. The lips to move. She would kiss them, if it was possible to feel at all.

"I'll let you know if things change." The surgeon spoke down at Jim, then glanced up to see the boy sitting with his small eyes shut in concentration, holding something in his closed hand. The girl's attention was making him nervous. Glancing to the side, he saw that she was still watching him intensely.

"Okay?" he indicated, not knowing what else to offer her.

Dogger slept stretched across the cushioned seat with his head resting on the killer's lap. The killer was attentively watching a nurse as she went about her duties behind the counter at the main station. He toyed with an outplay of ideas involving her confession, purifying actions that would make him well.

"It's like this," said Quagmire, sitting by Jim's side. "We're both playing with the same set of rules."

"I'm not interested," Jim curtly stated. He stood and stepped along the open area, too open, too confusing. Quagmire sighed and pushed himself to his feet, following the lawyer.

"You've been interested all your life," he said. "You're so sharp and logical. Pretending. But your fascination has actually been with good and evil. That's what it comes down to. You can toss all the philosophies and logic out the window. Syllogisms. Deductive reasoning. Foolishness. The first thing we learn when we're children is what's good and what's bad, and then we spend the rest

367

of our lives trying to explain these basics in every conceivable fashion. Pompous explanations. It only comes down to good and bad. Other formulations — no matter how intricate and comprehensive in their analysis — are mere academic scams. Fraud work for the ditherers, straining their dwarfish over-worked brains to invent principles that don't even exist. They make them up as they go along, yank them out of thin air. These principles have no substance in the real legitimate scope of things."

Jim ignored Quagmire. He folded his arms, steered himself off the path of white tiles, and sat back down in the chair.

Quagmire briskly dropped down beside him. "Look at your profession. Money, yes — score one. Truth, no — score zero. Good and bad, or bad and good. You get what I'm saying? Pick a number. It's how you want to look at it. Any argument can be backed up and proven true in this world."

Jim laid his hands against the seating, his fingers discovering a ragged hole in the vinyl covering. He picked at the stuffing, pulling it out in wide furry strands.

"Look at you sitting here. Good and bad in your head. I have the name and the address of the man who murdered your wife, and you couldn't care less. He is bad, no question, just the way you like it. Devoid of speculation. He slaughtered your wife. There's no grey area there."

"Stop it," Jim growled through his anguish.

"Why don't you do what you're supposed to be doing? Don't you have any pride?"

"Leave me alone." Jim sprang to his feet and headed for the elevator, savagely punching the buttons. The wall was close to him. He looked at it, not knowing what to expect.

Quagmire persisted, coming up close behind.

"I'll tell you anyway, because I like you." Quagmire fondled Jim's shoulder, but Jim jerked away. As soon as the elevator doors slid open, he stormed in, promptly leaning to press the button for the lobby, then concentrating on the floor.

"His name is Wilfred Payne. Three forty-nine Pinecrest Avenue."

The elevator doors slid shut. Quagmire pressed close to the crack, calling down the shaft, plainly spacing his words, "Check your pocket. You'll find what you've been searching for."

"Excuse me," the nurse anxiously called, leaning out into the corridor. "Can I help you, Father?"

"Just visiting," said Quagmire. He had taken the elevator to the fifth floor — Medicine — and wandered into one of the dim rooms, silently lifting an arrangement of wildflowers from a ledge before making his way back down to I.C.U. He held the flowers upright in his hand and gave a humble smile to the nurse.

"No visitors are permitted on this ward. You must be looking for another floor."

"No, my brother is in here. This is I.C.U., yes? He came in a little while ago. Oh, dear." Quagmire carefully dabbed a tear from the corner of his eye. "I'm sorry. I'm sure it's not very often you see a priest cry. It's just." Lowering his head, he sobbed openly, the flowers hanging weakly from his hand. "We're so close and...oh... Forgive me. I know I should be...strong. Faith in the Lord." He pulled a handkerchief from his pocket and blew his nose, his eyes glancing at the nurse. He saw that he had won; the nurse's face

369

was flushed with compassion. She was looking at his white collar, the one he kept in his pocket for such occasions.

"The man who was shot, Father?"

"Yes, yes, horrible. He's my brother. I talked with the hospital chaplain and he approved my visit. It's a special case." Sullenly he tilted his head. "I certainly wish it were not."

"Yes, Father. I understand perfectly. He's down this way."

Quagmire dried his eyes and smiled with humility at the stout policeman stationed outside the recovery room before following the nurse through the double doors.

"Hello, dear brother," said Quagmire, leaning over Brud, kindly touching his arm. "Shhh. I'm here, now. We will pray to the Lord."

"I think he'll be just fine." The nurse smiled at Brud, then regarded the priest.

"It certainly seems that way. God bless you." He read her name pin. "Nurse Whitley." He watched her with complacent eyes, his hand resting on Brud's arm, following the nurse until she had left the room. Quagmire pinned Brud with a triumphant smile. He darted a look at the screen, watched the line flicker, suddenly altering its pattern as Brud saw the face change and churn before him.

"Yes-no," sung the yellow-toothed man, "yes-no. It's off to hell we go. I've got your land, just like I planned. Yes-no, yes-no." He merrily whistled the rest of the tune.

Brud's heart began to speed. His skin broke out in a sweat.

"Feel the heat, hey. Mmmmm, yeah, yeah, yeah." Quagmire smacked his lips together, snatched the paper from his black raglan, and dropped it onto Brud's chest. "All I need is an X from you. Right here." His long fingernail stabbed the line above Brud's name, then he spun around, calling to the officer, "Excuse me?"

The stout policeman stuck his head in the door.

"I need a witness here," he quietly stated. "Funeral arrangements. Legal matters. Burial, that sort of thing. A mere precaution, you understand."

"Certainly, Father." The policeman stepped softly into the room.

"He's very weak. I'll have to assist him." Quagmire set the pen in Brud's hand, holding it in place at the beginning of the thin blank line.

Jim discovered the knife in his pocket. He held it concealed in his hand, knowing what it was as the elevator quickly sunk, then settled. The doors swept open. Stepping into the lobby, he sped toward the main doors and beyond. Outside.

Where am I going? he asked himself. *I know*, he insisted. *Do not think.* He took the knife from his pocket and drew it open. It was heavy, the blade long and stained. He walked with furious strides toward the dim parking lot, with the blade opened in his hand. He watched it as he walked, thinking of the address, repeating it with scorn, repeating the man's name and hating him keenly. Hating and hating, but the more he hated, the faster the energy wore itself out. Stepping distractedly, he wondered what he would do once he arrived at the address. Could he possibly kill the man? *Yes, of course*, he enthused. Then he interrupted himself, *I cannot bring myself to act hastily.* He argued, *My wife. MY WIFE*, repeating what he had lost. *My wife.* It was of no consequence. He knew that he had already defeated himself. It was not his nature. Halting in the middle of the parking lot, he morosely pondered his abilities. The asphalt was massive in dimension, with many parking spaces outlined in fresh yellow paint. *Order*, he thought to himself. He shivered and stared back, up at the hospital, the geometry of the windows alive with light.

Quagmire was quick to offer the information. Perhaps he was hoping to gain favour. No doubt Quagmire desired something. He was shrewd. Everything he did was flavoured with ulterior motives. Quagmire had bargained to see Jim gone. For what? His thoughts were quick and functioned explicitly. Yes, of course! He suddenly felt absolved from a breathless strain and turned to walk back. It made sense. He hurried his step. Hadn't Quagmire tried to get him to sign the papers? That's what it was all about. He wanted Jim out of the way so he could force Brud to sign over the land. The land that Brud must keep. He knew that Brud needed the farm. It was the only place he would be at peace. Jim also admired the land. He imagined himself living there, out in the country, with his wife. He did not know why he thought this way. The image presented itself, and he was convinced that he must stop Quagmire. He must stop him. By doing so, he would somehow save Andrea. She was there, the prospect of her recovery inseparably linked to the swiftness of his actions. She was waiting for him to see what he had so blatantly overlooked. The awareness was in his heart, and he would not deny it. Not this time.

Brud spoke to him. He heard Brud's voice as he burst through the doors, shouting across the lobby, "Yes, I'm coming."

Striding up the basement stairs, Jim shoved aside the

fire doors into I.C.U. Racing past the station, he was momentarily startled by a nurse shouting after him. He heard her voice calling, then flapping away behind the second set of doors as he went on.

Another nurse, at a smaller station, hurried out from behind her post to block his progress. He brushed close to her, and she flinched out of his way.

"You can't go in there," she called, furious. "Sir?! Sir, you —"

"It's an emergency," he panted. "Urgent." He bounded through the doors and saw Quagmire swing around with a triumphant tarry sheen in his eyes.

"Get out of here," Jim hoarsely shouted, noticing the policeman reaching for his revolver. The officer had been instructed to protect Brud at all costs. People had pledged to kill him for revenge. The stout policeman snapped the gun loose from his holster. Steadying himself, he aimed for Jim's heart.

"Too late," screamed Quagmire, shrieking and swirling the paper in the air.

The policeman, startled by the outburst of sound, turned his gun on the priest.

"I have it. Right here. Finally. Mine. Mine. With practically nothing left to claim, no pastures or fields, only this — the last substantial body of land. The sacred, divine body. And now I have it." He shook his fist at the ceiling. "Mine. Mine. Mine." Punching the air, he leapt off the floor, landing. "Yes!"

"Everyone out!" the policeman shouted uncertainly. "Everyone. Now."

Brud could not stop the smile that spread along his lips, his passionate struggle finally soothed. His eyes closed peacefully, and he imagined nothing. It was over. The line on the screen raced and chirped frantically, but his expression failed to defy its calm.

Furiously shoving through the doors, the nurse raced for the bed.

"I won't say it again," the policeman warned. "Let's move."

"I'm leaving." Quagmire tucked away the papers, shoving them down the front of his trousers. He winked and headed for the door, leaping with glee, and cracking his knuckles in one long scale of musical notes, like a bumpy harmony. "Snap, snap, snap, snap, snap." He heard the patients groaning through the intercoms linking the floors above him as he gritted the word "power" through his teeth.

Jim remained by Brud's side, desperately stroking his friend's bandaged hand.

"I'm praying, Brud," Jim whispered. "I believe you. I know you're innocent. I knew it all along."

Quagmire seized the occasion to glare back for one final revelation. "You've got it all wrong. So absolutely wrong." Kicking through the doors, he flapped away, disappearing with a loud "whoop."

The stout policeman slipped his gun back into his holster and stood close to Jim's side.

"Let's go now. I don't want to have to move you."

The nurse was on the telephone calling for assistance, sternly repeating the appropriate code.

Opening his eyes, Brud saw Jim's face, the severity of his hope and desolation.

"I'm sorry, Brud. I'm sorry. Will you please forgive me?"

The noise from the screen intensified, the frantic chirping filling the room. Bowing his head, Jim's lips moved in prayer. But he was thinking, *Lost. Dust, all dust.* He was praying, but the words were wrong. *Hail Inconsistencies Full Of Motivation, Blessed Art Thou Among Speculation...*

The policeman took Jim's arm and tugged him away. Jim held tightly to Brud's hand, yanking to free himself from the officer's grip.

Brud's small eyes moved kindly, slowly. He saw everything. His fleshy lips tried to retain the smile, but it was no good. It meant nothing. His lips were suddenly stricken, defeated, having lost their incorruptible tenderness.

"Like two stars," Brud mumbled. "Move but stay the same. Wrong. All wrong...time. Shooting from the sky. Fall down. Yes." He tried to shrug his shoulders. "Fall and goodbye."

Jim's chest heaved with emotion, and the warm impossible tears streamed loose. He was crying for his wife now, for his brother who had died, for all that had been lost. He saw each of their faces in Brud's eyes, all things beginning and ending there.

"I love you," a voice said, but it was not Brud's voice, even though it issued from the wide purplish lips. It was the voice of his wife, and the words were soaked with restful pleasure and abandon.

"Hold tight," she pleaded. "Come."

"I can't." Jim saw the blood seeping through the bandage on Brud's hand. "It's bleeding."

Two orderlies and a doctor came sprinting through the doors. The orderlies moved efficiently, dutifully helping the policeman pull Jim away.

The chirping sound bounced wild, as if it had been dropped. "Look," the nurse shouted emotionally, "at what you're doing!" She pointed at the screen.

"I'm helping him," Jim screamed, as he was dragged

away, kicking and pulling to release his arms. "I'm help-ing him see."

Brud let his eyes lag toward the screen. He was mildly impressed by how the line was scribbling loose, trying to lurch away and fly, jumping from the ground, landing, jumping again.

The nurse fumbled anxiously at Brud's side. He heard the doctor shouting, and felt another sting against his skin, like a single kiss of frozen rain. Shutting his eyes, carefully tuning in to the frantic noises, he then moved beyond, into silence, the faultless current carrying him, letting the line even out. He knew better than to fight what was certain to take him. The calamity coursed straight, smoothly racing off the screen. A storm. The rain stopping. A low peel of sound, like a melodious angelic scream, sustained and softening forever.

One note from an electronic trumpet, a blast of numb movement as the doctor called, "Clear," and charged Brud with electricity. "Clear, clear."

But he was gone.

The nurse watched the patient's face. She glanced at the even line on the screen, then down at Brud. The cool life-less lips smiled. The lips opened. She gently closed them, but they opened again, stirring with words. Her fingers darted away.

The dead lips speaking:

"Mom.

"Dad.

"Hello."

part four

ascent

chapter one

we all belong here

Brud smiled at the bright sensual colours of the farm. His father was tossing loose hay into the corral, and his mother, parting the curtains in the kitchen window, waved a welcome.

Brud wandered out into the field and stood staring up at the sky. He knew the earth was spinning. He sensed it once again, moving smoothly through space. Briefly, he wondered in what direction, then dismissed the vagueness. It was wrong to think this way. Confusion now clean from him, he squatted on his heels, running his wide palm along the flower petals. Sweet summer air filled his lungs. He would savour it. Drawing a luxurious breath, his smile expanded. The plain and simple consolation of it.

Through with admiring the flowers, he strolled back to the corral to stand beside his father. He stood close and stared at the appeased expression on his father's face. There was silence here. It belonged to them. Handing a bunch of hay to Brud, his father watched as his son fed the horses, the animals' teeth and big heads pulling the strands away.

"Where've you been, Brud?" his father asked.

Brud shrugged and looked over his shoulder, hearing his mother's distant voice calling to him. He saw that she was waiting on the front porch, waving for him to join her.

Brud instantly dropped the hay, obediently walking to where his mother leaned forward to hold him. She was warm and smelled nice. He kissed her on the cheek and lightly stroked her hair.

"Mom," he slowly said.

His mother held his face, her eyes softening with the spirit of unconditional acceptance.

"You shouldn't go away like that," she said, gently scolding him.

"Mom," Brud said again, thinking he would tell her what had happened, but his love limiting the words.

"I knew you were coming back, so I baked a pie. Apple, your favourite. And I have ice cream."

"Thanks, Mom," he shyly mumbled. He knew how what he wanted to tell her was impossible to say.

His mother began to turn for the kitchen. Pausing, a look of hesitation came over her as she remembered something. "Oh, I almost forgot. We have a special visitor to see you. She said she was a friend of yours. Sort of a friend, she said. She's resting upstairs. Poor girl was very tired. She needs to get her strength back."

"Okay."

"You know who I'm talking about?" his mother asked, proudly tipping her head forward.

Brud nodded, and nodded again, "Sure, Mom. I know. I know who."

"It's so good to have you back." She pressed her lips together and held her hands against her apron. "I love you so much."

"Me too, Mom." He leaned into her open arms, and they hugged tightly. Brud squinted, the pressure forcing him to laugh. When he stepped back, he saw the tears in his mother's eyes. She wiped at them with her palm and laughed once for him.

"Don't go away," she said, "ever again. I don't like it when you do that."

And Brud understood that she knew. She knew what he could not say. She was his mother. She understood and she was sad because of it.

He quietly nodded and saw a woman, moving beyond his mother's shoulders, flowing down the stairs.

Andrea smiled at Brud. It was a smile that never left her face. A meek and considerate smile.

"Hi," she said.

Brud swallowed and bobbed his head. "Okay?" he asked.

"It's such a beautiful place," she insisted. "But I guess you already know that."

Brud stared at her, until she felt she must look away. He was thinking of Joy. He knew that he would see her in a short time. Part of her was already here. He had sensed it out in the field, drifting alone, lost from the rest of her.

Andrea stepped closer and kissed Brud's cheek. Blushing, Brud pawed the kiss away, turning for a moment, and then glancing back with a huge, wet-eyed smile. He covered his mouth and hunched his shoulders, sadly blurting out a laugh.

"Jimmy will be here, won't he?"

Brud stared at her.

"I know that I'll have to wait. But I can see him from here. You can see everything, in all directions."

Brud turned to his father. He was glad that Andrea understood. He had wanted her to see things for herself, and she did see them, very clearly.

"Come over, Brud," his father called with a generous sweep of his arm. "What've you been up to?"

"Nothing." Brud said, trudging closer.

"You sure?"

"Nothing, been up to nothing. Uhn-uhn. No."

"You know what I like most about this land?" His father gazed off across the green and honey-coloured fields.

Brud said, "Yes."

"You know, don't you?"

"Yes, I know."

"What is it then? Tell me."

"Quiet, clear, and clean," Brud replied, as if counting things on his fingers, knowing he could go as high as eight, but never ten.

His father shook his head. "No, you're wrong. But they're pretty strong points all the same."

Brud looked deep into his father's eyes, and they were his eyes, and they smiled at each other.

"You know what it is?"

Brud shook his head. He liked the almost weightless feel of it moving back and forth.

"It's because I know we belong here. We all belong here. It's only natural. The land. You know what I mean?"

Brud stared, wondering about the words, hearing them even though his father's lips were not moving.

"Of course you do." His father smiled, then warmly hugged his son. "It's so good to see you. Always."

Brud laughed, openly, before he cried. Watching his father, he understood what was coming. A wisp of smoke in the air. The tractors. Eight but never ten. The impossibility right from the start; things never perfect in his hands.

Printed in Canada